I0788427

THE DEATH CHRONICLES II

By

J.E. Taylor

J.E. TAYLOR
SUPERNATURAL SUSPENSE
& DARK FANTASY AUTHOR

THE DEATH CHRONICLES
II

Death is the family business, but not one I want to pursue. Thankfully, it's been passed down from father to son for generations, so it should skip me as Death's daughter. Then I won't have to stop being alive and can actually live my life. Right?

Well, the reapers don't agree. And neither do the angels.

One thinks I'm destined to take over, the other believes I will destroy existence. Both want me dead to match their own agendas.

I have an agenda of my own, and Leviathan who has sworn to protect me. But once my family and friends start being targeted, the family business, while grim, might be the only choice I have to save those I love.

The Death Chronicles *II* includes the following titles
Grim's Daughter
Finding Death
Reap the Dead
Kissing Fate

Grim's Daughter
Chapter 1

I SAT OUTSIDE THE principal's office with my legs stretched out and my arms crossed over my chest. This wasn't the first time they had marched me to the office for telling the truth, but I couldn't bring myself to lie. Any time I attempted to fib, my mouth filled with such a bitter, sickening slime, it was as if I licked a bloody wad of snot. So, I would just rather tell the truth and pay the consequences than experience that horrendous taste.

I glanced at Holly Ryan in the chair next to me—my best friend, roommate, and partner in crime. She grinned at me and shrugged. She had the same affliction for getting in trouble that I did. It was as if whenever I got reckless, she gladly joined in. And here we sat. Again.

Movement caught my attention, and I looked out at the hallway as kids passed to their next class. Only one pair of eyes glanced into the principal's office. My heart jumped at the sight of Zane Bradley staring at me as he walked by. The corner of his lips tilted in a smile that made me momentarily forget that we were in serious trouble this time.

You see, my parents were Death and Fate. The Grim Reaper and the Queen of Providence in the flesh. But at least I wasn't Lucifer's granddaughter. Holly had that market cornered. Faith, Holly's mother, found out she was Lucifer's daughter just before her mother succumbed to cancer. That is not the kind of news anyone wants to find out when their world was falling apart.

On career day, when everyone was oozing over what their parents did, I got a little hostile, and inevitably blurted out my parents' vocations. Of course, on the heels of my announcement, Holly pipes in that she's Lucifer's granddaughter. It never ceased to amaze me how utterly comical the teachers' reactions were. They always, without fail, acted like we had just committed some horrifying sin. They wouldn't know the truth if it bit them in the ass.

I glanced back at Holly, and dimples dotted her cheeks. We looked away before we started to laugh. From experience, we knew that would get us into more trouble. Detentions were likely, but the number of times we had pulled this stunt might just get us suspended instead, and that wasn't great on college applications, which was something we'd have to deal with soon, if we didn't completely screw up our future with our time remaining in high school.

Our smiles disappeared when her father walked in the door. The glare he sent us stifled whatever humor had been dancing on our lips, and we both stared at the floor. Heat filled my face and a sideways glance at Holly confirmed the blushing embarrassment was there in her cheeks, too.

Alex Ryan was as much of a force as Holly's mom, who was a kick-ass redhead who sparked fire when she was angry. As far as parents go, I guess since mine couldn't be around, having the Ryans as my guardians was pretty cool, except for times like this when they had to come to the school to smooth over the waves Holly and I created.

A few minutes later, Alex walked out with the principal. Neither one of them were smiling like they usually were after one of Alex's conversations. Holly and I traded a glance, and I shifted in my seat. They stopped in front of us, and both of them crossed their arms, waiting for one of us to speak.

When neither of us did, Alex cleared his throat.

"I'm sorry," Holly and I mumbled at the same time.

"You two need to stop this, unless you want *me* to homeschool you," Alex said in such a way that I didn't dare speak. His warning came through loud and clear.

I kept my gaze on the floor and nodded. I gave Holly a sideways glance, and she captured my entire attention. She just stared up at her father. Her gaze turned more feral than I had ever seen it. Even I recoiled away from her.

"You dangle that in front of us like it's a bad thing." She crossed her arms and leaned back in the chair. "Papa always said he'd homeschool us if we wanted and I'd rather him do it than you." She pursed her lips at her father. Her hands clenched into fists, but I caught the blaze not only in her eyes, but the sparks that danced over her fingers like a moving wave of static electricity.

"It's okay," I whispered, trying to calm the inferno waiting to turn us all to cinders.

Holly glanced at me and shook her head. "But it isn't. We get in trouble for telling the truth, and then Dad dangles that threat over our head, like going through public school was our idea to begin with. I don't know about you, but I'd much rather sleep in and study on my own timeline and not the State of Maine's timeline."

Alex's arms fell to his sides and his mouth popped open.

Although I knew how Holly really felt, having her finally voice it in front of the principal was ballsy as Hell. She had hinted at home at how much she hated high school, but I was never sure whether Alex and Faith were actively ignoring her or just not listening hard enough. They certainly couldn't read her. Holly had the same natural block against their mystical meddling that I had. They couldn't see into either of our heads like they could with just about anyone else.

Holly's family happened to be the most powerful supernaturals in existence.

Ever.

Their power came from being the descendants of archangels. That apparently came with some mega magic that didn't seem to be found anywhere else but in York, Maine. Thankfully, none of them were into power, or politics, or world domination. Otherwise, the world would be bending a knee to these psychic superpowers.

The world was blissfully clueless as to the abilities they held in their minds and their blood. The only one who had been shoved into the limelight was Alex's father—Holly's paternal grandfather—and to this day, when he sang, people stopped and listened as though his voice were the Heavenly host itself. It was, but no one was the wiser. He just mesmerized the masses with his velvet croon whenever he was on stage.

The world also didn't realize both Death and Fate were real beings. Nor did they realize they had been just mere humans before they took the jobs some fifty years ago. My parents were closer in age to Nana and Papa than they were to Holly's parents. Yet, neither one of my parents looked any older than Holly or me.

Death and Fate were forever stuck in the bodies of eighteen-year-olds. If they weren't my parents, it might have been humorous. It gave a new meaning to the saying forever young.

"Why don't we go home and discuss this?" Alex's frustration made his voice more of a sharp bark of authority rather than the easy-going rhythm he usually had.

"Fine." Holly stood. She grabbed my hand and yanked me along. Whether or not I wanted to go.

I really wanted to go back to class and sulk in the back row while the rest of the class interacted. At least I could hear Zane Bradley laugh. That was always the highlight of my day in school. But it looked as if I was going to miss that today.

I didn't even have time to put up an argument before I found myself in the backseat of the car, in my usual place.

The tension bound by the silence inside the car made me shift in the seat. It was only a short ride, but it was enough to make me want to flee across town to Papa's house to avoid any sort of reprimand.

But it was no use. The moment we stepped inside the house, Holly turned on her father and let her hands fully engulf in flames of aggravation.

Alex pointed at her. "Cool your jets," he snapped.

I wouldn't mess with him if that dark warning glare was aimed in my direction, but I wasn't a true terror like Holly. She just laughed at her father's order.

Darkness passed over Alex's features, and I swallowed the fear that bloomed in my stomach, spitting acid all the way to the back of my throat. Lucifer had once possessed Alex Ryan, and every now and then, I thought the devil's essence still haunted the man.

Now was one of those moments.

I could almost see Hellfire burning in his irises, and I wished I could disappear into the wall. I stepped back to distance myself from this mounting fight.

Cold water rained down over Holly. Conjured out of who knows where, but it was enough to douse her flames and soak her clothing. Alex's furious gaze jumped to me before it went back to Holly.

"Go to your room. Now." His voice was nothing more than a low growl.

I went to move.

"Not you, Missy." He pointed at me and then toward the couch, sending a silent command that I was helpless to ignore.

My body marched to his will until I sat on the middle cushion. Although Alex couldn't get into my head to see what I was thinking, he certainly could make my body move against my will. Many a time he had marched us up to our room when we were in trouble. Holly climbed the stairs with the grace of an elephant. Each step bore her own mad exclamation points, rocking the floor as she went. When our door slammed, Alex turned his attention to me.

"Every. Single. Year." He closed his eyes for a moment and his nostrils flared. When his eyes opened, they were like a laser drilling into me. "Why? Why do you do this, knowing the outcome?" His exasperation filled the room like an uncomfortably humid day.

I shrugged. I didn't have an excuse. At least not one that I could articulate. Perhaps it was because my parents had been absent most of my life. I opened my mouth to say just that when he put his hand out.

"I don't need you to give me the same bullshit you've been shoveling for years about career day. Getting into trouble won't bring them here. You already know that."

Boy, he certainly knew how to cut right to the point. And he wasn't wrong. Sometimes I acted up just to see whether my parents would make an appearance, and career day was one of those days that drove me batty enough to test the barriers. I lowered my gaze and my cheeks heated.

He sighed and took the seat across from me. "Missy, we've been over this a thousand times," he said in such a deflated tone that I had to look up.

"Why was I even born?" The question slipped out before I could stop it.

Alex just shook his head and shrugged. "Magic. Destiny. The right mixture of possibilities." He looked out the sliding glass door behind where I was sitting and cocked an eyebrow.

The swish of the door made me turn and the blonde who stood in the doorway sent my heart thundering in my chest. I was on my feet and running toward her. "Mom!" I threw my arms around her.

She hugged me back, but then pushed me away and pursed her lips. "I understand you caused some trouble today, and this isn't the first time."

The disappointment pulling her lips into a frown was like a one-two punch. But that rebel inside me started revving her mini-motorcycle of aggravation.

"You and Dad haven't visited me since before I started high school, and you have the audacity to look disappointed in me?" My inner voice raged, and it seemed my mouth temporarily forgot its gag order.

"Missy, you know…"

"No. It's Melissa to you. Only those closest to me get to call me Missy." I crossed my arms, making my point even sharper.

My mother took a deep breath and let it out slowly, but the blaze of anger in her eyes and the rigid set of her shoulders announced her displeasure. "You know the situation…" She pressed her lips together and closed her eyes. Finally, she looked down at the floor as if she suddenly remembered high school herself.

"I'm sorry." She met my gaze. "You have every right to be upset. But every time we visited, after we left, you fell into a dark period." She traded a glance with Alex. "The last time, it was a little over a month before you came out of it. And we didn't want to trigger any more bouts of depression."

"Oh, and you think just ignoring my existence would help my frame of mind?" My voice barreled with enough snark to outshine Holly. "That's such bullshit!"

"Watch your mouth."

She pointed her finger at me, and it took everything not to snap it off between my teeth. Biting wasn't cool, but right now, that was the only thing I could think of to lash out and hurt her as much as she had hurt me. She must have sensed the violence rising, because she curled her finger in, tucking it safely in her palm.

"Julia, what brings you to York?" Alex asked, defusing some of the tension that had filled the room.

My mother looked beyond me, and she pressed her lips together before taking a deep breath. "Nick's been hearing some rumblings among the reapers." She glanced at me with her eyes shadowed, as though perhaps she shouldn't have spoken while I was in the room.

"About?" Alex asked.

My mother let out a nervous laugh. "Today might have been more à propos than you think."

I blinked and tilted my head, narrowing my eyes at her in a calculated glare. "Career day?"

The way she laughed next reminded me of a witch's cackle. "Why don't you go upstairs while I talk to Alex for a few minutes?"

"If it's about my life, I think I'm entitled." I didn't want to be sent to my room like a child in trouble.

"It has nothing to do with you," my mother said.

I knew she wasn't telling the truth. But it was Alex's raised eyebrow that got me moving. I ascended the stairs without the ruckus that Holly had made, but my bedroom door was another matter. I slammed that in an exclamation point of disdain.

Grim's Daughter
Chapter 2

“I'M SORRY,” HOLLY SAID from the bed on the other side of the room. Her wet clothes were in a pile in the center of the room and she had changed into a pair of cotton shorts and T-shirt that exclaimed she was something special.

The irony of the words on her shirt made me laugh under my breath. I nodded, accepting her apology. After all, it was her outburst that had garnered the wrath of her father and not necessarily our situation at school.

“My mother is downstairs,” I said softly and took a seat on the edge of my bed.

Holly's eyes widened, and she sat up. "Why in the world are you up here?"

"Because she wanted to talk to your father." I rolled my eyes and threw myself back first onto my mattress. My heart still raced in my chest at seeing her after so long, but bitterness had bloomed a near-hostile attitude that still clung to me. It burned that she had sent me away. Tears blurred my vision. I blinked, and hot trails slid down my face and pooled in my ears.

Holly crossed and sat on the bed next to me. "Your mom loves you."

I laughed my high-pitched laugh of disbelief and wiped at my face as if my tears were a betrayal.

"She does." Holly stared down at me. "Just like my parents love me. I know sometimes it doesn't feel that way, but they do."

Her words brought on fresh tears, and I closed my eyes against the fiery burn and covered them with my arm.

"You know, if you want to know what they are saying, we can sneak down the stairs."

I lifted my arm to look at her sly grin. Leave it to Holly to plant the most devious of acts into my mind. Of course, she would not miss out either. She grabbed my hand and pulled me off the bed, leading me right into the jaws of temptation.

We crept down the stairs until the whispers resembled words.

"What do you mean, she doesn't have an entry?" Alex's voice sounded somewhere between exasperated and worried.

I glanced at Holly, and we leaned closer to the wall.

"She has no Fate. There is no entry in my book and a small faction of reapers want to groom her for Nick's job."

My fists clenched. This was about me. I started to get up, intending to give my mother a piece of my very aggravated mind, but Holly's hand slammed down on my shoulder, keeping me in place. She shook her head.

"Why is that so bad?" Alex asked.

"Nick would die. And so would Missy."

My mother's words hit harder than a punch to the gut.

"Die, like in pass on to Heaven, die?" Alex's voice didn't carry that much concern. I guess when you've been possessed by the devil, death becomes almost blasé.

"No. Well, Nick would, but then Missy would be stuck in the job for the rest of eternity. And that is not something her father or I want for her." Something flapped. "And this damn thing doesn't outline her destiny like it does for every other living creature."

The slam of a book on the coffee table made both of us jump, and I bumped the wall with my elbow. We both held our breath, glancing at each other with wide eyes.

Alex peered around the wall. I didn't think his frown could get any deeper, but it did. I thought he would point us upstairs, but he waved us into the family room.

"What have I told you about eavesdropping?" He glared at Holly.

She shrugged. "Missy has a right to know what is going on." She jutted her chin out in defiance.

When his piercing gaze traveled to me, I met his stare head on before turning to my mother. Holly was right. I had a right to know what was happening, considering it was my life they were talking about.

"You totally lied to me!" I pointed at my mother. "And you didn't think I should know this?" I didn't even attempt to keep the snarl out of my voice.

She sighed and wiped her face. "No. You should not have this type of pressure laid on you when your focus needs to be on school. This is something for your father and I to deal with, but I wanted to give Alex a heads-up just in case..." She met my gaze. "Just in case some of the rogue reapers decide to intervene."

"What can a reaper do?" I asked. We had led fairly calm lives, but my understanding was there had been a time when monsters walked topside. Vampires, demons, shifters, and other things that went bump in the night. Neither Holly nor I had ever had an encounter with one of these so-called monsters. All our information came from fiction these days.

"They can kill with just a touch, if they choose."

"I'm sure they are no match for us." Holly laughed, and her hands engulfed in flames. "I'll just shoot them with one of these." She waggled her fiery fingers.

Fate crossed her arms. "They can appear as humans and you wouldn't even know they were reapers until you were already dead."

Holly's smug smile faded, and she dropped her hands. The flames dissipated into white smoke before they disappeared altogether.

Sometimes I wished I had a superpower like she did. I'm sure it could be a drag at times, but I'd rather have those problems than the normal, mundane teenage issues, like acne or periods that show up unannounced.

"None of your magic will work on them." She looked at Alex. "Not even CJ Ryan can stop a reaper."

Alex blinked and slowly dropped to the couch.

Her warning was scary enough to make my legs feel like jelly. I reached for the wall to steady myself. There was nothing Holly's Papa couldn't stop—at least, that was the belief embedded in all our hearts.

Alex's father was the strongest supernatural on the planet. If he ever had a bad day, he could snap the world in two with just a thought. If *he* couldn't stop a reaper, I was totally screwed.

"There is only one thing that can kill a reaper." My mother bit her lower lip.

"Heaven's blade?" Alex said with enough reverence to pique my interest.

My mother's eyebrows rose, and then she slowly shook her head. "Okay, two things, but anyone even nicked by *that* blade will cease to exist. It's not something I would recommend being in the hands of a child."

His jaw tightened. "You gave it to Faith when she was only sixteen."

My mother leveled a glare that could peel paint, and Alex shifted under it. I've never seen him uncomfortable under anyone's stare, so even though the subject matter was so black, I found a moment of levity and snorted a short laugh.

"What is so funny?" Alex snapped at me.

"Seeing you squirm under anyone's stare."

He narrowed his eyes at me just as Holly's mother walked in the door with an armful of groceries. Faith Ryan was a stunning redhead with the kind of complexion that Hollywood stars would do anything for, even with the sprinkle of freckles over the bridge of her nose.

Hell, I was even a little envious.

Faith paused when her gaze landed on my mother. "Julia. What are you doing here?" she asked and started toward the adjoining kitchen. She didn't wait for an answer, but she was back in a flash without the bags burdening her arms.

My mother ran a hand through her hair and sighed as she slipped the Book of Fates into her pocket. She glanced at me and then at Holly before returning her gaze to Faith. "I needed to warn you. Some reapers may be considering going rogue."

Alex glanced over his shoulder at Faith. And it was as if the two were silently communicating. Which they did a lot. I'd love to be able to actually send my thoughts out to someone and have them answer without uttering a word. It seemed to be really handy, especially if you didn't want other people in the room to know what you were saying.

When he glanced back at my mother, he said, "What else besides Heaven's blade kills a reaper?"

"I'm working on getting it here. It should be in your hands by Thanksgiving."

The realization that my mother hadn't come because I got in trouble at school dawned on me. That wasn't important enough for her to make an appearance. So, this truly had to be dire for her to show up. "And if something happens in the next few days?"

"Then you just tell them you are not interested in the job. I don't think they can force you, but they certainly can create a whirlwind of havoc just to make their point. Let's hope they aren't as dark as the ones who came after your father when he was your age."

"What happened when they went after my father?"

My mother's lips pressed together. "A lot of people who weren't supposed to die had the life yanked right out of them. Including *my* parents."

18

Grim's Daughter
Chapter 3

"WELL, THAT WAS A real downer." Holly took a seat on the edge of my bed and began tossing a fire ball from hand to hand.

It was a habit that unnerved me, but it also showed me she was just as unhinged as I was.

"Reapers." I shrugged. "Maybe homeschooling right now is not a bad thing." I thought about some of my friends, and then my mind wandered to my forever crush, Zane Bradley, whose smile made my knees weak, but he had never approached me. Maybe it was my jet-black hair or my almost golden eyes that scared him off. I don't know, but I sure wished he'd speak to me instead of sending those side glances as if he had a secret to share.

Holly said I was stunning, but I always felt like a shadow next to her utter vibrancy. I don't know whether it's the angel heritage or what, but she frickin' glowed at times.

"I think we'd miss our friends," Holly said. It was as if she had read my mind.

"But wouldn't it be safer?"

Holly tossed the flame ball back and forth a few more times before extinguishing it. Wisps of smoke trailed off her fingers and she shook them away. "I don't know. If we are at school, maybe we can avoid anyone we really care about, so no one gets hurt?" Her eyebrows rose with the same questioning inflection as her voice.

"But wouldn't that defeat the point? If we are there to see our friends, avoiding them would be stupid. Besides, being there could put everyone in danger." Although Holly had a protective reflex for those in her tight-knit circle, I tended to be broader in my protectivity.

She shrugged and picked at a hangnail on her thumb. "You'd rather be homeschooled than be in the school with all the other kids our age?"

Now that she put it that way, I saw her point, and no, I really didn't want to be homeschooled if I could help it. "So, all that posturing to get us to be homeschooled?" I couldn't help the chuckle that weaved through my words.

She smiled. "I guess when faced with the options, I really don't want to be isolated from our friends. Yeah, getting up whenever we wanted would be nice, but I think Papa would be so much more strict than even Mr. Jasper is."

Mr. Jasper was like a military drill sergeant where the periodic tables were concerned, and I couldn't agree more with Holly's assessment. Our grandfather was a genius, and he wouldn't give us a break. I'd bet my right arm that he would be ten times more stringent than old Mr. Jasper.

"We just have to stay out of trouble," Holly muttered under her breath and gave me a sideways look, which bloomed into a secret grin.

I really didn't think that was possible these days, but I nodded anyway. "Yeah, I won't mention my parents if you won't mention your grandfather."

She snorted laughter. "Did you see Derek's face when I announced my grandfather was the archangel Lucifer?"

"He went white as a ghost, and I thought his eyes were going to pop out of his head." I laughed right alongside her. Derek was new and had never seen our little show of solidarity on career day like the rest of the students. The rest of the class just rolled their eyes at us; they were so used to our wacky declarations that this wasn't anything other than a normal day for them. I guess Alex was right about my predictability, and that curtailed my laughter. "I really need to stop doing that, don't I?"

Holly shrugged. "It's always fun to shock people with the truth. Although they never seem to think it's real. I wonder if I should juggle fire balls just to prove we are more than what we appear to be." She winked at me. "You should bring in a scythe next time, too."

"Oh, and get expelled and arrested for having a weapon on school grounds? No, thank you."

"Yeah, but no one in their right mind would try to get near you."

I scoffed at her. "There are plenty of people who would be stupid enough to try to disarm me." I flipped my hair over my shoulder. "But I would hand it over to Zane Bradley in a heartbeat if he asked." I grinned.

Holly laughed. "You would do just about anything for that guy."

She wasn't wrong. "Unfortunately, he doesn't know I exist."

"Yes, he does. I've seen him sneak glances at you."

"Then why hasn't he ever come to talk to me? I think he's just looking because he thinks I'm weird."

"You could always go talk to him."

I snorted through my nose. "Yeah, right. As entertaining as that might seem to you, I'd probably fall flat on my face."

"Bull. You'd do just fine." She sighed. "But seriously, yeah. We kind of do need to keep this under wraps for a change. We wouldn't want to make waves, especially if reapers approach you."

All the humor bled out of the conversation. "Yeah." I glanced out the window at the snow-free lawn. The weather this year had been quite mild. Maybe we'd get to have one of our famous Ryan family flag football games this year. It was the best part of Thanksgiving, even more so than Nana's pies.

"I'm going to go get my homework done before dinner." She gave me a pat on the leg and headed downstairs to get her books.

I looked at my discarded book bag. I didn't want to open it right now and get lost in the mundane when everything was so upside down.

The air shimmered in the center of the room and my father appeared. I sat up, wide-eyed. He put his finger over his lips, shushing me as he crossed and silently closed the door. When he sat down next to me and ran his hand through his hair, I studied his handsome profile. I got my jet-black hair from him, as well as my creamy complexion. I really wish I had his eyes. They were the blue of a summer twilight sky and right now, they held worry so thick it nearly choked me.

"Mom's downstairs. Why did you come?" I whispered, conflicted by the sudden appearance of both my parents after not seeing them for a couple of years.

"Because shit is going to get real," he said softly. "Your Fate is not written. Unlike mine, and my father before me, and every single person who inherited the role of Death, all the way back to the very first one." He reached out and cupped my cheek. "Unlike us, you have a choice. You have a full life to live, and I don't want to see that ripped from you."

My lack of a Fate wasn't a new piece of information, but his fear of my life being ripped away certainly was. I wasn't ready to hang up breathing. Not for a job shuttling souls to their destination. "Why do you think it will be?" I cocked my head.

"Because the rumblings I have caught are not just a rogue faction. And since I set the reapers free many years ago, I no longer have dominion or control over them." He met my gaze. "They serve at their pleasure. Which means this coming war will be very dangerous."

I wrapped my arms around my legs. My mother hadn't framed what might come as war or even as a battle. That word had, at the very least, maimed bodies associated with it, and I blinked at him. "War?"

"I'm afraid so, and I am likely to be a casualty of it." He met my gaze. His blue eyes shimmered like diamonds on the ocean, giving me an eerie chill. "And if I am, I want the job to end with me. I do not want them insisting on it being you. This is unprecedented." He ran his hand through his hair again. "I don't think bad things will happen like when I questioned taking the job, because it was my destiny. I'm the last in line for this job. Just like your mother, I'll be in this role until time stops. But your destiny—" He pointed at me—"your destiny is not written."

"What does that mean?" I couldn't comprehend that. Not after everything they had taught me about Fate. Everyone has a predestined path. That was as certain as the moon rising at night or the sun rising at daybreak.

"That means you are free. Truly free to make your own choices. To blaze your own path." He smiled. "You are the only one who has that blessing. Everyone else, even those closest to you, had their entire lives and destinies scribed long before they were born."

I blinked at my father. I hooked my thumb toward the door. "The Ryans?"

"They are all in your mother's book of Fates. Although, they have changed Fates more than once. Which has a way of screwing things up, but they seem to be free of Heaven's wrath just through their heritage." He stood and crossed to the window, looking out. "You have a unique opportunity, Missy."

"So, my choices are mine and not some cosmic force directing me?"

"Precisely."

"And what if I make a mistake?"

He turned and met my gaze. He just shook his head. "I don't know. Every choice has a ramification. Yours are just not written. So far, there doesn't seem to be any sort of cosmic interruption with all your prior choices, so I think the same will be true as you move forward. Just be sure to weigh your options before you take a step in any direction."

"What if a reaper gives me an ultimatum—take the job or my family here dies?"

He closed his eyes and hung his head. "If you take the job, I die. There is no way around that. You need to make that choice. I know Alex and Faith have been more of a family all these years than your mother or I have ever been. I can't fault you for trying to protect them."

"Why are you telling me all this?" I crossed my arms and stared at him. The entire conversation left me cold, more so than the one with my mother earlier.

"Because you need to know what is at stake. I didn't. And I screwed up royally. Many people died because I wasn't given the benefit of information." He snapped his fingers and a German shepherd appeared by his side.

I grinned at the dog. Even though I knew full well it wasn't actually a dog. Levi had visited Faith and Alex enough over the years for me to hear all the stories, and he even revealed his true form to me when I scoffed at him, telling me he wasn't a dog. I had nightmares for weeks afterward, but he never caused me to doubt his devotion to our family. He was Leviathan, an ancient monster that used to guard the gates of Hell. And he was badass in either form.

"Plus, I wasn't given any protections like Levi here." He patted the dog's head. "You keep her safe, understand?"

"Yes, sir," the dog said as he looked up at my father. "I will keep everyone under this roof safe."

"You take him everywhere you go." He handed me a piece of paper.

I scanned the document and laughed. "An emotional support dog?"

He shrugged and grinned. "That allows you to have him with you at all times. He is one of three things that can destroy a reaper. So, feed him well."

His words sent a chill up my spine. Levi didn't eat like a normal dog. I didn't know what the Hell my father was going on about because I had never seen Levi eat anything but bacon, and I didn't think there was enough bacon in York to satisfy the beast. "Does Mom know you're here?"

He shook his head. "We didn't agree on how to handle this. She wanted to protect you, but

I've been in your shoes and I know being armed with information is better than being blindsided. You're a strong girl with a big heart, and while I know all this information scares you, I also know you are tough enough to deal with it." He pulled me off the bed into a hug. "I love you, Missy," he whispered into my hair. And then he was gone, as if he had been made of a whiff of smoke.

I looked down at my new shadow. "I can't wait to show you off at school tomorrow." I grinned.

Levi rolled his eyes and settled down on the floor next to the bed. I patted his head, expecting the feeling of fur under my fingertips. Instead, his head was solid and lizard-like, as opposed to soft and fluffy. It never ceased to amaze me how often I got duped by his disguise.

Grim's Daughter
Chapter 4

ALEX DROPPED US OFF at school and just pointed his finger at me as if I were the one who needed scolding. "Behave." His gaze dropped to the dog next to me wearing an emotional support animal vest, and he pointed at Levi.

The order was clear, but even I knew it was laughable. When Levi's tongue lolled out the side of his mouth, Alex pressed his lips together and brought his gaze back to me.

"Please try not to get into trouble today," he added, and then rolled up the window as I walked toward the school.

I loosely held the leash attached to Levi and headed inside to the principal's office with my note. Most people moved aside at the sight of the large German shepherd at my side, almost as if they sensed he was more than just a dog. Everyone gave us a wide berth. When I opened the office door, he sniffed the air tentatively and then stepped inside. I followed and handed the surprised school secretary my forged doctor's note regarding my service dog.

She read the note and eyed the dog. Then she pulled the pencil from behind her ear and pointed it at me. "Just stay right there."

The principal came out, pinching the bridge of his nose as he crossed with the letter in his hand. The secretary stuck her head out the door and watched with interest. When the principal's gaze landed on Levi, he stopped, and his eyes widened. "Oh, no..." he started.

The door squeaked open behind me. I glanced over my shoulder and cocked my eyebrow as Alex entered the office and closed the door behind him.

"You will let her have the dog in school," Alex said from behind me. The soft commanding tone rolled across the office and seemed to erase all animation from the principal, along with the secretary, looking out from his office.

The door swished closed, and I took one more look over my shoulder in time to see Alex slide out of the front door. Him and his damn sixth sense.

Levi huffed at me, and I met his gaze. I swear he shook his head. I almost launched into a tirade about me being able to handle this when I remembered where I was. I looked back at the principal and he was still staring at that piece of paper in his hand.

He sighed. "Fine, Melissa. But you need to make sure you clean up after him if he messes. And make sure no one gets bitten, otherwise I'm holding you accountable." He eyed the dog warily, but it wasn't enough to alter Alex's mind control command.

"Thank you." I think if I hadn't been sent home the day before, he might have put up a bigger stink, even with Alex's influence. But I was glad to have Levi with me. As soon as we stepped into the hallway, Levi's ears perked up.

"It's too damn noisy here," he muttered, quietly enough for only me to hear him over the din. Levi glanced up at me.

"It will settle down when the bell rings." I led him toward my first class of the day, but I didn't get far before Zane Bradley, my forever crush and the coolest senior in school, blocked my path. He grinned at Levi and then glanced up at me with eyes the color of glowing emeralds. His dark bangs fell across his forehead, and he swiped them aside.

"Cool dog," he said.

I stared at him. Zane Bradley had never once spoken to me in all the years we shared the same classes, and all it took was me bringing in a dog? I was too dumbfounded to speak.

He reached out to pet Levi, and Levi let out a low growl.

Zane pulled his hand back and glanced at me.

"He doesn't like to be pet. Sorry." I shrugged and put my hand on Levi's head. He stopped growling, but that wasn't what had sent my heartbeat into the stratosphere. *Zane. Bradley. And all I can muster was my dog didn't like to be pet? What an idiot!*

"Oh." He shuffled his feet and looked over his shoulder. "I gotta get to class. Maybe I'll see you and your dog later?" He met my gaze and smiled in a way that made my knees tremble. "Melissa, right?"

I nodded. I didn't even think he knew I existed before today. The timing was very weird, but then again, I had never walked the halls with a massive German shepherd, either. And for once, I was glad Holly wasn't with me. She would have flirted ruthlessly with Zane. Or worse, tried to play matchmaker.

He shoved his hands into his pockets. "I'm Zane," he said, as if we hadn't shared classes forever.

I almost said "no duh" but I bit back on the snarky response. "I didn't think you knew my name." *Jesus, it's like you've never spoken to a boy. Why can't you come up with something a little more witty?*

His cheeks turned a rosy hue. He shrugged. "I'll see you around." And then he was gone, down the hallway.

I glanced at Levi, perplexed by the entire conversation. "Why'd you growl?"

"Because he was using me to get your attention," he muttered softly and glanced up at me as we continued heading toward my English class.

Mrs. Wilson, my English teacher, smiled up at me as if I were a delicate flower prone to breakage, especially after the scene in class yesterday that got me sent to the principal's office. I crossed to my desk, ignoring her pity look. But it burned just under my skin and left me on edge. I took my seat at the back of the class, next to Holly's empty seat. She would be along any minute, most likely sliding in the door as the bell rang, or a millisecond after the clanging finished.

Levi heaved a heavy breath as he situated himself between me and the empty desk. I sat on the end of the leash to give the appearance of having him under control, but unless a reaper threatened me, Levi wouldn't move from his spot.

Just as the bell rang, the familiar crop of red hair slid through the door and grinned at me like some woman possessed. Holly nearly skipped to her seat and sat down as quietly as a bear plundering a honey pot.

Mrs. Wilson crossed her arms and looked down her aristocratic nose at us. With her light hair pulled back in a bun, the glare was more severe than it had been yesterday with our career day declarations.

I glanced down at Levi and a wicked thought crossed my mind. I had to press my lips together to stanch the urge to command Levi into his natural form. He glanced up at me and shook his head as if he could read my thoughts.

It would at least stop the snickering of the girls sitting in the front row who were casting me dirty looks. I guess they didn't like the fact that Zane Bradley had been talking to me in the hallway. After all, every single one of them had been hanging on his arm at one time or another over the last couple of years.

Levi rolled his eyes at me and laid his head down on his paws, watching the teacher as if the woman could actually enlighten him on some new source of entertainment.

As the teacher began writing on the blackboard, I leaned over to Holly. "Zane talked to me in the hallway."

Holly's brow creased. "Zane?" she asked louder than I think she meant to. Everyone turned around to look at us, including the teacher.

Mrs. Wilson's lips pressed together, and heat filled my cheeks at the total unwanted attention that I was now getting. Before she had the chance to scold us, a knock sounded on the door and the principal walked in with a student I had never seen before.

"This is Jake. He's new to York..." Mr. Webber started.

Levi sat up and stared at the boy. His nose crinkled back, and a low growl came from him.

I glanced at Levi. His gaze was glued to the kid, and his warning was clear enough for my head to snap in the boy's direction. That's when I saw it. The skeletal figure superimposed over the boy's body. It was as if I were looking at a badly edited film.

I gripped the leash. This was not the place or time to confront a reaper. Holly glanced at me, and then at Levi, cocking her eyebrow as she moved her gaze to the boy.

Her fingers began to spontaneously spark, as if her subconscious recognized the danger. She fisted her hands and put them under the desk. Only the three of us in the back recognized the threat.

"Hello, Jake." Mrs. Wilson waved to an empty seat up front at the far side of the room.

The kid gave a tense smile and headed for the seat. He stalled at the front of the row between Holly and me, and just stared at Levi. His eyes widened for a moment, and then his gaze jumped to mine. He obviously recognized the beast under my dog's disguise. Jake swallowed hard as he finished making his way to his chair.

He didn't once look back during the class. And when the bell rang, I swear he bolted out of the room as if it were on fire.

"Can I go eat him now?" Levi asked, soft enough for only Holly and me to hear.

"No. You can't just go eating random kids on school grounds," I said. "Even if they *are* reapers. But, if he is stupid enough to approach us and try something, you have my permission to eat him. Okay?" I patted Levi's head and the glare he gave me made me pull my hand back. I gathered my books and walked out of the classroom with Holly and Levi.

"Maybe we should just head home," Holly said as we entered the busy hall.

I bit my lower lip and blinked my eyes as my blood suddenly chilled. Whatever magic had let me see the reaper in the classroom swarmed my head again. Except this time, the number of superimposed skeletal forms was on people I had known for years. I gripped the leash tighter and gave Holly a nod.

"I'm not feeling so good." I scanned the hallway. Levi hadn't so much as growled when we walked through here before. I wondered what kind of voodoo would make my mind play this kind of trick.

"There weren't any reapers when we walked through this hall before," Levi said with an ominous tone. He sniffed the air. "There still aren't any besides the one they call Jake."

I blinked again, and my vision righted. At the end of the hall, the new kid stood in the center of the hallway with a demonic smile on his face. When I met his gaze, his smile faded. I narrowed my eyes at him and thought about unclasping Levi, but there were too many innocent victims between us, and I was not about to risk their lives.

"Come on." Holly tugged at my arm and pulled me in the opposite direction.

Once we were around the corner, out of Jake's view, my stomach stopped aching. Even Levi pulled me toward the nearest door, away from whatever dark magic the reaper had laid on us.

"What the Hell kind of voodoo was that?" I muttered under my breath as we stepped out the side door. Levi continued to lead me away from the school, with Holly trotting at my side.

"I don't know." Levi glanced back at me. "I saw it as well. But it didn't affect my sense of smell. If they had filled the hallway, as his illusion indicated, I would have known just by the stench.”

I unclipped the leash from Levi as we crossed the soccer field and headed toward the woods. If reapers showed up, I didn't want to be inadvertently dragged around behind him as he went into kill mode.

Holly's fingertips sparked, and my skin broke out in a rash of gooseflesh. Our gazes darted around.

“Hey,” a voice called from behind us.

We turned toward the voice. Jake stood at the edge of the parking lot and, although I could see his human figure, I also saw the reaper underneath. His human façade looked more like the skeleton overlays had looked on the other students in the hallway.

The bell rang in the school behind him and instead of going back inside like he should have; the idiot started to cross the field toward us.

“What the Hell?” Holly said, as we traded a glance.

Levi didn't wait for a command. He charged. I didn't call him back, either. Any reaper who messed with me would find out just how dangerous a line they were dancing on, and this jerk had tried mind games on me in the hallway.

Holly looked at me as if I should stop the inevitable. But I didn't care whether this guy was on the good side or the bad. He was here, and that was enough to damn him to Levi's wrath.

"Your mom sent me!" he yelled just before Levi's head elongated into a muzzle that looked more like a fantastical dragon's head.

I had a second to marvel at how badass Levi was as he lunged at the reaper. He devoured the reaper's entire form in one crunching snap, and Levi morphed back into a dog. He trotted back, with his tongue lolling to the side. I knew that look. He was either happy or he was mocking us. I had to press my lips together against a laugh. After all, he destroyed that reaper.

Holly's grip on my arm became hot, and I glanced at her. She was staring at the dog as if he had just stepped out of Hell.

"Ouch." I pulled out of her grip, inspecting my shirt to make sure she hadn't burned through it.

"I...I just never..." She waved at Levi.

I let out a laugh. "Seriously?"

She blushed and nodded. "Yes. Seriously," she snapped at me.

"You had to know he was more than a dog. Especially after all those stories your mom told us about her adventures with Levi." I raised my eyebrows. She had heard him talk before, but I guess she never connected the dots. "He is Leviathan."

Holly's eyes widened as Levi came up to us and let out a burp.

"I thought my mom was kidding. I just thought he was special because he could talk." She stumbled through the words, as if her brain was just now wrapping around the fact we had a prehistoric monster with us. He was probably older than all our parents' and grandparents' friends combined. And they had a few people in their social circles who dated back to close to the beginning of time.

I patted Levi's head despite his warning glare. "Oh no. He is much, much more than just a talking dog." An overwhelming certainty that someone was watching us took over, and I glanced toward the school just before the woods on the opposite side of the soccer field swallowed us up. I could have sworn I saw Zane on the sidewalk near the student parking lot, but then we slipped behind some trees and my view disappeared.

Levi trotted at my side. "You are not going to admonish me for eating someone your mother sent?" he asked when we were far enough away from the school to not be seen any longer.

"No. I'm not a pawn in anyone's war. Good or bad, if they come after me, you can eat them."

Holly's gaze found mine, and she seemed to be back in control of her momentary shock at seeing a flash of a legendary monster. She cocked an eyebrow. "You just let him kill that reaper."

"He messed with us. I'd rather be safe and let Levi do his job, rather than underestimate those things and lose someone I care about." She didn't look all that convinced. "Seriously. I won't be the monkey in the middle. I have a plan for my life, and it does not include seeing anyone I love die."

"You have a plan?" She stopped walking and crossed her arms.

I took a couple of steps beyond her and turned. "When don't I have a plan?"

Holly broke out in a smile. "Touché."

A twig snapped behind her and she spun.

I caught sight of someone, but Holly's fingers weren't sparking, at least not like they had in the field and in the classroom when the reaper showed up. Before Levi could pounce, I grabbed his collar. Although the intruder's dark hair blended with the trees, his green eyes glancing around the bark were familiar enough for my heart to jump into my throat.

"Zane?" I asked as Holly took a step back by my side, looking more shocked at seeing Zane Bradley in near proximity than she had been seeing Leviathan in his partially natural form.

"Hey. Um." He stepped out from behind the tree. "I..." He glanced down at Levi and seemed to shiver. When his gaze found mine, I knew he had seen more than he should have.

I traded a glance with Holly. Neither of us could bend minds the way her father had. There was no way we could erase what happened from his memory. Honestly, I really didn't want to, even though I knew there could be serious ramifications of letting someone on the outside in on the family secrets.

"What are you doing out of school?" I asked, to help him focus on something else besides a prehistoric monster eating what looked like another student.

"I think my vape must have been laced with something," he said. "Because I could have sworn your dog ate that kid in one bite." He pointed toward the school. "I just had to see with my own eyes."

He gave me an out, but a part of me didn't want to cover up the supernatural reality I lived in. I guess I needed more than just my immediate family to confide in at this point in my life.

Holly giggled next to me. "Man, you really must have gotten something bad."

"You've lived in York all your life, right?" I asked, ignoring Holly's sudden smack of her elbow against mine.

Zane nodded.

"Then you know all the rumors about me." I let go of Levi's collar and crossed my arms. "So why now? Why talk to me today?"

"You brought a cool dog to school. I just thought it would be easier for me to talk to you. And yeah, I've heard the rumors. I just never figured out a good opening to approach you with. I mean really, if I had come up to you and said, 'Hey, I hear you're a little off in the head,' you would have run in the other direction," he replied.

Levi let out a low growl at the dig.

"Shush, Levi." I put my hand on the back of his neck near enough to the collar to settle him down. "You could have tried a simple hello."

"His name is Levi?" Zane asked, ignoring my suggestion.

"Yes. It's short for Leviathan."

The way Zane started at the name made me smile. Everyone who watched the show *Supernatural* knew the reference. Although the lore didn't quite meet the reality. Leviathan was smarter and more of a badass than any of the monsters on the show. I exchanged a glance with Holly.

She shook her head to get me not to go where I was already headed.

"I'm still not convinced you just happened to pick today to approach me because of Levi." I left my hand on Levi's shoulder. "Anything smell funny to you?" I addressed the dog.

Levi looked up at me and then at Zane. He sniffed the air and growled low. "Just teenage hormones," he muttered, loud enough for all three of us to hear.

Holly rolled her eyes. "And there you go." She waved at Levi.

I smirked and kept eye contact with Zane.

The poor kid went all kinds of pale and leaned against the tree behind him. His gaze jerked from Levi to me. "That was real?" His voice cracked in a very unattractive, high-pitched tone.

"I'm not cray-cray." I twirled my finger next to my ear and gave him a wink. "There's shit out there that you do not want to mess with. Which is why Levi is here with me right now. He will make sure *that* shit doesn't come anywhere near me or my family."

"But that was just a person," he said after a moment of incessant blinking.

"That was a reaper." I raised a challenging eyebrow.

He started blinking again, and I honestly thought he was going to fall over. And then a crease appeared between his eyes. "Aren't you supposed to be Death's daughter?" he asked, straightening as if he suddenly realized this was all an elaborate joke. "Why would you kill your father?"

I rolled my eyes. "Reapers and Death are not the same thing." My tone said it all.

His face reddened. "Look, I'm new to this supernatural crap, so cut me a break. And I finally actually got the nerve to talk to you, so you don't need to make fun of me." He crossed his arms.

I took a calming breath and nodded, putting myself in his shoes for a moment. This was my normal. Talking beasts in a dog outfit. My best friend juggling the fire balls she created. Parents who were basically psychic deities. But for the normal kid down the block who thought the most traumatic moment of their life was finding out Santa wasn't real, this had to be overwhelming. "I'm sorry. You are right. I keep forgetting just how hidden our world is from the rest of the people around here. Reapers are just like the cab drivers who bring you to your final destination. Death is like the dispatcher who gives the directions, and Fate is the one with the where and when." I summed up the afterlife as I understood it, except right now those cab driver reapers were more like drunk drivers. A menace to society.

"Are you really Death's daughter?" He seemed more timid with the question now that I apologized for my snippiness.

I nodded, and he glanced at Holly. "And your grandfather..." He trailed off as the doubt crept into his tone.

Holly bit her lip and glared at me. I knew she would read me the riot act once we were alone.

But for now, she had my back. She put her hand out, palm up, and wiggled her fingers. Sparks danced along her fingers before small bursts of flame broke out. She closed her palm. "My dad is going to kill us," she muttered under her breath.

Zane laughed. This time it was more natural and not that high-pitched quality, although he certainly looked as though he were coming undone. "The devil exists?"

"He's dead now," both Holly and I said in unison.

Zane's laughter trickled away, and his eyes widened.

"He is not taking this as well as other humans have in the past," Levi said as he studied Zane. "Can I eat him?" He turned his sharp eyes in my direction.

"Levi!" I gasped and swatted his back. "No. You cannot eat the coolest kid in school." My eyes widened at my slip. I had not meant to say that out loud, especially in front of Zane.

Laughter snorted from Zane's nose at the unintended compliment and it seemed to snap him back into himself. "You think I'm cool?"

Heat filled my cheeks, and I looked at the ground as giddiness nearly made my knees buckle.

"For the love of..." Levi huffed and started the trek toward Holly's grandfather's house.

Holly leaned close. "Maybe Zane might want to come with us?"

I glanced at her, and she widened her eyes. Holly's grandfather could alter his memories even more efficiently than her father could. I was surprised she didn't have that power, but it seemed she only got her mother's fire curse and not the rest of the Ryan's ability pool.

I glanced back at Zane and smiled. "We need to get going. You probably should get back to school."

"Will I see you tomorrow?" he asked.

I glanced toward the school, and all giddiness evaporated. "It's not safe for me to be there. There's a supernatural war coming, and I would rather not have anyone caught in the middle of it, so no. I won't be there for a while."

His eyes softened, and he moved closer, taking my hand in his. The warmth flowed through me, and I could feel his essence. It was a strange effect, but one I really liked.

"Call me?"

"I don't have your number."

He reached into his pocket and pulled out a business card, handing it to me.

A business card? That was odder than my predicament. I glanced at the logo and his name in clean black block letters. "You have your own home improvement business?"

He nodded.

Shock filled me at the fact he owned his own business at seventeen. Truth be told, I was actually a tad impressed.

He tapped the card. "Call me when you can and maybe we can grab dinner or something sometime."

It was my turn to blink. *Did Zane Bradley just ask me on a date?* I nodded like a lovesick girl.

"See you around," he said to Holly, and headed back toward the school.

I turned to Holly when I was sure he was out of hearing range. "Zane just asked me to dinner." I grinned.

She glanced after him and nodded. "Yes. But wouldn't that put a big bull's-eye on his back?"

Dammit all. She was right. I still tucked the card in my pocket. I could at least call him. But I couldn't let him step into this craziness. I closed my eyes and hung my head. Holly didn't even need to reprimand me. "I shouldn't have told him." I opened one eye toward Holly.

She didn't say anything. Just shrugged and turned to trek after Levi. "So, tell me your plan."

I didn't really have a plan for the reapers, but I had a plan for my life. "I do not want to take the helm like the bad reapers want. I do not want any part of this ethereal war, either." I glanced at her.

Holly laughed. "That's not a plan. That's a declaration. And while you're at it, you've outed us to a guy."

"You've never said anything to anyone else outside of career day?" I slowed down and glanced at her.

She shook her head. "That would kill my dating life. No one would be interested in dating Lucifer's granddaughter. That's if they believed me. Besides, I don't know the entire story, just that my parents stopped him from launching the end of times."

"We're sixteen. You'd think we should know the entire story," I muttered as we caught up with Levi.

"Sixteen is just a blink." Levi scoffed at us. "When you have lived since the dawn of time, this all seems so juvenile," he added. "Fighting the devil with Faith meant something. This reaper unrest is just an annoying, petty bickering. A power play that holds human life hostage, so I am happy to oblige, eating whatever reaper dares to come near you or your family."

"So, where are we going?" Holly asked.

"Papa's house." I sighed and continued marching through the woods until we came out on Long Sands Road. I didn't want to head toward the beach, and the possibility of getting caught by the truancy officer, so I headed toward the library and Holly's grandfather's place beyond.

Holly didn't argue. She fell into step next to me as we navigated the side roads and tried to stay far from any attention. Skipping school, especially after the shit show yesterday, was likely to get us expelled. But Holly's grandfather could homeschool us easily. Unfortunately, there were no cute boys hanging around at her grandfather's house, so my nonexistent social life had no hope of revival.

We walked quietly and crossed the road near the Catholic church and down toward the Wiggly Bridge. We took the trail at the edge of the water toward where her grandfather lived, avoiding more roads than we normally would.

"What are you stewing on?" Holly glanced both ways before she scooted across the road and headed down the driveway to Harbor Beach and the cliff walk beyond, which would dump us out on the back portion of Roaring Rock Road where her grandfather lived.

I remained quiet as we navigated the rocks with Levi. He seemed surefooted, even with the misty slickness covering the path.

"How do we stop this war?" I asked under my breath, still turning it all over in my head.

"Easy. Destroy all the reapers." Levi glanced up at me.

Although I didn't want to be caught in the middle of the war, mass extinction did not seem like the right route to take. "We can't do that."

"You wanted to know. That is the only way to forever stop the power struggle. However, it would mean your father would work nonstop until the end of time. Or there would be far more ghosts just hanging around to haunt places if he could not keep up with the job." His tongue hung from the side of his mouth as he looked up at me.

None of the options were palatable. However, if reapers came for me or anyone I loved, I had no qualms about ending them.

"Are there any good reapers?"

Levi glanced back at the pathway. "Yes. They serve your father at their pleasure. Your father freed the reapers years ago, so I am unsure why this is happening now. My only guess is that the history of Death and his successors has been written in Fate's book since the beginning of time. They think you are destined to replace him."

"And if I have no interest in the job?"

Levi huffed. "You have far more choices than your father. You are a woman. There has never been a female Death. Ever."

I stopped and stared at him. "Never?"

"Not ever. The scythe is handed down from generation to generation, from father to son. I don't even recall Death ever having a female child. So, you are a true enigma."

"Fancy that." I laughed and met Holly's gaze. "An enigma. Just what I always wanted to be."

Grim's Daughter
Chapter 5

THERE WAS NO SNEAKING into Holly's grandparents' house. Not when the gate had a buzzer that went off any time it opened or closed. When we walked into their house, Holly's grandfather was waiting in the entryway to the back of the house with his arms crossed tight. Truthfully, CJ Ryan really didn't look much older than Alex. He could pass for Alex's twin. But seeing as he was Alex's dad, he must have been somewhere in his fifties.

When his gaze dropped to Levi, his arms fell to his side and the hardness around his mouth transitioned to worry. The only time this dog came out to play was when there were things going on in the supernatural realm that weren't kosher. And reapers wanting to overthrow Death counted as very unkosher.

"What's going on?"

"Reapers are getting restless," Levi said, and led me into the back of the house, where their open-concept kitchen and family room sat with a view of the ocean much like ours, except Papa had a pool between the sliders and the drop to the ocean. It was closed for winter despite the mild November we were experiencing.

"What does that mean?" he asked.

I took a seat on the couch. "It means I think it would be safer for everyone if you homeschooled us until this blows over. All I need is another reaper showing up at the school and killing people willy-nilly. Levi ate the one who showed up today." I met his gaze.

Papa's eyebrows shot up in perfectly manicured arches. "At the school?" His voice took on an incredulous tone.

"Outside the school. On the soccer field. No one saw us. Besides, I know better than to let Leviathan go hunting inside a high school." I rolled my eyes at him. I didn't mean any disrespect, but for such a genius, he sometimes asked stupid questions.

"What happened in school?" he asked in a measured tone. That crease of worry deepened between his eyes.

I blinked, and it took me a moment to realize my mistake. I laughed under my breath at my misuse of words. "No one died today except the reaper. I didn't mean to alarm you, and I'm not even sure if the one who was there was good or bad. Just before Levi ate him, he said my mother sent him."

"And you didn't hear him out?" Papa's expression nearly made me laugh. It was as if we turned down one of his famous ice cream sundaes he whipped up just for us.

Holly took the seat on the couch next to me. "Give us a break, Papa," she said. "Neither of us wants to be a pawn in this crazy dispute."

He glanced between the two of us as if we had lost our minds.

"And I've given Levi free rein to eat any reaper who comes near us."

"Is that truly wise?" Doubt painted his eyes darker, as if he might have more insight than we did.

"What would you do if you were in my shoes?"

My question seemed to snap him back into his normal analytical self. "What are the stakes?" He took a seat opposite me. He normally could pull out thoughts from people's heads just like Alex could, but for some reason, I wasn't one of those he could penetrate. He had never been able to read me, much like he was hit or miss with Holly or her father, Alex.

I sighed. "My father's life."

He let out a bark of a laugh and glanced out the door to the ocean beyond. "Sacrificing your father isn't easy." He looked down at his hands and then met my gaze. "Even if he's willing to take the hit. Is this what he wants?"

I shook my head. "He does not. And I'm not too keen on dying to take over the family business, you know." I picked at a hangnail on my thumb.

"I can see how that would be something you'd want to avoid." He nodded, and it wasn't in that placating way parents and grandparents sometimes had.

"But there are reapers who are not happy that they can't control my father, so they want me to step in, thinking they'd have a better chance of controlling me."

Papa smirked and looked away. "They apparently do not know you."

I laughed, but it faded quickly. "No. They don't. But they could hurt those I love to get me to agree."

His gaze snapped back to mine.

"And even you can't stop a reaper," I added, repeating my mother's words.

He cocked an eyebrow. It was more of a challenge than out of surprise. "Well, if one shows up, we'll just see about that."

He slowly grinned in a way that made me shift in my seat. There was no humor in his eyes, and I glanced away, unable to keep his silent challenge.

"You cannot beat a reaper," Levi said.

Papa's smile faded, and he glanced at the beast next to me. "Then why didn't your master bring an army of reapers to my house to collect the siren when I threatened him?" He crossed his arms.

Papa threatened my dad? I glanced between Levi and Papa, waiting for answers in this new development.

"Nick was fond of you and your brother. And he didn't expect you to toss me miles into the Atlantic. Besides, that would have been an unnecessary display of power." Levi settled down on the floor at my feet and crossed his paws. "Angel blood has no impact on a reaper. Neither does angel grace or supernatural powers. You may be the most powerful living being, but you have no powers on the other side. That is Death and Fate's realm."

He seemed to mull over Levi's words, and finally he nodded and met the dog's gaze. "Then what does kill a reaper?"

Levi's tongue lolled out the side of his mouth just before he burped.

Papa's eyes narrowed. "I can still kick your ass." He pointed at Levi.

"Perhaps, but you can't kill a reaper. I can." Tension thickened between the two of them.

"And my mother said a certain knife would do the trick, too," I added, to distract them both.

The color faded from Papa's face. "Not Heaven's blade," he said.

I had heard the stories. I knew Heaven's blade was something that was deadly in the extreme. One cut and it wiped someone from existence. One minute there, and the next gone. It had been used on Lucifer, and his exit from existence messed with the magical fabric of all realms for a spell, which in turn made me possible.

"That is one of the three things that can annihilate a reaper, but it isn't something my parents seem to trust me with. It's another dagger."

He seemed to relax in the chair, and he turned to Holly. "I'm assuming you want to be homeschooled, too?" His eyes seemed to sparkle at the prospect.

Alex always argued with his father on this one point. Alex wanted us in the town's public schools, even though he himself had been homeschooled. He said he didn't want us to miss out on our childhoods.

I guess I could see both points. We had a lot of friends in York who we wouldn't have met had we been homeschooled. Holly had been lucky enough to date a few boys, but hadn't yet found one who wasn't a tool.

Me, I hadn't really dated yet. I guess at some level; I was secretly holding out for Zane. My hand brushed the pocket where his card was. Just knowing he had given me his number made me lose my train of thought. Besides Zane, the only guys who seemed interested in me were the seasonal jerks who came to town with their entitled attitudes and only one thing on their minds. That was until today, when I brought Levi into the school and caught the coolest kid's eye.

"Seriously?" Holly said, pulling me out of my reverie.

"Hmm?" I blinked up at her. I hadn't heard a thing since Papa asked her about homeschool.

"I asked if you wanted me here with you."

I smiled. "It would be safer for both of us."

She rolled her eyes. "You're still thinking about Zane, aren't you?"

Heat filled my cheeks, and I glanced out the door, right into the angry eyes of my mother. I arched my eyebrows, and Levi sat up next to me. Her gaze dropped to him and her entire face turned red. She tried the door, and it didn't budge.

Papa glanced over at the sound and then traded a glance with me. Before he could get out of the seat, my mother transitioned through the glass and pointed at me.

"What happened to Jake?" she squeaked.

"I'm not willing to be a pawn in this war. I don't care that you sent him. He made me feel sick to my stomach and see reapers everywhere. That is not playing for the good team, wouldn't you say?"

She blinked, and her gaze dropped to Levi. Her eyes narrowed. "So, you just ate him?"

"I am here to protect Melissa and the Ryans, so yes, I ate the reaper, and I will continue to do so at the request of my ward." He glanced at me and then back at my mother. "So, if you truly have allies, then keep them away from these families."

"You work for me." She pointed at Levi.

He stood with a growl. "I am indebted to Nick Ramsay, not you. And he asked me to watch over his daughter. Do not mistake that for being your underling. Understand me?"

He started growing into his authentic form as he talked, and I reached out and touched his leg. He glanced at me, nodded, and shrunk back into dog form before he had the chance to ruin the house. If he had kept going, he would have gone clear through the ceiling, and who knew how tall he was in his native form.

"Nick works for me." She amended her comment.

"But I do not. I serve at *my* pleasure." Levi sat down next to me, giving my mother the stink eye.

"Are you two about finished?" Papa asked, pulling our attention away from the mounting tension in the room.

"Yes," both my mother and Levi said at the same time.

"Then will you tell me what we can do to make this go away?"

My mother sighed and shrugged. "I don't know. I don't think there's anything short of Melissa doing what they want her to do. And that means she dies and so does Nick." She shook her head. "That's not happening."

Papa crossed his arms and leaned back in the seat, gnawing on his lower lip as he mulled over what my mom had just said. "There has to be another way."

I raked my hand through my hair in exasperation. "I'm the only one who can stop this, even if it means annihilating every last reaper."

Grim's Daughter
Chapter 6

FIGURES. ALL THAT DRAMA in a single twenty-four hours and then nothing. Crickets. Maybe it was because Alex and Faith pulled us from school until this blew over, but I'm not sure. Maybe word I had Levi by my side got out to the rest of the rebel reapers. Who knows? But yesterday, Papa had drilled us relentlessly on mathematics, science, and English to the point both Holly and I wished we were back at York High School. The only highlight was texting Zane. I even asked him to join us for our Thanksgiving flag football game.

And much to my surprise, he said yes. Now I just had to figure out a way to break it to the family.

Holly and I rushed around, getting ready for the annual bash at Papa's house. I touched up my makeup and stepped back to look at the rings of curls in my hair. Today was always the family picture day for the latest Christmas card, so I wanted to look my best. Besides, Alex and Faith wanted us in our finest threads. But at least this year they didn't make us wear hideous matching stuff.

I smoothed down the front of my blood-red crushed velvet dress Holly's mother had put out for me to wear, and turned toward the full-length mirror hanging from the back of the bathroom door.

"You look stunning in that," Holly said from behind me. In a way, we did match, but with opposites. She wore black velvet, and her red hair complemented it in much the same way as my black hair complemented my dress.

"You look great, too." I smiled and headed back to the room, slipping on my black patent-leather shoes. I grabbed a pair of sweats and a T-shirt along with sneakers to change into for the annual turkey day football game.

This was one holiday I enjoyed celebrating, despite my parents never being there. And after the scare earlier this week, I was ready to have a stellar day with all Holly's aunts, uncles, cousins, and some pseudo family who weren't related to the Ryans by blood, but were considered family by some other unspoken bond.

Even with the anticipation of the day, my nerves remained unsettled, as if they were just waiting for the gauntlet to drop.

"You okay?" Holly asked as she squeezed by me and headed into the room.

I hadn't realized I had stalled in place. "Yeah, just looking forward to today."

"Is Zane dropping by?"

Heat filled my cheeks, and I nodded, thankful she broached the subject and I didn't have to figure out how to tell her the coolest kid in school was coming to play football with us. "I told him we play flag football around three. He said he'd be there. Besides, Alex wants to check him out to make sure he's legit before I can go anywhere with him." I rolled my eyes.

Holly smirked. "Dad is a bit overprotective of us. You'd think he'd ease up on us now that we aren't in school."

I snorted a laugh. If Holly really thought that, then she didn't know her father at all. With the potential for danger lurking in the shadows, he was more likely to be uber vigilant and protective to a fault. He didn't even like dropping us off at his father's house for homeschooling.

We climbed down the stairs and stepped into the living room just as her parents came out of their bedroom. Damn them, we were coordinated in red and black, after all. But at least this year it wasn't as gaudy as some years past. I was actually glad to be in this dress, and I hoped Zane would get there before I changed out of it. I wanted him to see me all decked out.

Holly and I traded a glance.

"I know. I know," Faith started once she saw our eye rolls. "But the family Christmas cards need to be done. So please..." She pointed to the hearth where Levi had already curled up at the base, leaving us a little room to gather behind the big shepherd.

The camera perched on a tripod and Alex fiddled with it as Holly and I took the center spots and Faith stood next to Holly in a dress that looked three times darker than my crimson red. Alex slid next to me, all decked out in black and, without prompting, we all plastered on our happy family picture smile.

"Really?" Levi said after the first picture snapped off and he looked back at us.

"You would prefer to sit?" Alex asked.

"No. I would prefer to be crouched, with my teeth bared, and look badass than like a docile family pet." He huffed and walked away. "Take the next one without me, please."

"Fine," Alex said, and we all focused on the camera.

Holly tapped me on the back, and I glanced at her just as the flash went off. Holly and I stepped away.

"I wasn't ready. One more." Faith pulled Holly back in place.

"Okay. One, two, three, smile!" Alex counted down and the second after the picture smiles appeared, the flash went off again.

This time, when we dispersed, no one called us back in place. Alex and Faith clicked through the images on the camera as Holly and I headed to the garage with Levi in tow.

"Humans are such techno-geeks," Levi muttered as he climbed into the backseat of the car.

I slid in next to him, and Holly took the remainder of the seat and tossed our bag with the change of clothes into the back as we waited for our parents to take us on the ride across town.

All the seasonal people abandoned York in October, and the town quieted into the slow Northeastern quaint lifestyle that we were used to. Our ride took a few minutes instead of the half hour it seemed to take at the height of summer. I didn't mind the hustle and bustle of summer like some residents did, but I preferred this time of year when the calm settled over all of us. I certainly hoped that calm would last.

The moment the front door opened, the scent of roasting turkey and all the trimmings wafted out at us, and my mouth watered. Levi bolted inside ahead of us with the hairs on the back of his neck raised in protective fashion. I hurried after him, because all we needed was for him to eat a guest just out of purely hyped-up adrenaline.

I skidded to a halt as soon as I slid through the door. My parents were among the familiar holiday faces. Levi backed up to where I stood gawking. My palm found the crown of his head as surprise raked its fine nails over my skin.

The lively conversation halted at our arrival, and all eyes fell on us as the rest of the family stepped in behind me. Holly darted around me and headed for the couch, where Alexis sat with her phone. Alexis's parents, Kylee and Michael, stood next to my parents. Whatever conversation they had been in the middle of stalled as they stared at me.

Abandoned by my best friend to grapple with the shock of my parents finally joining in on a holiday celebration, Alex put his hand on my shoulder and squeezed as if he knew I was reeling more than I let on.

I gave him a nod and followed him into the fray, with Levi at my side. I plastered a smile on my face as I said hello to Alex's twin sisters, Amber and Arianna, accepting hugs from them along with their husbands, John and Joe, who were also twins. They were weird that way, and the four of them were the only normal people in the family, although both Amber and Arianna had the dark hair and blue eye combination that seemed prevalent with the Ryan genes. Unfortunately, they hadn't inherited any of Nana and Papa's gifts, like Alex had. Even their cousin April had a touch of the angel magic. Maybe it was a twin thing, who knows, but they were the sweetest people, even without powers.

The back door slid open and Alexis's younger sister Naomi—who was the spitting image of her father Michael with dark hair, olive skin, and the same bright-blue eyes that seemed to be prevalent among angel kin—skipped into the house.

Behind her came Papa's personal pilot, Josh, and his wife Joanne, along with their two kids. I remember when he finally met Joanne. He was nice to begin with, but falling in love brought out an even more vibrant, joyous personality. He glowed more than his bride on their wedding day. Holly and I were nearly five and still remember dancing until we passed out on her parents' laps.

April—Alex's cousin—followed Josh and his family in from the backyard with both her girls jumping at her side asking to go down to the playroom. She nodded and they, along with Josh's children made a beeline down to Papa's famous kid zone in the basement.

Kylee slipped out of the room toward the front door and came back a few minutes later with another couple we only saw at this time of year. Her name was normal, Phoebe, but his name was just strange. Who names their kid Smoke? Even with the odd name, Smoke was the best flag football player in the group, and I always prayed he was on our team.

They both halted at the sight of Levi and my parents. "Is there something you want to tell us?" Smoke asked with a smooth New York accent, if there was such a thing. He pointedly stared at my mother with eyes as green as emeralds. Leave it to the New Yorker to ask a direct question. It made me like Smoke even more than when I found out he had been a cat for a couple of millennia.

The conversations that had started back up after our arrival stopped altogether, and all eyes swiveled to my parents. I guess no one really questioned why my folks finally showed up at a family event until this moment.

I crossed my arms and raised an eyebrow at my mom. The people here should know what kind of precarious situation they might step into.

Kylee pulled a knife out of what seemed like thin air and waved it in Phoebe and Smoke's direction.

"Another reaper from Hell?" Phoebe asked as her arms uncrossed and fell to her sides.

My father took a deep breath and glanced around the room before he met Phoebe's gaze. "Worse. A faction of the reapers wants me out of the job."

"What good would that do?" Phoebe asked.

"They want control," my father replied.

"But doesn't your wife have all the control?" Smoke waved toward my mom. It wasn't the least bit snarky, either.

"Technically, that's true, but they really want things to go back to the way they were before, which is ironic because they were basically Fate's slaves before we took over. So, they want both of us gone. They want someone green, someone they can control in our roles. They believe Missy is destined to take over as Death, but her future is not written. She is free from the binds of the family business, and we would like to keep it that way."

I snorted. Like reapers would have a prayer of controlling me. That idea nearly made me laugh, even as heat flushed my cheeks as all the attention in the room centered on me.

"I will eat any reaper who comes near Missy." Levi growled and leaned into my leg.

I patted him on the head, smiling. "Everyone here already knows that." I glanced around and shrugged. "Can we just enjoy a happy Thanksgiving today and deal with this another time?"

"I second that!" Holly said, as she popped up from the couch.

The doorbell rang, and Papa exchanged a look with Nana before he headed out of the family room. I crossed to the couch, but before I could sit down, Papa stepped back into the room and cleared his throat.

"Missy, can I have a word?"

His tone was cautious, as if I did something wrong. I glanced at Holly and then made my way through the crowd to where he stood. He pulled me into the foyer, and my heart dropped to the floor at Zane inside the front door.

It wasn't even noon yet, but that wasn't what made my feet move faster toward him. His right eye was swollen and discolored, and his lip still had dried blood on it. His shirt sported crimson droplets. He was hugging his right arm and leaning against the wall, as if standing were its own kind of Hell.

"I'm sorry." He shifted as he looked from me to my grandfather. "I didn't know where else to go."

I reached up to touch the bruise, and he flinched away from me. "Who did this?" I whispered.

Zane just shook his head.

"He said you invited him?" Papa asked from behind me, but his voice was softer than when he called me out of the family room. I was sure he knew what happened to Zane, and that I had indeed invited him to come over later today. He had a habit of peeking in other's minds to make sure they didn't have bad intentions.

I turned around and faced Papa. "I invited him for the touch football game."

"Well, since he's here, if he doesn't mind a crowd, he can join us for dinner, if you'd like." His gaze pierced through me as though he were trying to read my intentions. But, like Holly, I was totally unreadable.

I nodded and glanced over my shoulder. "Did you want to stay?"

Zane glanced at my grandfather and nodded. "If it isn't too much trouble."

Nana stepped into the room, wiping her hands. She glanced at Papa and then at Zane. Her eyes widened, and she handed the towel to Papa and crossed to where Zane stood.

"Take out the turkey while I tend to this boy's injuries." She took Zane's arm, leading him to the stairs as Papa left the room. "I'm a doctor," she said as he stared at her.

"I know. You've treated me before," he said.

Nana studied him for a moment and then, I swear, her eyes teared up. She nodded with her lips pressed together in an unhappy set. "I thought your father learned his lesson."

Zane let out a soft laugh, and his cheeks reddened. "For a little while. But as soon as his parole was up, he reverted to his old ways. Big Brother was no longer watching." Bitterness slid into his voice.

"It won't happen again," Nana said before she trotted up the stairs, leaving me with Zane. Before I could formulate the questions swirling in my mind and articulate them, Nana was back with her bag. She opened it on the floor and pulled out a small ice pack that she shook and then gingerly placed on his swollen eye.

Zane winced anyway and lifted his arm to hold it, but couldn't quite manage it. The ice pack fell into his lap. He picked it up with his left hand and put it back in place.

Nana reached into her bag for a bandage wrap. "Let me see that arm," she said, and as he held it out for her to inspect, my father stepped into the room.

"Who's this?" He waved at Zane. A crease appeared between his eyes as he studied Zane. As if he were supposed to know who he was.

"A friend," I said, but I couldn't meet his gaze as a chill gripped me.

Zane raised an eyebrow as he looked between me and my father. My father, who looked no older than I did. He hissed as Nana tried to straighten out his arm.

"Your arm is broken," Nana said.

Zane nodded, but kept his quizzical gaze on me. "Probably. I think a couple of ribs are broken, too."

It made me want to wrap my arms around him and take away all the hurt in his voice.

His gaze bounced between my father and me, and I realized the pain in his voice had very little to do with his physical injuries. He was trying to figure out the relationship between my father and me, especially given my father's disapproving glare.

"This is my father." I waved at my dad. "Dad, this is Zane. He goes to York High School with us. He saw Levi eat a reaper the other day." I couldn't let Zane think otherwise, not with that soul-crushing hurt in his eyes. Besides, I trusted him even though I didn't know enough about him, like why he was in such a sad state right now.

Nana stared right at me, with a wide-eyed look, as though I had divulged the world's secrets to a stranger.

"He saw. What was I supposed to do, lie?" I asked to her unspoken question.

Levi trotted into the living room, along with my mother. Zane shrunk back a little at the sight of the German shepherd.

Nana sighed and stood. "This is going to hurt a little." Then she leaned forward and pressed a kiss to the top of Zane's head.

"Mom," Alex said with a voice full of warning as he stepped into the room.

Sparks already had started down Zane's body, glowing in the darkened entryway. Zane hissed through clenched teeth.

"He saw Leviathan and didn't seem to flinch at seeing Missy's father, even though he had an inkling of exactly what he was. Besides, he's kept his own father's dirty secret for more years than a child has a right to—he can keep his mouth shut on mine." She looked down at Zane. "Isn't that right?"

"Yes, ma'am," he whispered, despite the pain carrying through his voice. Then his eyes rolled back, and he slumped on the stairs.

"Tend to your boyfriend," Nana said.

Before I could correct her, she corralled my parents to the back of the house. She even closed the pocket door and the noise level dropped enough for me to hear Zane's even breathing.

I sat down on the stairs next to him and bit my lip, debating on letting him just remain slumped against the wall. My urge to run my fingers through his hair won out, and I pulled him into my arms. His hair was just as silky as I had always imagined, and I sighed at the feel of it sliding through my hands. The ugly swelling melted away from Nana's healing magic. So did the dark-purple bruising.

I continued to stroke his forehead softly. I knew the effects of her mojo. It always made the receiver black out while their body healed, but those first few seconds were torture. I wasn't sure whether that was a blessing or a curse in itself, but I knew firsthand the pain of skin stitching together and the bliss of being unconscious through the bulk of the mending process.

Finally, his eyes fluttered open. He stared up at me, blinking rapidly as I pulled my hand away from his thick hair. And then looked around at the stairwell and then back at me as if his brain couldn't reconcile where he was.

"You passed out," I said. "It happens."

His eyebrows arched and he slowly sat up and rubbed his face, but stopped halfway through the action. His fingers touched the area that had been swollen and bruised, and then his gaze snapped to mine.

"It doesn't hurt." He moved his arm, turning his wrist this way and that, feeling his way up his forearm with his other hand. "What did she do to me?" he asked softly.

"Nana's a doctor."

"A frickin' witch doctor," he muttered, still inspecting his arm.

I hooked my finger under his chin and made him look at me. "Your father did this to you?" I couldn't fathom my father raising his hand to me. Especially with Alex and Papa around. He may have abandoned me for years, but he would never intentionally hurt me. As screwed up as that was, it was a truth I lived with.

He pulled away from me and stood, stepping toward the door. "I shouldn't have come."

I grabbed his arm before he could slip away. "You're safe here." I don't know why I blurted that out, but it had the desired effect.

He paused and put his forehead against the door. "I've never felt safe before," he whispered, and glanced at me out of the corner of his eyes.

I kept my hand on his arm. "You will be here." I stopped short at promising him. Not with the pending danger hanging over my head. But I'd do my damnedest to make sure no one here was harmed. Plus, Levi had my back, so I was pretty sure that counted as much as having my own army.

He turned my way. "Was that really your father?" he asked with a bit of sarcasm lacing his voice as a cocky smile formed.

"Death in the flesh."

He blinked again.

"You are serious." His arms fell by his sides.

"I've never lied."

He burst out laughing. "So, all those years you got sent to the principal's office for announcing your father was Death, you weren't trying to get in trouble?"

I shook my head.

"And that pretty blonde?" He glanced at the door.

"Is my mother. They are a few years younger than Papa is. He used to babysit my father when he was a kid."

He slowly sat back down on the stairs. "And how does Holly and her family fit in?" he asked as he studied his hands.

"They basically adopted me. My last name isn't Ryan. It's Ramsay." I took a seat next to him. "They aren't blood, if that's what you're asking. But they are my family. Everyone beyond that door is family in some way or another."

He nodded.

"Family doesn't end in blood."

He smirked. "*Supernatural* fan?"

"Ayup." I bumped his shoulder. "You staying for turkey and trimmings and then the touch football game?"

He glanced at his clasped hands. "I'm not ready for an in-depth conversation with the Grim Reaper. Besides, I'm not sure how to explain the black eye."

"Um. Stand up and look in that mirror." I pointed to the mirror on the wall above us.

Zane stood and glanced at the mirror and then stepped close to stare at his unmarred face. He touched his eye again. When he turned toward me, his eyes were wider and a brighter green than before. "I just thought she numbed the pain."

73

"Nana is pretty special, and she isn't the only one. Do you want to stay for dinner and get to know my family, or are you getting cold feet?"

He glanced at the door and licked his lips.

"I never would have thought the coolest kid in school was a bit of a chicken." I poked his chest.

He laughed and grabbed my hand. His grin faded as he met my gaze. "I'm not the coolest kid in school. You beat me by a mile."

He licked his lips and his gaze fell to mine. I just wanted him to kiss me, but I knew if he had those thoughts, someone was going to bust in on us and make this entire thing much more awkward than it already was for him.

I stepped back and pulled him toward the pocket door blocking out the crowd in the back of the house.

"Stay for dinner," I whispered and kept moving toward the door with his hand in mine.

He rolled his eyes. "I guess I can break bread with the famous Ryan clan," he conceded, as I reached for the door.

Grim's Daughter
Chapter 7

WE WALKED INTO THE back and conversation continued in little pods. The kitchen pod of women, along with Papa, were busy getting the food ready. Another pod was at the table already, and the kids were all gathered on the couches in front of the television watching the Macy's parade. I was sure others were downstairs, but I pulled Zane through to the couches and the group closest to our age.

"Hey," Zane said as we sat on the couch near Holly.

"You're a little early," Holly said, echoing my initial thoughts as she stared between us at our clasped hands. "Did something happen that I should know about?" She glanced up at me, cocking her head.

"Sorry." Zane actually tightened his grip on my hand.

"No apology needed," she said. "This is Alexis. She's from California." Holly smiled as if California were the most exotic place on the earth.

Alexis rolled her eyes and then smiled politely.

Holly started bouncing small flames from finger to finger as she focused on the kitchen. She was either bored or hungry. My bet was hungry because right about now, I could devour the turkey myself.

Zane's eyebrows rose so fast and so high, I thought they'd fly right off his forehead. I don't think he was handling all this supernatural stuff as well as he pretended, and it made me shift in my seat.

I cleared my throat, and she suddenly closed her hand, dousing the flame. It was as if she forgot someone was in the room who was not privy to all our insanely unique secrets.

He glanced around the room and then at me. Instead of answering his near panicked look, I took his hand and led him out the sliding glass doors into the backyard and across to the farthest point and a finely manicured rock wall that had stood for decades.

"No one even blinked when she did that fire thing with her fingers." He pointed back at the house.

I patted the stones next to me. After he sat, I nodded. "Yeah. Remember, this is all normal for us. Fire abilities, healing abilities, mind reading, and all sorts of other stuff, including being relatives of certain ethereal beings." I gave him a smile. "There are some normal people who know our family secrets in there. Loyal friends who know what side we are on."

"And what side is that?"

"We are on the side of good, despite some of our heritages."

"The villain always thinks he is on the side of good." Zane crossed his arms.

"They stopped the end of times." I nodded at the house. "People were lost in that battle, too." I had heard enough stories about Alex's uncle and the fact he sacrificed himself for Holly's mom. "I don't know the whole story, but I know it was bloody and devastating."

"What about you? Where do you stand?"

"I stand with the Ryans. Plus, I'm not interested in the family business."

He smiled and nodded. "Although I could see you with a badass scythe."

I laughed. "Not something I'm interested in. Besides, I have to stop breathing to take that job."

His smile disappeared and his eyes widened. "But your parents..."

"Dead as a doornail."

Speaking of the devil, my mother stepped outside and crossed the lawn to where we sat.

He stared at her as she moved closer. "Dead, like zombie-dead?"

I snorted laughter and shook my head as he glanced at me. Curiosity danced in his eyes. "Mom, this is Zane," I introduced when she stopped. "Zane, my mother."

"Mrs. Ramsay." He offered his hand.

"Nick said he briefly met you when you first arrived." She studied him, inspecting him for any tells that she could pounce on as she shook his hand.

"Yes, ma'am," he said.

I didn't like her sizing Zane up in front of me. If anyone had that right, it was Faith and Alex, not my absent mother.

"So, how do you know my daughter?" She crossed her arms.

"School. I've been in classes with Melissa since we were, what, seven or eight?" He glanced at me.

I shrugged, but I was impressed. "I didn't think you even noticed me until I walked into the school on Monday with Levi."

He grinned. "I guess I've kept my secret pretty well all these years, then."

I leaned to the side and stared at him. Zane hesitated and glanced at my mom. She scowled until I cleared my throat, sending her my best *please leave us alone* look.

"Dinner is almost ready. We can resume this conversation after supper," my mother said in a tone harsh enough for me to want to deck her.

"Touch football is after dinner." I cocked my head in a silent challenge and stood.

My mother turned and headed toward the house.

I spun back to Zane when my mother was out of earshot. "What secret?"

"Oh, come on, you had to have known I've had a crush on you since, like, the fourth grade." He laughed.

My eyebrows arched. I had no clue. And here I had the same feelings that I kept under wraps because the cool kid wouldn't ever fall for my skinny ass. I was goth at best, not some hot tart like I had seen hanging on his arm almost every day. But it was never the same girl and every now and again, I'd see him looking my way. It was almost as if those trails of girls were supposed to make me jealous. No way I was telling him it worked. Not with this little revelation.

"Why wouldn't you, I don't know, ask me out on a date?" I asked.

"That would have meant revealing what a monster my father was," he said under his breath and looked away.

My heart broke for him, and I covered his hand with mine. Instead of acting on my instinct to just hug him, I pulled him back toward the house to the waiting turkey and all the trimmings.

I stopped at the door and turned toward him before we stepped inside.

"This isn't some dare that one of your friends put you up to, is it?" I glanced up at him, still unsure whether he was really sincere. "Or some dare to get the goth girl to sleep with you?"

"You sure are blunt," he said, but he kept his hand in mine.

"Well?"

"No. This isn't some stupid high school bet. I think your dog would eat me if I wasn't sincere." He glanced over my shoulder at Levi inside the house. "And I have a feeling he would know if I was full of shit or not." He met my gaze again.

"Just a word of warning...if this does end up being something like that, I will happily let Levi tear you apart."

"Duly noted."

He smiled down at me in such a sexy way that I was the one to let go of his hand and step inside, where everyone had already gathered around the table. The gap for where we were supposed to sit looked like a missing tooth and I hurried over to fill the space with Zane by my side.

Everyone joined hands, and Zane squeezed mine while Papa said grace.

The minute everyone's hands dropped and people took their seats, pandemonium broke out. Conversations started or continued in some cases, as food and plates were passed around the table.

Zane looked a bit overwhelmed by it all, but that didn't seem to stop him from loading his plate like the rest of the guests. It wasn't until I had my last forkful of mashed potatoes that a tingle started at the base of my spine and the room tilted enough for me to pause with my mouth hanging open.

I shot my gaze to where Levi had been sitting. He was already on his feet and halfway across the room when everyone turned into that superimposed version of reapers like the kids in the school hallway had. I forced it away. No one else seemed to sense the mounting danger in the room besides my favorite ancient beast.

Not even my mother or father seemed to notice the change in the air. An ominous presence was about to make themselves known. The low growl in Levi's throat caught the attention of Faith, who sat on the other side of Zane. She looked at the dog and then around the room, almost in the same way as I had.

Our gaze met, and I shrugged. I didn't know what was coming, but something clearly was. Papa, Nana, and Alex exchanged a quizzical glance, and then darkness blanketed the room.

Reapers cloaked in black surrounded us, looking like a wall of skeletal monks. But they were not here in peace. The malice rolled off them and there was at least one reaper for every person at the table, and they were close enough to us that my heart galloped in my chest. I was the first one on my feet, and I spun to look at the reaper behind me. Levi growled at my side.

My skin buzzed in a way I had never experienced, and I just wanted to protect everyone in the room from the hatred coming in waves at all of us.

"Come with us and there will be no harm to everyone here," the reaper I faced said. He grabbed my wrist.

This reaper wanted me dead. He wanted my father dead. He wanted control, and that was not in my plans at all. If I didn't comply, every living being in this room would find their end with just a touch from the reapers poised behind each guest.

A chill bit at my skin and then that buzzing ballooned into something I had no idea how to control. It pounded in my veins, and I gritted my teeth together, steeling myself for the worst.

My protective reflex flared, and I imagined a cocoon around everyone else, protecting them from harm. When I met the reaper's gaze, a rush of the power building inside me ran down my arm, right to the spot where he had me in his grip.

The reaper gasped. His jaw fell slack and his gaze shot to the spot where we were connected, flesh to bone.

My arm turned crimson around his skeletal hand, and then he flaked away like ash from a firepit on a particularly windy day. He wasn't the only one in the room disintegrating, either. A handful of reapers had reached out to the humans around the table, but their touch never reached their destination.

Each reaper's destruction resonated in my cells. I bit my lip so I wouldn't cry out with the darkness bleeding into my veins like a thousand deaths clawing at me from the inside. I grabbed the back of my chair to steady myself. If I fell now, everyone else at the table would meet their end. And I was positive, now that I was connected into the afterlife in some strange way, I would feel their deaths just as acutely as I felt the reapers'.

I had to get them out of there while they were dumbstruck with fear. Before I lost the fight against the darkness trying to drown me.

"Leave before I do the same to every one of you." By some miracle, I kept the shakiness out of my voice and moved my gaze to the nearest reaper.

I guess my threat was worth something because, after a moment, it pointed at me. "This isn't over." And then the lot of them blinked out of the room.

I turned back toward the table, to the shocked expressions of everyone in the room, including my parents. The buzz filling my ears got louder and louder as my vision narrowed into a pinhole.

"Catch her!" Levi said loud enough to penetrate my brain, and then all went black.

Grim's Daughter
Chapter 8

THAT BUZZING PERSISTED, BUT when I opened my eyes, all I saw was Zane's concerned green eyes hovering over me. More faces beyond his came into focus and I blinked away the fog clouding my brain and pushed myself up into a sitting position on the couch.

"I'm okay," I said with a voice that sounded more croaky than clear. My arm throbbed where the reaper had gripped me. So did the rest of my body. I felt as if they had used me as someone's punching bag.

My father sat in the reclining chair across from me, paler than usual. He glanced at my wrist, and I followed his confused gaze and gasped. The skin around my wrist had blackened, as though they had branded me with the shape of a skeletal hand. No wonder it throbbed.

I looked at Nana, and she just shrugged and slowly shook her head. I leaned back against the soft throw pillows and closed my eyes. Nana usually could erase damage with a healing kiss like she had with Zane. This burn wasn't within her power to fix, which meant it was made of a more powerful supernatural magic, or curse—which felt like a better term.

Levi strolled up to me and sniffed the mark before letting out a decisive growl. "Next time I will not hesitate like I did today."

"People would have died if you had." I touched the burn and winced.

Zane took a seat on the couch next to me and ran a shaky hand through his hair. "I'm not sure I'm really ready for any of this," he mumbled under his breath, and glanced my way.

Alex reached out to touch Zane's forehead, and I grabbed his hand, intercepting what was akin to erasing his memories of this day. It was far more effective than the neuralyzer from the movie *Men in Black.*

Alex's eyebrow arched, and I narrowed my eyes, trying to convey *don't you dare* without words. I seemed to have broadcast the message clearly because he stepped back the moment I released his wrist.

Zane glanced between the two of us. "Did I miss something?"

I sighed. And for once, I didn't say yes or no. Alex's powers were not mine to discuss, even though I intervened. Zane had a right to know what was happening with me, especially if he had intentions of staying in my life in any form. Friend. More than friends. It didn't matter. He deserved to make the decision with all the facts.

"I know this is a lot for you, and if you want to forget all about me, that's okay, too."

Zane's eyebrows lowered, morphing into an almost mad expression. Like I had dissed him in some way. Enough so that I shrank back into the couch.

"You think a little"—he twirled his finger—"cosmic weirdness is about to run me off after waiting so long to talk to you?"

The smirks around the room caught me as off guard as his words.

I stood.

"You might want to take it easy," Alex said, and I cast a glare in his direction.

I didn't need to be coddled, even with every cell in my body throbbing with whatever leftover magic had knocked me on my ass. But I needed a private conversation with Zane.

I reached my hand out to him and he took it, allowing me to lead him back outside. The wind had picked up, along with enough of a nip in the air for my arms to break out in gooseflesh. I glanced over my shoulder to make sure we weren't followed. No one came out to stand watch except my trusted shepherd.

Levi trailed behind us far enough to give me a sense of privacy, but near enough to defend me if the reapers returned.

Instead of going out to the rock wall, I took a seat on the closest lounge chair facing the pool and waved Zane to the one next to me. It took a great deal out of me to get this far, and there was no way I'd make it all the way across the yard. I felt like a puddle instead of a person.

"This cosmic weirdness that you referred to in there is deadly for anyone with a heartbeat."

"Nothing like softening the blow," Levi muttered from close by.

Zane snorted a laugh. "I live in a house where just a single word can trigger a deadly experience. You think this scares me?"

I stared at him. "If one of those things touched you, you would have died like that." I snapped my fingers and noticed that my hand shook despite my attempt not to let all this get to me. But saying the words out loud actually undid my calm composure. It was as if I had the delayed reaction of the sudden drop in adrenaline, like most trauma survivors I had read about. Shock was a tricky thing, and I was experiencing the full force of it.

I dropped my hand as quickly as possible, but I couldn't hide the fact the chair was vibrating with the shakes gripping me.

Zane moved to the edge of my chair and took my hands. "Take slow breaths," he said in the calmest manner. "You're okay. You just need to breathe right now."

I looked into the green depths of his eyes and instead of concern, I saw understanding and it made my stomach clench. The reason he recognized the signs hurt in the depths of my soul. He had been there, but not because of a bunch of rogue reapers. No, his father's beatings gave him this calmness in a crisis.

I closed my eyes and listened to his soft instructions on taking breath after breath until the shaking subsided. I squeezed his hand.

"Thank you," I whispered.

"For?"

"For talking me off the ledge." I shrugged. "For being willing to stay when it isn't in your best interest."

He reached out and palmed my cheek. I leaned into his hand, relishing the warmth of it. "I admit, I was not prepared for all this supernatural crap, but as I said in there, I finally got up the nerve to talk to you and I'm not so keen on running away like a scared little kid."

I huffed a soft laugh. "You don't look like a scared little kid."

He grinned. "Well, I'm good at hiding it."

My smile faded. "I'm sorry. I really shouldn't have dragged you into the middle of this."

Instead of saying anything, he leaned in and pressed his lips gently against mine.

They were as soft and silky as I had always imagined, and the kiss made my head spin. My skin tingled with the rush of heat that engulfed me, and I pulled away, searching his eyes. I'm not sure what I was looking for, but what I saw reflected in his gaze was enough to make me glad I was already sitting. If I had been standing and in his arms, my legs would not have held my weight.

"Don't look so surprised," he said.

His voice carried a husky quality that turned on something deep inside me. I could listen to him talk with that tone for the rest of my life. I laughed out loud at both his words and my reaction to them. "You must have a death wish." Then I pulled him back into a more insistent kiss.

Levi cleared his throat.

My heart launched into the stratosphere and we both pulled away from each other, expecting the worst.

"You have an audience," Levi said.

I glanced over my shoulder and my father stood in the doorway, with a frown pulling his lips down at the edges. And right next to him stood Alex, wearing the same look of disapproval. Even with their scowls, it was a relief because I don't think I could deal with another reaper onslaught.

When I turned back to Zane, he had shifted far enough away that another kiss seemed to be out of the question.

"Rain check?" He winked.

The coolest kid in school just asked me for a rain check on a kiss. Who was I to argue?

Grim's Daughter
Chapter 9

"SO, IS HE A good kisser?" Holly asked after Zane went off to use the bathroom.

I forced my lips to remain straight, fighting back a smile. For once, I was the one getting some action and not her. It felt good, but I wasn't going to give out any details. I glanced at the kitchen. Everyone was packing up the leftovers and cleaning the dishes, leaving only the teenagers in the family room.

"He shouldn't be here," my mother said as she sat down next to me on the couch. "And you should tell him to move on for his own safety."

Leave it to my mother to kill whatever high I had from Zane's kiss. I glared at her. "You already know his Fate, don't you?" I crossed my arms.

She glanced down at her hands and shook her head. "Something happened here today, beyond whatever you did to those reapers." She took her little Book of Fates out of her pocket and started scrolling up and down through the list. Even plugging in searches for some people in attendance at the house. "There is no record for anyone here anymore."

I let out a bark of a laugh. "How is that possible?" From everything that was ever explained to me, everyone had their Fates written in that little database of hers. It was written the moment someone was born and never changed. Every single choice a person made led them to their predestined Fate—unless, of course, they were a Ryan. But even they had entries, even though their Fates changed; the entries in my mother's books were still there, just with the goalpost moved.

She shrugged. "I don't know." Her haunted gaze landed on me.

Holly leaned forward, her brow creased. "Were some of the people here supposed to die today?"

Leave it to her to be blunt, and my mother's shift in her seat, along with her non-reaction, announced the answer loud and clear.

"So, I changed their Fate?"

She opened her mouth and then closed it as she glanced around at the sudden quiet. Everyone had stopped talking and was now concentrating on us. Even Zane was close enough to catch the conversation. He had stopped just behind the couch and his wide-eyed gaze caught mine.

"I don't know." My mother kept scrolling through her little Book of Fates and finally looked up at me.

"Is that why you two were here today? Because some of us were on your death list?" Alex crossed his arms. The bite in his tone matched the spark of anger inside me.

I thought they were here because of the reaper revolt and the danger that I could be in. I nearly laughed when my mother avoided my gaze. She also avoided Alex and his question.

My mother tucked the reader back into her pocket and met my father's gaze. "Yes," she finally said. "We knew Missy would need us." She looked at Alex and shrugged.

I leaned back against the soft down of the couch, blinking. I saved people in this room when I did what I did to the reapers. How many deaths had I felt before I blacked out? Six, maybe seven. I glanced around the room. At least a third of those here had been destined to die today.

Had I felt the reapers' deaths, or theirs? All the heat in my face disappeared, and a humming started in my head.

Zane must have seen something in my expression, because he moved faster than anyone else. He slid into the space next to me on the couch and took my hand in his.

It gave me the strength to focus back on the room before the buzzing overwhelmed me. I gulped, trying to reconcile what had truly happened. I glanced up at Alex. The reaper behind his chair had evaporated just like the one in front of me. Same with the one behind Holly and Faith and Nana and Papa.

My stomach rolled. Those bastards planned to kill those closest to me. Those who had protected me all my life. Tears blurred my vision, and I understood why my parents had chosen this holiday to be here.

I yanked my hand from Zane's grip and bolted for the bathroom. I got there in time for my dinner to violently exit my mouth into the toilet. I heaved until acid burned my throat. The door closed, and I glanced up after flushing.

My father took a seat on the ground next to me and pushed my hair away from my face. "We couldn't let you face that alone."

"I felt their deaths. I thought it was the reapers, but now I'm not so sure. It was as if I was dying," I whispered, and spit to get rid of the vile taste lingering in my mouth. I wiped my lips with a tissue, flushed, then leaned against the wall.

"I don't know how you did what you did. But you changed the book of Fates for everyone here. Not just those whose fates were supposed to be realized today. And I don't know what the ramifications of this will be."

"Ramifications?" I blinked. Like today could get any worse.

"There always are ramifications when Fate is messed with. At least there have been in the past, but this is a new situation. Something that has never happened in the history of time." He ruffled his hair with his hand.

A soft knock interrupted us. "Are you okay?" Zane's voice traveled through the wood.

"Yeah." I climbed to my feet and so did my father. "I'll be out in a minute," I added and turned to the sink to rinse my face and mouth.

My father grabbed my arm when I reached for the door. "He changed his Fate when he stepped into this house."

"What do you mean by that?"

"Zane Bradley was supposed to pass away from internal bleeding today." He glanced at the door. "Valerie..." he started and shook his head. "Nana changed his Fate, and then you erased any record of him in your mother's book."

I pulled away from him. "How is that possible?"

He laughed. "The Ryans have screwed with Fate for decades. That angelic healing thing they have has moved the stakes for many people. It makes for some disruptions in the universe's fabric, but because of their lineage, it is overlooked by the Heavenly host. But we know every time it happens."

I reached for the door again and hesitated, still processing the information I had been given. Despair wrapped its icy hands around my heart, and I shivered. "They won't stop, will they?" My hand rested on the knob.

"I think they were hoping for a coup of some sort by taking them all at once, but you put a wrench in that plan." He sighed. "I don't know when they will strike again. It depends on how much you freaked them out." He let a half smile capture his lips, and I had a moment to understand why my mother fell for him in the first place. "If how freaked out your mom and I are is any indication, it could be a little while. I don't understand how you did what you did. But perhaps you are coming into some of the special powers that come with our reaper lineage. Although dusting reapers wasn't ever part of our repertoire of powers. That's as new as not having an entry in the book of Fates."

"It didn't come without side effects." I held my wrist out, showing the skeletal print burned into my skin. But that was the least of it. Feeling Death grip my heart was a chilling experience that I did not want to experience again.

I had a feeling that wish was as futile as my situation was becoming.

Grim's Daugter
Chapter 10

I STEPPED OUT OF the bathroom to find Zane leaning against the wall on the other side of the hallway. My father gave him a nod and left the two of us to talk. Although I had no idea what to say. I didn't know whether I should tell him the beating he took today should have killed him.

I met his concerned gaze. "You can't go home," I blurted.

He cocked his head like a lost puppy. "Why not?"

"Your father..." I couldn't finish my sentence. The horror of his situation transcended my own.

"He'll be passed out by now," Zane said with that bitterness that I wanted to wipe out of his tone.

"You don't understand." Heat filled my veins like a locomotive, making my heart thunder in my chest. I couldn't let a panic attack render me useless, so I took a deep, soothing breath while keeping his gaze. "You cannot go home. Understand?" The command came out in almost a bark.

Enough so to make Zane stand straighter and narrow his eyes. "I can take my old man."

"Yeah? Well, you would have died today if you didn't come here," I snapped, and then I covered my mouth in shock.

"I almost died at dinner." He waved to the kitchen beyond us.

I closed my eyes and sighed. "No. What I am trying to tell you is if you had not come here, you would have died because of internal injuries." I opened my eyes. "Nana changed that, and then I erased all mention of you in the book of Fates, just like everyone else here."

"Who told you that? And what the Hell is the book of Fates?"

"My dad told me. A lot of people should have died today, but like Nana, I seemed to have changed things. And as far as what the book of Fates is, it's where everyone's destiny is spelled out. Everyone is in that book from the moment of conception. And everyone here except for me had an entry before the reapers came. When I killed them, I erased all your destinies." I took a breath. "You would have died if you hadn't come here," I repeated around the lump in my throat.

He blinked a few times, and then sagged against the wall and looked up at the ceiling. I guess when confronted by the Grim Reaper's words, it actually sunk in. The muscles in his jaws jumped as he ground his teeth and digested the bleak truth. It was bitter and vile, just like the taste of vomit clinging to my throat.

A tear slipped out of the corner of his eye, and I stepped toward him.

He shook his head and put his hand out to stop me, but I didn't heed his silent plea. I knocked his human stop sign out of the way and wrapped my arms around his neck, nuzzling my head under his upturned chin. At first, he didn't move, and then slowly, he encircled me, pressing me tight to his chest like a cherished teddy bear. His lips pressed against my forehead and he trembled the way I had in the chair outside.

"I have nowhere else to go," he finally said in a husky whisper.

"Yes, you do. You can stay with us," I said, knowing that might be its own fight when I put that out there to Alex and Faith. We had extra rooms and Zane's father did nearly beat him to death, so I couldn't fathom them turning him away, especially with the current situation.

Plus, if he was at the house with us, then I would at least know that my immediate family was safe. As for everyone else here, I didn't have a clue how to keep them from falling into harm's way, especially if I wasn't physically there.

Zane peeled out of my arms and stepped into the bathroom without another word. The water went on and then off, and a moment later, he stepped back into the hall. But his eyes still carried that haunted quality that I wanted to erase.

"You ready to go back into the mayhem?" I nodded toward the now very noisy back of the house.

He let out a laugh and shook his head. "No, but we probably need to."

We stepped into the room and everyone was shouting questions at my parents, as if they caused all the trouble happening today.

Levi strolled over to us and sat down next to me. "I've never seen so many people unraveled over a single event." He chuckled.

The only one who wasn't part of the yelling match was the New Yorker. He leaned against the kitchen counter with a glass of whisky in his hand, sipping it while he looked on, amused. Smoke turned and met my gaze. He shrugged as if the worst thing in the world hadn't almost happened.

"Hey!" I belted out as a surge of irritation rose to the surface.

Silence clanged down on the room as everyone turned toward me.

I scanned the guests. "Who is at risk here?" I directed the question to my parents.

"Anyone you care about," my dad said.

I rolled my eyes. I cared about everyone in the room. I also had friends at school who I cared about and teachers and kids I had babysat. The list was pretty big, and his statement was way too broad to take any action on.

"Seriously, you already said they were after those who have protected me. So, Nana, Papa, Alex, and Faith are the primary targets. Holly, too."

"And it looks as if your friend there might climb the list fast, too." Alex nodded toward Zane.

"So, who in this house is safe to leave?" Kylee looked between my parents and me.

"Everyone is in danger," I said. "I wiped everyone's Fate clean. That puts a target on all of your backs, and I don't have the foggiest clue of how to hide any of you from them."

Kylee cleared her throat. "I may be able to help with that."

Now everyone in the room looked at her.

She moved her hair, turned her back to me, and pulled her shirt down over her shoulder, revealing a tattoo that looked like a weathervane with squiggly lines and dots between the four points.

I remember seeing it at the lake a couple of times, and every time I saw it, a weird dizziness overtook me. Now was no different. I had to lean into Zane to steady myself.

My mother's eyes widened, and she paled, reaching out for the wall for support. It seemed that tattoo had a similar effect on her. "That's why I became blind to your whereabouts?"

Kylee chuckled and shrugged. "I'm almost as old as the original Fate, so I know a few tricks that you young'uns don't. I'm pretty rusty on my sigils, but this one saved my ass more than once." She tapped her tattoo and then covered it back up and turned toward the group again.

The dizziness disappeared the moment the sigil was covered. I blinked the cobwebs away and noted my mother didn't look as pale as she had. That was some kind of serious voodoo to make both of us sick.

Kylee was still talking, so I focused on the conversation again.

"...seeing as it's a holiday, I'm not sure we could find a tattoo parlor open right now. It's not like we are in New York or Los Angeles."

"You didn't get that in San Diego, did you?" my mother asked with her head tilted, as if she were digging through her memories.

"No. I drew it on my wrist with a Sharpie. I also drew it on the walls of my home. Neither you nor the old Fate ever set foot in my home because of this." She tapped her shoulder.

"I have a bunch of Sharpies in the kitchen." Nana stood and headed into the kitchen and came back with a handful of colorful pens. Red, yellow, green, blue, purple, pink, and three black Sharpies. "You can draw it on their skin, right?"

Kylee nodded. "Yes. That would work until we can get something a little more permanent."

"Will that really work?" Alex asked, a skeptical eyebrow raised.

"Ask Julia."

"Yes," my mother said. "You went off the radar and only came back for a brief flash in Arizona and then again in Utah and crossing into Colorado, and then everything came to a grinding halt."

"Sweating makes it fade enough to fail." She glanced outside. "But seeing as it's November, I don't think we have to worry about that too much. Colorado was where I got this tattoo."

"So, wait. You don't know where she is at all?" Phoebe asked. "How did you know where to find her to get that knife for me?"

Julia pulled a cell phone out of the ether. "Modern technology." She waved it.

Silence fell on the room and then Zane let out a guffaw that pulled attention to us.

"I'm sorry," he said through the laughter. He pointed and continued to laugh until he bent over, holding his knees.

Josh cracked a smile and started chuckling, and then it caught, and we all found ourselves laughing in the way maniacs laugh when they've finally snapped.

When our laughter wound down, Kylee leaned forward and picked up a Sharpie. "Who's first?"

"Me! Me!" Naomi raised her hand.

"You already have one. So does your father and Alexis." Kylee bopped Naomi's nose with her index finger.

"What?" My mother's question was phrased in shock.

"I covered all my bases," Kylee said. "It's kept me alive, and I didn't want any supernatural to know where the Hell my family was. This covers more than just you, darling. It is one of the oldest protection sigils."

"Why did you wait so long to use it?" Nana asked.

Kylee shrugged as Josh escorted his kids to sit next to her. She changed pens for each of the pieces of the symbol until she had a tiny, colorful replica on each of the children's shoulder blades. She did the same for Josh and his wife Joanne before moving onto the rest of the crew.

Every time Kylee finished a drawing, it was as if the breath was ripped from my lungs for a moment and my head spun. I had to grip the dinner chair I had slid into after the second drawing was done. I noticed my mother had to do the same.

It took an hour before everyone, including Zane, had that sigil drawn on their shoulder blade. When Kylee waved me over, I shook my head. If I had a reaction to seeing it completed on others, there was no telling what would happen if that sigil was drawn on my skin. The thought was enough to make me break out in sweat.

"Come on, it doesn't hurt," Kylee said.

"It may not hurt any of you, but seeing it makes me feel sick to my stomach, like I'm coming down with the flu or something." I swallowed the bitter taste in the back of my throat and ignored their raised eyebrows. "I have a feeling it would do more harm than this." I raised my arm with the reaper burn.

"Maybe we should skip Melissa," my mother said. Her complexion had not truly cleared up, either. "Because what she described is pretty much what happens to me as I looked at the mark, too."

Kylee looked at the pens on the table and back at me. She chewed her bottom lip and nodded. "It will protect you," she said, trying to coax me over as if I were just a scared horse. "What's the harm?"

"It could nullify that nifty reaper demolishing trick she has," my father said from the back of the room.

Kylee capped the pen. "None of us want that."

Oh, hell no. Without that, I might as well dive off the ledge in our yard to the jagged rocks below. And I wouldn't have a prayer of keeping the people I cared about safe, and right now, that was my primary goal.

"Can I have a few pieces of paper?" Kylee asked Nana and Papa.

Nana went back to the drawer in the kitchen where she had found the pens and pulled out a pad of paper, handing it to Kylee.

I turned away as she drew a sigil on the paper.

"Copy this and put it on every door and window in your house and they'll never find you," Kylee said as the swish of pen on paper reached my ears.

I counted the tearing of paper from the pad Nana had given Kylee. After the eighth page was torn out, I turned back to see Zane folding his piece of paper. He slipped it into his pocket, and I was grateful. The others hadn't followed suit yet, and my stomach rolled, and a bout of dizziness struck. I reached for Zane's arm to steady myself.

I guess the others noticed the fact I was swaying on my feet. Everyone tucked their drawn sigils away and the vertigo suddenly shifted to clarity. Relief swept through me.

"We need to go see what we can find out about the reapers' next move." My father gave me a quick hug. "Stay and keep her safe," he directed at Levi.

"I wasn't going to leave her," Levi said with an eye roll.

My mother gave me a hug. "Stay safe," she whispered and brushed a kiss against my cheek.

"When will I see you again?" I asked as that familiar sinking feeling gripped my stomach.

"As soon as we can."

That was their normal fallback. It could mean in an hour or in a year. Before I could argue, they blinked out of the room, leaving a small whirlwind that immediately dissipated.

"Does anyone want dessert?" Nana asked before I could fall into what Alex called a funk.

Every time they left me, it felt as if someone had yanked a piece of my soul out. Between that and my father's earlier revelation, I certainly didn't want any more food. Even Nana's pristine pies didn't entice me.

I guess I wasn't the only one who didn't have an appetite, either. It seemed the holiday spirit had been sucked out of everyone.

Josh and his wife were the first ones to take off, and then the twins left with their families, followed by April and her family.

Considering my ability to toast reapers, Kylee decided our home was already protected and handed over the reaper-killing knife to Papa.

"It's about time we call it a night," Kylee said as she and Michael rounded up Naomi and Alexis. "We've got plans at the lake tomorrow with Smoke and Phoebe and, with all the excitement, I think we should get out of your hair," she added.

All six of them doled out hugs before they took off, which left us with Papa and Nana and Zane.

Just when I thought we would escape any more stress, Alex turned to Zane. "Now that it's just us, do you want to tell me what happened to you today?"

"Alex," Nana started.

Alex put up his hand to quiet her. "I want to hear his side of the story."

As if he didn't already know the entire story. Neither Alex nor Papa would have let Zane in the house if his intentions were not pure. I nearly said something, but I had a feeling what Zane said would make a difference to whether Alex would allow him under our roof.

Zane glanced down at his hands and took a deep breath before meeting Alex's gaze. "My father beat the shit out of me."

"Why?"

Alex's question ruffled my nerves, but he didn't ask it in a demanding way that would insinuate this was Zane's fault, so I gave him a pass.

"Because I wouldn't give him the money I earned doing the Smiths' basement this past weekend."

Alex noodled on that for a few minutes. He chewed on his lower lip and then glanced at Papa.

"Some people are just assholes and don't need a reason to beat on their kids," Papa said, as if Alex had voiced the questions reflected in his eyes. Papa glanced at Zane. "If you need a place to stay, we have extra rooms here. Or if you're more comfortable in the company of Missy and Holly, I'm sure my son has room for you in his home as well."

I don't know whether he had been privy to my conversation with Zane or not, but I could have given Papa the biggest hug. He had just saved me from having to fight with Alex on arrangements of any kind.

Alex nodded. "I'm just having a hard time wrapping my head around this." It was his way of apologizing to Zane without actually saying the words. "I guess I'm just used to supernatural jerks, not human ones."

"Supernatural jerks?" Zane leaned forward in interest.

"My son was a little sheltered," Papa said, and smiled at Zane. "He's never really seen the dark side of humanity."

"Oh, and you have?" The words slipped out of my mouth before I could stop them. Papa led as charmed a life as any.

He chuckled at me. "You're right. I never dealt with the dark side of human nature, but my brother had more than a few brushes with them. And my father had a step-father who seemed to like to use him as a punching bag, so while I haven't been subjected to those kinds of horrors, I have seen them in the memories I now hold." He tapped his temple, referring to the memories of his father that he now held. He rarely mentioned that side effect of his powers, but I guess if you can read minds, it is pretty much the same as absorbing memories.

Papa glanced at Zane. "Since you've seen a glimpse of Leviathan here, and got a dose of my wife's healing mojo today, you have a right to know what associating with us means."

He glanced at Alex and raised an eyebrow, as if some silent communication were happening between them.

"There's a world of supernatural out there," Holly burst out from next to us and waved at the slider. "Of course, I've only seen reapers, but there are angels and demons and vampires and everything in between."

"There aren't any more vampires," Papa said with a dark smile. "We took care of them a long time ago."

Alex put his hands out, palm first. "Back to what my father started to say," he said, addressing Zane. "Associating with us is dangerous because of the supernatural world. So, you have to truly weigh the pros and cons before you decide what you want to do."

"Considering I don't know if I'm going to survive on a daily basis at home, this all seems juvenile in comparison." Zane waved a hand at the group. "Besides, if I'm going to be a target, I'd rather be a target with Melissa by my side. She's pretty badass." He glanced at me and one side of his lip twitched into a fleeting smile. "I know what she is and what Holly is, but I have no clue what your wife is."

"What is Holly?" Faith crossed her arms.

"Holly is Lucifer's granddaughter. Which makes you Lucifer's daughter?" Zane said in a timid voice.

The color in Faith's cheeks faded, and she glanced at me in a way that made me gulp.

"I told him," Holly said before her mother could read me the riot act.

"I am a trinity," Papa said. "The first child born with three archangel bloodlines. Alex has four archangel bloodlines. Faith is the only true direct descendant left. The rest of us are so many layers removed...well, except for Michael. He is the grandson of the archangel Gabriel."

"Trinity?"

"Yes." Papa smiled. "And some of us have exceptional powers, while others are normal. Val here inherited the ability to heal by being the safekeeper of my parents' powers."

"Who else has powers?" Zane asked.

Papa tilted his head and stared at Zane as if looking deep into his mind.

Zane winced, and then his eyes widened. "You can talk in people's minds?" He gasped.

"I can see inside your mind, too. So can my wife. I knew what happened to you when I opened the door to let you in. I also know how you feel about my granddaughter."

Zane glanced at me. "I thought you said he babysat your father, not that he was your grandfather."

"Missy may not be by blood, but she became my granddaughter the moment Alex and Faith signed the adoption papers."

"You don't need to do all this posturing." Levi stretched out next to me. "The boy doesn't have ill intentions, unless you consider his attraction to Missy an ill intention."

"Levi!" I swatted him lightly.

He raised his muzzle toward me. "I would have already eaten him if his intentions were not in the right place. He is less hormonal than Alex was with Faith."

Alex pressed his lips together, and I couldn't tell whether it was to suppress a smile or whether he were truly irritated with Levi.

"You can stay with us, but if you so much as go near Missy's room, I will know, and you don't want to mess with me. Understand?" he said, this time with authority and a pointed finger to bring home his words.

"Yes, sir," he said.

"Then I think we are going to head out, so we don't invite trouble here again today," Alex said.

"Before you head out, I have a question for Zane," Nana said, and a heaviness drew down her lips. "What do you want us to do about your father?"

Zane licked his lips, and his gaze dropped to the ground. "It's kind of hard to have him arrested without proof of what he did."

She nodded slowly and traded a glance with Papa. "Do you think he will try to come after you?"

Zane laughed. "He doesn't have a clue where I went. He smashed my phone to smithereens before he started punching me. So, no. For all he knows, I died in a ditch somewhere." He shook his head. "He won't look for me, but he might pack up and hightail it out of there when he wakes from his drunken stupor and sees blood on his fists."

"Is there anything you need at your house that we can get for you?" she asked.

He shook his head. "I have a backpack in my locker at school with some clothes and stuff. If we can stop by there on the way home, I can grab it and I'll be all set."

"We can stop," Alex said with a nod.

With that, Papa stood, and so did Nana. She went to the refrigerator and pulled out a couple of containers of turkey and fixings and handed them to Faith, along with a Dutch apple pie for us to indulge in later.

After hugs and kisses, we headed back home by way of the school. Alex went inside with Zane while he gathered his stowed backpack.

"It's sad that he has to have an emergency backpack hidden away at school," Holly said, as we waited for them to come out.

"I can't imagine what kind of hell he lives in daily." I could not comprehend it, and it made my heart ache all the more.

"Well, he never has to go back to that," Faith said from the front seat as Alex and Zane stepped out of the darkened school.

I prayed that was the end of the holiday excitement. I was looking forward to an evening of football and pie, but in the pit of my stomach, I knew darker days were ahead for all of us.

Grim's Daughter
Chapter 11

THE SCENT OF APPLES and cinnamon in the car on the ride home was too tempting and when we got inside, the first thing Faith did was heat the pie in the microwave and then cut five pieces—one for each of us—before piling on vanilla ice cream. She didn't even ask whether we wanted any. She just handed us each a plate with a smile and turned on the television.

"But the game," Alex said, waving at the television as she surfed through the channels.

"I don't want to watch a bunch of men pounding each other for a pigskin ball. Not today." She gave him a look that shut him up.

I had to smile at the dynamic. Faith usually got her way when she disagreed with something that was being done. I never knew whether it was because of a healthy fear of her powers or whether Alex really didn't mind compromising. Either way, he was a good man to let his wife have her way most of the time.

Faith settled on a channel with *A Charlie Brown Thanksgiving* on it.

I sat on the couch, sandwiched between Holly and Zane, and we dug into our pies with little conversation.

"What's the deal?" Zane finally said, glancing at me after he finished his pie and put his plate on the coffee table. "Why do they want you?"

"They think they can control me."

"After today, I doubt that," he muttered and shoulder bumped me.

I pressed my lips together against a smile and shoulder bumped him back before taking the last bite of pie from my plate. I went to put my plate down and gasped. Every muscle in my body cramped. This was the same feeling I had at the house when the reaper had me in his grip, but we were alone in the room. Levi hadn't even stirred at my feet.

The mark on my wrist turned a burning red, and I folded over in the seat, nearly launching the pie from my stomach. I swallowed the bile that crawled up my throat and could hardly hear Zane and Holly asking me what was wrong. My cells felt as if someone had set off an atom bomb inside me. Liquid fire filled my veins, and I cried out.

My eyes rolled in my head, and darkness blanketed over me.

WHEN I FINALLY CAME to, it was dark out, and Zane had my head in his lap. He was combing my hair with his fingers with his gaze glued to the television. I didn't move for fear I had broken something critical. Every inch of my body hurt, as though someone took a bat to me. I glanced toward the other couch. Alex and Faith sat together with tissues in their hands.

I glanced at the television to see what everyone was concentrating on and my mind couldn't grasp what I was seeing. A small plane went down and there were no survivors. They didn't have names or faces, but they had the flight plan and the corporation that owned the jet. Beaumont Travel Enterprises.

I sat up too fast and bumped my head against Zane's chin, which only made my headache bloom into bright lights across my vision.

"Ouch." Zane rubbed his chin.

"Is that who I think it is?" I said with a raspy voice, ignoring my pounding head. My chest squeezed at the thoughts racing through my head. If what I experienced was any indication, they hadn't died instantly.

Alex glanced at me and nodded.

Well, shit. Now I knew what happened. I felt their deaths, and now I was convinced I was tied into the afterlife more solidly than I wanted to be. "Were they on the list?" I asked the ceiling, hoping my mother would pop in to confirm or deny it. Those closest to me were supposed to die at the dinner table, but I stopped it. Did that mean Josh and his family were the ramifications of changing Fates?

"Those bastards got him." He glanced at Zane's somber expression. "Josh is a pilot for Beaumont Travel Enterprises." Alex waved at the television where the caption read the same flight company. "He flies up with his family for the holiday every year."

Zane bit his lip and nodded. Then he glanced down at me. "Why did you pass out?" His quizzical gaze reminded me of a puppy.

There was only one answer. It was the same reason I passed out after toasting those reapers, and it wasn't the act of letting that power loose. It was much darker. "I felt their Deaths."

"Oh," Zane said, and squeezed me in what seemed like support.

Levi growled, and a note fell on the table in front of me as if just thrown from the ether. He sniffed the paper and opened his mouth to eat it, but I snatched it from his mouth before he could dispose of it.

As you can see, those sigils won't help your friends. We will reap them all. Yield and we will spare the rest. The words on the paper leaped out at me, and I had a moment of regret in not letting Levi chomp it down. Slowly, the reality settled into my bones and with it came the darkness I was so familiar with.

"Assholes," Zane muttered from next to me, and I turned to look at him. He stared at the paper in my hand and the muscles in his jaw jumped. *If he saw the note...* I crumpled it up and tossed it on the table before glancing at Alex.

Because Zane had seen the note, both Alex and Faith were privy to the content, and they both stared at me.

I couldn't handle the weight of anger in their eyes, and I buried my face in my hands. Images of Josh and Joanne and their children accosted my eyelids, and their loss battered my already aching muscles.

"I should have gone with the reapers," I said.

Alex's gaze blazed right through me, and he pointed at the television. "This is not your fault."

"What if it was Nana and Papa?" I said, trying to make him understand this nightmare was far from over. I was going to have to make a choice or sacrifice everyone I loved.

Alex shook his head. "They have the knife. We have you."

"What if they came here while I was passed out and unable to protect you?" Panic crept in at the verbalization of my frantic thoughts.

"We have Levi," Faith said, reminding us we had a one-beast army already. And she would know more about what he was capable of than anyone in this room. After all, she and Kylee gallivanted through Hell with Levi.

That made sense, but it still didn't ease my mind at all. "I can't..." I stood and walked to the back window, unable to finish that sentence.

"You cannot make a decision that takes your life, understand?" Alex was on his feet, facing me. His reflection looked just as frazzled as I felt.

"I might not have a choice. Not if your lives are at stake." I met his gaze in the reflection.

"Why do you have to take the role of Death?" Holly asked.

"Because that is what they want of me," I answered with a glance over my shoulder. She already knew the stakes, so her question sent a rush of aggravation through my veins.

"Why can't you take both roles? If you are Fate, you rule the reapers, right?"

I turned back to the raging ocean and pondered her question. She had an interesting point, one that was worth some thought. Because if I could do that, then at least my parents would be together. But I didn't know whether the powers that be would allow that. Then again, I existed, so maybe it was as unorthodox as my existence. "I don't think one person can have both roles," I finally said, acknowledging her question.

"But either way you die, right?" Zane asked.

I nodded. That was the catch. Although my parents would be together and everyone else would be safe, I would not be in this realm anymore. And any future with Zane was rightfully forfeited.

"Then no." He crossed his arms, like he could change my future just by wishing it so.

It was kind of cute considering he had only really spoken to me a handful of times, and of course kissed me as though we had been together for a lifetime earlier today. But as sweet as his sentiment was, I could not base my future on blind hope.

I LAID IN BED with Holly snoring on the other side of the room and Levi on the floor next to me, tossing around the idea that Holly had presented earlier. Although I didn't want to die, I also didn't want my family to be killed because I was being obstinate. And whatever was happening with Zane would have to be put aside. I wasn't hauling him into the afterlife with me just to keep me company.

"That is not a feasible option." Levi's rumbling voice came from his position on the floor. "But then again, I never thought anyone would ever free me, and yet your father did. And there is no precedent for your birth. So perhaps it is possible for you to take both positions."

I leaned over the side of the bed and stared down at the monster in drag. "Stop digging in my head." While I liked the idea of silent communication, I really hated the reality that Levi could get into my private thoughts that I did not want to share with anyone.

"Your thoughts are so damn loud. I cannot ignore them like I can with the rest of the humans."

I grunted at his answer and went back to my lament. "You really think it is possible?"

He met my gaze with eyes that shined in the darkness. He didn't confirm or deny my question. If I could see him clearly, I'm sure I would have seen a shrug, but his glowing eyes stared back.

Instead of waiting for him to impart some legendary wisdom, I threw the covers off me and pointed at him. "Stay and protect Holly," I ordered.

A low, rumbling growl started in his throat.

"I'm serious. I don't want you following me to the bathroom or anywhere else right now."

"You are going to see the boy," he grumbled.

I bit my lower lip. I needed to use the facilities, but I did not intend to come back to this room right away. It was odd that this creature could get into my head when no one else could, but it was a comfort not to have to tell him my thoughts and feelings. Especially when they were so jumbled in my head. "Just stay," I said. "Please, so I know she is safe." I nodded toward Holly.

"Fine." His head slowly dropped back down to the floor.

I took that as my cue to go before he changed his mind. I left the door open so if I needed Levi, he could get to me without taking the door down. My mind was full of possibilities and every one of them meant my death and an eternity alone. I did my business and wandered down the hall past Alex and Faith's room to the guest room at the end of the hall.

The door was closed, and I tried the doorknob. I couldn't remember whether or not it had a lock. Ours didn't, but Alex and Faith's door did. The knob turned easily, and I stepped inside the dark room, trying to be as quiet as I could, closing the door behind me.

I took a step, and the floor creaked. I held my breath and moved my weight away from the creaking plank. The light on the bedside table turned on.

Zane's wide and worried gaze met mine. He glanced at the door and back at me before his eyebrows rose in a silent question. His bare chest greeted me. For seventeen, he had a nicely cut six-pack, and I tried not to stare.

I crossed and took a seat on the edge of the bed. "I'm thinking about what Holly said earlier."

He wiped his face and then laid back on his pillow. He stared at the ceiling. "If I had spoken to you sooner—"

"I'd still have a decision to make." I interrupted him, shutting off whatever lament he was starting to launch.

This time, his eyes locked with mine. "It means you stop breathing. It means you die."

I shrugged. "Better me than everyone I care about. Besides, I can visit."

"That's not the same thing, and you know it. It's just really shitty timing."

He couldn't be more right, and I felt that melancholy of "*if only*" starting in my head. My parents gave me up for a reason. They couldn't be in this realm all the time, not without the world going to Hell. I would have the same limitations.

Zane propped himself up on his elbow. "So, if you've made up your mind, why did you come to my room?" His question was as soft as his eyes.

"I know when I tell Alex there will be a yelling battle, and I just wanted some calmness with you before the bottom drops out from under me."

His lips formed that tilted half smile that always made my heart rate pick up and at this moment, it pulled the heat right to my cheeks. He reached up and ran his hand into my hair, pulling me toward him as he sat up.

He covered my mouth with his in an insistent kiss. Like he actually read my deepest desires and acted on them. My mind went blank and heat enveloped me in a warm embrace. It took me a moment to realize where this was meant to go as his hand slid down my shoulder and didn't stop there.

I pulled away with a gasp. Although I was headed for a death sentence, I didn't want to do anything that would compromise my morals either. As easy as it would be to slide under the sheets and let Zane have his way with me, I would not be able to look at myself in the mirror in the morning. I was not cut out for a one-night stand, and this certainly felt like it was leading to that single taboo.

He pressed his lips together as he searched my eyes for some explanation, and then he fell back on his pillow again and covered his face in a gruff rub before he met my gaze again. "Why does this all feel so final?" he asked, quietly enough that I nearly missed it.

"Because it is." My throat tightened and I stood, but Zane grabbed my wrist, stopping me from leaving.

"Don't go," he whispered. "I promise I won't try anything else. I just want..." He closed his eyes. "I just want to feel safe a little longer."

I blinked, and I think my mouth popped open for a moment before I closed it. His absolute vulnerability melted my heart, and I nearly stumbled where I stood.

"If you are going to make an insane choice to sacrifice yourself for your family, I'd like to hold on to you for a little while longer, if you don't mind." Words tumbled from him as though he were trying to backtrack and save face.

I knew better from the small glimpse of him I got earlier. He had never felt safe, and the fact he did around me with all this supernatural crap going on was beyond me. I nodded and stepped toward the bed.

He scooted over and lifted the covers in a silent invitation. When I hesitated, he said, "I promise, no funny stuff. I'd just like to know what it's like to wake with you in my arms, and since this may be the only shot I have of knowing that..." He shrugged.

So many conflicting emotions overwhelmed me. I blinked back the sudden mist blurring my vision and crawled under the covers despite the fear that gripped my bones. Zane was a complication I didn't need right now. But as I clicked off the bedside lamp and his arms wrapped around me, pulling my back into his chest, I pushed it aside and just let the cadence of his breath on the back of my neck lull me to sleep.

Grim's Daughter
Chapter 13

THE BANG OF THE door made me jump, and I blinked at the sunshine bathing the room before I glanced at the door. Alex stood just inside the door with a scowl as big as any I've ever seen, and his arms crossed so tight that the oxford he had on looked as if the arms would split.

The bathroom door opened, and Zane stepped out fully dressed before Alex could blast me for being in Zane's room.

Alex's gaze swiveled to Zane, and his eyes narrowed. Zane winced and stumbled back. The anger etched in Alex's face smoothed out.

"You could have just asked instead of forcing your way into his memories." I threw the covers back and sat up.

"He what?" Zane rubbed his temple as if he now had a headache.

"Because I was once your age," Alex said. It wasn't much of an answer. "But I have to give you credit," he said to Zane. "You showed much more restraint than I ever did at your age." When he glanced at me, he shook his head. "And you shouldn't sacrifice yourself for us."

"But how many more have to die?"

"People die every day," he said. "You can't control that."

"It is my choice to make." I got up and instead of arguing with Alex or Zane, I slid by them and went back to my room. Holly wasn't in the bedroom, and neither was Levi. The bathroom was open, so I just grabbed my clothes and settled in for a nice, long, hot shower.

The water felt heavenly and I let it wash away the horrors of the prior day. The only stark reminder was the skeletal handprint on my wrist. I stared at the charred relief map and sighed, wondering, yet again, whether I could step into both roles.

At least my parents would be together if I took both stations, but that also meant I would forever remain alone. No soulmate by my side, no one to lean on when all the Death and destruction got to me, and I'm sure it would. I couldn't see myself allowing a child to be reaped. Just the thought sent a rash of goose bumps across my skin, and I turned the water to near scalding to wipe that thought out of my head.

I forced myself to stand under the water for a few more moments before I shut it off. I had isolated myself long enough and needed to hit this head on. The room was so steamy when I stepped out that I could hardly see my pile of clothes on the side of the sink. I wrapped my hair and then dried the rest of my body before pulling on my underwear and jeans. Usually I would put on an old pair of sweats the day after Thanksgiving, but I didn't want to wear ratty but comfortable clothes in front of Zane.

My bra and a nice warm sweater with a plunging V-neck came next, and I used the towel to squeeze the rest of the water from my hair. The wet towel provided me with a means to wipe the steamed mirror. I got just a swath cleared before I gasped at the reflection of a reaper right behind me. I spun around. Nothing was there but the pounding in my chest. The tingling in my blood told me my mind was not tricking me. I swore a reaper had been right behind my left shoulder. A reaper reaching for me.

I turned back to the mirror and the swath I had cleared had already fogged up again. Growling from outside the bathroom door reaffirmed I was not seeing things.

And if a reaper was in here with me, then there might be more in the house.

Instead of giving my knotted wet hair any attention, I moved to the bathroom door and swung it open. Levi was in the hallway with his teeth bared at the stairwell. I didn't even look. I closed my eyes and pushed the surge of power that pulsed alongside the sudden panic in my blood out like a massive wave in all directions, so I covered the entire house.

A reaper in human form had a fistful of Holly's hair with his human hand, but his other was in skeletal form. "I don't want to hurt her," he said. "But I needed some assurances that you wouldn't vaporize me without hearing me out."

"Let my sister go." I wasn't interested in mincing words on my relationship with Holly. But one thing was for sure: if this reaper had bad intentions like the ones at the dinner table had, I think he would have turned to dust already. If he truly meant Holly harm, she would have already been dead, and I would have probably been out cold on the bathroom floor.

"Promise you won't kill me."

I cocked an eyebrow and crossed my arms. "If you were truly here to hurt these people, you would have been poufed out of existence the minute I stepped out of the bathroom. Now, let her go. Or I'll let Levi here have his way with you." I gave Levi's head a soft pat to make my point.

The reaper slowly dropped his hand and its skeleton disappeared behind human-like skin. He released Holly's hair, and she jabbed her elbow into his side with a growl.

"How dare you use me as a human shield!" Her hands engulfed in flame and she raised them toward the reaper.

"You realize we are inside, right?" I asked her before she shot a blaze at the thing in the hallway and set the entire house on fire.

My calm tone slammed right through her fury, and she glanced at me and then quickly fisted her hands. Smoke billowed from her palms and the fire alarm above our heads started wailing.

When Zane appeared at the top of the stairs, I put my hand out for him to stop. "We are okay. Just please stay where you are." I didn't want him anywhere near the reaper. "Just do something with that thing on the ceiling, please?"

Zane stopped and reached up to the ceiling. With a quick twist, he had the fire alarm in his hands and, a moment later, he disconnected the battery. He glanced at the back of the reaper's head. "Who is this?" He waved at the teenager in the hallway.

"He's a reaper in disguise like the one Levi ate at the school. He just made the mistake of trying to use Holly as a shield in case I decided to turn him into that nauseating dust." I glanced at Holly and gave her a head nod toward our room.

She got the message immediately and stepped away.

Zane's jaw tightened, and he glared at the poor reaper. Any closer and he would be within the reaper's reach. With just a touch, this thing could extinguish life. I certainly didn't want that to happen today, especially considering I finally got all the knots in my back out in the hot shower.

"What do you want?" I snapped at the reaper and had a moment to wonder where Alex and Faith were. They should have been the first ones running toward the alarm.

"I serve your father." That really didn't answer the question, and it did not settle my nerves.

"And?"

"And I'll serve you."

I rolled my eyes. "I have no intention of taking over for my father." No need to let this little slimy bastard know I was planning to take both helms so my parents could be together. Yet the lie coated my mouth with its awful tin-like taste and I nearly gagged on it.

He bit his lower lip. "More will die," he whispered, as if saying it with a normal voice would make it so. His eyes begged me to agree to his unspoken terms.

I glanced over his shoulder at Zane, and his gaze met mine. I saw the spark of hope ignite in his green irises. *Damn, I wish he wasn't here to hear me lie outright to the reaper.*

Even Levi glanced up at me. "We will all follow her if she makes that choice." He sent a narrow-eyed glare at the reaper. "But she is not of age. She cannot step into the role until she is at least twenty-one. So, this little rebellious play of yours isn't even timed correctly."

The reaper blinked, as though he didn't understand the reapers had staged an ill-timed coup. "Her father wasn't of age."

Levi sighed and looked up at me. "Can I eat him now?"

"You have exactly sixty seconds to tell me what you want before I let Levi eat you." My heart had already started to pound. But I hadn't experienced any losses today. No blackouts. So, everyone had to be okay, right?

Levi rubbed his shoulder against me, and I glanced down. He gave me a nod. I kept forgetting the beast could hear my inner dialog as if I were speaking aloud, and the nod of affirmation released a majority of the tension filling my muscles. If the damn reaper hadn't been in the hall, I might have collapsed into a puddle of relief. Thank God for the little things.

"They won't stop until you have taken the helm," the reaper said, as if I hadn't already been given the warning. "And that will cause more damage than you can imagine."

"What kind of damage?" I didn't really want to hear about the Death of those I loved, but I remember my father telling me about ramifications if people were taken before their time.

He wiped his face and glanced around, as if there could be ears nearby. "Breaches. And with breaches comes battles and death and destruction, the likes of which this earth has never seen."

Scare tactics. Great. Now the world's survival was on my shoulders. It wasn't bad enough to just have my loved one's heads hanging over me—now it was the world?

"Bullshit." I crossed my arms. "Levi, it's breakfast time."

Before the sentence was even out of my lips, Levi pounced. The reaper didn't have a chance. I guess I should have felt guilty about his demise, but the fact he had ruined my morning bliss made it easier to swallow. I turned and trudged back into the bathroom to comb the ungodly knots out of my hair as Zane and Holly stared at me with wide eyes, as if I had just committed an unthinkable sin.

Grim's Daughter
Chapter 14

WHERE WERE YOU?" I snapped when I finally made my way downstairs to find Alex and Faith in the kitchen.

Holly and Zane's gazes fell on me with open mouths at my impatient tone. Levi chuckled.

"We went to the store to grab milk." Alex held up a new gallon of milk in his hand.

I glanced at Holly and Zane. "Did you not tell him what happened upstairs?"

They shook their heads and Levi burped.

Alex stopped what he was doing, narrowed his gaze for a moment and then glanced at me, his eyes widening, telling me he'd just snuck into Zane's mind because he was the only one in the room Alex's mind reading could penetrate.

"Yeah. A reaper was here." I jammed my fists into my hips, but refrained from tapping my foot with the annoyance running through me. Although I wasn't sure why I was so aggravated. If they had been here, the outcome would not have changed.

But being out of the house, outside of my protections, made them vulnerable. That was where my irritation came from. Knowledge that they could have ended up like Josh and his family.

Alex cocked his head and then slowly shook it, as if he could read my train of thought. Perhaps it was already written on my face, because Faith put the pan she had set on the burner to the side and crossed to me. Without a word, she took me in her arms.

"I'm sorry we worried you," she said.

I accepted the hug and gave her one back, pressing my lips together against the sudden tremble. This whole thing had me more unhinged than I thought. After all, until I finally made the sacrifice, any of them could be taken. And the thought of my death was even worse. What I was contemplating was so final.

What if it didn't work?

If I messed up, that was it. Game over.

Faith kept her arms around me. "I've already had one person sacrifice his life for mine. Please don't take that route," she whispered and pulled back, meeting my gaze. Alex's uncle's death still affected her, and any time his name was mentioned, guilt reflected in her eyes.

Her emotions pierced through the wall I tried to build, crumbling it to the ground. I put my forehead on her shoulder. "I have to," I whispered. "There is no other solution. No other way that will save you all from harm."

"There has to be another way." She pushed me away from her chest and made me look at her. "Understand. You have an entire life to enjoy. Taking the helm is not a job for a child."

"This from the woman who took on Lucifer when she was only sixteen?" I laughed and wiped the tears from my face.

"My dad wanted me dead. Be glad yours wants you to have a full life."

Zane snorted a laugh from the couch. "Been there. It sucks," he muttered, pulling our attention away from each other. "She's right, though. If your parents don't want that for you, why are you so set on it?" He leaned back against the cushion, studying me with his arms crossed. There was a fire in his eyes, as though he were going to get ornery about my choices any minute.

Instead, he stood and went out to the covered veranda, closing the door behind him as if he couldn't stomach any more talk about supernatural things.

"He's struggling with all this," Faith said, looking after him. "He really cares for you." She raised an eyebrow. "Pining after you all these years and just when he got the nerve to talk to you, everything falls apart." She shrugged and jutted her chin out, silently telling me to go to him.

I took the cue and gave Holly a little hug as I walked by her. I had largely ignored her since Zane walked into the house yesterday and a little guilt crept in, especially with her eyes reflecting the same hurt Zane's had. After all, Holly and I were sisters by circumstances, and I would take a bullet for her without a second thought. I knew she had my back the same way.

"Listen to Mom." She sniffled as she hugged me back.

I didn't acknowledge her request because it tore me up inside. I crossed to the door and slid outside. The cold plastic webbing of the chair creaked as I settled into it.

Zane continued to stare at the ocean view as if the roiling waves had all the answers he needed. I didn't dare interrupt him, either.

"I thought somehow, after all the continuous beatings I've survived, I would someday be rewarded for my sacrifices." He shook his head. "There is no reward at the end of the tunnel. No light. Just a bunch of disappointing nothing."

"Zane."

He shook his head. "Don't."

"What would you do in my shoes?" I didn't want to see him broken like this. He was supposed to be the cool one.

He picked at the cuticle on his thumb, still staring at the water and not looking at me. He sighed. "I honestly don't know. And I am aware what I want really has no bearing on your choices, which makes it that much harder to stomach."

"Why do you say that?" If he hadn't shown up at the door, he was right; it was just a couple of texts and a brief phone call between the scene at school and Thanksgiving. I wouldn't have given him much of a thought in this grave decision. But he showed up. And my world got so much more complicated because he tugged at my heart, whether I wanted him to or not.

"Look, I know nothing about you, and vice versa."

"Excuse me?" I crossed my arms.

"I know who your parents are, and you know my father is a monster. But I don't know your favorite color, or what you want to be, or what schools you're looking at for college, or anything meaningful." He glanced at me. "All the shit I wanted time to find out. All the reasons to fall even farther than I have all these years." He challenged me with a raised brow. "All the little things that matter."

Oh, the boy knew exactly which buttons to push to make me melt. "If I stay, I get to feel your death when they come for you. And make no mistake, they will come. You can't cheat Death."

A smile formed. "But didn't I already?"

"You don't have nine lives, like Smoke," I snapped.

He gave me a sideways stare.

"Don't you give me that look."

Now his eyebrows arched.

I rolled my eyes. Now I needed to explain yet another person's secrets beyond ours. "He was a cat for thousands of years, thus the nine lives reference."

"Really?"

I was glad to move his thoughts away from my pending death to something else. "Yeah. Fate, the original one, turned him into a cat. And Phoebe, apparently, was one of the best torturers Hell had before she escaped. She sold her soul, and her penance was making sure those bound for Hell earned their eternal damnation in the most unpleasant of ways. My mom gave her a chance to get her soul back. Same with Kylee, except she was a siren before she became totally human."

He blinked at me and shook his head. "Don't change the subject." He met my gaze. "As interesting as all that verbal click-bait is, we are talking about you." He pointed at me and repositioned himself on the seat, so he was leaning toward me with his feet firmly planted on the ground. He turned my chair and trapped me in place with his hands on the arms of my chair. "What do you want from me?"

His blunt question threw me. I opened my mouth and then closed it. I wasn't sure what I wanted. If I hadn't been timebound, I would have said to be his girlfriend. To find out all those little things like he wanted to. But I didn't have the luxury of that now.

"Melissa?" he asked after I couldn't answer.

"I don't know, okay? If time was on our side..."

"Pretend it is. What do you want?"

"I would want to explore this. I've had the same crush on you for years, so yeah. I would want to see if this went anywhere." Heat bloomed in my cheeks and I leaned back in the chair to get some distance from the intensity in his green eyes.

He licked his lips. "And now? Now that time is playing a cruel trick on us, you don't want to even try." He leaned back in the seat.

"It's not that cut-and-dried." But wasn't it? My head said puppy love wasn't enough to damn my family to certain death, but my heart wanted his arms around me and his lips on mine.

He slowly leaned forward, with his elbows on his knees. "You do want to try?"

I closed my eyes and rested the back of my head against the chair. "I don't want to ignore what is between us. There is something, right?"

He didn't answer, but before my eyes opened, his lips captured mine. The non-answer made my heart soar, and a lump formed in my throat. The more he played with my emotions, the harder it would be to make the choice when the time came.

My damn body betrayed me. I wrapped my arms around his neck, and he pulled me into his lap. Good lord, this guy knew how to kiss. He knew how to make me melt with his slow tongue dance, as if we had all the time in the world.

The slider opened, and a throat cleared. Alex stood with that disapproving frown. I glanced at Zane and his eyes were brighter green, like I had revved his engine to a point of near flash-over. Which explained Alex's intrusion on our moment.

"Your parents are here."

I leaned my head into Zane's chest, annoyed by the interruption. It was as if they knew there was trouble brewing. And not the type of trouble that warranted a visit from Death and Fate.

Grim's Daughter
Chapter 15

THE LAST THING I wanted to do was talk more about the reapers' dark plan. My mother put her electronic Book of Fates on the table while she argued with Alex and Faith about what needed to happen. She and my father wanted to take me somewhere the reapers wouldn't find me, and Alex and Faith didn't want me abandoned somewhere while my parents went off and fought this war.

I couldn't have agreed more, because if they left me alone locked in some ivory tower so they could battle the reapers, I would be pissed.

Instead of engaging in the conversation, my gaze kept wandering back to my mother's Book of Fates. I reached over and picked up the tablet out of sheer curiosity. My hands tingled with the ethereal power emitting from this thing. All the Fates of everyone and everything on earth were held within the binary code flitting on the screen.

The room got silent, and I glanced up. My mother's eyes were wide, as though I had done something gravely wrong. It wasn't until I saw her skin flake away that my stomach plummeted. The tablet dinged, and I looked down at the screen. Two names appeared. Mine and my mother's names blinked on the screen, and then intertwined together in a wild spin that leaped from the electronic list into the room. My mother's signature exit, but this time she didn't just fade away into the light like normal—no, her essence wrapped around me like a whirlwind, blinding me to the rest of the people in the room.

I could hear Alex and Faith and my father yelling for both of us, but whatever had kept my mother animated all these years slammed into me with such a stabbing force that I screamed. She never made a sound, but like the other Deaths, I felt this one acutely. Even so, I kept a grip on that tablet as knowledge flooded into me. The knowledge of space and time. Of life and Death. Of the Fates. It accosted me, pummeling me like a prize fighter hitting a trainee in the ring.

Mercifully, the cold wrapped around me, seeping right down to my core. I curled up into a ball, soaking up everything I could before darkness draped over my vision and an emptiness filled my heart.

"JESUS CHRIST, THIS SHOULD not be!" My father's frantic voice pulled me from the darkness.

"What shouldn't be?" I asked without opening my eyes. I already knew what happened. I had all the knowledge fed down from the creation of Fate at the dawn of time. By picking up that tablet, I had taken my mother's place. I was now Fate, and my mother had moved on. Sorrow squeezed my chest, and I opened my eyes.

They all stared at me. All but my mother. She was laid out on the couch across from where I had fallen. Zane had my head in his lap and a cool cloth on my forehead.

I stared at my mother's form and her chest rose and fell in the cadence of sleep. She was not still or shrouded in death like I had assumed. "But she..." *She had moved on. Hadn't she?* I looked at my father.

"You are alive," he said to me. "So is she. I don't know how that can be."

Whoa.

Wait. What?

My brain couldn't filter what he said. I glanced at the tablet still in my grip. I had seen our names. I had felt her go. We both should be dead, and I should be sending her over that great rainbow bridge in the sky.

I climbed to my feet and swayed as I tucked the tablet away safely in my pocket so no one else picked it up and inadvertently became the next in line for the job.

Zane held my arm to keep me from losing balance.

"Alive?" I finally asked, still not operating on all synapses.

"Yes. You are, and now it seems Fate is," Levi said. Even his eyes were wide, filled with an awe, as if I were some sort of god instead of just a teenager.

"I, um, I don't think she's Fate anymore." I met my father's gaze.

He stumbled to the couch and took a seat, looking as confused and defeated as I've ever seen a man look. He looked between my mother and me, perplexed.

A thought popped into my head and before Levi could say anything to dissuade me, I put my hand out. "Give me the scythe," I ordered, knowing full well he would have to comply with an order by Fate. I didn't want to stumble into this one by accident like I had with my mother. Who knew what the ramifications would be? But if my gut was right, they would live a full life together, here in this realm.

His mouth dropped open, but his hand pulled the ancient weapon from the ether. The silver arch of the scythe glistened in the sunlight and the ancient writing on the blade nearly glowed, beckoning me. Before anyone could stop me, I grabbed it from him and held tight as the same whirlwind encompassed us.

I wished both the Book of Fates and the scythe were charms on a charm bracelet instead of such heavy weapons. Damned if they didn't morph into what I wanted. Either that or I was truly dying and experiencing some strange hallucinations while transitioning to the other side. My father's passing was strangely tranquil as opposed to my mother's, but it still rang through me like being locked in the belfry while the church bells rang.

When the blackness came, I thought perhaps this was it. I could not possibly be alive with this much power pulsing in my veins or the flood of knowledge that filled my brain to an inhuman capacity.

COOLNESS STROKED MY FOREHEAD and hushed whispers caressed my ears. My entire body buzzed like an electrical current, yet my breath was calm and deep, like slumber.

"Did she wake up yet?" a familiar voice asked.

My eyelids flew open, and I sat up to stare at the face of my father. I looked down at my bare arms and the charm bracelet glittered in the shards of sunlight peeking through the blinds of my bedroom. Both the scythe and Book of Fates dangled from the bracelet, warming my skin whenever the precious metal touched my flesh. Whatever clothing I had been wearing had altered into something out of a movie. It reminded me of Athena's gown made of spun gold with silver accents and looked as if I would fit more in ancient Greece than in modern times. It did not fit my goth sense of style in the least. I would prefer a skintight black leather outfit with a plunging neckline and duster to match than this willowy toga type outfit. It was definitely over the top, more like what I always envisioned my mother in than something suited for me.

My skeletal scar was still there, but that was not where my gaze was pulled. On the crook of my elbow, a tattoo of a skull was etched into my skin along with vines crawling up my arm to my shoulder. It stretched down to the reaper's burn. The flowers at the top of the vine were in full bloom, but on the vine going down, the flowers had already wilted and blackened, as though the reaper's touch had killed them. It was ornate enough for me to wonder just how long I had been out.

"You've only been unconscious for a few hours," Levi said from the floor.

I glanced back at my father and then looked at the person sitting next to me. I don't know why I expected Zane, but I recoiled a little at my mother sitting there. Their life-forces were visible, giving them a healthy glow from the inside. They were indeed alive, but hell if I knew how that happened.

I glanced at Levi. "Did I do what I think I did?"

He chuckled in a good-humored, creepy way and nodded. "But instead of ushering your parents into the afterlife, you seem to have revived them. And you did not pass on like you should have." He glanced at my father. "And while he had been one of the most powerful Deaths in all of time, you seem to have surpassed that tenfold."

I what? My father was a legend, or so I had been told on many occasions. How could I be more powerful than he was?

"This isn't what I wanted for you." My father came in and sat on the bed. "But you are now the queen of the underworld."

I laughed, but he didn't.

"You have the knowledge. You know the responsibility that falls on you even if you are here and not there, for the time being." His deadpan delivery had me recheck that light glowing from within him.

My smile faded, and the fog lifted from my brain, bringing with it horrible clarity. My father had sacrificed himself for my mother. That's why he was in the role so young. My mother had stumbled into the position in a similar way as I had, by taking possession of the Book of Fates, without knowing that was how the role was passed on.

I shook those thoughts away. I had one task right now. I had to gain full control of the reapers before they created a genuine tragedy. But I didn't know how to do that from this realm. I still carried the glow of life in my veins, along with the power of Death and Fate combined.

I glanced at my parents. It seemed I also had the power to put a moratorium on Death. But that could have its own consequences, as well. It was too much right now and a dull headache captured my attention. I closed my eyes and pressed my fingers against the bridge of my nose to stave it off.

"Is Zane still here or was he rightly freaked out enough to have run like the devil was chasing him?" I dreaded the answer.

"About that..."

I lowered my hand and opened my eyes, feeling the weight of his cautious words.

"What about that?" I whispered, suddenly afraid for them to speak any more.

"You need to be really cautious about touching people." My father shoved his hands into his pockets and looked down at the ground.

My heart leaped into my throat, pounding with each frantic beat. *What had I done?* "Is he okay?"

He nodded. "But you did freak him out. Hell, you freaked everyone out." He kicked at the floor without meeting my gaze. He didn't sound freaked out, though. Just unemotional, as though something were missing.

Even though I was afraid to ask, I had to know. "What happens when I touch someone?"

"It seems you absorb spiritual energy," my mother said in a tone that made the alarms in my head sound.

Her tone said it was more than just making someone tired; same with the sadness in her eyes.

"What does that mean?"

"It means if you touch someone long enough, you can strip them of their soul." My father met my gaze.

"I kill them?" I gasped, without really thinking it through.

He shook his head. "No. You just leave them soulless. Which means they have no moral code. No filter. And they can no longer feel emotion—at least, according to Alex."

I blinked at him. Alex had once lost most of his soul, but he got it back when he and Faith went up against Lucifer. On the plus side, at least my touch wasn't lethal. "Did I do that to Zane?"

My father shook his head. "No. Zane is fine."

"But not everyone is fine," I said, taking in both my parents' expressions.

"It depends on how you quantify fine," he said.

I tried to think of who was close to me besides Zane. Faith and Alex were nearby. So was Holly. And then I felt a hand cover mine. I stared at it and my gaze jumped to my father's. He squeezed my hand and shrugged.

"You?"

"I'm fine with it. I'm breathing. So is your mother. So are you. Besides, I've been Death for so long that I kind of forgot what emotions really were." He waved it away, but one glance at my mother told me something significant was gone in him now and it saddened her.

He was shoveling so much bull in my direction that it nearly made me choke. "I'm so sorry." I was now a true menace not only to evil-seeking reapers, but to humankind.

"It is a sight to behold, though. Or so I'm told." He glanced at me with a crooked grin. "I never knew you could see the transfer of a soul, but apparently it's very majestic."

I rolled my eyes and glanced at Levi. "Can I touch animals?" I asked.

Levi shook his head. "They have souls."

"You?" I asked him.

"I don't think you want me soulless." He offered me his dog grin, lolling tongue and all.

Levi without a soul would be more of a nightmare than I was. Thunder rumbled in the distance, matching my mood.

"We'll leave you to digest all this," my mother said, and took my father's hand, leading him out of the room.

Just seeing their fingers intertwined was a stark reminder of my future.

I threw myself back on the bed and covered my face. Not only was I now a dual deity, but I couldn't touch anyone. No hugs, no lingering kisses with Zane, no handshakes or high fives.

Life was going to suck.

Grim's Daughter
Chapter 16

LEVI REMAINED IN THE room, vigilant and silent, as if he knew I needed to toss my situation around in my head before I could fully accept my new normal. I seemed to have just scratched the surface with my powers.

If I could breathe life back into someone, couldn't I retrieve their soul?

"No. You absorbed his soul. It's like me eating someone and thinking that by shitting them out the other end I might be able to salvage them," Levi said from the floor.

I disliked his analogy just as much as the fact he could read my thoughts right now. They were dark and devastating, especially with his response.

"That is my curse. I get to hear your juvenile laments." He huffed and put his head back down.

I sat up and looked at Levi. "So, when they say I absorbed my father's soul, basically I destroyed it the way you destroy reapers?" I asked, to make sure I understood what exactly I did with a touch.

He nodded.

"So how long did it take to strip my father of his soul?"

"Moments. They were being kind when they told you that you had to watch how long you touch someone. Your father caught you as you transformed into the vision you are now, and his soul was ripped from his body. It was a sight to behold, but not in the pleasant sense."

So, I couldn't even hope for a peck on the lips from Zane. I closed my eyes and fell back on the bed. I needed to figure out how to nullify this new curse. I refused to think of it as a power. It was vile and destructive, like I had somehow inherited a dark streak from Lucifer himself.

"Stop with the melodrama." Levi growled.

"What would you do in my situation?" I finally asked when my overtaxed brain couldn't come up with a solution.

He sat up. "I don't like people, so I'd be good with not touching any of them."

I tried to think of something that would impact Levi in the same way it impacted me.

"What if you couldn't eat demons or reapers anymore?"

He glanced at me. "I would not like that."

"That's what the thought of never touching Zane or hugging Holly or Alex or Faith, or anyone for that matter, feels like to me."

"I would find a way around it," he grumbled.

Finding a way around it meant people would lose their souls just to satisfy my need for touch. Having a town full of soulless supernaturals would be just as much a disaster as letting the reapers get away with what they had been doing. I had a life before they screwed around with me. They were going to find out just how unhappy their boss was soon enough.

I started to get up, and the door opened. Zane stood in the entry, looking unsure of himself. He pointed to the end of the bed and I nodded, curling up my legs so there was no chance of him touching me.

He crossed and took a seat carefully. His gaze landed on the ornate tattoo on my arm, and he let out a high-pitched laugh.

If I thought I was undone, he looked a feather away from a total freak-out.

"I'm okay." I didn't know what else to say to wipe out that crazed look in his eyes.

"Well, I'm not." He ran his hand through his hair.

"Hey, I'm alive," I said to ease the pain radiating in his voice.

"But I can't touch you, otherwise you'll suck my soul out like you did to your father." His irritated glare caught mine.

I shrugged and offered a half-hearted smile. "This way you can get to know all those small little things you wanted to," I said, trying to see whatever silver lining there was to this new curse. "And, hey, I apparently can bring people back to life," I added.

His lips twitched. "Be serious for a moment."

"I can't be. If I do, I might just annihilate every reaper out of spite."

"Missy!"

A yell from downstairs startled me, and a moment later, I popped into the living room. I didn't know how I got there and the momentary shock of transporting out of my room made the scene before me even more surreal.

Another reaper in human form had Holly, and his skeletal hand was close enough to her skin for me to see red. Rage filled every pore.

The reaper looked between my parents and me, and his jawbone dropped open.

"Let her go." The growling command came from my lips at the same time Zane came into view on the stairs with Levi by his side.

The reaper pulled his hands back as if Holly were the one with the power to destroy it. His eyes widened. "You..."

"Are done here." I waved my hand. The power I exercised at the dinner table took a blink's-worth of energy this time, and the reaper exploded into a dust cloud as opposed to just flaking away like those before. Unlike the Deaths I felt at the dinner table, there was no pain that accompanied his exit from the universe.

"Why did you do that?" my father snapped, and I turned on him.

"I will do that to every last reaper who threatens my family," I shouted at him. "If they continue to test me, none of them will be left standing," I added in the same growl I used before.

My father stepped closer, crowding me, but his expression was frighteningly neutral. "You need them. Otherwise, you'll be collecting all the souls and helping them transition." He poked my chest to make his point.

"I don't think they know anything has happened," Faith said from the kitchen and although I heard her, I didn't pay any attention to her with my father in my face.

"People can find their own way to Heaven or Hell!" I was not in the mood for a lecture from him. I wasn't in the mood for anything except finding a way around this damn curse.

My father blinked and cocked his head, studying me. There was an absolute absence of emotion there and a chill skittered up my spine. "You don't mean that."

Oh, but I did. They put me in the position to make a dire decision, where I had no idea what the ramifications were. Death would have been better than living without human contact.

"I think Faith is right," my mother said from behind me.

Both my father and I turned.

"What?" we asked at the same time.

"I don't think the reapers know you are..." She waved at me without saying I was now Fate and Death combined into a mega entity.

The doorbell rang, and everyone exchanged a glance. There had been no warning for visitors.

Before Alex could move, his father and mother came in with a harried Kylee and Michael.

"They drove here as fast as they could," Papa said, out of breath.

"Where are your kids?" Faith asked, looking around them.

"Smoke and Phoebe are watching them at the lake. They are safe." Kylee looked at me, pointing an accusing finger. "But you've gone and pissed off Heaven."

Grim's Daughter
Chapter 17

NANA RAN BACK TO the car and brought in leftovers. She apparently had enough of a heads-up to pack a cooler. I guess, considering we didn't really eat yesterday, that Nana decided we needed to eat while Kylee told us the reaction of the Heavenly host. If it wasn't such a morbid topic, it would be kind of amusing.

"Michael went to visit the cove to say hi to his mom and dad and brother. He came back paler than the ghosts that visited him," Kylee said while she nibbled on a roll.

Michael tried to smile, but he didn't manage it. He also wouldn't quite meet my gaze. "Heaven said you cannot be both deities."

I stared at my plate, unable to bring myself to eat. Not with all the turmoil happening in my stomach. "Where was Heaven when the reapers were threatening my family?"

He caught my glare and shrugged. "They said if the reapers knew, they would have already swarmed Missy. So there is a window to correct this."

"If Heaven knows what is going on with the reapers, why haven't they interceded?" my father asked with a full mouth of potatoes. He was shoveling food into his mouth as if he hadn't eaten in decades.

"You know better than I do, but my guess is that they don't meddle in the affairs of the earth. They only take up arms when something extreme happens," Michael said.

Kylee stared at my father with a crease between her eyes, and then her gaze jumped to my mother.

"They aren't okay with you two living, either. They think this whole thing is a massive cluster." Michael focused back on his plate and pushed the food around, picking here and there without bringing much to his mouth.

"I'm not dying just to make them happy." My dad reached for more food, as if they were discussing the weather and not his life.

"What is wrong with you?" Kylee asked, glancing at my mother before looking back at my father.

"No soul." He shrugged and kept eating.

Kylee looked at my mother. She knew more about the soulless than anyone. She used to strip humans of their souls when she was a siren. But since Papa and his brother saved her with the help of my mother, she has been just a normal human. Albeit one with some mad fighting skills and millennia of history stored in her pretty head.

"I have a soul, but it seems if Missy, um, is touched, she absorbs souls. After she did whatever to transfer the role to her, she passed out. Thankfully, Nick was lucid enough to catch her, but in doing so, his soul was sucked out of him and into her. We witnessed it." Julia twirled her fork around, indicating Faith and Alex and Holly and Zane.

"I'm fine with it," my dad said. "Continue, please." He rolled his wrist for them to continue.

"Heaven is in an uproar."

"Big fucking deal," he replied. "If they had helped instead of just sitting up there on their high horses, none of this would have happened."

"Dad. We are at the dinner table," I said, embarrassed by his casual swearing in front of everyone. Now I understood the no-filter issue with the soulless.

"Was I like that?" Alex asked Faith. After all, he had lost most of his soul in the fight against Lucifer. But he was able to get it back in the end.

She smirked and nodded. Papa and Nana's smirks matched Faith's.

"Anyway," Kylee pulled us back on topic. "The last...whatever..." She waved at me. "Deity that had such absolute power was reduced to dust, and Heaven vowed to never let that happen again." She took a sip of water. "That dust storm created our universe. The big bang was the destruction of that god."

We all looked at Michael. He nodded and took a bite of food.

Great. Just what I needed. "So, what is the bottom line?" I was tired of this conversation. I just wanted to know what Heaven expected of me.

"There's a snag." Michael finished his food and pushed his plate back. "You are alive."

"And?"

Kylee put her hand on his arm and said, "This is as unprecedented as your birth. They don't know how to handle it because all life is precious. However, I can tell you from experience, the taking of souls is going to be a problem once they find that out."

"I don't intend on doing it again." At least not on purpose, but I couldn't control people around me. My mind drifted to Kylee's children and my cheeks went cold. They doled out hugs like a child abductor handed out candy. I pushed my plate away in disgust. "I can't be here, can I?"

I didn't wait for an answer. It was my turn to flee from the crowd, and I ended up back in the chair on the veranda, staring out at the ocean. This time the cold didn't seem to penetrate, even though I wore this weird outfit.

Zane strolled out and took the seat by me. He clasped his hands together in front of him.

"You know, I could have Alex wipe me from your memory." I didn't want him saddled with all this and pining for me from afar.

He turned on me like an angry viper. "You think you can take every memory of you from my mind and it wouldn't leave a hole that I would never know how to fill?" He turned my chair toward him, barely avoiding my knees.

I gasped and recoiled.

"You would have him take away the only thing that gave me the strength to get out of bed every morning and cover up my bruises so I could go to school and see you?" He shook his head. "I'd rather be soulless and holding you than have no memory of you."

"That's the thing about being soulless," Alex said from the doorway. "You would lose all that passion you have locked up. You wouldn't give a damn whether or not you were holding her."

Zane stared up at him. His anger slowly transitioned to sorrow. He looked down at me and leaned back in his chair.

"I can do what she said, if you'd like."

Zane shook his head. "No. Then I wouldn't understand how the Hell I survived daily. It would remove the only thing I ever clung to."

I had no idea how paramount I was to his daily existence, and it hurt more than I expected. I wanted to reach out and touch him, but instead I curled my hands into fists and shoved them under the sides of my thighs so I wouldn't be tempted.

Alex gave a nod and went back inside to continue whatever conversation they were having about me and the current predicament.

"So, this is as close as we can ever get?" Zane asked. The edges of his lips turned down as the reality slammed into him.

"Seems so. Unless I can figure out a workaround." Somehow, I would figure this out. I needed to. Otherwise, I would go truly insane.

"Well, get on that." He gave me the beginnings of a smile. "Otherwise, I may just say screw it despite what Mr. Ryan says."

I glanced at him and he gave me a shrug.

"I'll do that just as soon as I get these pesky reapers off our case."

"Sounds like a plan."

I actually laughed, and so did Zane. It felt good. I hadn't really laughed in a long time. When we both settled down, I sighed.

"I never in my wildest dreams thought I'd be in this predicament, even with knowing who my parents were. Now I have them back in the land of the living, but my father is without a soul, which means he doesn't feel anything anymore and as you saw at the table, he has no filter. They both are in the bodies of eighteen-year-olds, but they are old. And yet they still have an entire life to live out." As I summarized, a horrible thought entered my mind, and I sagged in my seat. "He has no soul."

"You said that." He looked at me sideways.

"You don't understand. It's not like Alex, who was able to get his soul back. My father's soul is gone. When he dies, that is it. There is no afterlife for him." I wiped my face and nearly doubled over at the reality of what I had done.

That was why my mother looked so damn sad. Whatever life they had, whatever forever they thought they earned together, was gone. It was only here in this life, and then she'd move on without him while he just turned to dust.

This could not happen again.

"Breathe," Zane said softly.

I hadn't realized I was hyperventilating until that moment, and I met his wide-eyed stare. He reached for me, but pulled his hand back at the last second, remembering why I was having trouble breathing.

That familiar tingle hit, and I heard Papa's name being called.

"Shit," I muttered and then followed the psychic signal of the call. One minute, I was sitting in the backyard with Zane and the next, I stood in April's living room, staring down a reaper who had cornered her. This one was there to take her life, and anger burst forth from me before he could register who had entered the room.

"There's more," she said, and ran out of the room toward the stairs.

I looked up and sent my angry power out until every crevice of the house was clear of reapers. I turned to go, and Papa stood behind me with the reaper knife. He met my gaze. He gave me a nod and started to fade.

"Wait."

He solidified again. "You got them all," he said.

"I know. I just don't know how to get back without walking." I had popped downstairs when Holly had called my name and I had no idea why I heard April's call for help when it was aimed at Papa, but it was as if a switch turned on and within a blink I was here to defend my family.

"You will it. Just like you did to get here." He put his hand out to take mine.

I stepped out of his reach. "Don't touch." I hadn't meant for it to come out so harshly, but he paused, curled his fingers into his palm and dropped his hand with a nod. "I can't be responsible for someone else..." I pressed my lips together and shook my head.

"Okay. Then close your eyes and feel the pull of where your body is."

I laughed. "Papa, you don't get it. I didn't astral project like you did. I am physically here." I pointed to the floor. "And walking down the streets in this getup will get me thrown in jail." I waved at the pretty and skimpy dress I had on.

"Oh." He glanced at my clothing and then around the house, and bit his lower lip. "Well, then just hang tight and I'll be over to pick you up in a few minutes." In a blink, he was gone.

I waited at the window while April tended to her family upstairs.

"Thank you," April said from behind me after a good ten minutes had passed.

I turned and nodded. When she went to give me a hug, I put my hand out to stop her and moved out of range. "You can't touch me. Please." I moved even farther away.

Her brow furrowed. She glanced at the ground and then back at me. "I can't see anything about your future," she said. April had the ability to glimpse the future for most people.

"You've never been able to see my future to begin with," I said, reminding her of all her failed attempts.

"True. But how did you get here? Did CJ bring you?" She shot the questions at me as the pitch of her voice got higher. "And why are you wearing a toga?" She was just now noticing my inappropriate clothing.

I splayed my fingers. "Calm down."

"They came after my family," she yelled at me.

"It's my family, too," I said. "And I'm just as pissed about it as you are." She blinked at me. "Papa didn't bring me here. I did that all on my own. If you noticed, I didn't pass out when I took out that reaper or the ones upstairs like I did yesterday at Thanksgiving."

She cocked her head.

"There have been a few recent developments. Which is why you cannot touch me." I wiped my face and glanced out the window, wishing Papa would hurry and get here. I didn't like being away from home right now.

"What developments?" Her voice trembled.

I glanced back at her. "I took over for both my parents. But I didn't die, and neither did they. The reapers don't know because normally, the people holding the roles pass through to their final destination. But they are sitting at Papa's house right now, arguing over what to do with me."

Her arms dropped to her sides, and her jaw popped open.

"And the kicker? If I touch anyone, I apparently suck out their soul. Leaving them soulless. So please, as much as I'd love a hug, just don't." Tears blurred my vision and hot streaks slid down my cheeks.

"Aw, sweetie." She stepped toward me and stopped. "Who did you leave soulless?" she asked in a whisper.

"My father."

"Alex?" she asked with wide, scared eyes.

I shook my head. "No. The former Death."

I saw her shoulders slump with relief. She had lived through the era of Alex with no soul, too. But she didn't understand the full ramifications of this. "It's not something he will ever get back, either. Not like Alex did." More tears made my voice raw, and it cracked on almost every word.

The front door opened, and Papa walked in. He gave April an awkward smile and then focused on me. "Zane was rightfully freaked out when you just disappeared. I guess that freaked him out more than my unanimated form. He's in the car." He hooked his thumb over his shoulder.

I nodded and glanced back at April. "They won't be coming back again. I promise you that. This ends tonight."

"Thank you for protecting my kids, but don't promise something that you can't deliver," she said.

"I will end this tonight." I wasn't dicking around anymore. If they thought they had any prayer of control now, they needed to be put in their place or put in the ground. I stormed past Papa and made my way to the car. Zane was in the front seat, so I slid into the back.

I needed Levi to take me to where the reapers gathered. I wasn't totally sure that I could get there while breathing, but if I had to die to end this threat to my family, so be it.

Zane glanced at Papa as he got into the car and then over the back of the seat at me. "You just disappeared. No swirl of air or anything. One minute you were there and then gone," he said. "Just like in the bedroom."

"I didn't have time to explain." I glared at him. "And when I get back to the house, you all will stay inside while I take care of this once and for all."

"No," both Papa and Zane said at the same time.

"Yes," I growled from the backseat. "They need to know who the Hell is boss now, and I'm not some sweet pushover like my mother. They will bow to me or they will die."

"Yes, my queen of dragons," Zane said in a snide voice with a glare to match. His reference to *Game of Thrones* was not lost on me. The fact he knew to throw that out there and hit the right nerve was impressive.

It knocked me down to the appropriate peg.

I leaned back in the seat as Papa glanced at him. Zane was right. I was acting irrationally, but they sent their thugs after my family. "Fine. I won't kill them all." I sighed and glanced at him. "Happy now?"

"I won't be happy until I can kiss you again."

The car swerved a little, and we both looked at Papa. He gave Zane the evil side eye.

"Sorry, sir," he said.

"You will not kiss my granddaughter until she is eighteen, you understand?" He pointed at Zane.

I snorted a laugh from the backseat and his blue-eyed gaze shot to the rearview mirror just as he pulled into Alex's driveway. I hurried out of the car so I wouldn't have to hear another word about kisses.

When I stepped into the house, I put my hand up to stop whatever arguments Alex and Faith were going to launch. "They went after April and her family."

That pretty much killed any conversation. I looked at Levi and then at my father. "May I speak with you both outside for a moment?" I pointed to the backyard.

My father pointed to his chest as Levi got up and started toward the door.

"Yes. You." I grabbed his arm as I walked by, careful to avoid bumping into anyone, especially Levi as I got closer to the door.

Zane followed, and I shook my head at him. "No. Please don't complicate things right now. I need to figure out what has to be done, so just stay inside with the family."

He crossed his arms, but he yielded. Although he stood planted in the doorway with a full view of the backyard.

I walked out to the end of the veranda and across the lawn until I stood at the bluff. It was at least a thirty-foot drop to a rocky bed covered with the crashing waves. No cliff diving from here, for sure. I took a deep breath of the cool sea air and let it settle in my lungs before I blew it out. I loved the smell and taste of the salt air. It grounded me enough to focus on what needed to be done.

I turned to my father. "How do we stop them?"

"There's no we. It's up to you now. Since I'm not sure you can pass to the reaper realm

168

without an escort, I think you will need to summon them here. And then give them an ultimatum."

"And if they scoff at the ultimatum?"

He shrugged. "They are free. They can choose to follow or not. They can choose to threaten harm to those you love to get you to bend to their will." He glanced at the house. "And considering what they tried to do with your mother and me at the helm, I'm not sure much will dissuade them."

"So, I need to become the queen of dragons," I muttered and turned back toward the sea. As much as I was fine with taking out reapers, Zane's words in the car sunk in deep. I didn't want to be the crazy queen who kills off everyone who disagrees with her. I wanted to be fair. I wanted to be more like my parents.

"How do I call them here and protect everyone in the house from the rogue assholes?"

My father glanced around the backyard. He shook his head. "This won't work. The house is too close to others. There isn't a barrier between the edge and that drop, so they could potentially gang up on you and cause you to fall." He looked down the cliff. "And that would be deadly, since you don't know how to jump realms. Which you really can't do unless you're dead or have a guide and anyone or anything you touch that has a soul ends up like me."

"Well then, where? Where the Hell do I have this standoff with the reapers?"

"The Mojave Desert," he said in all seriousness. "Nothing living around for miles."

"In York. Where in York can I do this?"

"What about Fort McClary? It's not in York, but it's pretty damn remote and it's closed at night."

I glanced at him with a bit of appreciation. That was the perfect spot, especially after dark.

"The only thing you have to worry about is cops. If they show up, it could be a major hassle."

I glanced at Levi. "We just have to figure out how to get there." I wasn't going without Levi. I needed him by my side to show the reapers that I had an ally. A very powerful and very loyal ally.

"I'll drive you," my father said.

"With what?" He didn't own a car, and I doubted anyone inside would lend him one. Not for this task, anyway.

He shrugged. "They have cars." He pointed toward the house. "I'll just take one."

"You can't just take a car without asking."

"Sure I can. Besides, Alex and Faith won't mind if I borrow their car."

Good lord, he was going to be a real problem after this. Without that moral compass, he didn't recognize wrong from right. And he certainly didn't get the protective reflexes of my guardians. "Um. I doubt they'll let you take me somewhere that neither of us discloses, to do something that is dangerous to my health."

My father shrugged. "I'd be there with you. So would Levi. What's the problem?"

I rolled my eyes and looked down at Levi. "A little help?"

"It's a plan," Levi said. But his lack of enthusiasm didn't give me a sense of confidence.

"Fine." I threw my hands up and turned back toward the ocean. The hardest part of this plan was convincing my family and Zane to let me go handle this without fanfare. I thought I'd be able to convince Alex, Faith, and Holly, but getting my mother and Zane to agree to this crazy plan would be nearly impossible. I needed to get a handle on the reapers; otherwise, someone else would die on my watch. And that just wasn't acceptable.

Grim's Daughter
Chapter 18

"I HAVE TO DO this!" I yelled from the corner of the room. Alex and Papa had cornered me. Faith had conceded that although it was dangerous, it was something that none of them could do.

Kylee didn't say much either way; neither did Michael. They just sat back and watched the arguments rage on.

"You are a teenager. You should not be put in this position!" Alex shouted at me.

Papa's head snapped in Alex's direction. "Faith went after Lucifer when she was only her age."

I blinked at him. It seemed as though he were coming around to my corner with that nugget, but I could tell from the set of his expression, he was not happy. "I can handle this." I looked at both of them. "Now please, give me a little breathing room."

They glanced at their proximity and both took a healthy step back, giving me exactly what I requested.

"Do I have a say here?" Zane said from the couch.

"No. None of you have a say. This is my mess. I need to fix it without an audience. Because if you are there, the likelihood of you getting hurt or killed is pretty damn high. If I don't do this, the same odds are still in play. They will get to you eventually while we sit on our hands and do nothing just to spare the teenager from...from what?" I threw my hands in the air.

"Death," Zane said.

I shrugged. "That doesn't change things. In case you didn't notice, I *am* Death. Alive or dead, I'm still in the damn role and I still won't be able to touch anyone."

"Damnit, Missy," Holly snapped. She had been so quiet with all this, and now I turned my attention to her tear-stained face. "What happened to our forever pact? *If you go, I go*? Huh?"

"Holly." I sagged against the wall. My partner in all my crimes. My rebel sister. I already felt the bond between us breaking. "I'll be here for you."

She shook her head. "You've already made the choice." She turned, crossing to disappear up the stairs. She knew me better than anyone in this room. But if she was there, I would falter. If anyone in this room was there, I would fail or do something drastic to save their lives. And then Heaven would come down and squash me like a bug.

I turned back to the rest of them. "I need Levi with me. I can't touch him to take him along, so my father has agreed to drive us. Please don't stop us."

"Sit down." Alex pointed at the couch.

Normally, when he uttered a command, my body did exactly as instructed. But I didn't even feel the pull of his words like I usually did.

I crossed my arms. "You sit," I challenged.

His expression fell as his body marched to the couch and sat down. Everyone stared at him and then at me. Even my father.

"Shit. I could only control the elements when I was in your position."

My gaze snapped to his. "You could control the elements?" That would be quite handy. Fire. Water. Earth. Air. Man, that would be a hoot and a half.

He grinned and nodded, as if all this were normal.

I thought about the reaper here and my command to stop. "What about reapers? Could you control them?"

He shook his head.

A new hope bloomed inside me. "I did."

"I commanded them, but I couldn't control them," my mother said.

Even Levi looked at me with interest. "You may be able to command them to stop, and it would stick for a while, but as your father said outside, they are free. And they wouldn't take too kindly to that once it wore off."

Damn him for speaking the truth and bursting my bubble.

"Can I get up now?" Alex said through clenched teeth.

I didn't realize I was holding him in place. I waved my hand for him to go ahead, and a tiny rush of release filled me. I would need to explore that more later. I turned to my father. "Tell me what you could do."

Before he could launch into his litany of powers, the doorbell rang. We all looked at one another while Nana went to get the door. A moment later, Kylee's two kids ran in. Smoke and Phoebe followed, but they weren't smiling like I've always seen them. Even Smoke's expression was a warning of sorts. Nana didn't come in right away. When she did, her expression was guarded in a way I had never seen, and she met Papa's gaze. Papa stumbled back into the wall. Even Alex and Faith paled at whatever she was announcing in her silent voice.

I recognized the person who walked into the room behind Nana, but I had only seen pictures of him before. I glanced at Papa. After all, it was his brother in the flesh. Now I knew why the lot of them faltered. Nana had announced his presence before he even walked into the room. I should have been just as shocked as the rest of the crew in the house, but considering what I had done with my parents, nothing shocked me.

"Tom?" Papa asked, as if he saw a ghost.

The man smiled a crooked smile and shrugged. "It was either me or Dad." He glanced at Faith. "Sorry for the shock, but they gave me a pass in order to make sure Heaven's demands were heard."

Faith clung to the doorway wall as if the house might fall down around her. I don't think I've ever seen her that pale, either. She was reliving his death in her mind, and I kept catching snippets of images. And every last one of them was disturbing.

I shook my head to clear it and stared at Papa's brother. "I assume the ultimatum has to do with me."

He nodded. "I got Heaven's version. You want to tell me the real version?"

"I thought Heaven's version would be the real version." I glanced at Papa and then back at his brother.

He scoffed. "Angels all have sticks up their asses. I don't trust their version of the truth as far as I could throw one of those winged bastards."

I arched an eyebrow. "Well, I guess the reapers wanted my father out of a job and someone in the position of Death who they could control. They just never thought I'd take both Fate and Death on instead of leaving my parents separated for all eternity. Unfortunately, that's kind of what happened, because instead of all three of us dying and them moving on, all three of us are alive and if I touch anyone, I end up absorbing their soul. My dad doesn't have a soul anymore because of me." I shrugged and bit my lower lip. I really wanted a hug or a hand squeeze to tell me I was doing the right thing, but that would not happen, so I had to pull up my own bootstraps and take this on like the fighter I was on the inside.

He took a seat at the kitchen table and tapped his fingers as he studied me.

"Death doesn't have a soul?" Smoke asked, pulling my attention away from the newest guest raised from the dead.

"No," I answered and focused back on Papa's brother.

Faith finally seemed to reanimate now that the initial shock had worn off.

"How are you alive?" she finally asked and took a seat across from him.

"I'm not. Well, not in the same sense as you and Alex and CJ are. If you put a stethoscope to my chest, you'd hear a big fat nothing. So... Alive may be pushing it. I don't know how long I'm here for, either."

"*The Walking Dead*?" Zane glanced at me.

"More like *Warm Bodies*," I whispered to him, but it was loud enough for the entire room to hear, and I earned a couple suppressed smiles from my witty comeback. "And I don't think he survives on brains. Do you?"

Papa's brother smiled and shook his head. "No. I'm not a zombie, if that's what you're asking."

"What's the message?" Papa asked, returning us all to the fact his dead brother was sitting at the kitchen table drumming his fingers to the point I wanted to scream for him to stop.

"She isn't supposed to be," he said. "I was sent to put an end to her."

Papa stood, and it was as if the Heavens had opened up. Light shined from within him and wings right out of a fantasy book spread behind him. The look on his face made everyone seem to flinch away from him. Neither Holly nor I had ever seen Papa with wings, and we stared in stark fascination. "Not going to happen."

"Jesus, CJ, cool your damn jets. Did I say I was actually going to follow the orders of those dicks?" he asked, while still sitting calmly at the table. Papa's display didn't even make him blink, never mind cower in fear like he probably should have.

Papa blinked and both the light and the wings faded, but the vision would forever be burned in my mind.

"Angels are the bane of my existence. Besides, she is a child no older than Faith was when she went after Lucifer. This whole thing is as much of a clusterfuck as that was." He slung his arm over the back of the chair. "I'm not hurting a kid, no matter how much Heaven wants her destroyed. It's not like she's the antichrist or the devil reincarnated." He glanced at me. "Right?"

I stared at him and shook my head. "Neither. Just the daughter of Fate and Death, who has now taken over both jobs," I said with a half-hearted smile.

Heaven sent an assassin to take me out. How was I supposed to deal with *that*? The more pressing question was, how would I deal with this guy if he decided to make good on Heaven's threat?

I couldn't chase off the reapers and fend off Heaven's assassins. I had to at least take out the one who put my family at risk, and get that off my plate before I dealt with this Heaven business.

I turned toward Alex. "You can at least let me try to get rid of one of the pending disasters tonight. Please."

Alex glanced at his uncle and then back at me. "I can't let you walk into that alone, though."

"I won't be alone. I'll have Levi there."

Alex glanced at Levi and then back at me. "And what happens if your father does not listen to your instructions? What happens if he gets caught in the crossfire? You need to assume there will be shots fired."

"He will not be there. He needs to make sure no one comes up to the fort."

"Say what?" my father asked, now focusing on our conversation in full.

"You aren't part of the standoff."

"The Hell I'm not. I've been Death for what..." He glanced at my mother. "Julia, help me out here."

"Fifty-eight years." She sighed.

"I've been Death for fifty-eight years and all that time, those bastards have been free. Fifty-eight years and not one of them came to me to tell me they were unhappy. Perhaps if they had grown a pair and confronted me with their issues, we wouldn't be here right now." His eyes blazed.

I guess the soulless could still feel anger. Go figure.

"I'm serious. I can't have you in the crossfire. You have no soul. What if they decide to kill you? That's it. There is no Heaven for you."

My father recoiled at that statement with a mask of confusion marring his smooth skin.

"What the Hell did we miss?" Phoebe looked back and forth between my mother and father.

"A lot. It seems my daughter is both Fate and Death now, and as she said before, we are all alive. Like breathing, heartbeat alive, versus the animated stiffs we were before," my father said.

"How?"

"A determined sixteen-year-old and just a split second of me leaving my tablet on the table." My mother waved at me. "It went downhill from there."

Phoebe chuckled, exchanging a humorous glance with Smoke. "You're alive and stuck in an eighteen-year-old's body? Does that mean you need to enroll in college and get actual jobs now?"

"Oh, go pound sand," my mother snapped and took a seat next to Holly and Zane on the couch. She crossed her arms with the perfect pout.

They seemed to find it just as funny as Smoke and Phoebe and didn't even try to hide their smirks. I glanced at my father. He just shrugged.

"Are you going to listen and stay at the entrance of the park so that no one wanders in and gets killed?" I asked my father.

"Fine." He rolled his eyes. "Let's go." He headed for the front door and swiped a pair of keys off the kitchen island as we passed. Levi followed him.

I glanced at Alex. "I promise we'll be back."

"Wait," Zane said from behind me before I passed through the front door.

I stopped and glanced back at him as he approached. He got close enough for me to feel the life pulsing in his veins. I could almost smell his essence, and I licked my lips, meeting his sad-eyed stare. He reached for me, and I shook my head.

"Not even a quick peck?" he asked.

My gaze fell to his lips and my entire being wanted to kiss him. "No. Not even a peck," I whispered and met his gaze. "But as soon as I deal with these reapers, I'll start looking into how to fix this. I promise."

He leaned against the wall. "Just come back in one piece, okay?"

That was the plan. I nodded and opened the screen door.

"And remember, don't go all psycho on them if you don't have to."

"I'll try not to." I had to refrain from pushing up on my tiptoes to kiss him. Instead, I headed to the car that my father and Levi were in and slipped into the backseat. I had to come up with a solid plan in order for this to work. Otherwise, Levi might eat good tonight.

Grim's Daughter
Chapter 19

TWENTY MINUTES LATER, WE stood at the park entrance of Fort McClary. The steel barrier gate was closed, so vehicle traffic wouldn't be able to enter, and my father turned around in the small space, parking as far on the side as he could to be inconspicuous. I got out of the car and opened the front passenger door to let Levi out with me.

"How do I summon all the reapers?"

"You need both the book of Fates and the scythe in your hands, and then just command the reaper federation to appear before you."

"That's it?"

He nodded. "Then just hold the book of Fates so they can see it and you've sealed your position. But then you need to tuck that away so no one can snatch it from you. Turn it back into the charm where they can't see you do it, but be cautious of turning your back on them, even with Levi next to you. Because if they get a hold of either of those things, I'm not sure what would happen."

"Thanks, Dad." I leaned in, giving his cheek a quick kiss. But I couldn't go up against the reapers dressed like the goddess Athena. I needed something more fierce and more goth, like me. "How do I change my clothes?" I asked. After all, he could manipulate the elements as Death. I should be able to do a magical wardrobe change.

He grinned. "You will it. Think of what you want, close your eyes and wish it so."

If only things were that easy. I took a deep breath and closed my eyes, envisioning a badass leather duster dress with a plunging neckline and slits up to my thighs. The wind changed, circling around me as I visualized the details.

I opened my eyes and although the clothes were leather; they looked like a child had stitched them together. I looked more like a zombie cast member from *The Walking Dead* than an entity to be respected. I bet if a brisk sea gust came along, the fabric would fly off in a snap. That was all I needed, to make the stand in front of the reapers naked.

My father tried not to laugh, but humor at my failure danced in his eyes and the poorly hidden smirk didn't help. "Well, that is…different."

I rolled my eyes. "This wasn't what I was going for," I muttered.

"I should hope not," Levi said from his spot next to my father.

"Let me try this again." I closed my eyes, thinking about a cross between Kate Beckinsale in *Underworld* and Gal Gadot in *Wonder Woman*. I needed it to be fitted up top and drop in a long skirt with slits to my thighs. Something that would make Zane drool, but something that I could also move in if I needed to. Fabric shifted on my skin and I suppressed the urge to open my eyes. If I didn't do this right, I would end up looking like a reject and that wouldn't do. I wanted to look like a queen.

A slow clap made my eyes fly open. My father was clapping as if he were impressed, and I glanced down at my threads, expecting to see either the silver and golden flowy thing I came in or another nightmare of a leather mess. Nope, I was as badass as I had imagined this time.

"I did it!" I smiled and gave him another hug.

"Go get 'em, tiger," he said. But there wasn't the enthusiasm that should have accompanied those words. It felt very superficial and false. But his tender smile was more like his old self.

I nodded and turned to face the battle alone. If I had to take a page out of *Game of Thrones*, I would, but I prayed it didn't go that route.

When I got to the farthest point on the park green, which gave me the highest land elevation to look down on the expanse of lawn hidden behind a berm, I took a deep breath, closed my eyes, and wished my charms back into existence. The weight of the scythe snapped my eyelids open, and I stared out at the darkness, wondering whether a sea of reapers were any different from the blackness of the night surrounding me and Levi.

"Now or never, huh?" I asked, and Levi nodded. "I command the federation of reapers to appear before me now," I said with authority.

Nothing happened. I waited and then asked Levi, "What did I do wrong?"

"Reaper federation. The order of words makes a difference."

Of course they did. Damn semantics. "I command the reaper federation to appear before me now!" I used the right string of words this time because the air shifted, and a legion of reapers appeared, shrouded in their black cloaks with only the whites of their skeletal faces peering out from their hoods and their skeletal hands poking out of the sleeves.

Silence fell on the crowd and then murmurs rippled among the reapers as they leaned into whisper to one another. Some even pointed at me.

"Yes, I have both the book of Fates and Death's scythe. So, your little rebellion to control Fate by making me Death has ended. I am both." I held both my hands in the air so they could see the tools in my hands. Then I tucked the Book of Fates into my bra, wishing it to become a charm again. When I pulled my hand free of the fabric, the book charm caught the lighthouse beacon, shimmering for a moment before I dropped my hand to my side.

"That can't be. You're alive."

"Yes. And apparently a person can't be made into Death until they're twenty-one or older, either. Yet reapers forced my father into the role early, just like you tried to force me into the role. You wanted the rules broken? Well, they are broken. Blown to Hell and all." I raved at the shrouded reapers, spreading my arms out wide for all of them to see. Life pulsed inside me, alongside the magic of both Death and Fate.

"I am very much alive, and I expect you all to kneel before me and pledge your allegiance to my reign." A part of me cringed at the words tumbling from my lips. Perhaps just having the power in my veins was corrupting, but I couldn't help it. I needed them to back off and the only way to do that was to lead by force, considering they were the ones who took the first shot at trying to kill my family.

None of them moved. I glanced at Levi. He licked his lips and then let his tongue loll out the side of his mouth in a dog grin that was unmistakable to the people closest to us. They knew his penchant for gobbling reapers and demons up in a feeding frenzy. A couple of the reapers in the front bent a knee, with their gaze glued on Levi.

This wasn't what I truly wanted. Not an allegiance based on fear. But then again, I didn't really want an allegiance with the ones who rebelled and caused all this crap to go down. The more I stewed on it, the angrier I got.

"You know what? I'm pretty pissed at the developments of late. You all—and I mean all, since there really were no clear sides in this little coup d'état that the rebels staged—you all need to learn who is boss."

"You are just a child. You can't possibly have taken on both roles." One reaper yelled from within the crowd, and the crowd reacted in agreement.

"You realize I have the power to turn you to dust right here and now, right?" I asked.

"Bull!"

Levi growled next to me as the crowd got a bit ornery and the current in the air darkened.

I needed to take control before I lost this crowd. That righteous power had roared to life the moment the reapers showed up, and I harnessed it. The dissent was growing around me, and I launched my power with the force of a steamroller over the entire legion. My target was anyone who had ill will toward me or my family.

I needed to know that those who were left to follow wouldn't stab me in the back just as easily as smiling at me. My wave of power sought the evil amid the neutral. Over half of the legion burst into dusty embers that floated on the air like spoiled confetti. One of the two kneeling in the front row became a casualty of this short-lived war. The others stared up at me with wide eyes.

I remained standing as the mass of deaths hit me. It wasn't like at the house when I took out the one who threatened Holly. This was pain, like those first ones around the table. But this time, it was the Death of the reapers I was encountering. I clenched my fists tight so I wouldn't reach out to Levi to keep me steady. Even through the pain, a part of me rejoiced in annihilating the bad seeds in the crowd. However, the old me cringed and admitted I had done exactly what Zane had said not to.

But I didn't wipe them all out, so I showed some restraint. The print on my arm glowed and more flowers seemed to bloom at the top of my tattoo. I didn't understand what that meant, but it couldn't be all that bad, especially because they were colorful blooms that glowed in the same way as the reaper print.

"The Fates of those of you who are left still remains to be seen." I wasn't dicking around. They stood by and witnessed the rebellion without stepping up to say how wrong it was. "You don't harbor feelings of retribution or thoughts of harming me or my family. That is why you remain in this realm instead of snapping out of existence like the dust bunnies hanging in the air." I waved at the ash still floating around us. "But my kindness won't last unless I see some type of allegiance."

Silence layered over the remaining crowd.

"If you make a choice to rebel instead of coming and having a civilized conversation with me, that will happen." I pointed at the ash in the air. "I take no joy in wiping them out of existence, but you must know, I am equipped and ready to take you all on if you continue to put my family in your devious cross hairs."

My father appeared at the far side of the field. "She is what she professes to be," he said, and they all turned. "And so much more. So please, bend a knee to your new boss and show some respect."

Standing in the darkness, his life-force was like a beacon in the sea of the dead. I imagined mine was, too, and when they turned back to me, their skeletal faces seemed to radiate awe. One by one, they bent down in respect until the remaining legion was all bowed before me.

Although my father didn't listen to my explicit instructions, his support was certainly welcomed.

"One down," I said to Levi, and he nodded. I reached out to pat him on the head and stopped short. "I'll have to take a rain check on that for when I figure out what to do with this soul-sucking thing."

For now, all was well in the land of the dead, but that wouldn't last too long with Heaven's displeasure now on the forefront of the battlefield.

"Dismissed," I said, and the sea of black robes disappeared.

Grim's Daughter
Chapter 20

I SAT IN THE front seat on the way back home, quietly contemplating what was next. My father reached over and squeezed my forearm. I think even as a soulless being; he knew how much I needed human contact. And I patted his hand in appreciation.

"You did well," he said.

"Thanks." But I didn't feel like I did well, and with so much more hanging over my head, I couldn't count this as a win. "I need to figure out how to undo this curse of mine before it drives me crazy." I looked down at my hands and sighed. "And I have a feeling that Papa's brother is just the first in a long line of Heaven's assassins coming to take me out."

"Levi can handle them." He glanced in the rearview mirror.

"With pleasure," he replied.

"Or you can just use that curse you have to strip them of their souls." My father grinned at me.

I shook my head. "That isn't an acceptable answer. It's as good as erasing them from existence."

"If it's your life or theirs, you may not have a choice. Just bask in your win from tonight. We can deal with the rest tomorrow."

"Agreed," Levi said from the backseat. "Enjoy your victory."

I glanced out the window and sighed. Tonight wasn't what I would call a total success. I still annihilated more than half of the legion of reapers, and the other half only bowed down to me after my father interceded. But they were right: I walked away without so much as a physical scratch. But their deaths would forever haunt my dreams.

The End

Continue reading on the next page with book five or THE DEATH CHRONICLES II, FINDING DEATH.

Finding Death
Chapter 1

I AM THE FIRST.

I'm the first offspring of Fate and Death that was conceived *after* they had taken the roles. In other words, they were not living, breathing beings when I was born. But the annihilation of the devil made so many weird things possible, including me.

I have no entry in the Book of Fates. Having no entry isn't normal. Every soul has an entry, a timeline that can be searched in the Book of Fates, but not me. In all of Earth's long and rich history, there has never been someone without an entry. To make matters more bizarre, I apparently can wipe out the entries of those I protect. So, now there are almost two dozen people running around like me with no written path.

The power to kill reapers has been solely Leviathan's gift. That, of course, does not include wielding either Heaven's blade or another ancient knife that was made just for that purpose. Those were the only things that could rid the world of a reaper. Until I unleashed my true potential. So, I am the first human to harness that little trick, and that was before I became a dual deity.

Which leads me to my current predicament. I now hold the role of both Fate and Death—while breathing, I might add, which is another historical event. Blood flows through my veins with every beat of my teenage heart.

I'm not the only one alive, either. It seems I've given my parents a moratorium on death, too. For the first time in decades, they have a steady heartbeat.

But all this mojo, all this ethereal juice, didn't come without a side effect, and what a doozy it is. I can't touch anyone. Well, except my father, but that's only because he touched me after my transformation into duel-deityship.

My touch isn't deadly per se. It's so much worse.

I absorb souls when my flesh connects with anything harboring a life-force.

So, although my dad is breathing again, he has no soul. Once his life is over, there will be no happily ever after for him and my mother in the land of the dead.

My only saving grace: Heaven does not know about my latest curse.

However, when they find out, I'm sure they'll send an army of assassins after me. Even now, just having a single being at the helm as both Death and Fate was enough to get Heaven's panties in a wad.

The trees pass as my father drives down the winding roads leading us home from Kittery. I glance at him for a moment as the silence surrounds us. His dark hair falls onto his forehead unchecked. The man doesn't look a day older than I am, and yet he had been Death for fifty some years. He gives me a smile and then looks back at the road, navigating us home. Well, to the only home that I've ever known, anyway.

My father seems pleased now that the first of my obstacles has been taken care of. Taking on the reapers wasn't all that challenging, in retrospect.

I guess having the power to annihilate reapers who harbor ill will toward me and my family helped, but it certainly made it anticlimactic. I mean, as soon as I wiped out half the reaper legion, the remaining horde of reapers bowed to show their alliance pretty damn quick.

Although stripping the reapers from existence didn't feel like my finest hour.

I huff at my internal dialog as my father pulls into the Ryans' driveway. The house is a pretty two-story colonial on a bluff overlooking the ocean. We can actually see Papa's house on Roaring Rock Road from our backyard.

"What?" my father asks from the driver's seat.

"She is just mourning those she killed," Levi, the German shepherd in the backseat, says.

He really isn't a dog but a monster in drag, protecting me from harm at the direction of my father. You see, Leviathan is seriously loyal to my dad because before my father even became Death, he set Leviathan free. I guess if I had been chained since the dawn of time and someone freed me, I'd be protecting them with everything I had, too. It's actually kind of sweet.

I look over the seat and roll my eyes at Levi. I'm not mourning the reapers I killed. Not really. Well, maybe. Damn, I hate he could read my deepest feelings.

The house looms before us, and I bite my lower lip. Before we left to deal with the reaper uprising, an emissary from Heaven had been sent to annihilate me. Thankfully, he has a mind of his own.

You see, Heaven sent Papa Ryan's dead brother back home to take care of the situation, but none of us truly knew what that meant. Luckily, Papa's brother didn't seem all that keen on carrying out their orders to destroy me. But that was before I took care of the reaper uprising.

Now that that particular roadblock has been taken care of, I don't know what will happen next.

"Are you coming?" My father had climbed out of the car while I was lost in my own mental

196

review of my situation. He opens the back door for Levi.

The front door to the house stands open and the person in the doorway erases all the random thoughts piling up in my head.

Zane Bradley stands at the front of the growing group. His bright-green eyes lock with mine and the relief that washes over his features is enough to get me moving. He's really stunning to look at, with his dark hair gently shifting in the ocean breeze and his muscular physique that supports his side gig as a home improvement guy, but I would never in my wildest dreams tell him that. Just seeing him brings a smile to my face. I guess having my lifetime crush still present after the insane weekend we've all had is enough to light the fire underneath me.

My best friend, and de facto sister, elbows her way through to stand next to Zane. Her red hair blows in the breeze and if I could freeze this moment, I would. My victory seems small compared to the love that radiates from the house, and I slowly climb out of the car.

As I round the grill and step into the rays of the garage spots, Holly's mouth drops open. But it's Zane's slow smile as he scans me from head to toe that makes my heart skip a beat.

You see, I never changed from the leather outfit I conjured for my face-off with the reapers. And it is kick ass, with a fitted bodice and flared skirt with a slit that is probably too high for a sixteen-year-old. I guess I composed it right because it certainly has the effect on Zane that I had been going for when I put it together in my mind.

He licks his lips and starts toward me. But then his smile fades, and he draws to a stop. The glaring truth extinguishes his momentary excitement. He cannot so much as brush his hand against me, never mind wrap his arms around me and kiss me like I want him to.

My momentary spike of anticipation falls to the ground as effectively as a mic drop. It crushes my insides, turning my mood darker, and dropping me on the edge of despair. I almost turn and run because although I feel their love in waves, being near these people is dangerous.

At this precise moment, my father, who is the only one here who can touch me, throws his arm over my shoulder as if he knows I'm a flight risk and smiles at the crowd at the door. "She had them shaking in their hoods," he says with a grin, breaking through whatever darkness grabbed hold of me.

I roll my eyes and shake his arm off my shoulders. His explanation doesn't paint me in the light I want, although it's totally accurate. I had them quaking and dropping to their knees, but it wasn't out of respect. It had been out of fear. I was serious, too—if they ganged up on me en masse again, I would annihilate the lot of them, despite the ramifications.

Zane cocks his eyebrow and I know what the question floating in his mind is. I shrug. I had gone a little GoT on the reapers. The disappointment that flashes in his eyes and rounds his shoulders turns my stomach sour.

I'll have to fill him in later. I have one more dangerous enemy to deal with and its emissary steps out of the house. His dark hair blows in the breeze and his piercing blue eyes echo all those related to him by angle blood. I jut my chin out, staring him down like we were going to be thrown into a cage to fight to the Death.

His lips twitch into a cocky grin, as if he would welcome a bloody fight. But then he gives me a nod, like I have done something that he respects instead of something worthy of destroying me. Holly's Papa had once said he was the wild one of the two of them. The one who didn't always walk on the right side of the law, but he had lived through hell after their father died. Despite whatever trials Tom Ryan had been put through, Papa said he definitely had the bigger heart.

I certainly hope so, and that somehow I've won him over. Otherwise, I am walking into an ambush I am ill prepared to defend.

Finding Death
Chapter 2

IN THE FAMILY ROOM, I pull a kitchen chair into the corner, away from any chance of knocking anyone. I don't need another soulless person around who had no eternal future. The guilt over my father is enough to carry; I can't imagine that burden multiplied.

My mother remains in her spot in the kitchen, her gaze jumping between my father and me like she didn't know whether she wanted to hear what happened. She brushes a stray blonde hair out of her face and puts down the dishcloth she had been using when I walked in.

Zane drags a chair next to mine and sits as close as he dares without touching me. It's oddly comforting because I can feel his essence. It leaves me warm enough to sigh, even though everyone else is acting odd, as if I am a stranger.

Holly sits on the floor so the adults in the room can either congregate on the couches or at the dinner table that ends where the family room begins. She leans against the edge of the couch and crosses her arms. "So, are you going to clue us in as to what happened?"

I glance at the rest of the people in the house. Alex and Faith, Holly's parents, lean on the kitchen island with coffee cups. Alex runs his hand through his dark hair as he waits for me to answer, and Faith just keeps twirling a strand of her fiery hair on her finger. It is one of her nervous habits and I wonder what exactly was said while my father and I were dealing with the reapers.

Holly's Papa takes a seat at the kitchen table, along with his brother. I can tell who is related to the angels just by glancing around the room. Every single one of them has piercing blue, iridescent eyes. It reminds me almost of neon blue, especially in the low lights, like now. I've never seen eyes like that outside the family.

Usually, being the center of attention with Holly isn't a problem, but tonight it gets under my skin like a bad case of poison ivy. I refrain from itching my skin in response. Papa's brother's stare makes me shift in my seat. He is the one Heaven sent to destroy me, but he doesn't seem all that eager to follow Heaven's orders.

Although I'm leery of him, he isn't the one who sets off alarms in my head as my gaze passes over him. It's Kylee and her husband Michael who make me want to wield my scythe in self-defense. Every sense of mine tingles just looking at them, and Michael won't so much as look at me. Even Kylee averts her gaze when I glance her way.

Something is gravely wrong here, and it takes me a moment to realize what is missing. I scan the room and then tilt my head, listening for a television somewhere in the house. Nothing. No electronics of any kind are on.

"Where are your kids?" I address Kylee.

She barely meets my gaze. "We sent them over to CJ's house with Smoke and Phoebe to put them to bed."

Zane's nod confirms her statement. And it sounds reasonable, given it's late enough, but that didn't stop the warning bells in my head. Twisting, turning doubt blooms in my belly.

"Why wouldn't you go with your kids?"

"We, uh, we wanted to be here for you when you returned." Kylee stumbles on her words.

I nod and glance at the ground, rummaging around through Fate's memories swarming in my head. Alarms are sounding like the house is engulfed in flames, but I can't read Kylee. She is acting completely squirrelly.

"What happened?" Holly asks again.

I shrug. "Unfortunately, they wouldn't listen, and now there's a lot of dust and ash floating around Fort McClary."

She grins and her eyes sparkle as if this were one of her freaky supernatural shows instead of real life. She's enjoying this, but then again, Holly has always been twisted, so this is right on point for her character. She's warped, and for a minute, the binds of our friendship seem solid. But then she asks, "So, you toasted all of them?"

"No. I only eliminated those who would harm you." I let that sink in. I don't want the people closest to me to think I am some kind of bloodthirsty fiend. "Any of you." I glance around the room to make sure they know that extends to everyone here and not just my immediate family. "And any reaper who had a violent reaction to me taking both roles. The rest were willing to kneel to show their loyalty." At least, I hope they were going to be loyal.

Michael fiddles with something under the table and Kylee stares at him with a crease in the space between her eyes. They seem lost in their own thoughts, and those thoughts don't seem all that kosher.

I glance at Alex and then over to Michael, silently relaying my blooming concern with my eye movement. He's never been able to read me, but Alex and Faith and Papa can get into most of the people's heads in this room with their psychic connection. The silent communication between Alex, Faith, and Papa begins. Papa's eyes narrow and he cocks his head as though he picked up a bad wavelength.

"What are you doing?" he asks Michael, pulling everyone's attention away from me.

Even Papa's brother now looks at Michael with curiosity.

"Nothing," Michael says, but he continues to stare at the table, avoiding eye contact with anyone.

"Heaven sent you to kill me?" I ask, reading his face with a certainty that left me cold, but Papa's expression is downright chilling.

Michael hisses and reaches up to his temple, bringing his hands into view from underneath the table. One hand goes to his temple and the other stops with a glistening crystal-blue knife.

Whatever headache Papa is creating eliminated Michael's surprise attack, but he keeps his grip tight on the handle despite whatever pain he's experiencing.

Both Faith and Alex gasp at the blade he holds.

"You brought Heaven's blade?" The growl in Papa's voice slams home.

Faith's gaze jumps to my father. From what I gathered from all of Faith's stories of her run-in with Lucifer, she left Heaven's blade with Death.

But it clearly is now in Michael's possession. Anything even nicked with that blade ceases to exist.

My chest tightens. Heaven got to him, too. How many others in my close circle were doing Heaven's bidding?

My father's gaze narrows, as do his lips, and his eyes shift to Kylee. The former siren who procured ancient weapons as a hobby. She has almost every known weapon in the universe locked up tight in her fortress in San Diego. Except this one. Heaven's blade is here.

The last time Heaven's blade had been out in the general human population was when my mother faced off against an escaped demon. It was used to turn that rebel into dust.

And now, from the look on Michael's face, he means to turn *me* to dust.

One minute, Michael winces in pain, and the next, he launches the blade at me. I stare at it as it circles, end over end. If I dodge right, I plow into Zane and strip him of his soul. To my left is a wall. I'm stuck and as helpless as I've ever felt.

I'm not the only one shocked in the room, but someone recovers their wits because the blade stops less than a foot from my chest. He aimed it at the biggest part of me. The one surefire way to at least nick me if I wasn't fast enough to get out of the way.

Except Michael forgot one very important fact. He's in a room with the most powerful supernaturals on Earth. If he didn't forget, then he was betting on the shock factor.

The fact it came so close was a testament to his surprise attack. I don't know who saved my ass. It could have been Papa or Alex or Faith, because all three of them can control matter.

The knife hangs in the air for a moment and then drops straight down as if it were batted out of the air. It clangs on the floor and all eyes shift back to the one who had the audacity to try to kill me.

Michael pales and his gaze shoots to the ones with the actual power in the room. The ones who could crush him with just a thought. Alex actually growls and steps toward Michael. I thought he looked angry on career day, but my God, he looks like steam is coming out of his ears.

Papa puts his hand on Alex's chest, stopping him from giving Michael a physical beatdown with his fists.

Levi jumps from his position next to my father, and he lands on the table crouching, his nose elongating enough to show his true head, with teeth bared that are strong enough to bite through titanium steel.

"Levi," I say in a stern voice. He snaps back into regular form, looking at me in a cross manner. "No." I may be mad at Michael, but I don't want him dead. Beaten and bruised, maybe, but not killed. He was only following orders from Heaven, and I am not sure he understands the total ramifications if that knife nicks me.

Movement diverts my attention away from the table. Papa's brother crosses and picks up the knife, causing everyone to freeze. I hold my breath. He's close enough to wield that weapon, and there'd be nothing anyone could do if he tried. He's already dead and risen by Heaven's grace, so killing him wouldn't work.

"So, this is the famed blade that annihilated Lucifer." He studies it, careful not to touch the business end of the knife, and then he turns to me. For a moment, I think he's going to finish what Michael had started, but then he hands the knife to me, hilt first.

I hesitate and meet Tom Ryan's humor-filled eyes. I reach out slowly, waiting for him to pull the knife back and brandish it, snuffing me out of existence. But he never flinches or looks away. I think it's his way of making peace with me. I now understand the kinship. I understand

I'm more a Ryan in their eyes than I am a Ramsay.

I take the blade and do the same type of inspection that he had, wishing for the proper sheath to put this baby somewhere safe. A scabbard made of leather and steel appears at my waist. I stare at the conjured sheath and then carefully slide the knife into the case. It fits like it is made for the blade. This little trick of conjuring what I wish comes in handier than I thought.

Zane's eyes are locked on the blade at my waist, as if he is still trying to come to terms with this entire ordeal. I think Michael looks pale, but Zane looks a breath away from passing out. I want to reach out and squeeze his arm to reassure him, but I can't. Not with this godforsaken curse.

Touching him puts him in mortal danger. So, I ignore him for now and focus back on Michael. Anger fresh enough to make my hands shake accosts me, and I cross my arms. "Why?" I demand.

"You are an abomination. Borne of Lucifer's magic," he says, as if reciting what Heaven pounded in his head.

"Last I knew, Fate and Death were my parents, not Lucifer," I snap. I am done with this little show of morality. Especially from a vampire's son.

"How could you?" Faith snarls, her voice shaking. Faith's anger displays in sparks lighting from her fingertips. Hell, sparks are coming out of the ends of her hair, turning from the orange-yellow flame into a white light that I have never seen before. And I've seen Holly's mom angry before. This seems to be more like fury, almost to the point there is no reasoning with her at all.

"After coming into my home for so many years and breaking bread with us? How could you try to kill her?" Faith's voice even booms, rattling the dishes on the counters and the table. She clenches her fists as if she's afraid whatever manifestation inside her would be released into the entire room.

Nana puts her hand on Faith's shoulder, and although I can see the disappointment in Nana's eyes as she looks in Michael's direction, she has the desired calming effect Faith needs. The dishes stop rattling.

"It's a better alternative than true Armageddon. If the angels come..." Michael shakes his head. "We'll all die."

"You really think I'd let them harm you?" I shout, standing up to make my point very clear. "You really think I'm capable of that?" I want to reach across the table and shake him like a rag doll, and I take a step closer before I realize if I touch him, he'll be soulless. At least right now he looks a little remorseful; without a soul and with Heaven's directive, he'd stop at nothing to destroy me.

He leans back in the seat with wide eyes at my outburst. I usually take things pretty calmly with everything except where my parents are concerned, so me yelling is a big deal. The thing that sucks is no one can lay their hand on me to rein in my anger like Nana had with Faith.

A hand drops on my arm.

Well, my dad still can, but it did nothing to quench the burn in my veins. I stare at him.

"Cool your jets. I'll pound his fucking head in," he says with such malice that I think everyone blinks. I certainly do. He moves faster than anyone expects. Before I know it, he has a handful of Michael's shirt and his right fist smashes square into Michael's face.

Blood spurts from his nose and mouth, and Michael falls back in his seat, stunned.

"That is my daughter you just tried to kill."

"Dad, step away," I pull him back before he launches another punch. "An ultimatum from Heaven can't be easy to ignore."

Papa's brother scoffs. "Angels are dicks. I'll fight them with you." He gives me a cocky grin.

"You aren't equipped to fight against Heaven anymore." Faith steps closer to me. "But we are, so let them come." She glares at Michael. "So, you just run back to that goddamned portal and tell them they just screwed with the wrong family." She glances at Tom. "Or better yet, why don't you take me to Paradise Cove. I opened that portal. I can close it, too." She flips her hair over her right shoulder with an arrogance I had never seen in her.

Michael's eyes widen as he continued to cup his nose and mouth. Blood drips from his hands, enough for me to glance at my father. He has a mean punch for a mere mortal.

Papa glances at Faith with something akin to horror on his face. I know how much everyone in this room relies on the only portal to Heaven in the known universe to see their relatives. Even Faith goes from time to time to talk to her own mother, so the magnitude of her threat shakes everyone in the room to the core.

"What do you mean, everyone will die?" Zane asks from the chair where he still sat. He is blinking fast, as if his brain can't digest the past few minutes. He looks at Michael and then at me as if he just awoke from a nightmare, only to find it's real.

"They told him he needed to take care of this now before the world went straight to Hell. This is an imbalance that can't be. Earth will collapse under the weight of it. Literally. So, if we don't do this, they will come down and do it and that will cause another big bang event."

"And what would have happened if you had cut me with Heaven's blade? What happens if there is no Fate or Death?" I ask, curious whether anyone knows the answer. My parents both pale. They held the knowledge crammed in my head. I cross my arms and wait. When no one answer, I add, "If Heaven kills me while I hold both positions, what happens?" I tap my foot, glancing at everyone in the room except for my parents.

"Everyone dies," Michael says slowly from behind his hands. His voice has a nasally quality as if he'd developed a terrible cold.

"Yup. And what happens if someone here kills me while I hold both positions?"

Michael starts to shrug and then his hands drop to the table, leaving bloody handprints on the wood. His eyes widen. Heaven's duplicity finally shines through. He understands, and from the faces surrounding me, everyone is already there; we just had to get both Michael and Kylee there, too.

"It makes no difference who kills me right now, does it?" I cock an eyebrow, spelling it out for him in simple words.

He slowly shakes his head as the reality of the situation sinks in. I am still a time bomb waiting to wipe out all of humanity. He glances at Papa's brother as if he would have some reasonable answer that would make sense.

"I told you. Angels are dicks." He shrugs. "They would be just as happy with or without humanity in the picture."

"They sanction mass murder?" Kylee gasps.

I slowly sit down. The reality of the situation claws at my insides. Heaven is not only ready to sacrifice me, but all of humanity.

Finding Death
Chapter 3

FAITH STILL LOOKS READY to kick some Heavenly ass, or at least close the only portal that gives angels access to this realm. Her fire hasn't faded since we all gave it a rest for the night. And today hasn't been any different.

We had been at this all day—arguing over who should do what—and the longer Heaven's portal is open, the more chances of being attacked come into play. Although with Alex and Papa setting their protective barriers around the houses, the angels had about as much of a prayer of entering as the demons of old.

The sun went down about an hour ago and my stomach rumbles. I am sick and tired of this conversation. I'm not one to sit around. I'm more of an action girl and all this inaction is driving me batty.

"Why don't you just give us the book and the scythe again?" my father asks after hours of discussing options. None of which are appetizing to anyone.

I glance at Levi and receive a cock of his eyebrow in response. Before I can second-guess myself, I hand my father the scythe, intending to let him take over again. Cringing, I wait for the transfer, but nothing happens. No swirl of wind, no ethereal light. Nothing. It's as if the scythe rejects him.

He looks down at himself and then back at me. "I don't feel any different."

"That's because nothing happened." I yank the scythe back before he can swing it around and hurt someone.

He glances at his empty hand and then at me as if I imparted some magic instead of ripping the ultimate instrument of death from his grip. He cocks his head. "Why didn't it work?"

I have one guess, but I keep my mouth shut. He is an empty vessel. Soulless. And I think the scythe knows it. The alternative is too weird to entertain, but it creeps into my head anyway. Perhaps the scythe, like the reapers, wants me in this position. Instead of answering him, I busy myself with shrinking the weapon into a charm again. I will not attempt to give my mother the Book of Fates and tempt the darkness weighing on me. Not when my gut tells me she will die, and I will be stuck forever with my mother telling me what to do. That is not a plan I can get behind at all.

Besides, knowing the person who takes over for either job will die makes this a categorical no for me to transfer the position to anyone else but my parents. And because the powers that be rejected my father, that was the end of the conversation.

"Seems like you're a little impotent there, kid." Smoke's New York accent is filled with mirth. He leans on the kitchen counter, picking at the leftovers. Smoke grins, enjoying my father's suffering just a little too much.

I would understand it more if he was yanking my mother's chain, considering Fate had kept him in cat form for millenniums. But that had been the entity before my mother. My mom actually found a loophole in Smoke's contract that allowed him to come back in this suave form. I wonder whether he can still shift into the fearless form he had before Fate cursed him into a housecat.

"Fuck you." My father glares at him, but my mother's hand on his shoulder shut up whatever else was poised to slip out of his mouth.

Phoebe smacks Smoke on the arm. "Leave the boy alone." Phoebe and Smoke had come back with the kids during our earlier spirited debate, and neither of them had contributed much to the conversation at all until now.

"Give me the scythe." Zane holds his hand out.

If I could have batted it away without harming him, I would have. Instead, I just level the type of glare that had him pulling away without another word. Having him take over for Death isn't an option, especially considering that means he stops breathing.

"You idiot." Holly smacks his hand away as if she read my mind. "If anyone is going to step into this with her, it's going to be me," she says, and my gratefulness disappears.

Just as I'm ready to launch into a tirade, Alex does it for me.

"No way!" He yanks Holly back as if I am daft enough to hand her the scythe. "This isn't some fantasy game we are playing. This is Death. Death!"

"Yeah, and what better way to spend the rest of my life? With my best friend." She turns to me. "Think of the trouble we could get into!"

She grins in a way that makes me nervous and sad at the same time. I want her to go to college. To get married and have kids. I want to see her grow old with a husband who loves her more than I do. I cannot strike that down. Just like I can't let Zane do the same. Even though the relationship with him is much more complicated, it would still end messy.

"I'm not sure we would still be friends after a couple thousand years with only the two of us and Levi to keep us entertained."

Her shoulders drop and she seems to deflate before me.

"Look, while I appreciate the sentiments from both you and Zane, no one is taking over either role. If it had worked with my dad, I would have gladly given my mother the book of Fates. But it didn't, so I'll continue to hold these roles until all of Heaven is convinced I am not a menace."

"They'll keep sending more." Michael's voice is still nasally, and both eyes blackened like a raccoon from my father's earlier punch. He at least had gone into the bathroom to clean up before his kids arrived with Smoke and Phoebe. "But I doubt those they send next will be able to be reasoned with."

I roll my eyes. "Who are they going to send that these guys haven't already beaten?" I point to Papa, Papa's brother, Alex, and Faith. "They took on the devil and won. They hold the grace of all the archangels inside them, so who can they send? Who can beat them?"

Heat drains from my cheeks. There is only one being stronger than the collective power in this room. God himself. If they send the supreme being who made all of Heaven and Earth, we are screwed.

"God hasn't been around since they crucified his son," Levi says from the floor. "But that might be the only being that could snuff us all out."

My hand falls to the knife at my side and the thought that blooms in the back of my mind is unthinkable. I move my hand away and cross to the sliding glass doors. I am not about to voice my thoughts. Even having them at all is blasphemy.

"We need to close that portal," Faith says, but at least this time it is with a more reasoned tone. "That will stop them from sending more..." She waves toward Michael. "More gullible idiots."

"I agree with Faith," my mother says, and I turn toward her. She hasn't said much through all of this. Not since my father agreed to take the roles back, and the transfer didn't happen. "We can at least mitigate the number of people gunning for her."

"If we close the portal, does that prevent them from launching this war?" Papa asks. The worry lines around his mouth and on his forehead express his unease.

I totally understand his hesitation. That portal is the only place the family can see their loved ones who have passed on. If that was the only way I could see my parents, I'd be hesitant, too. I don't think he is prepared to say final goodbyes to all who he has lost in his life. He glances at his brother.

Tom shrugs.

"They'd have to go through Purgatory." My father glances at Levi. "And no one is guarding the gates there anymore. After she wiped out half the federation in Kittery, I doubt the reapers would put up much of a fuss if the angels went through that way, either."

That was my fault. I close my eyes and lean my forehead against the cool glass, berating myself silently. I didn't exactly instill loyalty with the reapers last night. Fear, yes, but true alliances? Not a chance—and that's really what I need. "Can we do this in the morning? I'm not up for a midnight drive across New Hampshire."

"You aren't going," Alex says.

My eyebrows rise in the reflection, and I turn away from the glass door. "If closing that portal puts Faith in danger, you bet your ass I'll be there."

He scoffs at me. "You aren't equipped to handle that kind of attack. We are."

"I can toast reapers. You don't think I can conjure up some powers to take on angels?"

My father snorts a laugh.

I give him the side eye, but that doesn't stop his continuing chuckle. Although his laughing at me is aggravating, he is right. I am not sure my personal karate training from Alex and Papa was enough, especially because I haven't trained in a while. I know my way around a multiple attack scenario, but even if I wanted to get a few sparring sessions in before we leave, I can't train hand-to-hand.

"If you are going on this crazy mission, so am I." I cross my arms. "I'm not letting anyone get hurt because I acted on impulse." Taking the scythe from my father had been on impulse, especially considering I somehow made it so my mother was living. I hadn't wanted them separated. That bleeding-heart part of me is exactly what made me grab it from his hand and caused this lousy touch side effect.

"You can't step on that hallowed ground," my father says after he winds down. "You are Death. You can never cross over into Heaven's territory. Just like you will never cross into Hell's territory either. Your domain is the between."

I blow a raspberry at him. "Everything about me challenges the status quo. You really believe I can't step into their domain? Especially when they've decided to invade mine?"

He wipes his face and looks at my mother for help.

"Honestly, she has a point," my mother says.

"Well, if you're going, so am I," Zane says.

"No," everyone in the room says at the same time, including me. I don't want him anywhere near the angels. That's like handing them the ultimate leverage.

Zane leans back in the chair and scans every face in the room before his gaze lands on me. And damn, he's got a stubborn jaw. "I'm going."

"For Christ's sake!" Faith throws her hands in the air and walks out of the room.

No one moves. Then a car engine starts up.

"Damn it," Alex snarls and stalks out after her.

"I guess we are all going to the lake house," Papa says with a shake of his head. He glances at the food strewn about the kitchen and closes his eyes. A small vein on his forehead bulges, and then a drawer opens and the press-and-seal wrap comes out as if carried by the invisible man. Each item is wrapped with speed and precision, and then everything floats in the air toward an open refrigerator. When everything is placed on the shelves, the door closes.

Papa doesn't even break a sweat at the effort. Sometimes I wish for that kind of juice. But my own powers aren't anything to scoff at. Although I would not want to be pitted against Papa.

"That just about does it." He glances at Michael and Kylee. "If you two want to stay here and put your kids down, I'm sure Alex and Faith won't mind."

"I think I'd like to say one last goodbye to my folks before Faith wipes out the portal," Michael says.

I glance at Papa's brother. "Are you going with us?"

He nods slowly. "My wife and daughter are up there, and as much as I'd like to join your war against the angels, I don't wish to be separated from them for what is likely to be the rest of eternity." He glances at Papa. "I kind of screwed the pooch on this one, so I'm not sure they'll allow me back, but I have to try."

"And if I could pull them out?" I ask. After all, I pulled my mother and father's life-force from wherever it had gone, reanimating them after fifty some years of not being alive.

"You can't," my mother says, as if my suggestion is too terrible to even consider. As if it is more horrifying than Heaven's intentions of taking me out and all the fallout that will come from that debacle.

"Why can't I?" I cross my arms. "What if I could bring them all back?" I wonder whether I really have that sort of power. It would be interesting to find out. I even had the list of names in the back of my mind.

"Because it would cause a major imbalance in the universe."

"So? There already is an imbalance, according to Heaven."

"It's not the way to win brownie points with them. Stealing souls from their care is frowned upon. Just like screwing with Fates."

At this moment, I don't give a damn about winning them over. Heaven burned that bridge when they sent Michael and Kylee to kill me. Closing the portal will hurt those I care about. I can see it in their eyes. If Heaven can reanimate Papa's brother, why can't I do the same with the people my family cares about?

"We can talk on the way." My father grabs one of the key sets on the wall next to the garage entrance. "Missy gets the passenger seat. Zane, Levi, and Julia, you get the back. The rest of you need to move your cars out of the way. I'm taking whatever these keys go to." He jangles a set of keys.

"I'm going with you." Holly follows as my mother starts toward the door with Levi. Zane joins our mini entourage.

I weave through the remaining guests until I am clear of the family room congestion. "We'll see you up there." I don't wait for anyone's response. Closing the door, I press the garage opener and by the time I climb around to the passenger side, the door was up, and the cool night wraps an unspeakable dread around my heart.

Finding Death
Chapter 4

"DO YOU EVEN KNOW where you're going?" Holly asks from the backseat.

We arrived in Brooksfield, New Hampshire twenty minutes ago and all my father has done is drive in circles, muttering under his breath. He sends a glare into the rearview mirror.

"Do you?" he barks at Holly.

"Yes." Holly doesn't bother explaining where we need to go. She just crosses her arms and cocks her head at my father.

"You want to drive?" he snaps and pulls the car to the side of the road. Without another word, he throws the shift into park and steps out of the car. He opens the door behind him and waits for Holly to get out.

She looks at him with wide eyes.

"You're old enough to drive, so get us where we need to go before your mother fucks everything up."

Wow, dude, chill. I don't think I've ever seen my father this annoyed.

Holly climbs out of the backseat. "Are you sure?"

He sighs and stares her down in a way that would move my butt just as fast.

"Fine." She slips into the driver's seat and before my father can close the backseat door, she shifts into drive. With no one on the road in front of us, she does a U-turn, turning back the way we came.

"Do you know where we are going?" I never paid attention to the roads and turnoffs to get to the lake house. My nose was either in a book or taking in the scenery, so when she nods and takes a left turn into an overgrown driveway, I am impressed.

She glances at me as she slows to a crawl, maneuvering the road like an old woman. But in her defense, the driveway is narrow, and she is an inexperienced driver.

I want her to go faster. I want to get there because my nerves are dancing like I'm sitting on a bomb made of liquid nitrogen and dry ice. The explosion is imminent. When we round the corner, Holly slams on the brakes. The driveway is already full. Our wandering aimlessly left us last to arrive instead of right after Faith and Alex got there.

I don't wait for her to throw the car in park. I am out of the passenger side of the car, running toward the light show strobing through the trees. I stop halfway across the lawn as a body is thrown clear of the woods by what I assume is some righteous agent of Heaven in Paradise Cove.

The motion sensors on the house trigger and the back lawn lights up like it's midday. It takes my eyes a moment to adjust. Tom Ryan slowly sits up, his face forming a mask of anger and disgust. The names of the dead related to our family flit through my mind. I don't have much time. I kneel and place my hands on the ground. I believe I am close enough to the gate to affect the dead, so I call the souls forth.

I am not sure where to start until my eyes land back on Tom. I need to start with the one who defied Heaven's orders, because he is right—Heaven will never let him back in. I recite their first names aloud, including his. Wishing life into forms that come forth in my mind's eye.

"Tom, Ty, Jessica, Steve, Jennifer, Raven, Hannah, Damian, Naomi, Gabriel."

Light brighter than the spots settles over Tom, sparkling the way Nana's healing magic does when she uses it, making me pause before I complete the list in my mind.

I doubt Tom notices. Not when his mother and father step out of the woods. His father, Alex's namesake, is a spitting image of Alex, with those piercing blue eyes and dark hair and the kind of looks that make most women swoon. But he wasn't a saint when he was alive. From what I understand, Ty Ryan was quite the opposite, enough so that I don't know how he ended up in Heaven. Maybe it had to do with having angel blood. Tom's mother, Jessica Ryan, is pretty in a way that is just as striking as Ty Ryan. But it is her eyes that draw me in. Calico eyes like Nana's, but in tones that seemed to settle into a soft brush of color surrounded by that angel-blood blue.

Next comes Tom's guardians: Steve and Jennifer Williams, the original owners of the land I stand on. Although they really never understood their property housed the only portal to Heaven. He had been an FBI agent before he and his actress wife settled in New York City. Both of them look as lost as Alex's grandparents.

Tom's jaw drops open and his eyes bulge when the red-haired mother and daughter step from the woods. Raven and Hannah, Tom's wife and daughter, don't seem as bewildered as everyone else, and their faces split into broad grins at the sight of Tom sitting on the lawn.

I hear a gasp from behind me and glance over my shoulder as Michael rounds the corner, with Kylee following close behind. Michael's parents and brother had already stepped onto the grass at the edge of the woods.

One by one, they glance around as if they had just woken from a long, drawn-out nightmare.

"Stop," my father orders from behind me. "You can't raise the dead," he hisses, and I glare back at him.

"That is precisely what I'm doing." There are more souls I want to call from Heaven, but before I can utter Faith's mother's name or my grandparents' names, a blinding white light fills the woods, making shadows run.

Screaming filters out of the woods, and curses that would make a pissed-off sailor proud carry on the wind. Papa stumbles out of the forest, followed by Alex, who is dragging a ballistically furious Faith with him. She never curses, but the foul words still spitting from her lips make everyone stare at her with open-mouth shock.

I wonder just what transpired in the portal. What words could Heaven have delivered to set the normally calm woman into this holy terror, complete with sparks shooting from her fingertips?

Papa draws short at the sight of the growing crowd and Alex bumps into him. It's almost like watching a comedy show, except everyone is too shocked to laugh. Silence descends on the clearing as the view of the crowd quiets Faith. Papa blinks as if his brain can't comprehend what he is seeing and then he turns toward where I still crouch.

I'm pleased by the arch of his eyebrow and the hint of a smile that captures his lips, like he can't quite believe what I've done. I shrug and offer a smile of sorts in his direction. Heaven may have initially given Papa his brother back, but I made it permanent, like I had with my parents. I yanked these souls from Heaven's grip and willed their bodies back into existence. None of which took any effort. I didn't even break a sweat.

They are here, living and breathing and just as fragile as the rest of us, but they don't have whatever powers they had when they were here. They had already passed those on and there was no time to recreate that. They are no longer gods among men. That is reserved for Papa, Nana, Alex, Faith, and Holly only. And from the awe widening Papa's eyes, apparently, I fall into that category, too.

No one moves at first, and then pandemonium breaks out in the form of hugs and even tears as they realize they've been given some strange gift. A chance to pick up where they had left off.

"What have you done?" My mother gasps. She goes to grab me, but my father intercepts her hand.

He shakes his head, his eyes warning her against touching me. "There's no sense in you losing your soul, too," he says to her.

I climb to my feet, satisfied with what I have accomplished. "If Heaven is going to send assassins to kill me, I need an army of loyal people to stand with me. And we both know the reapers will not fight at my side." I meet my father's gaze.

"You could have persuaded them," he says. "Instead, you brought these people back, only to face Death at the hands of the angels?"

I blink as his words scrape over my skin like an unwanted rash. I glance out at the people hugging and crying and expressing such joy that it fills my heart with dread. I signed every one of them up for doom unless I can figure out how to take on the angels without anyone being harmed. Maybe I need the reapers after all.

"How do I persuade them?" I ask as the crowd moves in our direction.

"I don't know. But this will have huge ramifications. You're supposed to reap the souls and escort them to their final destination, not revive them." He runs his hands through his hair and glances at my mother. For someone without a soul, he looks more worried than his current state allows.

I don't want to address his comments, not with everyone coming toward me like I am their savior. Tom puts his hand on his chest and his eyes widen. He stops short and a couple of the resurrectees bump into him.

"My heart," he says with his eyes glued to me. "What kind of necromancy shit is this?"

"It's not black magic," Raven, his wife, takes hold of his arm. "It's pure." She sniffs the air as though there is something sweet and decadent cooking.

He glances at her as if she has two heads.

"Can't you taste it? It's like a bowl of strawberries and whipped cream. Sweet and wholesome. Dark magic does not taste like this."

I stare at the redhead next to Tom and a plethora of information bubbles to the surface. She knows her way around practical magic, the kind I might need to lift this damn touch curse. But we have bigger worries, like what ramifications this little event will cause. I do not know, but my father is right. There will be hell to pay for my actions.

Papa's father, the feared Ty Ryan, steps forward and sticks his hand out toward me like he expects a handshake.

I jump back, colliding with my father.

"Don't touch her unless you want to become soulless like me," my dad says from behind me. "While she can make you come back to life, she can also ruin any chances of anything more than the here and now with her touch."

"Thanks, Dad," I mutter under my breath. I press my hands together and give a slight bow in salutation instead of accepting his handshake. "My father is right. He's the only one who can touch me at the moment, and I certainly hope that doesn't change."

"Who are you?" Ty asks. His question is framed in reverence.

"She's my daughter," my father says, pride oozing over every word.

Papa's father looks him over, his eyes narrowing. "And you are?"

I forget, most of these people never knew Death and Fate existed before they passed and went to Heaven. Tom knew because he had personal experience with my parents when the Ryans met Kylee, but the rest of them had already died by that point.

"I used to be Death and my wife here used to be Fate. But now our daughter has taken on both those roles and given us the ability to breathe again after fifty-four years." He shrugs like this all makes perfect sense and this is just another normal day.

Eyes move back to me.

"And Heaven is pissed at her." Faith speaks for the first time since Alex carried her out of the woods. Her voice is hoarse and bitter. "They want her dead, except killing her wipes out the world, and Heaven does not give a shit if this world dies." Faith spits on the ground as if she had just tasted something vile. "So, I closed their damn portal to Earth."

"You what?" Papa's father glances at his wife and then back at Faith.

"I used angel fire to destroy the only portal Heaven has." She points toward the cove. "It will take them forever to drill through to this realm." She crosses her arms as if she has just conquered Heaven herself. "And I'm fine with that."

"Mmm." My father cocks his head. "You forgot one little hiccup."

Faith glances at him and cocks her head.

"Purgatory and the reaper realm."

Her stubborn expression falls, turning the edges of her lips down.

None of the reapers will put up a fight to stop my demise. I need to figure out a way to get them on my side before Heaven compromises that entry to Earth.

With this crew and the reapers on our side, we'd be unstoppable.

Finding Death
Chapter 5

THE LAKE HOUSE IS a tad tighter than Alex's house. We really should have gone back to Papa's place in York, where there is plenty of room for the crowd. Every time I move, I'm afraid I might brush someone by mistake and eviscerate their soul. It is far from a pleasant feeling.

I've shoved myself in the farthest corner and my father took it upon himself to take one side and Zane sits on the other side of me. At least Zane is far enough away that if he talks with his hands, he will not brush into me. I can't say the same for my father. It's as if he doesn't recognize personal space at all.

I'm antsy to get back to Maine, to where I know my surroundings and have ample room to work with. If we had stayed outside, I don't think the anxiety pulsing through me would have been quite as bad as it is right now.

One thing is for sure, these people can talk a subject to Death. We've all introduced ourselves, but I think the newly living are still having a hard time connecting all the dots.

"So, you are Lucifer's daughter?" Damian asks in a tone filled with disdain as he stares at Faith. He grips the arms of the chair so hard his knuckles turn white. It's the same type of reaction that Faith said Tom had at one time before he got to know her. He obviously changed his mind about her because he died so she could live.

Naomi, Damian's wife, reaches out and covers his hand. "She is the one who used Heaven's blade on him."

"While he possessed my daughter," Damian nearly growls.

Faith made me possible when she killed Lucifer. Her actions seventeen years ago changed the course of many lives. And saved the world from Armageddon. Unfortunately, we are back at another Earth-ending point. You'd think the Ryans would have this planet-saving down by now, but they are stumbling through it right alongside me.

"Yes," Faith answers, and there isn't an ounce of apology in her tone. The tension in the room thickens.

"Dad," Gabriel interrupts, trying to be the one to smooth over the friction before it blows up on all of us. "Faith did the right thing then, and she did the right thing now by closing that portal." He looks at his brother, Michael. "I still can't believe they'd sacrifice the world because some sweet teenager holds the role of both Death and Fate. And they didn't tell you this before they sent you to kill her?"

The fact he refers to me as sweet is humbling. I'm not sweet. I just did what I thought was necessary to win this war, and I didn't want Tom separated from his family after he defied Heaven's orders for a complete stranger.

Michael slowly shakes his head.

"So, let me get this straight. Heaven is just as fucked up as Hell?" Smoke asks. He's leaning against the wall, with Phoebe lounging against his chest. He glances at my mother as if she should know all this.

"I wouldn't know. I just had the reapers escort people to their assigned destination." She picks at her thumbnail. "I went by what the book told me."

I glance at the miniature book hanging from my charm bracelet and then back at her. Fates of men are already predestined, but their final destination isn't scripted. It's based on how they live their lives, but now I wonder by whose measure it is based.

"We got the files on those coming through Hell. They all deserved to be on my table." Phoebe crosses her arms.

Damian swings his darkening gaze to her. "Who are you?"

I've had enough of the posturing and climb to my feet. "Everyone in this room is family. So please leave the attitude outside." I glance around the room at the angel descendants I called from Heaven. Bright-blue eyes stare back at me. Every single pair holds almost an iridescent glow. They all carry an aura I can almost see, unlike those not born of angel blood. Steve, Jennifer, and Raven don't have those features, although Steve's eyes are an enviable blue. Smoke and Phoebe don't carry that same angel quality, either.

My father has the blue eyes that rival the angel kin. But he was born into an ethereal bloodline himself. My eyes weren't. My original color falls into the golden category, but now they seemed to have changed to a weird lavender. I really envy the neon blue of those with ethereal blood.

Papa's father chuckles. "Damian's not used to having others as old as he is in the room." He gives a head nod to Phoebe and Smoke.

"Aww, he's just a young'un." Smoke smiles. His New York accent drawls through the words like a car wreck.

"Actually, we are older than he is," Kylee says from next to Michael.

Damian turns and stares at her before his gaze moves to his son.

Michael shrugs. "She kind of fell right into my lap." He grins and drapes his arm around Kylee's shoulders. "But you knew that already."

"All this is well and good, but we really need to figure out what Heaven's next move is. Otherwise, we are going to be blindsided. And that never turns out well." Alex stands from the dinner table. He turns his back on all of us and stares out the window.

"We need the reapers," Levi says from his position on the floor.

Everyone who I called from Heaven turns ashen when the German shepherd speaks.

"Since when are there talking dogs?" Steve says.

Levi chuckles. So do Alex, Faith, Kylee, my mother, and my father. I crack a smile and meet Zane's gaze.

"Well, sir." Zane speaks first. "He's not really a dog."

"Yeah, he really wouldn't fit in the house if he was in his natural state," Faith says.

"What is he?"

"Leviathan," my mother says. "The guardian of the gates."

"Like, as in the fabled Leviathan?" Steve says, his eyebrows arched.

"Yes," Levi says. "And I'm bound to protect Missy," he adds. "So, anyone in this room thinking about harming her," he looks pointedly at Michael, "I will eat you." As if to make his point crystal-clear, he lets his head transform into his natural form, and then he snaps his sharp teeth with a ferocious growl before shrinking back into a dog.

Steve shifts back in the chair with wide eyes. "And I thought vampires were a stretch," he mumbles loud enough to make most of us smile.

"There are far more things out there than you silly humans can truly comprehend," Levi says with an eye roll.

Smoke snorts and glances out the window. A crease between his eyes appears, and I follow his gaze.

Alex steps backward as a sea of black accented by the spotlight stands out against the green grass. It looks like the entire reaper federation has shown up on the lawn, unbidden. I get to my feet and, without a word, head outside to deal with this mess. Before the door closes behind me, Levi shoots out and trots next to me like a sentry Hell-bent on protecting his charge.

By the time we round the corner, Levi has stripped himself of his dog persona and towers over all of us. It is a less than subtle warning. With one sweep of his tail, he could destroy the reapers and the house behind us. I ignore the gasps from inside as we step into view. I imagine those newly living are reeling at seeing the full effect of my trusty sidekick, or at least what they can see of him considering he towers over the trees. It's like looking out and seeing the hindquarters of a dinosaur in the window.

I keep my hands free, although I itch for my scythe. Pulling that into my hands would be seen as a sign of aggression, and I do not want to project that the way Leviathan is. I stop and turn, facing the skeletons as they look up at me with what I assume is malice. But without bodies, I can't tell, and I rely on body language to give me proper warning. I press my lips together, wishing they all had their original forms so I could truly tell their intentions.

Light fans out from me, touching every reaper. The scene reminds me of the lightning that shoots out from the ark in that old Indiana Jones movie. Except the reapers don't turn to dust at the touch of my light.

Instead, they grow human forms under their black capes. I step back, just as surprised as the reaper federation in front of me, as the light dims and faces of all shapes and colors stare up at me. Some with awe, some with confusion. Some just stare at their flesh-colored hands as though I have given them an unspeakable gift.

My father steps out from around the corner and halts as he scans the crowd.

"What is she?" one reaper in the front row asks, glancing at my father.

My dad is at a loss for words. He just stares at the reapers with human skin, his eyes blinking rapidly and his mouth forming a little O of shock. When he turns to me, he asks, "Did you just bring them all back to life?"

I don't know. All I wanted was to see their faces, and here they are. I shrug. "I don't think they are alive." I turn to the dark-haired woman who asked what I am. "Are you?"

With wide eyes, she puts her hand on her chest.

My heartbeat thunders in my ears as I wait for her to answer. If I truly breathed life into them, I was screwed. There would be no one to escort the dead.

She moves her hand again. And again, and then shakes her head. "No heartbeat." She glances at the reaper next to her and puts her palm on his chest. "None there, either."

The tension between my shoulders relaxes. I hadn't screwed up after all. "What's your name?"

"Amanda," she says. "But my friends call me Mandy." She sticks out her hand for a handshake.

I'm regretting our customs. Why couldn't I have been born in a place that bows as a salutation instead of shaking hands? I stare at her offered hand, wondering whether it's an invitation to call her Mandy or not.

"I am not trying to be rude, but this"—I wave at my form—"came with a nasty side effect and I'd rather not do any harm to your soul." I know better than most that reapers are souls who had agreed to forgo their final destination to serve Fate.

Mandy lowers her hand slowly. She swallows and glances over her shoulder. "Heaven sent us." She looks back at me and then down at her human hands.

Levi growls, and I put my hand out to calm him. I don't need to touch him to silence him; my motion is enough to quell any thought of an attack.

"If you try to harm her, I will destroy every single one of you," Levi growls.

"I think they get that." I look up at him as a few nervous laughs break out in the crowd. I glance back at the sea of faces and although I don't see any malice visible, I have to ask. "What are your intentions?" I aim my question at Mandy while suppressing the urge to send out my sweeping guide to snuff out the infiltrators.

"Heaven wants you destroyed." Mandy shifts as she studies her flesh-covered bones as if she has never seen skin before.

"And you came to do that?"

She continues to stare at her hands. Her mouth opens and closes a few times before she looks up at me with pleading eyes.

"You realize killing her takes out the entire world, right?" my father snaps.

Eyes widen and Mandy's gaze shoots from her hands to my face. She blinks as my father's words sink in.

Murmurs build to a crescendo all around us.

I laugh under my breath. Heaven seems to have left that little nugget out of the equation. And it matters to the reapers. It matters a great deal. When the world ends, they automatically move onto their final destination. Although some are headed for the pearly gates, especially those who were relatives of Death's, many chose to be reapers because the alternative was not Heaven.

Reapers, as a whole, aren't saints.

"I don't know if any of you were around when Death and Fate were created, but they were one entity like Missy here, and I guess Heaven wasn't too happy about that then, either. When Heaven destroyed that entity, this universe was created. I am not too keen on doing that to the Earth. Are you?"

Mandy opens her mouth and closes it and then stares down at the ground. "Heaven said you stole some souls from them." She looks beyond me at the picture window of the house, where everyone is watching.

"I figured if the person who raised me was going to close the only portal to Heaven, I'd pull out those they visited with the most. Unfortunately, I didn't get everyone out before she destroyed the portal with angel fire." I nod.

"So yes. I did technically steal souls from Heaven and breathed life back into them."

"You raised the dead?" Her voice cracks. "That isn't supposed to be one of your powers."

Now I do laugh. "Neither is turning reapers to dust. But I seem to have had that power even before I became this god-awful entity."

"How?"

The answer to that question seems so much more complex. I don't understand how it truly works. All I know is when I wish for something to be, it happens. I wished them alive, and they lived. I wished reapers to have forms so I could see their expressions and here they are. On Thanksgiving, I wished for my family to be safe from harm, and they were. Even at the fort in Kittery, I wished the reapers with bad intentions gone. Maybe it isn't as complex as I thought, but it certainly is a dangerous gift. "I willed it," I finally say.

A new thought dawns. Could I will my touch not to be lethal to the soul?

I blink the thought away and refocus back on Mandy. "I haven't exercised the same magic that I did back at the fort to ferret out those who wish me ill will. But I can if I need to." Some reapers shift from foot to foot. I switch my gaze back to Mandy. "I'm assuming you are the one speaking for the rest?" I raise an eyebrow.

She nods slowly.

"What are your intentions?" I cross my arms. I am still uneasy about their alliances.

She takes a deep breath. "Well," she starts and looks at her hands. Her thumb strokes the side of her palm. "Before we knew the ramifications, we were going to follow Heaven's orders." She looks up at me. "Or at least die trying. Then you did this." She raises her hands, turning them palm forward and then palm back and lets out a huffing laugh. "And you brought back the dead." She points to the house. "So, honestly, I don't quite know what to do now."

At least she is honest.

"Do we get to keep this form?" a male reaper from a few rows back calls out.

"I can turn you all back if you'd prefer," I say, unsure whether he is happy about the change or prefers the skeleton form that they've had for millenniums.

"Oh, no. Please don't!"

Almost every reaper seems to agree, but I catch a couple of unsure expressions. If there is even one dissenting voice in the group, I can't expect them to be united with me against Heaven.

"Whoever would like their skeleton form back, raise their hand." I wait.

After a moment, two hands slowly rise in the air. That's it. Only two in a sea of hundreds. The rest of the reapers wrap their arms around their new substantial forms, as if to safeguard it from whatever may be coming.

"It's okay. Come forward, please." I wave the two hands toward me.

They step to the front of the crowd. They aren't the most stunning creatures in the pack, but they had their own beauty hidden within the thinning blonde hair and ruddy complexions. They look as if they feel like squat makeup artists in a room full of supermodels. The two are noticeably similar, as if they were siblings in the real world before they passed on. They shine in their own unique way.

"You really want to be a skeleton?" I ask, unsure whether that is their true want, or whether they are just embarrassed at their former bodies in comparison with the others. "Because you two are beautiful." I don't want them to regret the decision, and I certainly know all too well what it is like to feel different and gawky, even though others tell me I'm beautiful.

They look at each other and then around them. "We aren't..." They glance back at me.

"I only ask because I don't want you to regret your decision." Honestly, I don't know whether I can just zap only two of them back into skeleton form or whether it would affect the entire federation, but I don't want to say that out loud. This wishing or willing or whatever thing I'm doing is not an exact science, and I do not want to jeopardize what I think I've accomplished with the rest of the reapers.

They entwine their hands together and take a deep breath, searching each other's gray eyes.

I wait and scan the rest of the reapers, silently praying they will accept themselves as they are right now, because if I try to turn them back, and turn the rest of the group with the effort, I will lose my edge.

After what seems like eons, they turn back to me. "We will stay in human form for now," the shorter of the two says, satisfied with whatever silent communication they had between them.

The relief almost makes my shoulders sag, but I don't want to show any weaknesses right now. Something deep down forces me to remain strong when I really want to drop into a de-stressed puddle.

"So, now what?" Mandy asks, pulling my gaze to her as the other two fade back into the crowd.

"Now you bring me back to Purgatory so I can make sure no punks from Heaven break through the barrier to this realm," Levi says from next to me. He shrinks down into his dog form and steps closer to Mandy.

I'm not ready to lose my trusty sidekick. Without him, I'm not sure I'm the pillar of strength that I project when he's got my back.

Levi glances at me and gives me an eye roll, like he thinks my thoughts are juvenile. I suppose they are, but still, he makes me feel invincible.

"There's a war coming. Are you sure you want to be on the front line?" I ask him. I know it's a stupid question. This is Leviathan, after all. He glorifies war and eating whatever suits his fancy, whether it be demon, or reaper—or, in this case, angel. He cocks an eyebrow at me in an echo of my own thoughts. I glance around at the reaper federation surrounding us. "I don't want them on the front lines, either. Much less you." I meet Levi's gaze.

"This is what I was created to do," he says. "Heaven. Hell. Neither one is supposed to be able to punch through the fabric safeguarding Earth. It is the reapers' job to protect the reaper realm from attack as much as it is to escort souls to their final destination. It is mine to make sure nothing gets out of either Heaven or Hell through Purgatory."

Damn, he was one loyal creature. And I know that's what he is designed for, but it doesn't make the lump forming in my throat any smaller. I swallow it anyway.

I can't let the reapers see me cry. I blink back the swell of tears and glance at Mandy. "I'm trusting you with him. Make sure he gets to Purgatory without harm. And God help you if you try to chain him up." I point my finger at her, trying to sound like the voice of authority, but my words don't come out as strong as I hoped. I sound like a whiney teenager pouting because her best friend is moving away.

Levi's tongue lolls out of the side of his mouth. He is silently laughing at me. His misplaced humor slaps the steel back into my spine.

Mandy nods and then drops to her knee, with her right arm crossing her chest in a bow. Others follow. It is completely mortifying.

"Get up," I hiss. Although I expected that at the fort, I really don't want them kneeling before me in this manner. I am not a queen. And I certainly am not a god. I am just me, and with the audience in the house behind me, this show of loyalty is embarrassing.

They rise with creases between their eyes and unsure expressions on their faces.

"I know I demanded it back in York, but we are beyond that." I take a deep breath and glance over the crowd. Even though it would have settled my nerves, I don't send my radar out to see whether there were dissenters in the pack. I meet Mandy's gaze, still feeling antsy about the plan. "I trust in you to do the right thing for this world."

Weighty words and they have the desired effect. The reapers nod, and Mandy reaches out to grab Levi's collar.

I swallow, wishing I could just wrap my arms around his neck in a goodbye hug, but that is not possible. I don't know if it will ever be.

When the reapers dissolve in the air, along with Levi, my eyes blur from the sudden mist of tears.

Finding Death
Chapter 6

"YOU DID THE RIGHT thing," my mother says from the backseat of the car as we pass under the Welcome to Maine sign on the Piscataqua River Bridge on Interstate 95.

I glance out the window at the passing scenery. I miss Levi already. His sideways humor always brings me back from the edge of a dark abyss. Exhaustion racks my bones, and my stomach growls as loud as Levi.

My father gives my arm a pat and focuses back on the road as he hangs back from the rest of the pack of cars traveling from the lake house.

"I'm still all confused about what just happened," Zane says. "I thought the reapers weren't on our side?"

"The ones that remain seem to be, but they left their post for long enough for Heaven to get some assassins to our side." My father turns the blinker on and takes a different road, peeling away from the rest of the crowd. He glances at the rearview mirror. "What's your address?" he asks Zane.

My stomach lurches. "No, Dad." I don't want to put Zane in that position. Especially when we don't have Levi with us to intervene if Zane's father steps out of line.

"Your father is right, especially if there are assassins on the loose already. 213 Birch Hill Road," Zane says. "You'll be safer there. Besides, if you can control an angel descendant, you can control an asshole human."

I glance in the backseat, barely making out Zane in the shadows. "I don't think this is a good idea." If his father comes at him, I know I wouldn't hesitate to strike him dead on the spot, especially after seeing the condition Zane was in on Thanksgiving.

"I won't let anything happen," my father says. "If he so much as flinches in Zane's direction, I'll lay him out flat."

"That's if he's even there," Zane says under his breath as the car crosses over the highway to the west side of the town.

I rarely come over this way. This is the poorest section of York. To the north is Mount Agamenticus and the rolling estates leading to it. The shoreline has the same air of wealth. Just like Papa's home, there were gated estates, but as we continue, the modest homes turn to a collection of farms and nothing bigger than double-wide trailer homes. They are larger than some of the run-down summer cottages on the shoreline, but they seem more worn, if that's possible. Maybe it's just the darkness creeping in around us that makes them look that way.

When my father turns in to the driveway of a small single-level home, I blink at it and swallow the pity that wells up. I live a charmed life on an estate by the sea. This is a landlocked home next to a quarry. Everything around it is covered in a fine gray dust, making it look almost ghostly in quality.

Zane sits up straighter in the car and his jaw goes rigid. "My truck is gone," he says in almost a growl. "The asshole took my truck!"

"Well, we have Faith's car," my father says as he rolls to a stop, and then turns the car off.

"The difference is you intend to give the car back." Zane gets out of the car and heads to the front door. He leans down and picks up a rock under the bush, and a moment later, has a key in his hand. Even he has a hide-a-key.

I press my lips against a smile as we all get out of the car and follow him. He doesn't seem to be in the mood for any ribbing, so I keep my humor to myself.

Zane pauses with the key in the door, as if he's having second thoughts. The lost look in his eyes makes me want to reach out and touch him, to reassure him that whatever lay beyond the door wouldn't change my feelings.

"This isn't what you are accustomed to." He glances back at me.

"It will be fine," my father says before I can say the same. He puts his arm around my mother and gives her a squeeze. "Right?"

She rolls her eyes. "Nick's right. It can't be any worse than our friend Noah's house in Florida. That place was barely standing. If a stiff wind came along, we were always afraid the walls were going to collapse on us."

Something about the way she says it seems to soothe whatever doubts Zane has because he swings the door open and reaches for the light switch on the inside wall. He flicks it a couple more times in frustration.

"Shit." He looks back at us with more aggravation written in the creases on his forehead and the low drop of his eyebrows. "Do any of you have a flashlight?"

I turn on my phone and flip the flashlight on. I went to hand it to Zane and my brain catches up to my actions before disaster strikes. I yank the phone away before Zane takes it from my hand. Scolding myself, I hand the phone to my father. "Can you give him this?" I nearly slam the phone in his palm.

I don't know if touching such a small thing at the same time will harm his soul, but I am not taking any chances.

My father does as I request with an eye roll and we follow Zane into the dark house. Zane stands in the empty living room—devoid of furniture, devoid of anything hinting at the fact people had lived there—just staring at the nothingness as he turns the light in all directions.

I wish there was enough light in the room to see his expression because the waves of conflicting emotions he's broadcasting wash over me in continuous succession. The overhead light in the kitchen flickers on.

Zane spins toward it with wide eyes, like he expects Levi to leap out of the cabinets or something. He glances at me.

"Did you just do that?"

Truthfully, I'm not sure, but I had wished for light and I guess that's the only light in the vicinity that's still here. "I wanted light because I could feel you freaking out. So, probably?" I shrug.

He gives me a nod and heads down the hallway with the phone light, leaving us in the stark kitchen light.

My father crosses to the refrigerator and opens it. Not even a crumb remains. It's like the Grinch had paid a visit while Zane was at our place. The freezer is just as barren. No dishes or glasses grace the cabinet shelves either.

Zane's face says it all as he slowly comes back down the hall to where we all wait. In the living room, he sits on the faded carpet and tosses my phone a few feet away. When he buries his face in his hands, I step toward him and stop, grinding my teeth together at my lack of being able to comfort him. He stays that way—his elbows on his knees and his hands covering his face—while his breath wheezes out from beneath his palms.

I want to string up his father. The asshole
stripped the place barren and ran like the
coward he is. My guess and probably Zane's as
well is the bastard took off in a hurry when Zane
didn't come home. Who knows, he's probably in
Canada by now.

My mother approaches him because I can't
console him the way I'd like to. She kneels next
to him and places her hand on his back, rubbing
it slowly. He stiffens, but she doesn't speak. She
doesn't need to. Zane's loss weighs on the air
like the thick Maine fog.

When he finally looks up, his tear-stained
eyes meet mine. "He took everything I had," he
says with such bitterness that I shiver. "That
bastard thought I was dead and ran with
everything. My truck. My equipment that I've
spent years collecting. He even found where I
had stashed my cash in my bedroom. Everything
I've built... Gone." He closes his eyes and shakes
his head. "I don't even have clothes besides what
was in my backpack at your house." He waves in
my direction. "And it isn't even Monday yet," he
adds as he rakes his hand through his hair.

"You will be fine," my mother says.

Zane glances at her. "You're in the same boat
as I am," he points out. "At least I still have my
wallet and the measly hundred dollars that I
keep as pocket change. But you two look like
teenagers and right now, you've got no home, no
clothing except what you are wearing right now,
and I'd venture to guess money isn't something
you've ever needed before. So, telling me it's
going to be fine is pretty comical, considering."

My mother's hand stops moving on his back and her gaze jumps to my father's in that deer in the headlights manner, as if she is just now grasping what being alive truly means.

"Where do you think he went?" I ask.

"Probably Mexico. He has always hated the cold." Zane wipes his face and stands up, crossing into the kitchen. He pushes the lever for water, and nothing comes out. He bangs it down again. "We can't stay here."

"Why not?" my father asks.

"No water, no electricity, no heat." Zane stares at him as if he's daft.

My father points at the empty fireplace. "I saw wood out back, right?"

Zane glances at the fireplace with a sigh. "No matches or paper for kindling." He looks back at my father.

"I'm sure we can find something to light a fire with." My father crosses his arms, challenging Zane with an eyebrow raise.

"Dude, there's no food. No water. No toilet paper." He shrugs with his palms up.

"Look, this is the safest place for Missy. No one knows where you live. Not the Ryans, not the reapers, and not the angels. If you are so concerned about roughing it, you said you had a hundred dollars. Order a pizza and we can pick it up and grab sodas, water, napkins, and matches at the same time. And toilet paper, if that's such an issue." My father makes an exaggerated eye roll.

"I have money at home. I can pay you back," I add, just to ease his mind. I don't want him to panic about money. Not while I'm living under the roof of one of the wealthiest men in America.

"Fine, but I don't have a phone."

"Use mine." I point to the phone still shining a light on the ceiling. He picks it up and shows me the lock screen before he puts it down and slides it across the floor to me. It comes close, and I lean over and swipe it off the ground. The local pizza place is practically on speed dial and with a couple of swipes of my finger, I hit the call button. "What kind of pizza do you all want?"

"Hawaiian," both Zane and my mother say.

"Hamburger," my father says a beat later.

Well, at least Zane and my mother have exemplary taste in pizza toppings. Although a hamburger pizza doesn't sound all that bad. My stomach growls again and I order two large pizzas and an extra-small Hawaiian, so we don't run out. At the pace my stomach seems to be devouring my insides, I could probably suck down an entire pizza by myself.

"They said twenty minutes." I slide my phone into my back pocket.

"I'll drive," my father says and offers Zane a hand to help him off the floor.

I can tell Zane isn't all that thrilled with the prospect of being alone with my father. I open my mouth and my mother interrupts me.

"We'll stay here and figure out what we can scrounge in the way of wood and kindling based on what's in the yard. Okay?"

"Seems reasonable to me," my father answers. He didn't even wait for Zane. He starts toward the door and glances back.

I send a seething glare at him, purposely narrowing my eyes. I'm not sure I want him alone with the guy I'm... I suddenly realize I don't know the status of what we are. Friends? Girlfriend-boyfriend? I'm not sure what to even refer to him as besides his name. Regardless of our precarious status, I do want to hear from Zane. "Is that okay with you? Because if it isn't, I can go."

"I'll be fine," Zane says, but he does not follow with the same enthusiasm. "But there isn't anything here. I've already looked."

"We'll just do another once-over and see if we can at least get the water on. Now go." My mother makes a shooing motion toward the door.

We watch from the entryway as the car pulls out of the driveway and my mother closes the door and turns to me.

"You have the ability to conjure things." It wasn't a question, especially when her gaze dropped to the lovely knife holder I created for Heaven's blade.

"So?"

"So, turn on the water, just like you turned on this light, so we can at least go to the bathroom. And while you're at it, conjure up some sleeping bags and pillows." She points at the empty floor.

My skin suddenly itches uncomfortably at the orders she utters, and I shift in place. "Is this what you did?"

"When I needed to, yes."

"So, this is more Fate's powers rather than Death's?"

"No. Your father could conjure things much easier than I ever could. But I learned over the years. By the time you came along, I could conjure whatever I wanted to wear or however I felt like having my hair on any day. Or if I needed a weapon, and it wasn't hidden away wherever Kylee hides things, I'd wish it out of the ether and voila." She spreads her arms like a goddess used to getting her way.

I had difficulty with my first outfit, but since then I hadn't had any missteps. I glance at the floor and bite my lower lip, debating. "How many sleeping bags?" I finally ask. I don't want to assume they'll sleep separately, even though I'd feel a hell of a lot more comfortable that way.

She chews on her nail as she studies the floor.

I can almost hear her internal dialog arguing for and against one sleeping bag. Silently, I wish for separate to be the answer because just the thought of my mother and father going at it in the same room makes me puke in my mouth a little.

"I don't think either of you will want to hear our shenanigans, so four would work."

Oh, hell no. Four sleeping bags and four pillows it is. I close my eyes, envisioning those sleeping bags that were used to keep warm in the arctic. A cool flow of air seems to breeze through me like I'm not solid flesh and bone. It's the same feeling I got when I pulled this outfit successfully together. When I open my eyes, four bags stretch out on the floor, as if an invisible hand unrolled them at my bidding. I smile and glance at my mother.

She just nods her approval and I concentrate on pillows.

I like mine soft and fluffy, so everyone is going to have to deal with that. Fluffy pillows that match the deep green of the sleeping bags appear on the openings of the bags.

I turn to my mother, feeling very accomplished by the magic that tickles my mind.

She points toward the sink. "Think you can turn on the water and the electricity and keep it on for a couple of days?"

That isn't quite as easy as conjuring something I can envision, like sleeping bags or clothes. That's a mechanical process, and I don't know if I can just wish running water through the house or not. The light had been a fluke. I wanted to see Zane's face and the only overhead light in the place happened to come on at the same time.

I decide to tackle electricity first because I don't think trying to do them at the same time is a really sane choice. Now, if I had a death wish, that might be a feat worth performing. But considering I don't want to die anytime soon, I cross to the wall and gather up every bit of my science know-how and put my hands near the light switches.

Electricity must have a signature of some kind, since it is just a mass of energy moving from one place to another. I close my eyes and take a deep breath, reaching for the energy.

It takes a few minutes to find any pulse, but I keep having to widen my search beyond the house until I find the source near the edge of the road running parallel to the house. My senses scan the source until I feel the underground wire that connects this house to the source. With a push, I clear the block the power company put in place, and the surge of energy that flows into my hands nearly knocks me across the room. The kitchen light flares bright and a couple of ceiling lights in the hallway come to life.

I catch myself before I pinwheel onto the floor and shake the sting out of my hands. I certainly don't want that same rush to happen when I try to do that to the water, otherwise every pipe in this house will burst. I am amazed that the surge didn't blow the electrical circuits.

My mother smiles at me, beaming like a proud parent.

I cross to the sink and push the lever to the open position. I stare at it for a moment. Maybe there's an easier way than using my magical skills. I glance down the hallway, wondering whether this one is as simple as turning on a valve. I head down the hall, trying each door as I pass. A closet. A bedroom. A bathroom. Then I finally find stairs that lead down. I flip on the light switch and grin as the light bathes the way.

The stairs are not rickety like most old houses and I'm thankful as I climb down them. I cross to where the water heater sits in the far corner. In Alex's house, there's a lever near their water system that turns off the water drawing from the city line.

My mother is close enough to make me nervous, and I glance back at her, raising an eyebrow. She moves a couple of steps back with a nod.

Starting at the water heater, I scan the pipes in the ceiling.

"What are you doing?"

"Looking for the valve to turn on the water." There are plenty of pipes overhead, but I'm looking for the one that goes through the basement wall. That's usually the one that has the turnoff valve on it, at least according to what Alex had told us when he was adding a bathroom in the downstairs family room area.

On the far side of the furnace, I catch a red-handled valve set to the off position. I'm glad I looked first because had I willed water to the house, it would have destroyed that valve. I crossed and stood under it on my tiptoes. Even jumping, I couldn't quite reach it. I don't even consider my mother. She's shorter than I am.

I glance around the barren basement, wishing for a darn step stool or ladder. Before me, the air shimmers and a three-step ladder appears, already open and waiting for me to climb up it.

I have to suppress a laugh. I really like this conjuring ability. I step up and turn the lever to the on position. The moment I do, the rush of running water reaches my ears.

I climb down and smile at my mother. "I didn't need to will that one after all."

She smiles back, with her eyes sparkling with pride. "I'm impressed. How did you know about that?" She waves at the valve.

"Alex does a lot of stuff around the house. He showed me where it was and explained that when they go away for any extended period, it's a good thing to turn off. Especially in the winter. It could save the pipes from bursting."

She follows me back upstairs.

"So, he doesn't just fix things with his mind?"

I laugh and shake my head. "No. And he wants us to be self-sufficient, so he tries to teach us the things he thinks are important. Like changing tires on a car or knowing where the water turnoff valves are in most houses."

"Hmm." We stop in the living room and she stares at the empty fireplace. "Care to conjure some wood for the fire?" she asks before I cross the room.

"There's wood out back. We can grab it after we eat." My muscles already feel strained, but I think some physical exercise of moving wood will actually help me sleep later.

I sit on the farthest sleeping bag, putting distance between me and the nearest bag, so I don't have any possibility of hitting anyone near me if I flail in my sleep. I rarely have nightmares, but this whole thing has me on edge enough to want to prevent a soul-sucking mistake.

As much as I find this conjuring stuff amazing, I'd trade it all to kiss Zane again.

"I'm sorry about Dad," I say after a moment. I haven't said anything to my mother since the jobs passed to me and I consumed my father's soul.

She takes a deep breath and gives me a sad smile. "You didn't know. Neither did we. Out of everyone there, I am glad it's your father. While he is off, if you know what I mean, he's not so far off from himself. It's hard to explain. He still is fiercely protective, and he still takes my hand when we are walking or puts his arm around me, although I think it's more out of habit than feeling." She sits down on the third sleeping bag, keeping her distance. "It could have been worse," she says, but I catch the way she averts her eyes.

"Why are you placating me?" I blurt.

She meets my gaze as her smile fades away. "I'm not. There are times he's more like his old self and then others when all his manners disappear. It's not consistent." She shrugs. "And there isn't anything we can do about it, so I'm choosing to live with the circumstances dealt to me and try to find the good in everything."

This is by far one of the longest conversations I think I have ever had with my mother, and I realize if we were in school together, we might have been friends because her inherently good view of the world is just so innocent. I don't know how, after all these years as a deity, she can still exude innocence.

I pray if the day ever comes that I must pass on the torch to someone else, that I'm as poised and wholesome as my mother.

Finding Death
Chapter 7

ZANE AND MY FATHER arrive with the pizzas, sodas, waters, paper plates, napkins, and a package of toilet paper. He drops the pies on the ground between the sleeping bags and heads down the hallway to the bathroom with the toilet paper.

When he returns, a crease between his eyes deepens. He crosses and takes a seat on the opposite side of my mother. As far away from me as possible. My father hadn't taken the spot next to me yet, so Zane's choice of where to sit has my curiosity climbing. Along with the fact of how skittish he seems to be acting.

I glance at my father as he takes the seat next to me. "What did you say to him in the car?"

My father opens his mouth to speak.

"He didn't say anything that hadn't already been said," Zane says. It takes him a few moments to actually look at me, as if I'm something to be feared.

I glance back at my father. "Seriously, what did you say?"

"I told him that if it had been anyone else in that house who you touched, they wouldn't just have had their soul sucked out of them, they would have died." He breaks open the seals on the pizza boxes and flips the tops open one by one, setting them toward the foot of the sleeping bags in the middle of us all. "You are Death," he adds when I just gawk at him. "That comes with curses all its own. And you have about as much control over that as I had."

"You didn't die." I reach for the untouched pizza. If no one else is going to dig in, I will. My stomach has been rumbling since before we left for the lake house and I had exercised a lot of magic in these few hours. I need to replenish my energy.

"No. But I think that's because we were technically dead when you stripped us of our roles. I probably should be dead right now, but I think it kind of backfired because you brought us back to life."

"But you didn't kill me when you became Death," my mother says as she reaches for pizza, too, except she uses one of the paper plates Zane dropped on the floor near our bedding.

"I had the benefit of a warning from my father. I knew my touch was deadly unless I wrapped those I cared about in a protective cocoon. You and Noah were protected because I willed it."

"Wouldn't that be the same with him?" I wave at Zane and dug into my pizza. "If you could will your touch not to be deadly, couldn't I will my touch not to suck out his soul?"

"I don't know the limits of your power," he says. "I could never bring someone back to life by sheer will. I had to turn back the clock to do that."

My mother turns her head and stares at my father.

"You knew I did that," my father says to her questioning eyes. "And then I screwed up by giving you the book of Fates to hold on to. I could instill ideas into people too, just like I've got control over fire and water." He glances at the fireplace. "Or had those powers before Missy took the helm. But back to the here and now. I never could raise the dead at will, or eviscerate reapers, either." He looks straight at me. "Neither of those powers were in our wheelhouse before."

Just as Zane reaches for the pizza, the front door bursts open.

I am on my feet, facing the intruder, before my brain catches up. Zane is on his feet too, his pizza cast aside carelessly.

"You!" The man points at Zane, and the stench of bourbon fills the room.

"Where's my stuff?" Zane says as he squares his feet, waiting. Every muscle in his body is visibly tense and just waiting for the first fist to fly.

It's as if the man doesn't even see the rest of us in the room. "You were supposed to die out there," he growls and then charges at Zane, hitting him full out like a linebacker.

Zane goes down with a heartbreaking thud. His head bounces against the floor.

My feet move as fury fills every cell.

I don't care that I can strip this bastard of either his soul or his life. He is hurting Zane, and all I can feel is the burn of retribution.

My father is faster. He tackles Zane's father, ripping him away from Zane and throwing him to the ground. My dad isn't large by any means, but he is scrappy as hell.

I want to help Zane, but I just point my mother to him instead. I cross as Zane's father climbs to his feet with the sourest expression I've ever seen scrunching his ugly face. I guess Zane must have gotten his good looks from his mother because this man isn't even in the same stratosphere as Zane.

I shove my father aside and block access to Zane as I will my scythe into existence. The blade glistens in the light, casting its deadly intent to everyone in the room.

"Do you know who I am?" I pound the blunt end of my weapon on the floor to get his attention. The charm on my wrist dings and a chill skitters through me, especially when the knowledge of the name listed flows into me.

His father reaches inside his shirt and pulls out a gun.

I am not allowing that entry to come to fruition. Before the bastard can raise the gun to take aim, I bring the business end of my scythe sweeping down as fast as a bolt of lightning.

His severed hand holding the gun drops to the ground, where it can no longer do any harm.

Blood spurts from the clean stump of his wrist and Zane's father blinks a few times before the pain renders a wail. He grips his arm above the bloody stump.

"Missy, don't." Zane's shaking voice comes from behind me.

"He beat you practically to death," I say, but I don't dare take my eyes off the shrieking man messing up the floor with his blood. Can I protect this idiot from my powers? The thought flits through my mind, changing him from a sure kill, to my first test subject. "Besides, I want to see if I can control my powers."

"Who the fuck are you?" he screams at me.

I smile and step forward.

"He may be an asshole, but he's the only family I've got," Zane says.

Now I do glance over my shoulder at Zane. He pulls his hand away from the back of his head. Blood smears the soft skin of his palm.

Darkness fills me, along with the need to enact justice. It pounds in my temples like a freight train. Seeing Zane bloody again is all I need to test my hypothesis out. I stalk forward, willing protection around the asshole from both my deadly touch as well as the soul-stealing ability. I grab his good arm.

He stiffens, and his eyes widen. His cries of pain hitch in his chest just before the room goes white. This time, his soul rips from his body with such force, the tearing of it sounds like wet flesh being torn apart. His soul is not the white light I expect—it's yellowing as if it's diseased—and I recoil from the sight just before it slams into my chest, absorbing into my skin whether or not I want it to.

His soul is as black and evil as I imagined Lucifer's was. A vile taste fills my mouth, and I nearly gag at the essence of the man. He does not have an ounce of any redemptive quality in his heart, and he hates Zane with a passion that creates a loathing in me I abhor.

This man hates that he was saddled with a spawn he didn't have any party in creating.

The transfer only takes a few seconds, but when the light dies down, I stare into his still living eyes. Eyes now devoid of a soul. His eyes are wide, as if he is seeing me for the first time, and I catch a hint of fear blooming there.

I'm not proud, but that fear gives me a hint of satisfaction. I'm glad this bastard has an inkling that his lousy existence is about to be snuffed out. I am just sad he isn't going on to Hell to live through the same pain and fear that Zane dealt with daily.

My willing him safe didn't save him from my curse. It only saved him from Death's touch. But that is about to change. "I revoke my protection," I snarl.

He wheezes a rattling breath as his good hand flies to his chest. As efficiently as I had sucked his soul from his body, I recklessly stomp the life out of him. I let go of the husk of a man and he crumples to the ground in an ashen-colored heap.

"You just killed my father!"

I turn to see both my father and mother holding Zane back. The horrifying taste in my mouth increases. Zane cared for this bastard, despite all the horrible things he did over the years.

"He came here to kill you."

"You don't know that," he growls as tears cascade down his handsome face.

I will the Book of Fates into existence and stare at the name I knew had been scribed in the book. I inhale and glance down at the shriveled carcass without an ounce of regret before turning toward Zane with the book facing him.

The name Zane Bradley is scrawled across the screen.

Zane pales and meets my gaze.

"I made a choice." I will not apologize for choosing him over the loser on the floor, and when I turn the book back around toward me, the name morphs from Zane's name to his father's. "I was not willing to let that cold-hearted bastard kill you. He wasn't even your real father." I will both my weapon and the Book of Fates back into the charms on my bracelet. The weight of them seems a little heavier this time. After all, I had taken a human life. I had committed an atrocious sin.

I turn toward the corpse; we can't have him stinking up the place and we really have nowhere else that is this safe to hide out. Lifting my hands, I will the body into a fine dust that I force up and out of the chimney and into the cool night air.

I dust my hands on my thighs and then, without a word, I cross and sit back down, focusing on the pizza and ignoring the open-mouthed stares of all three of them. I need something to wash out the vile taste of his soul from the back of my throat.

My parents let go of him and settle back down on the sleeping bags, as if nothing horrific had just happened. I guess it really isn't for them. After being Death and Fate for so long, the shock of human indecency doesn't seem to faze them the way it's throwing me.

"What do you mean, he isn't my real father?" Zane finally takes a seat, slower to return to the pizza feast than the rest of us. In fact, he pushes his plate away.

He still looks pale and I'm not sure it's because he just witnessed someone's death. Worry creeps under the hardened crust I built to deal with my actions. "How bad is the cut on his head?" I nod toward him and my mother goes to take a look.

She winces as she moved some of his hair aside. Her fingers come out of his hair smeared with red streaks. "I think you might need stitches."

"I'm okay." Zane brushes her away. "I just need a wet towel or something to use as a compress and a little soda."

I blink at him and glance up at my mother. She shakes her head, silently telling me it's worse than just a little cut. I will some liquid bandage into her hand. Her eyebrows shoot up at the little vial of liquid she now holds.

"She's going to fix you up, so hold still," I say and nod to my mother.

Zane glances over his shoulder at her and then back toward me.

"Stop ignoring my question."

He winces as my mother parts his hair with her fingers and applies a line of the adhesive to the cut.

"Hold still," she says and seems to press the edges of the cut together.

"Tell me what you meant," he directs at me through clenched teeth.

Zane has a right to know. "He isn't your biological father."

"How the fuck do you know that?" He shoos my mother away and then reaches for a paper cup and one of the bottles of soda.

"You tend to get a huge download of information about someone when you absorb their soul. Although I could do without his. It's awful and I wish I had just killed him so he could have an eternity atoning for his sins." I put the pizza down, no longer hungry.

Zane pours himself a glass of soda and then pours me one, pushing mine toward me instead of handing it to me. That small gesture warms the chill right out of me. It also tightens my throat.

My hand shakes as I reach for the cup. The adrenaline finally fades and my horrible actions hit home. Tears fill my eyes and my chin quivers. "I killed him."

Zane goes to move toward me, as if he wants to still protect me from the pain those three words create.

I put my hand up to stop him. "It's my sin to bear, not yours," I whisper as hot tears spill down my cheeks. "I'll be fine."

I don't want him to touch me. It isn't safe, and God knows I want him, of all people, to be safe.

I'd just need to learn to breathe through this crippling dread on my own.

LONG AFTER THE FIRE Dad and Zane built in the fireplace turned to embers and my mother and father's snoring filled the space, I tire of staring at the ceiling as my mind continuously relives my mistake. Although I can't really categorize it as a true mistake. At least now I know my protections only apply to letting someone continue breathing. I imagine the results if I had tried that on someone I care about. That leaves me more restless and intent on protecting those I love.

I climb to my feet and find the door that leads to the backyard. A weathered picnic table sits in the open yard, and I cross and stretch out on the top. The deep, clear night surrounds me, sending a chill around me as comforting as a wet blanket.

The vast galaxy shimmers across the moonless sky, uninhibited by any streetlight.

The creak of the door makes me tilt my head back to see who else can't sleep. Zane crosses and takes a seat on the bench. He stares at me and bites his lower lip.

"I should be angry with you."

I just nod, because he has the right. After all, I killed his only known family, even if he was a major dick.

"I'm not." He crosses his arms on the table and props his chin on his hand. "The longer I think about it, the more I wish you had filleted him with your scythe."

I raise my eyebrow at him.

"I know. Sick, right?"

I glance back at the sky. "It's not like the thought didn't cross my mind."

His audible sigh reaches my ears, and I glance at him again. "You have no idea how much I just want to climb on top of you and kiss you right now." He smiles in a way that flushes my entire body. "Among other things." But instead of doing just that, he stretches out on the picnic table seat and stares up at the cosmos with me.

"Even with what I did today?"

He doesn't answer and my stomach flips. If what I did alienates him, I'm not sure I can deal with that. I roll onto my side, peering down at him. He just continues staring at the stars above like they have answers we need. His gaze moves to mine.

"It hurts not being able to hold you. Weird, huh?" He attempts a light laugh, but it falls flat. "I needed you earlier. I needed your arms around me." He shakes his head and studies my face. "And it hurt worse than my head not to be able to hold you. Hell, the more time I spend with you, the less I seem to care about whether or not I have a soul."

He reaches up to touch my face.

My heart slams a panicked beat and I move away fast enough to jab my ass into a sliver of wood sticking up from the table. I stop the wince from hissing from between my teeth. That would be a surefire way to bring Zane right into my arms. Or worse, have him insist on getting the sliver out.

I cannot strip him of his soul. Not with how much his heart bleeds through his every word. If he didn't have a soul, I would not have fallen for him the way I have—hard.

As far as the sliver went, I'd have to have my father take it out with some tweezers later so it doesn't fester into something that could land me in the hospital. Although mortifying, it is still better than making a hospital full of the morally corrupt.

"So, what's next?" he asks, but his voice has an edge to it, one that my actions created.

I slowly lay back and search the constellations. I don't have an answer that would ease his mind. I am going up against Heaven, and if I die, the world dies. But there aren't any palatable alternatives.

"I could take one of the roles," he says quietly. "Then Heaven wouldn't have you on their hit list."

"No." He needs to have a life, even if it's without me. "You will die."

"You didn't." He sits up and rests his elbows on the table.

"I'm not..." I look away.

"Normal?" He chuckles. "Thank the fucking stars for that."

I glance at him. He's starting to sound a lot like my father in the loose language department. "No. I wasn't supposed to be. Levi called me an enigma."

"Well, you are, and you are now some sort of mystical immortal. One with a much kinder heart than mine."

"Excuse me?"

"I would have made my father suffer." He meets my stare. "I would have escorted him to Hell myself."

"I needed a test subject," I say, defending my actions. "I needed to know if I could safeguard someone from losing their soul and I saw an opportunity."

He rolls his eyes. "I'm not judging you. Don't go getting all defensive on me." He reaches out again, but this time he stops on his own, pulling his hand back and clenching it into a fist. He pounds the table. "Goddammit all." He gets up and heads back into the house, muttering under his breath about life being unfair and all.

I realize with a sick certainty that I need to get away from Zane. I am more lethal to him than I am to anyone else.

I want to be in his arms.

I want to feel his body against me, and not just spooning in bed like the other night.

I want more, and the longer I am around him, the deeper he gets under my skin. If I stay, he will be soulless in a matter of days.

Finding Death
Chapter 8

THIS TIME, I WAIT until I hear three distinct snores and then I go out the front door as quietly as humanly possible. I need to hone my skills, and I need to get away from any more mistakes. Zane is safe with my parents.

I walk to the end of the driveway and look toward home. Yearning pulls my midsection that way, but I turn and trudge in the opposite direction, putting time and distance between me and Zane's house. In the wee hours of the night, I blend in with the woods surrounding me.

I know I need to find somewhere to sleep, but I can't stop while I'm still in Maine.

Just as the sky lightens with dawn, the air shimmers next to me. Mandy appears by my side.

I stop, and she takes a couple of steps before she stops, too.

"Why are you here?" I ask and then, as my brain fog clears, I add, "And where is Levi?"

"He's fine. He's happily devouring whatever tries to come into Purgatory."

"So, if he's okay, why are you here?"

Mandy looks down and then back up at me as she shifts from foot to foot. She reaches into her pocket and pulls out a folded piece of paper. "Well, one of the angels got by him and spared me so I could give you this." She reluctantly hands it to me.

I use the tips of my fingernails to take the note, but instead of opening it and reading what an angel from Heaven has to say, I am more concerned about Mandy's comment.

"How many did the angel not spare?"

Mandy winces. "I think there may be less than a hundred of us left."

I blink and slowly drop to the ground. I didn't even feel them go. I should have. Mandy crouches down, her face transforming through the tears filling my eyes.

"You...you care about us?" Her voice cracks and she reaches out to touch me.

"Don't," I snap, and she freezes in place. "Don't touch me. I'm cursed, and I don't want to harm you."

She slowly pulls her hand back. "You care?"

I let out a high-pitch laugh. "Of course, I care. Why would you think I don't?"

"Well, you annihilated more than half of us."

Point taken. I close my eyes and hang my head. "They wanted to do harm to my family." I open my eyes. "I know you weren't party to what happened. If you were, you would not be here. I'm sorry I wasn't there to help you fend off the angels that got by Levi."

She glances off into the distance. "I don't know if you can survive their smiting."

I'm not sure either, but I have a host of allies who harbor angel fire. And they had toasted an archangel with it in the past. But even so, they haven't had to fight a host of angels from Heaven.

"And how did you survive?"

She winces and stands, glancing at the road. "They promised to spare me if I brought them through to this realm."

My senses itch, and I stare up at her before I glance around for the ambush that seems imminent. "Where are they?"

"Read the note." She points to the nearly forgotten paper in my hand.

I open it and stare at the scrawl.

You have sentenced the world to death by not heeding our warning. You are an abomination that cannot exist and will be terminated by Heaven's might.

Those who stand with you are just as damned as you are.

As punishment for your sin, we promise each and every one of those who stand by you and those who you stole from our grip will endure an eternity of torture alone.

We promise none of you will see each other ever again.

My chest tightens and I slowly look up at Mandy as I climb to my feet. "And you are standing with Heaven?"

She shakes her head. "But some are. Most of us scattered when we got here. Especially since we don't look like reapers anymore. We have a chance of blending in and hiding from their wrath."

I glance at the note again. "Can you get Levi and bring him back without getting hurt?"

"No. They left guards."

My heart pounds and I narrow my eyes, studying her. "Levi isn't okay, is he?" There was no way short of him being chained again that he would ever allow angels through. Not under his watch.

She glances at the ground. "When they couldn't smite him, they caged him."

"Why did you lie to me before?" I hiss the words out and refrain from grabbing her.

A pair of headlights approach, making me step into the grass and nod for Mandy to follow. The truck slows to a stop, and Zane glances out the passenger window at the two of us. He lifts my cell phone.

"Holly texted."

He doesn't need to say anything more. The glare he gives me says everything. I abandoned him and there is no level of forgiveness in his eyes.

"Where are my parents?" I ask as I stare at the decal on the passenger side door. This is Zane's truck. I hadn't even noticed it in the driveway when I left. That explains how his father came barreling in like a wrecking ball last night.

"They went to Papa's house. Everyone is there." He glances at Mandy. "Why is she here?"

I wave the note in my hand. "There's been a breach." I open the passenger door and step aside to allow Mandy to get into the backseat.

"She can walk," Zane says, pulling my attention back to him. "We have some things to discuss."

That's the last thing I need, but I give Mandy a nod, knowing she doesn't really need a lift to wherever we are going. She probably wants to go off and blend in as she was saying, and I don't blame her for wanting a last hurrah before the worlds as we know them end.

Zane does not take me to Papa's house. Instead of driving by his house, he pulls in and leaves me in the truck, slamming the front door behind him with a bang. I wait for him to come back, and when he doesn't, I think about driving myself, but he has the car keys.

I climb out of the truck and with every step closer to the house, dread wraps another frigid finger around my heart. He stands by the fireplace with his arms on the mantel, just staring down at the embers in the hearth.

I close the door behind me and his entire back tenses. He turns and stalks toward me like he wants to shake sense into me. I press my back against the door, trying to literally push my way through it. When Zane's hands slam into the wood on either side of my head, I gasp. He leans close enough for me to feel the heat and anger radiating from his skin.

"Please don't," I whisper. My chin quivers.

"Why not? You don't seem to give a damn about me."

Hot tears spill over and run down my cheeks. I don't dare move. I want to push him away and call him a pig-headed fool. I want to bridge the slight distance between us and crush his lips with mine. Damn him, I want his arms around me.

"I care too much." I meet his wild-eyed glare. "It's only a matter of time before..." More tears spill over. "Before we..." I can't finish the sentence. "I'm not that strong, and I can't protect you," I finally sputter. "This hurts me just as much as it hurts you."

He pushes back and takes a step away to give us both some breathing room. "That's not a good enough reason to leave in the dead of night."

"Yes. It is. You would do the same damn thing if you were in my shoes," I yell, moving as close as I dare. "You would do anything to protect me if the roles were reversed. Even if it meant leaving." Tears blur my vision, and I run my hands through my hair. "And now everything is going to shit, anyway." I throw the note onto the floor between us and step back against the door as sobs rip from my chest. "They smited most of the reapers, and Levi has been caged by the asshole angels somewhere in Purgatory, so there is no one holding them back." I swipe at my face as he picks up the letter and reads it.

He pales as Heaven's horrifying promises of wiping us all out are outlined in gruesome detail. "They would do this?" He waves the letter. "These are supposed to be the good guys. Why would they slaughter your whole family?"

"To break me." It is simple, and it is working.

Finding Death
Chapter 9

HE DRIVES SLOWLY, AS if he doesn't want us to arrive in time to see whatever slaughter is coming. Without Levi blocking the gates, they are free to swarm the reaper realm and slip into ours. The thought terrifies me.

"What did Holly say?"

Zane remains quiet and tosses me my phone. This grand, silent treatment is grating on my nerves. He never admitted he would have done the same thing, either. He refuses to acknowledge the danger of coming with me. And he would not let me go alone to the house, not with the possibility of the world ending tonight.

But he also wasn't going to stop me from coming home and making sure my family was safe. So here we are, in the truck. Me with my arms crossed in the passenger seat and him giving me this damn attitude.

I pick up my phone and swipe the text app open, finding Holly's text. She asked whether I was okay. And there isn't just one text. There are a dozen of them trying to get me to answer, each one increasingly frantic until she finally called. "What did you tell her?"

"That you were sleeping and would call her when you woke up. I told her we were fine."

I glance out the passenger side window with that lump permanently lodged in my throat. I swallow, blinking away the mist that springs over my vision. I take a few moments to catch my voice. "Thank you," I finally squeak out.

He grunts. Both his hands grip the steering wheel to the point his knuckles turn white. The muscles in his jaw stand out like he's clenching his teeth. Everything about him is as tight as a coiled snake ready to strike.

"What?"

"You're walking into a trap."

"What choice do I have?"

"Let me take one of the roles. That way, they have no beef with you. Either give me the book or give me the scythe."

"There is no guarantee that it will work. You saw me try to pass it back to my father."

He sends a searing stare in my direction before looking back at the road. "I have a soul."

"I cannot risk your life on a maybe. If I'm touching the scythe at the same time, there's no guarantee I won't strip you of your soul and kill you. I'm not losing you that way."

"You can bring me back." He glances at me.

"I don't know how to do that without a damn portal. And don't say I brought my parents back from the dead because I don't have the foggiest clue how that happened."

"If they kill you, we all die."

"I don't intend on dying by their filthy hands. Besides, if we all die, then we all pass on together."

"Not according to that note." He points to the paper on the console between us.

Heaven not only swore the Deaths of all who stood by me—which meant everyone who attended Thanksgiving at Papa's house—but every being I brought back from the dead. They also promised each and every one of us would be ushered through the gates of Hell for an eternity on the racks, with no chance of ever getting off.

Basically, if I don't give myself up freely, none of us would ever see each other again.

"It's total bullshit," I mutter under my breath. They are hoping they'll scare me to the point I won't be able to see straight. But on the other side, I am in control. Purgatory is my domain, and they killed my federation.

I can feel my blood pressure rising, along with the anger rushing to the surface and drowning out all remnants of fear. They are screwing with the wrong girl.

What had Tom Ryan said earlier?

Angels are dicks.

If the angels try to smite me, that will be their last mistake. I really believe I am not smitable. Not with the incredible power flowing through my veins. Not with the absolute uniqueness I bring to the table. Not with the ability to turn reapers to ash. And from the wrath and spite outlined in their note, I am ready for a bloody battle.

I am prepared to strip every one of those bastards of their souls before I blow them into oblivion with Heaven's blade. That's my secret surprise. They have no clue I possess the ultimate weapon. Although my scythe can do damage, Heaven's blade will blink them out of existence like it did to Lucifer.

I have years of self-defense lessons, and I know how to handle multiple attacks, especially multiples with weapons. That was Papa's favorite test for obtaining a black belt, and I moved fast enough through my forms to impress the entire family. I just need to keep control of Heaven's blade throughout the battle, and not end up nicking myself in the mayhem.

That kind of mistake would snap me, and probably the rest of humanity, right out of existence. It is also the reason I had to face the angels alone. I can't take a chance of scratching anyone who is on my side of the equation.

That's my plan.

I take a shaky breath. But the boy driving the car will never let me go out to the battlefield alone. The only reason he let me go before was Levi, and I no longer have the benefit of Levi to protect my back.

"I can't let you go up against Heaven alone."

It's like he read my mind. I mop my face as we turn onto Papa's road. I have no idea how to make him understand. "You have to. Otherwise, I will be powerless."

He slams the brakes, and the seat belt tightens from my forward momentum. "Despite what it looks like, I can fight." He turns hard eyes in my direction.

"I will have Heaven's blade. If I get moving too fast and not paying attention to where you are, I could slice you into oblivion."

"You can't fight." He laughed.

"What? Because I'm a girl?" I glare at him, and he has the audacity to shrug. "I will have you know, I'm a second-degree black belt. If I could touch you right now, I'd kick your ass just for laughing at me."

"That still doesn't mean you have actual fighting experience," he says.

"Being someone's punching bag doesn't qualify as fighting experience, either." I know the moment the words slip out of my mouth I should never have uttered them. But now that they were out, I can't take it back.

He presses his lips together and the muscle in his jaw jumps. The truck moves slowly forward as he lifts his foot off the brake. We are back to the silent treatment, and this time, I don't think I can break through his purposeful barrier so easily.

"Damn it, Zane," I whisper and look out the window at the sun breaching the horizon, bathing us with a new and uncertain dawn.

Finding Death
Chapter 10

PAPA'S DRIVEWAY IS AS crowded as I had ever seen it. Zane pulls up alongside the gate on the road outside instead of blocking everyone in. I open the gate and step inside, hitting the button to reengage it as soon as we are clear. We walk down the driveway in silence, but a noise like crunching leaves under a boot behind us makes me glance over my shoulder.

An angel is coming at us with a feral grin on her face. Her skin glows, reminding me of when Papa had gone all angelic on his brother. The gate slams closed behind the winged being, emitting a sound that I had grown accustomed to. The gate is armed, but not with the normal electrical charge. No, I had only seen this a few times. It is charmed to not let anything or anyone in—or out, in this case—that doesn't have the access codes.

It takes a moment for the creature to realize she is locked inside the protective bubble with me. I sidestep her first flailing attempt, easily avoiding the edge of the weapon she holds and putting distance between Zane and me.

He reaches to grab the angel.

"Don't!" I warn.

He halts as if his life depends on it.

I am sure it did, but that little distraction cost me some blood. The angel's sword slices down my left shoulder with her second attack. The sting barely registers, but the oozing heat running down my arm does. Before she can get another blow in, I step closer, reaching for her wrist with as much speed as I can conjure.

I yank her forward, making it impossible for her to cut me again with her long sword. Her eyes widen, and I let a satisfied smile form. I relish her sudden terror as her ethereal soul slowly strips from her earthly form. It is glorious, but in some ways worse than Zane's father had been.

"I am so much more than any of you heavenly assholes ever thought. It will take an army to crush me," I snarl in her ear as I unsheathe Heaven's blade. I sink it right into the angel's stomach.

She sucks in her breath as her gaze drops to the knife I still grasp.

"Heaven's blade?"

"You bet your lily-white ass." I yank it out of her just as the last of her soul peels off her body.

Light radiates from where the blade pierced her, and she screams, throwing her head back with the force of it. I almost didn't catch the ding from my wrist announcing her death. Her body lifts off the ground and a millisecond later, she explodes in a wave of light that throws me into the air.

I land on the grass and the wind sucks out of me as if I am stuck in some weird vortex. I blink up at the brightening sky and try to take a full breath; I can't quite manage it. My ears ring as I push myself into a sitting position. The blade is still in my tightly fisted hand. I somehow am lucky enough that the ethereal blast hadn't sent me in Zane's direction. I sheathe it before I do any more damage and then look around. I am halfway across the yard.

The cars we were near had been pushed a few feet toward the house, and in some cases, into each other. I scan the yard for Zane and my heart jumps into my throat when I can't locate him. I scramble to my feet and run toward the mass of metal.

In my mind, I scream for Nana, because in the pit of my stomach, I know something terrible has happened. But at least the Book of Fates hadn't rung its foreboding ding more than once, so he had to be alive.

The front door opens, and Nana runs out onto the front path like the world has gone up in flames. Her bare feet and nightgown tell me I woke her from sleep, abruptly. "What the..." She skids to a halt.

"Zane." I point at the cars. We both run toward the twisted mess. When I can't see his body above the crushed cars, I drop on my hands and knees, but the shadows play tricks on my eyes.

"Move!" Nana snaps, and I scramble out of the way. I'm breathing heavy, more from the panic than exertion.

The creak of metal sends a flurry of shivers through me and then one of the cars rights and slides to the side. Nana only has the power to heal. I glance up in time to see Papa's drapes fall back into place. She must have used her telepathic powers to call for his help and he moved the cars out of the way for her with his power of telekinesis. Light fills the space between cars, and I round the corner and stop in my tracks. My hand flies over my mouth at the sight before me.

Zane is still breathing, but barely. He was nearly crushed to death by the mass of metal that he had been thrown among. I sit down hard on the pavement. My throat tightens at the thought of losing him.

"Thank you," I squeak out.

"He's going to be out for a while." She wipes her face. "You don't look like you got through whatever that was unscathed." She nods toward my arm.

I glance down at the deep cut. I won't have the benefit of Nana's magic to heal it. "You have your medical bag here, right?"

"That needs stitches," she says as she comes closer.

"You can't touch me." I point at her. "But you can walk my father through patching me up." I glance around as Papa comes out of the house with flannel pants on.

"What happened?"

"An angel got through the charms you have up, and I used Heaven's blade." I climb to my feet and wave at the metal disaster surrounding us. The world tilts under my feet, and I reach out to the nearest car to get my balance.

"Can you help get Zane into the house and on the couch?" Nana asks Papa. "I'll go get your dad and get my bag." She nods toward the house. "Go sit at the kitchen table, please."

I weave my way inside and collapse on one of the wooden kitchen chairs, welcoming the dark room. I don't know what I am going to do. My plan didn't account for the bomb-like annihilation that happened when Heaven's blade was employed. I lean back and cover my face with my hand just before the overhead lights blink on.

Nana comes in, carrying her medical bag. She sets it on the table and puts on a pair of rubber gloves. I stare at her latex-clad hands and raise an eyebrow.

"Your father is on his way down to help, but I need to at least clean the wound before he stitches you up." She puts a package of fresh gauze on the table along with a bottle of iodine. "I want you to put your head down on the table and your arm out straight. This way, if you end up passing out, you will not fall. Okay?"

"But the blood."

She waves my words away and points to the table. I slide the chair so the arm rest is underneath the table and move my hair so it is as far away from my throbbing arm as possible and I lay that straight across the wood just like she instructed.

"That's perfect. Just don't move."

"What the Hell?" My father's voice echoes in the kitchen, making me jump a little.

Before I can speak, cool liquid douses my arm. The coolness transitions into a nasty burn, like fire had been poured in the cut, but I force myself to stay still. But that does not exclude the wailing curses that slip out of my mouth. I normally don't drop f-bombs, but right now, with the pain radiating from my arm and up my neck, I don't care whether I am grounded for a month for my inappropriate language.

"Take deep, slow breaths," Nana says. "I know it burns like holy hell, but I need to get the dirt out before your father stitches you up."

More burning sensations take hold and tears blur my vision. I don't even twitch this time, but man, my stomach becomes decidedly sour. I swallow the awful taste creeping up my throat and will myself into a state of relaxation. Focusing on the light reflecting in the middle of the large-screen television, I force myself to breathe in through my nose and breathe out through my mouth, like all those meditation videos I've seen recommend. I concentrate on each breath, counting the ins and outs, even when the prick of a needle pierces my skin and my vision blurs from tears.

You can do this, I tell myself. *Breathe.* I can almost hear Zane's calm tone saying the word in my head. God, I wish he was awake and in here so I could get lost in his green eyes and the sound of his voice.

If I could have, I would have leaned over and vomited on the floor, but I can't move. Not if I don't want my father to screw up what he is doing. Nana coaches him through each stitch. Her soft instructions are lost on me because I have to keep counting my breaths to keep my stomach in check through each pierce of the needle and tug of the sutures. My eyes and throat sting from the continuous flow of my tears.

Then comes another round of burning iodine, but by this time, the sting isn't as teeth clenching as the first two rounds.

After what seems like a lifetime, Nana says, "You can sit up now."

"I don't think I can," I say. "At least not without throwing up."

Something shuffles next to the chair.

"It's okay. There's a garbage can right next to you if you need it."

I push myself up and stare at the blood smearing the nice wood table. My stomach rolls, but settles down after a few deep breaths. By some miracle, I don't vomit. I lean back in the chair and close my eyes.

"Is Zane okay?"

"He's passed out on the couch in the living room," Nana says as a warm cloth wipes at my arm.

I looked up as my father attempts to clean the blood off my arm. His lips are set in grim determination. When his gaze meets mine, I see a flash of emotion. It isn't anger, either. I blink at him. He is supposed to be soulless, but that look tells me otherwise, like there is still a small piece of him hidden away underneath.

"You did amazing," he finally says. Then he crosses to the sink and rinses out the bloody cloth before returning and helping to clean up the table with Nana. The shuffling of feet upstairs makes me look up at the ceiling and then over at Nana as she tosses another soaked paper towel into the garbage.

"Everyone is here. We thought it best to hunker down in one place after what happened in New Hampshire." She keeps mopping up blood and spraying the disinfectant on the areas she has gotten clean.

My father drops to his knees to sop up the mess on the floor before the rest of the house comes in for breakfast. I bet there would not be a soul that could eat after taking one look at this mess.

"We were worried about you, though." Nana glances at my father as she continues to clean off the table. "Your dad filled us in a little."

"You have charms against angels?" I know they had charms against other things, but I didn't think they worked on heavenly beings.

She smiles. "When Lucifer is your sworn enemy, you invoke the most powerful magic that you can muster. My sister-in-law restored it to its former glory." She throws the last of the paper towels that are now soaked in only cleaner in the garbage can and packs up her medical bag before she grabs a soda and sits down across from me. She pushes the ginger ale across the tabletop. "I wanted to thank you for bringing them all back." She takes a heavy breath. "That really was quite a feat."

My father slides the chair out next to me and takes a seat. "It isn't without ramifications. Any time you cheat Death, there are consequences." He lets out a small laugh. "But damned if I know what they are, with Heaven throwing such a hissy fit over nothing."

I bite my lower lip. Why would Heaven risk short-circuiting the world? Granted, we humans had slid into the gutter recently, but that can't be it. If it is, why don't they just launch a meteor toward Earth and end it like that?

No. This feels more personal. More fearful, as if I am more powerful than Heaven. I blow out air. The angel that showed up here hadn't attempted to smite me. Instead, she attacked with a sword. "They can't smite me, can they?" I glance at my father.

He just shrugs. "I don't know what they can do to you. But I sure know what they can do to us. They've made that perfectly clear in that note of yours." He crosses his arms. "I, for one, am not going down without a fight."

Finding Death
Chapter 11

MOST OF THE DAY slips away as I sit in the chair across from the couch in the living room, just watching Zane sleep. My heart weighs heavy with how pale he still seems. Nana assures me he is healing, but he was in such awful shape when she got to him. Thankfully, I hadn't found him first. Otherwise, my freak-out would have been much more magnified.

The pocket door is closed, shutting off most of the noise from the back of the house, where everyone who had been at the cottage congregated. I wonder how many more I could have brought back before I collapsed from exhaustion if Faith hadn't closed the portal as quickly as she had.

If I had been thinking, I would have brought Zane's mom back, too. I close my eyes. She hadn't even crossed my mind. With a heavy sigh, I stand up slowly. Any fast moves make the world spin. Nana says that's from blood loss, but as long as I eat and drink, it should go away fairly soon. Which is good, because if I have to fight in this condition, the world will end in a matter of minutes.

I cross and sink to my knees as close to Zane as I dare.

"I'm sorry for being a bitch earlier."

Zane's eyes open, and he turns his head toward me before looking around the room. "What happened?"

"You nearly got crushed by a car."

He glances down at his body and then back at me. "Dr. Ryan?"

I nod and his head falls back on the pillow. "How bad?"

I don't answer, but all I can envision is his mangled body between the cars, with her healing light cascading over him like a faithful blanket.

"What happened?" he asks again and turns on his side, tucking his palms under his cheek as he faces me. His gaze lands on my arm and he sits up as though his memory just turned on full force. "You got hurt."

I let out a huff. It's nothing compared to what he's been through. He had been unconscious most of the day, healing under Nana's magic. "I have an ugly line of stitches under this gauze pad." I tap my arm gently, careful to avoid my injury.

He closes his eyes and creases develop in his forehead. It takes a moment for the memories to fully form, but when they do, his eyelids fly open, zeroing in on me. "The angel blew up."

"That pretty much sums up what happens with Heaven's blade." Faith and Alex had recounted their experience with the blade. My mother and father testified as well. In all cases, that is the result of sticking Heaven's blade into the flesh of an enemy. "It also makes me need to reconsider my grand plan of stealing their souls and stabbing them with Heaven's blade. That explosion would likely kill me, along with anyone in the vicinity."

He snorts at me, as if I am feeding him a line of pure bullshit.

"You don't believe me? Look at the cars in the driveway." I hook my thumb over my shoulder.

He rises slowly, testing out his legs as if he doesn't quite trust them. When he seems surer of himself, he crosses to the bay window. He stares at the car pile-up and lets out a slow, soft whistle. "It looks like someone plowed into all of them."

"Yeah. I bet you're glad you parked on the road."

He lets out a bark of a laugh as he glances back at me with a nod. "At least we have one undamaged vehicle if we need to make a quick getaway."

I snort a laugh, but as I think about this morning, my smile fades. "You were crushed in between that mangled mess."

He turns toward me with wide eyes.

"I told you. You were nearly crushed to death."

He glances down at his tattered and bloody clothing as if to make sense of it all. But his gaze keeps landing back on my bandage. "I caused that." He points at my arm.

I can't bring myself to lie and tell him he didn't cause me to get hurt. If he had backed off and let me handle it instead of trying to march in like a savior, I wouldn't have taken my eyes off the angel in attack mode. I meet his gaze and shrug.

"Maybe now you'll listen to me when I tell you I have to do this alone."

The look he gives me crushes that hope. He makes his way back to the couch and stretches out on it again, as if the effort to walk to the window has sucked what little energy he had from his muscles. I guess having another near-Death experience will do that. Hell, I am exhausted from the day's emotional and physical toll. My muscles throb with it. What I wouldn't give to stretch out beside him on the couch and snuggle.

"You look so sad," he says.

I nod. I am. All this is too much for me. At sixteen, I am not prepared for this much drama. "I'm completely disillusioned. Everything I believed about good and evil..." I glance down at my hands and shake my head. I don't want to voice the words flowing through my mind. Everything has turned upside down in my world.

"I know. And right now, I couldn't give two craps about forever." He puts his hand out for me to take it.

I stare at his sweet offering. What I wouldn't give to take his hands and fall into his arms. The number of emotional hits his gesture gives me nearly closes my lungs. My chin trembles and my eyes mist over in response, because as much as I want to, I can't. I blink and hot streaks slide down my cheeks.

"That's worse than escorting you to Hell myself." I move back in the chair, scraping it a few feet out of his reach in case he throws caution to the wind completely instead of letting me make the decision about his soul.

Heat continues tracing paths on my face, and I swipe at the tears, trying to regain my composure.

The air surrounding us shimmers, then fades, almost like a warning. Someone is in trouble.

Zane sits up, as if he can feel the disruption, too.

My gaze lands on the door and everyone else who is dear to me beyond it. My feet move before my brain registers, and I fling the pocket door open. Everyone is crowded against the far end of the family room, across from the sliding glass doors leading to the backyard.

The slider is open, and two reapers hold a bloodied Mandy in their grip. My father has his arms out for everyone to stay back. Even without a soul, his protective reflex is amazingly astute.

I filter through the room, mindful not to touch anyone.

"We tried," Mandy says when I get closer.

"Put her on the couch," I order. The other two reapers—one young enough to be my age, and the other probably in his fifties—bring Mandy to the couch and lay her down. Her left arm is torn through just above the elbow, leaving a jagged, dripping mess. Everything about her screams she is near drifting away. I turn with my heart pounding in my chest.

"Nana, please help her." I point at Mandy and make sure I extend my mental power to protect everyone in the room from the reaper's touch. The same protection that I shot out around Zane's father fans out over my family standing with wide eyes, observing this crazy scene.

"She can't," Mandy whispers.

"Yes. She can. I am protecting her and everyone else in this room from Death's touch." Just like my father before me, I protect those I care about from our deadly touch.

Nana steps forward and casts me a worried glance. "It won't grow back," she says, waving to the reaper's severed arm.

"I know. We'll find her a mechanical arm after all this if we need to, but if you don't help her, she's not going to make it."

"I don't know if my healing power will work on a reaper." Nana bites her lip and wrings her hands. She takes the final steps, but the closer she comes to Mandy, the paler she becomes.

"It's okay. The reapers can't hurt you. So, please just try," I say softly enough for her to hear.

Some of her color returns, and she leans down and presses a kiss to Mandy's forehead.

At first nothing happens, but then Nana's healing light blooms bright, nearly blinding us as it dances over Mandy's battered body. Mandy groans at first before she grits her teeth and stares wide-eyed as the unnatural jagged angles in her body straighten back into their natural state. The bruises in her already pale skin clear and even her severed arm heals up, as if someone repaired the raw end. At least her skin grows back, but Nana is right: the arm itself doesn't regenerate.

Mandy blinks and glances up at Nana and then at me with her mouth open.

I stifle a smile. I know how awe-inspiring Nana is and seeing it in the reaper's gaze makes me want to laugh. "What did you try to do?" I lower onto the edge of the coffee table now that she seems to be doing better.

"Malcolm, Jenny, and I tried to get Leviathan out of the cage they've got him locked in."

I glance at her arm, afraid to ask the question that pops into my head. "Did he do that?"

"No, the griffin standing guard did."

"Griffins exist?" I blurt the question and glance over my shoulder at my father.

"Beats the Hell out of me." He turns to Kylee, who stands near him. "Have you ever seen one?"

"No." Kylee glances at Phoebe and Smoke. "How about you?"

"Nope," both Smoke and Phoebe say in unison.

"There was one at Heaven's disposal," Papa's father says from the back corner of the room. "Nasty motherfucker, too."

Oh great. Leviathan is being guarded by another mythical beast. Just what I need. I wipe my face and turn toward the family still backed up into the wall area.

"You don't have to remain stuffed into the corner anymore. They won't hurt you. You all now have my protections against a reaper's touch." I glance around the room and my gaze lands on my father and his proud grin that is totally misplaced in the current situation.

"That's my girl."

I roll my eyes and grab one of the kitchen table chairs and pull it into the corner nearest the couch Mandy is on. The other two stand behind the overstuffed seat like sentries. I need to find out whether they have any other information about Heaven's impending attack.

None of the reapers seem eager to leave either. I'm not sure whether that's by design or whether they can't leave. After all, the protections on the house were pretty robust.

"How'd you get in?" I ask.

"You're our boss. We can get to you anytime, despite these rudimentary sigils." Mandy points to the piece of paper with the drawings Kylee had done to make everyone's whereabouts blind to the reapers.

"It protects the humans from us knowing where they are, though," the older reaper said. His grimace told me the sight of that sigil makes him as logy as it makes me feel.

Zane wanders over and takes a seat near me. I can tell he isn't exactly comfortable being near my emissaries. And he recognizes Mandy. He gives her a curt nod and sits as close to me as he can without touching me.

I scoot my chair into the wall, putting some distance between us. "Zane, you've met Mandy, but this is Jenny and Malcolm. Guys, this is Zane."

Zane sticks out his hand. "I'm Missy's boyfriend," he says, surprising the Hell out of me.

I stare at him like he had suddenly grown a second head. I am so conflicted where he is concerned, especially given our current no-touch circumstances, and I thought he was in the same mindset, but apparently not.

I guess my shock is on full display because Mandy asks, "Does she know that?" before she accepts his handshake.

He smiles and shrugs. "I don't know. But whether she likes it or not, I am not going anywhere."

"Must be nice to have such loyal subjects." Mandy gives me a raised eyebrow.

"They are not subjects." I don't like the way she refers to the people in this house. They aren't my subordinates. They are family—and some pretty powerful family members at that.

Mandy puts her hand out, splaying her fingers wide. "I meant no offense. It has been a very long time since I interacted in this realm."

I rein in my aggravation as Holly makes her way over to our growing circle. Although I am relieved to have the distraction, the closer people get, the more uncomfortable I become. I go to scoot my chair farther away, but the wall stops me. There is nowhere for me to go.

"Holly, this is Mandy, Malcolm, and Jenny. Guys, this is my best friend in all the world."

Holly gives handshakes all around. "I heard you say it's been a long time since you've been here. So, how long has it been?" Holly asks. Leave it to her to ask the questions no one else will voice after Mandy's awkward slip.

Mandy's mouth moves silently as she stares at the ceiling, counting on her only hand. "About sixteen hundred years. And that was just a brief visit." She glances around. "Things certainly have gotten advanced in the ways of comfort."

"What about you?" Holly asks Malcolm.

He shifts and puts his arm out to lean on the counter near me. When his hand brushes my arm, I gasp in horror. Light blooms from within him and flows into me in a rush that steals my breath just as efficiently as I've stolen his soul.

"No, no, no," I mutter, trying to stop the transfer. But I am helpless. If I lean too far away, I will connect with Zane, and my body will not allow that.

Malcolm's lips draw into a grimace and then he crumbles away like the reapers I destroyed at Thanksgiving. It isn't the same as a living being; they seem to be able to survive without a soul. But not a reaper. Without his soul, he is nothing but dust.

"No!" I cry just before his face disappears.

I can't stay inside. I can't deal with the shocked stares of everyone in the house, and I bolt out the back door, away from everyone.

However, I can't outrun the truth of what just happened. My breath comes in distressed pants at the horror of an innocent mistake. With just a brush of skin, I destroyed that reaper.

"No!" I scream at the Heavens and fall to my knees as sobs rip from my chest.

A cold rain spritzes down over me, soaking my clothes and chilling me as I cry. No one comes out to collect me. Not even my father.

I can not do this. I can't live in a world where I am a monster. It's not in my makeup to be alone, never mind alone forever. My breath hitches again as the sobs turn to more like hyperventilating. I can almost hear Zane whispering "breathe" in my ear.

Just the thought of him both soothes the growing anguish and creates an emptiness in my soul. Tears mix with the rain as I take breath after breath like a fish gasping out of water. Somehow, oxygen finally flows into my veins, loosening my chest. My teeth chatter and as soon as I get my lungs under control, I glance over my shoulder at the house.

The door is closed and although my father leans against the glass watching me, he doesn't budge to try to console me. He's probably doing damage control inside. Everyone knows I'm dangerous to touch, but that little horrifying display certainly solidified the genuine threat.

I turn back toward the ocean when I spot Zane on the lounge chair, watching me. He gives me a half-hearted smile and pats the seat next to him. Damn him. He has such a wonderful heart.

Tears spring again and I blindly make my way to the chair next to him, mindful of where he is in relation to me.

"I didn't mean to…" I wave at the house and then collapse into the chair.

"I know. He barely brushed against you." He stares out at the ocean as if mesmerized by the sound of the rain and the waves. "It wasn't your fault."

"How long have you been out here?" The leather outfit I'm still wearing isn't as comfortable when it's wet, and I wish for a comfortable pair of dry jeans and a button-down shirt instead. The air around me swirls, and Zane's eyes widen.

My kick-ass boots remain, and they look just as good with jeans as the black duster. The sheath for Heaven's blade hangs comfortably on my hip from a stylish belt. And I don't really know why I chose white, especially considering it's raining, but the white button-up shirt seems to fit just right. Thankfully, we are both under the awning. Otherwise, my choice in color would be questionable at best.

"That seems like a handy power," he says, impressed.

"I'd forgo all these powers if I could get rid of this curse." As much as the willing of clothing and other items is fun and handy, I'd give it up in a heartbeat just to hug my family and kiss Zane.

Finding Death
Chapter 12

WHEN THE CHILL HAS my teeth chattering, we head back into the house and this time people give me a wide berth. It is enough to trigger a chuckle or two. Mandy and Jenny hadn't bugged out like I assumed. If I had been in their shoes, I wouldn't have stayed put. I would have been gone in a flash. They sat with the only witch in the group.

Raven Ryan leans over the coffee table, examining each of the items laid out across the wood.

I glance over Kylee's shoulder at the array of spices and crystals. "What are you doing?"

"After that disturbing display, your father was kind enough to explain what happened to you and why Heaven is in such an uproar." Raven glances up and meets my gaze. "And Kylee and I were going through some of these ancient magic tomes that Mandy retrieved for us. I think we may have found just the right spell to rid you of that curse," she says with a smile that only lasted a blink before it fades. "Unfortunately, there is an ingredient that is tricky."

"What's that?"

"The blood of a demon."

I straighten, and my stomach tightens at the thought. What the Hell would they need demon blood for? "How exactly does this spell work?"

"It's an ancient rite from the dawn of time. Or at least that's what I think, from some of the language. Of course, my decryption skills are rusty now that I'm back here, but in Heaven, I could decipher any language. With that said, it's risky. Especially if I translated it wrong. If even one stone is out of place or we miss an ingredient, it could backfire," Raven says, lulling me with her Irish accent.

"How so?" Zane says from a few feet away. Even he is giving me a wide enough berth to make my heart ache.

Raven huffs and glances at the paper with the entire translation written out in plain English, along with the laundry list of items. Most of the ingredients lay on the table, from crystals to pieces of wood and weeds to cinnamon and other spices that I know well enough from our kitchen, along with a handful of essential oils. It looks like a natural healing center instead of Papa's family room.

"It could capture her soul in the bloodstone." Raven meets my gaze.

I inhale and glance at my father, who doesn't seem the least bit fazed by her admission, so I turn to Tom Ryan, Raven's husband, and the one the angels originally sent here to destroy me. "How sure are you in her skills?"

He goes to speak, but Papa raises his hand, silencing him. "She saved Valerie from possession," Papa says. "I would not hesitate to put my life in her hands."

Raven glances over her shoulder and gives him a smile and a nod of thanks.

But it still leaves me itchy and uncomfortable. Sort of the same way Kylee and Michael had made me feel just before he tried to kill me.

"I'm still not sold on this," Zane says. "She is Tom's wife, right?"

"Mhm," Papa confirms.

I am sure he knows where Zane is going with his questioning. After all, Papa can dig into any mind he wants with no effort. But I am glad someone else besides me is having difficulty with this very convenient development. I hadn't even asked anyone for help with trying to find a mystical cure for my problem.

"Wasn't he sent to kill Missy?" Zane crosses his arms and glances at Kylee. "And didn't your husband actually try to kill her?" His sharp glare dances across them and lands on Mandy. "And you're a reaper. Weren't you part of the rebellion that caused all this shit to rain down on us?"

Holly cocks her head as she steps closer, inspecting those who had come up with this marvelous plan to get rid of my curse. "He has a point," she says, giving Zane's line of questioning a more solid ground. "What if the goal is to capture her soul and then destroy her?"

"Oh, child," Raven says softly, scanning the contents of the page. "Capturing her soul in the bloodstone won't doom us all."

Tom steps around in front of Raven, but she won't look at him. He sinks to his knee next to her. The crease between his eyes deepens and his lips turn into a deep frown of disappointment. "Really?" he says. "You're taking Heaven's side?"

She presses her lips together and stares at the ground.

Mandy looks between the two of them and then at me with wide eyes, as if she isn't in on the ruse.

"Do you know what that really means?" he asks.

Raven still avoids his gaze. "That we are all safe?"

Tom slowly shakes his head. "No. If she dies while she holds both roles, the world ends." He snaps his fingers. "Like that."

Raven finally looks up at him. "They said we'd all be safe."

Zane pulls the note that Mandy had given me out of his pocket and throws it on the table. "Does that sound like safe to you?"

Tom doesn't even spare the note a glance, but he does look at me. "I'm not willing to wipe out the world just because Heaven is afraid of a sixteen-year-old girl." He looks back at his wife. "No one here should be willing to do that. Hell, even the reaper looks sick at the thought." He waves at Mandy.

Raven glances at the dust-bound book in front of her and leans back on the couch, meeting my gaze. "They said you would destroy the world," she says to me.

"I don't plan on doing that. That seems to be Heaven's grand scheme."

She shakes her head, unable to grasp what we are telling her.

"Angels are dicks," Tom says. "You know that as well as I do."

I cross my arms and tilt my head. "How did they know I'd bring you back?"

She blinks. "They didn't. I was supposed to slip through in the event Tom failed." She glances at him. "And they promised we'd all be together again when this was over." She looks at the other side of the room where the kids were playing board games. "We were dead."

"And she brought us all back to life." He points at me. "That is God's power, not something made of evil. Heaven could have come and saved us from Lucifer. They could have saved all their blood, but they stayed up in the garden, saying that they couldn't fiddle with Fate. Well, Fate just interceded. And I'm placing my bets on her."

Kylee moves back on the couch, too. Her face is a mask I can't read. She shakes her head. "I thought you were genuine," she finally says in a tone that carries the same disgust I taste in the back of my throat.

She glances around at the people I brought back from the dead. "How many of you were coerced to do the same?" Kylee asks.

"I told them to go pound sand," Papa's father says. "I never trusted those bastards. They smile to your face and then rip you to shreds behind your back."

All of this talk is really grating on my nerves. If this is where people are trying to get to all their lives, it must be a horrible letdown. "I have a question," I say, capturing everyone's attention. "Is Heaven really that bad?" I look at Papa's father because it seems he has the most reservations of anyone in the room, even more so than Tom.

He tilts his head from side to side. "Heaven itself as a place isn't bad. It's quite peaceful, but the angels that run it remind me too much of my sadistic older brother to really buy into it all. They don't like free thought." He shrugs. "That's the best way I can describe them. They want people who kiss their ass and believe they are the perfect creations. They aren't. They are just as flawed as we are, but they are blind to that. And anyone or anything that is stronger than they are, they fear."

"They do things that conflict with what they are supposed to represent," Tom says. "And with all the archangels graceless, it makes it difficult to restore any semblance of order. Even they are pretty much shit on at this point."

I blink at that. Archangels shit on? That just did not compute at all. "It seems they are sending the people closest to Papa, or to Alex and Faith, to do their dirty work, but I'm not sure there is anyone else at their disposal to send, based on all of you." I wave my hand toward the people who I pulled out of Heaven and breathed life into. "They've locked Levi away in Purgatory somewhere, and they are planning on attacking us all in the next twenty-four hours." I scan the room, making eye contact with the thirty or so people, including the kids, who were present. "You know how I came to be this..." I hold up my hands and slowly fist them before I let them drop by my side again. "This cursed thing. So, what would you do if you were me?"

Raven sighs and pulls the book back in front of her.

"What are you doing?" Holly asks.

"Instead of crafting a way to bind her, I need to see if there is anything in this book to free her of her curse." She pushes all the contents of the table into the corner and flips open the book.

"Thank you, but that doesn't address the angels."

"No, but it will give them one less reason to want to destroy you." She meets my gaze and then looks at the space surrounding me the same way Tom had.

Tom leans back on his heels. "You can see her aura?"

She nods and glances at her hands. "I just didn't want to believe what I was seeing."

"It's the reason I immediately discounted Heaven's orders."

"What's wrong with my aura?"

"Not a damn thing," Tom answers. "It's actually the most stunningly pure aura I've ever seen, and that includes CJ's." He points at Papa. "Sorry bro, but hers is brighter and it looks like it's infused with rainbows. There is a total absence of darkness, like I'd expect from being Death." He shrugs. "Not even the angels in Heaven have auras like that. I just wish I had met her before she took those positions to see if it was the same."

"It's always been like that," Faith says from the kitchen table. She smiles at me. "The only time it seemed to dull at all was after her parents visited and she dipped into her separation depression."

I shift my feet and glance over my shoulder at Zane. This conversation isn't helping me. I clear my throat. "That's all well and good, but I need to talk battle strategy while we all still have our wits about us."

"Are you really going to trust them?" Zane asks, scanning the room with a skeptical eye.

"I have no choice. Everyone knows the stakes. And if they cross me, there will be some sort of reckoning that won't make anyone happy."

I glance at Mandy and then Raven, Kylee, and Michael to make my point. I wonder whether I had the ability to test alliances like I had with the reapers. I close my eyes and send the same power I'd used to ferret out traitors in the reaper federation across the house like a bomb plowing over the wicked.

I open my eyes. Jenny, the other reaper, gasps as her fingers turn to dust and the ash gray spreads until all that is left is a human form of ash before it explodes outward and disappears before it covers everything in the room.

"What did you just do?" Mandy asks with her eyebrows riding high on her forehead. The rest of the room mirrors her.

"Sorry, but I had to be sure. I did the same mental sweep of the room that I did in Kittery with the federation," I say, a little rattled that even one being is toasted by my protection sweep. I don't know what I would have done had one of the living people in the room dropped dead, but I needed the comfort of knowing that when I turn my back, I wouldn't find a butcher knife embedded between my shoulder blades.

Finding Death
Chapter 13

FEEDING NEARLY THIRTY PEOPLE seems to be a challenging thought. Challenging enough for Papa to order pizza and wings instead of trying to figure out what they have in the way of food in their pantry. It'll take a while for them to arrive and the newly living use the time to catch up with those around here.

The doorbell rings and all talk halts. There's no way the pizza place made ten pies and delivered them in less than ten minutes.

"Relax. It's April. I thought she might want to see her father." Papa meets Tom's gaze before he leaves the room.

A moment later, April steps into the kitchen. Her normally manicured hair looks like she ran over from their house across town. She is breathing hard too, so maybe she did. When her gaze lands on her father, her hand flies to her mouth. Tears spring from the corner of her eyes and then her gaze shoots around the room until it lands on me.

"You?" she asks.

Although Heaven had originally sent him, I brought him back to life, so I take the credit with a nod.

One minute, she's standing still and the next, she's in a full-out run, closing the distance between her and her father. She jumps the last couple of feet and throws her arms around her father's neck, nearly knocking him back into the wall. Her shaking sobs fill the room. Even though she's seen him in Paradise Cove over the years, I guess having him there in the flesh is different.

My throat tightens because I know just how she feels. Every time I saw my parents, that rush of gratefulness is overwhelming. I glance at my parents watching from across the room with wine glasses in their hands. That warm rush fills my veins and I blink back tears.

It is nice to see the good that I had done by bringing them back to life.

As I scan the room, families form cliques. The elder Ryans and Williamses hang together near the front window. All the Andreas clan stand in their little circle except for Kylee. She is talking with my folks and Phoebe and Smoke on the other side of the kitchen island, almost as if they are all removed from the dynamics of the family reunion going on.

Nana and Papa follow April and stand with their brother and his family, along with Alex and Faith.

That leaves us, my little clan of Zane, Holly, and Mandy, by the sliders to the backyard and the younger kids between the Andreases and the elder Ryans.

The dynamic in the room is odd and, despite the multitude of conversations going on, a stressful undercurrent still thrives in the air.

I know I'm stressed just by the dull ache from having my muscles clenched for so long. Even my jaw hurts. But hunger partly fuels my tension. Despite Nana's continued offerings of food, I hadn't eaten much today. My stomach just doesn't want any part of food. At least I drank enough juice and soda during the day to feel like myself again. Well, all except my arm. That just throbs with an underlying itch. It'll drive me mad if I don't have anything to keep my mind occupied.

My lack of appetite changes the moment the pizza arrives. The scent of Italian spices and tomato sauce makes my mouth water. Zane seems to have the same reaction, too. He licks his lips as the tops are thrown back from the pizza boxes on the island in the kitchen and the counter. Once my plate is piled high with Hawaiian pizza, I find my way back to my seat in the corner, thankful that no one has claimed the chair.

I don't care that it's the second night of pizza. I could eat this every day of the year if given the chance, but Alex and Faith limited our pizza runs to once a month. They wanted us healthy, with a rounded palate. Whatever the Hell that means.

The only thing that would make this the perfect meal would be a tray of Goldenrods fudge. I love good, rich chocolate fudge, and Goldenrods has the best. I wish we had one of the fudge trays they display in their picture windows to entice the public to come into the store. I can almost smell it and damned if that would make this horrific situation flow a little smoother.

The air over the counter shimmers and within a blink, an industrial-size tray of fudge appears.

I let out a soft laugh and meet Zane's gaze. He smiles. It seems like the first genuine smile to grace his lips since he saw me in the school hallway with Levi. It reaches his eyes, making them sparkle.

We reach for the sweets at the same time and both stop. He waves for me to go ahead and I know as a guest in the house, he should go first, but I am craving the decadent dessert. I grab a corner and tear off a piece. It isn't cut, so a fair-size chunk comes off and I grin at his dropped jaw. Although I could devour the enormous piece in my hand, I break the piece in half and put the smaller part back in the pan for him.

He does not hesitate. He scoops up the fudge and nearly shoves the entire piece in his mouth.

I'm not much more civil about it. After all, it is Goldenrods fudge, which is on par with their salt-water taffy. Knowing he is just as crazy for their fudge makes my heart carve another notch on the "do not let go of him" pole, regardless of our hopeless situation.

"I could eat this whole pan," he whispers low enough for only me to hear.

"You'd have to fight me for it."

Thunder cracks outdoors and we both jump. Our gazes swivel toward the glass sliding doors. Darker clouds roll in at an unnatural pace, blocking out the late afternoon sun that had temporarily broken through. It's something you would see in a horror movie. Lightning dances on the water in a deadly march straight toward the bluff where Papa's house sits.

Papa steps to the window and closes his eyes. He dips his head and the surrounding air electrifies.

His power tastes like the sweetest cotton candy, and I swallow my last bite of fudge to drown out just how insignificant I feel next to Papa. His power could split the world in two, and yet Heaven never once tried to kill him because of it. Maybe that's because he's angelic in nature, but his magic could be just as deadly as my touch.

"Don't you already have the property protected?"

"It only goes in a complete circle around the house. The far end of the yard near the rock wall isn't covered. Besides, a little stronger incentive to keep them away never hurts." He smiles down at me and I can't disagree.

A single angel lands just inside the rock wall near where the protection charms on Papa's property end. Papa reaches for the door, but my father stops him.

"I got this. Just don't toast me in the process." He steps outside. He puts his hand out and gives me a curt shake of his head when I slip from my chair to join him, and then he closes the door behind him.

He crosses to the edge of the pool on this side. The angel comes closer but stops after a few steps as his eyes widen and he looks beyond my father, right at Papa. Even I can see the fury building in the intruder just by how red his face gets. His gaze snaps back to my father. My father had to have warned him in some way, but I couldn't be sure.

"What are they saying?" I ask. The rest of the people in the house gather around as well, upping my unease.

"I don't know. I can't read your father's mind and I can't read the angel, but from his stance, he's not happy with whatever your father is saying," Papa said.

Thunder rumbles in response, rattling the windows.

I move back into my corner, careful not to bump into anyone. I reach for another piece of fudge. A hand grabs my wrist and I gasp, snapping my gaze to the one stupid enough to touch me. Gabriel's eyes are wide and I'm sure mine are the same.

Zane goes to grab Gabriel.

"Don't touch him!" I can't help the panic in my voice, but at least Zane heeds my warning.

Light flares around us and I breathe him in. Purity and Old Spice. That's what he smells like and his soul—despite the horrific trials that he suffered and died from—fills me with calmness, followed by a hollowed-out feeling that I'd ruined yet another person with this curse. The brightness that had surrounded him before fades and he looks at the connection of his hand around my wrist.

"I just cut that piece," he says in a deadpan voice.

My eyes follow where I was reaching. A kitchen knife lays next to a neatly cut square. Gabriel lost his soul over a piece of Goldenrods fudge.

How asinine is that?

"Oh." That's all I can muster. "I'm sorry," I add as an afterthought. My heart aches for him and he lets go of my wrist, scoops up the chocolate and wanders away as if nothing happened.

I know better. Everyone in the room staring at me knows better, too.

I turn toward Zane, feeling that welling panic attack coming on.

The slider door opens, and my father steps inside, closing the glass behind him.

"What the Hell just happened?" my father asks.

"I was reaching for a piece of fudge without looking and Gabriel grabbed my wrist."

My father looks beyond me. "Goldenrods?" He points, as if the fudge had made him forget his question.

"Of course. Where else would I conjure a tray from?" I roll my eyes. "But that's beside the point," I add as he crosses and cuts himself a piece, too.

"Well, if you're going to lose your soul over something, this fudge isn't a bad thing to have it happen over." He plops it into his mouth and smiles.

"What happened outside?" Papa asks with a tone as impatient as I feel.

My father doesn't answer right away. He closes his eyes and puts up his finger, announcing silently that he'd be with us in a moment. "You want a piece, hon?" he asks my mother around a mouthful of the confection.

"Dad," I snap. Everyone is focused on him and waiting to hear our Fate since it's no longer written in my handy-dandy Book of Fates.

"I bought us another twenty-four hours before all of Heaven's angels descend and smite us to Hell." He cuts another piece and holds it in his outstretched hand for my mother.

She rolls her eyes and crosses to him, plucking the fudge out of his hand. I can almost hear her "Oh my God, really?" but she doesn't speak. Instead, she nibbles on the fudge. If we had been in any other situation, she would have gobbled it up as fast as either Zane or I had before the angel came.

"Minus the archangels. They did not want any part of this," he adds after he swallows a second piece. "However, after that light show in here, I'm not so sure they'll abide by the terms. I think that angel recognized the transfer of a soul."

"What do you mean, transfer of a soul?" Gabriel asks as he finishes licking his fingers.

"Wait. They are going to kill us?" Jessica Ryan, Papa's mother, asks from the far side of the room.

"That's their current threat. But the fact that angel was afraid of CJ's barrier, I'm not so concerned. Now, if something were to happen to him, well, then we'd have to have another conversation." My father reaches for another piece of fudge.

I slap his hand and shake my head. "I'm sure others will want some of that," I say when he tilts his head like a damn puppy.

The creases on his forehead smoothed out. "Sorry."

"You all need to get some rest if we have a prayer of figuring this out." Papa looks pointedly at me, as if he knows just how exhausting all this is. Although Gabriel's soul had given me a boost of energy, unlike the reaper earlier.

He crosses to me. "I think you should stay in the panic room with your family," Papa says softly. "It has almost every kind of warding and protection known to man."

"What if they come for us while I'm sleeping?"

His lips twitch into a secret grin. "They can't get in. And if they get through the protections we have in place, they'll have to deal with me." He shakes the smile off his face and meets my gaze. "You need sleep." He nods toward the stairwell. "Alex knows the code. The couches pull out and there are already linens down there." He turns to Zane. "See that she actually gets some rest."

Zane nods, but we all know that if I decide to get up and leave, there is no possibility of physically stopping me without someone else losing their soul.

Finding Death
Chapter 14

THE ROOM IS PITCH black. I lie on the pull-out closest to the door. Zane's on the other bed. I am shocked that Alex and Faith let us come in here alone, but they, along with my mother, insisted that I get rest.

"You're still awake," Zane says from the other bed.

"Yes."

"Why?"

I sigh. "Because I can't stop thinking about that binding spell. If my soul was captured in the bloodstone…"

"No. Just no. If you become soulless, you won't have any inclination to save us, and I think you'd be very dangerous without a soul." He sounds annoyed. "Besides, if you won't entertain me losing my soul, why the Hell should I contemplate you losing yours?"

"Didn't anyone ever tell you life isn't fair?"

The springs of his bed squeak, and I hold my breath. But hands scraping against the wall searching for a light switch fills the dark just before all the lights blaze on, blinding me. Zane glares at me.

He crosses to the end of my bed where all that separates us is sheets and a comforter. "That was pretty shitty." He climbs on the end of the bed, crawling with his legs on the outside of mine, the same with his arms.

"What are you doing?" I pull the blankets up to my chin as the weight of him pins me under the sheets. My breathing labors and I will him to stop moving. I will him not to touch me, even though every cell screams for him.

He stops moving, frozen by my wish, and his jaw tightens as his glare pierces through me. "Let me go."

I shake my head slowly. "No."

"How can I love someone and hate them at the same moment?" His green eyes nearly glow with malice and underneath a caring so strong that I nearly falter.

"You hate me?"

He closes his eyes, still stuck mid-crawl. "I'm angry," he finally says. "I want to slam you against a wall and then kiss you into oblivion. If we are going to all die tomorrow, I at least want a damn kiss."

"I can give you fudge," I say softly and try on a smile.

His eyebrows rise as if he's considering the alternative. "As much as I like candy, it's not the same."

"Please go back to your bed," I plead, allowing him to back up if he chooses. But if he uses the sudden release of my mental hold as a sign of weakness and starts forward again, I'll make him go to his own bed. If I think he's mad now, *that* would make him furious.

"Fine," he says after a few minutes of a staring showdown between the two of us. He crawls off the bed and stomps to the light switch, slams it off, and stomps across the room. Flesh connects with metal in a subtle bang, followed by him cursing under his breath, "Goddamn it!"

"You okay?"

"Yeah," he groans. "I didn't need that little toe on my left foot."

"Ouch."

"No kidding. These bedframes are fucking dangerous in the dark."

"Yeah, well, you could have just left the light on, you know."

"You won't sleep if the light is on."

Damn, he actually knows me better than I gave him credit for. I would have totally just stared at the ceiling until someone came and got us out of the room. Still, I might just have that issue in the dark, too.

I don't answer him either. He knows he is right. I don't need to confirm it, and if I denied it, he would know I was lying. Besides, I don't want the awful taste lies leave in my mouth, so I say nothing.

Silence fills the absolute blackness surrounding us. I can't see my hand in front of my face, never mind the ceiling.

"I'm sorry," I whisper.

"For what?" he says, as if I had just pulled him from the edge of sleep.

"For bringing Levi to school."

The quiet stretches out between us as the wedge I just shoved in place pushes us apart.

"So, you'd rather have me dead?" There is a bite to his words.

"No. I..." What can I say to erase his aggravation? "I just wish you had never..." I close my eyes and growl in frustration. Anything I say right now will be wrong, and I certainly don't want to wish us back in time to change things, because that would mean that Zane Bradley died on Thanksgiving. "I wish I could lie in your arms and sleep."

"You can."

"No. I can't without harming you worse than your father ever did. Don't you see? Your soul is everything I love about you. Destroying that destroys you." My voice rasps out of my throat as I try to regain my composure, but I can't get hold of my emotions, so I lay them bare for him to see. "I can't voluntarily give you either the book or the scythe just to see if it will work, knowing you will die either way. I can't kill you. I can't strip you of your soul, and worst of all, I can't touch you."

"I can't let the angels slaughter you. *I* can't watch that."

"How do you know that's how it will end?" Irritation flares up. Hadn't he seen what I was capable of on a small scale at Thanksgiving when I annihilated the reapers who wanted to cause us all harm?

"Because everything good in my life is eventually crushed to dust."

That is a conversation killer, and it wipes the mounting frustration right from my bones. It isn't his lack of faith in my abilities, and that makes me feel better and worse at the same time. The circumstances of his life differ vastly from mine and if I, for a moment, were to put myself in his shoes, I would cling to whatever this insanity is between us, too.

"I'm not going to die."

"Can you guarantee that, or is that just to appease my insecurities?" The growl is back in his voice.

"Why do you think the angels are so afraid of me?" I ask, trying like hell to avoid making a promise I myself am not sure about. I have no intention of dying, but then again, the best laid plans always seem to go awry.

"Changing the subject?"

I let out a soft laugh. "Trying to, yes. I keep coming back to why would the angels want to destroy me. And the only thing I can think of is they are afraid. But I don't know why, and I feel that is the key to all this."

"It's simple. They know you are a force, and a wild card at that. You've done things no one else ever has. At least that's what your father said when we went to the pizza place." He sighs heavily. "You are the unknown."

"Levi once called me an enigma." I curl up on my side, facing the direction he is in. "I miss that monster. At least with him near, I felt like I had a fighting chance."

"I wonder how they caged him. That seems odd."

"Do you think the griffin is as big as Levi in his natural form?" Worry etches its way under my skin. I hadn't given much thought to how they got Levi under control. "And do you think their attempting to smite him actually hurt him?" My chest constricts. "And then the griffin attacked him?"

"Stop." Zane's voice holds authority. "Don't speculate. That will drive you bonkers."

"Bonkers?"

His chuckle warms me. "Better than batshit crazy."

"It is, I guess. Right now, everything seems a little more batshit crazy than it has all year, and that's certainly saying something."

"Agreed. I need some sleep."

"You slept most of the day."

"Being unconscious and sleeping aren't the same and you know it. You're the one with a visible wound. Get some shut-eye. That's an order. Or I'll just come over there and bother you again."

"Fine." Instead of staring at nothing, I close my eyes and start counting my breaths.

Somewhere around the two hundred mark, I drift off in earnest.

341

Finding Death
Chapter 15

BLINDING LIGHT FILLS THE room, and for a moment, I think the angels are attacking. I sit up and raise my hand, squinting.

Holly's giggle breaks through the cobwebs in my head and her red hair forms beyond my hand as she comes closer to the bed.

"What time is it?" I glance over at the fold-out couch next to me where Zane had been. It is no longer out. The couch has been put back together and the sheets and comforter are folded up neatly on one side. I glance at where the bathroom is, expecting the door to be closed, but it's wide open.

"Where's Zane?" I look back at Holly.

"He got up a few hours ago and said to let you rest. But damn, girl. It's almost two in the afternoon."

My heart skips in my chest. I nearly slept the day away. And it could be my last damn day. "Why didn't anyone wake me earlier than this?" I jump out of bed and don't wait for her to answer. Instead, I bolt for the bathroom because I don't want to end up soiling the floor.

Holly follows to the door and waits until I throw it open after doing my business and splashing water on my face. I open the door to her standing near enough to give me a start.

She continues the conversation. "Because you needed the rest, and they used the time to figure out a way to break your curse."

I hurry by her, and then stop and spin around. She's still leaning on the wall. But the grin on her face causes my pulse to pick up. Hope shines down on me. "Did they?"

She nods. "At least they think they did."

My entire form jolts with the news and I don't wait for more information. I bolt upstairs and almost plow over Smoke as I round the corner. Thankfully, I am able to pivot enough to not brush into him. I stop in my tracks at the array of spices, crystals, oils, and patterns pasted to the walls. The house smells like burned rosemary, and smoke still lingers in the air.

"You found a way?" I ask, out of breath, to no one in particular.

"We think so. It's not tested, but I think it will work," Raven says, studying the book on the counter.

A chair sits in the center of a pentagram within a circle they had drawn on the floor. There are more crystals at points along the circumference. Under the chair sits a smooth oblong beach pebble in a shallow grinding bowl.

Distrust blooms and I meet Zane's gaze from across the room. "What do you think?" I need to know his gut feeling about all this. As excited as Holly was downstairs, I can't help but let hope bloom, especially considering she was the first to truly question their intentions beyond Zane.

He lifts one shoulder. "I don't know enough about it to comment, but they seem sincere this time."

I meet Raven's gaze and she doesn't look away, unlike her earlier bid that included demon blood in the equation. "What are the risks?"

"You might get a stomachache from the drink. It's not all that pleasant." She pushes a cup across the counter and hooks her thumb toward the couch. "Your mother tried it to be sure it wouldn't harm you."

My mother waves from the couch and sends a half smile as she feeds some round disks into her mouth.

Raven taps the opened canister of Tums. "You'll probably need a few of these when it's done, too."

I lean over and take a whiff of the concoction. It smells like Papa's bourbon gone bad, mixed with twenty-week-old vegetables that had browned in the vegetable bin. My throat closes and I step back. "What's in it?"

"Kale."

That explains the bad vegetable smell.

"Dandelion greens, peppermint, cayenne pepper, lemon juice, and brandy, mixed with the blood of angels and ancients alike."

No wonder I want to vomit at the smell. I glance at my mother again. "How long ago did she take it?"

Raven glances at the clock on the stove. "A couple of hours ago. She's not as green as she was before."

"How much time is there before the angels come?" I ask my father. My heart has already made the choice for me. I am doing this if my time hasn't already run out.

"You have about five hours. Do you want to try this now or after you kick their asses back to Heaven?" he asks.

The way Zane looks at me is enough to decide. If there is any possibility of granting his wish, I am taking it. "Now." I grimace at the cup and then meet Raven's gaze. "What do I need to do?"

"Drink that and keep it down. And then sit in the chair and we'll do the rest."

I pinch my nose and pick up the cup. Without overthinking it, I tip it into my mouth, swallowing until it is all gone. The nose pinching helped, but I still shiver and gag my way to the chair. I concentrate on one of the sigils taped to the wall, willing my stomach to accept the drink.

My eyes burn from it. So does my throat. My stomach makes a roaring growl as it begrudgingly keeps the liquid in check.

I don't dare look away from that drawing because if I do, I will hurl. Zane steps in front of the picture and for a moment I think I'm going to lose it all over the floor, but the hope in his green eyes gives me the courage to swallow the vileness in my throat and keep that drink down.

"Breathe," he whispers and then others join him, clasping hands as they line the outer edges of the circle drawn on the floor.

From behind me, Raven chants words in a language I've never heard. The rest join in, including Zane. I watch in fascination as the words form tendrils of smoke, each one drifting toward me. The more times they chant, the more tendrils join the fray inside my circle.

I still keep Zane's gaze, ignoring the gathering smoke. Until miniature lightning bolts rain down around me. His eyes widen, but he keeps on saying the incantation, increasing the smoke and the clouds building above me.

I grip the arms of the chair. My heart races in my chest, making me forget about my sour stomach. I jump with every strike of light and so does Zane.

They all keep going, as if the energy being created in the circle is also fueling them. It is strange and scary and exhilarating. Rumbling starts above me. Then a blinding light encompasses me. I think I yelp, but I can't be sure.

All I know at this moment is absolute weightlessness, and then I crash down in the chair with enough force to rattle my teeth.

Zane looks a little pale, and he's pressed to the wall. I glance around at the rest of the group. Holly's hair looks as if she's been standing near the rock wall in the backyard during a nor'easter windstorm. My mother stands next to Holly with the same windblown features, but at least she doesn't look green anymore. My father stands on the other side of Zane with a grin, like whatever happened entertained him.

Alex, Faith, Nana, and Papa, although windblown, didn't look as rattled as Zane and Holly looked. Behind me, Raven, Tom, and Papa's parents fill in the circle.

"What happened?"

Zane remains speechless.

"Did it work?" I ask when no one speaks.

"There's only one way to find out," my father says. "Who wants to be the guinea pig?"

Zane went to move.

"No." I point at him. "You just stay right there." I turn around and look at Raven. "Since this was your thing..."

She pales and glances at Tom.

"Oh, for Heaven's sake." Kylee pushes through, breaking the neat little circle surrounding me, and grabs my wrist.

Light flares around us and her soul yanks from her body so fast, I don't even feel the transition. One minute, it was just me, and the next, Kylee's essence surrounds me before absorbing like the fading froth in a cooling bubble bath.

She stares at me and blinks. Her eyes widen for a moment and she lets out a soft laugh. "I wasn't Heaven bound, anyway." She winks at me.

"She's not wrong, you know," my father says.

"Did she just..." Michael points as Kylee heads back in his direction.

"No one was moving, so I took on the role of test subject. I really have nothing to lose. Well, I could have died if she didn't have that save-the-people-here spell going on all of us."

"But your soul?" Michael says.

"I'm not going to Heaven, Michael."

He glances at his father. "But he was a vampire for centuries and was still in Heaven."

"I'm not like your father. He is the archangel Gabriel's son, and before that he was human. I'm not."

His eyebrows arch as if this just doesn't compute.

"I'm not immortal anymore, but I wouldn't say I'm human."

"Technically, I think you became human once your siren was removed," my mother says. "But I don't think you could end up within the pearly gates."

"See? So just accept that I'll be a little less subtle and we'll continue raising our kids and hunting things like we normally do for as long as we are here. Of course, that could end this evening, but let's cross our fingers that Missy doesn't get snuffed out by those winged bastards." She smiles.

Disappointment flows in like the tide. Sneaky thing, too. One minute, I am fine and the next, my stomach decides that the crap I drank needs to be forcefully evicted. I make it to the kitchen sink without vomiting on anyone or touching them before the liquid escapes my tightly clamped lips.

I turn on the water as I heave, trying to clean the vile splatter from the spotless stainless steel. Someone pulls my hair away and rubs my back softly. When I finally spit out the last of the gross stuff, I take a mouthful of water from the faucet, swish it around my mouth, spit and then look at who was helping me.

Kylee gives me a soft smile. "It's the least I can do, considering I had been part of a plot to kill you and fulfill Heaven's asinine plans." She hands me a paper towel.

I wipe my mouth and shut off the water. "Sorry," I whisper, unsure of what I am apologizing for. She took the chance by stepping in and touching me when she wasn't sure whether it would strip her soul.

As far as my sins are concerned, my list is growing, and I don't even know where to start to atone.

Finding Death
Chapter 16

I TAKE A SEAT in the corner near Papa's sound studio entrance and stare out at the ocean. The world has just a few hours left before its possible demise and my entire mood sours with the thought. I can't seem to figure out my next move, except to fight.

The group has exhausted the options left to us. We even discuss trying that first spell to trap my soul in the bloodstone. But Zane won't have that. To be honest, no one is really for that, considering the price for failing.

"What if Missy were to give up both roles to two others?"

"I'm not killing anyone in this room to save myself," I snap and glare at him. "I'm not planning on losing, so you all can stop this little exercise in futility."

"I've already told you I can take on one of the roles." Zane crosses his arms. "Wouldn't that call off this insane battle?"

"You will stop breathing. What the Hell do I have to do to get that into your thick skull? Besides, we all saw the failed attempt to give the role back to my dad." I wave at my father. "I'm not trying something on you or anyone in this room, only to have you die and still be in this situation."

"She has a point," my father mutters, staring out at the ocean.

"He doesn't have a soul. Don't you think that might have something to do with why it failed?"

"I'm not betting your life on something so thin." Truth be told, that is the reason I initially thought the scythe wouldn't bond with him like it had with me, but I am not about to admit that to Zane. Not when so much is at stake.

"Everyone's life is already on the line."

An alarm buzzes and my father looks at his watch and then at me as those weird thunder clouds form again. But this time, they are gathering faster and more violently than before. Instead of retreating, I open the door.

"Make sure no one comes out," I say to my father and then close the door behind me. I cross far enough away to keep those in the house safe and stand on the lawn, using the pool as a buffer. If I can use that mass of water to my advantage, I will.

I close my eyes and wish for the leather battle gear I wore for the reaper standoff instead of the jeans and button-up I still have on.

The wind swirls around me as my outfit morphs into what I want. My scythe and Book of Fates also grow to their normal size, as I will them. I face the ocean, waiting.

A throat clears behind me, and I turn to Zane standing within a few steps from me. I glance at the door and my father is sitting on the ground, rubbing his jaw with the door still open.

"Did you hit my father?" I swing my sharp gaze to Zane's.

Zane glares at me as I hold both the Book of Fates and Death's scythe, waiting for Heaven's promised onslaught. I'm sure I look like a deity. At least, that is what I am trying to project. And he knows I am prepared to battle all of Heaven to keep my station and not put anyone I care about in harm's way.

He knows I don't want anyone saddled with the burden of forever, either.

Yet he still has his hand out, expecting me to concede. He is in. He is willing to sacrifice his entire future to keep me safe. He is too much like me in that respect. But for him, it is only about keeping me safe. For me, it's my entire family. Hell, the entire world—because the last time Heaven's wrath took out the single entity, the big bang happened.

If they kill me, who knows what will happen. It could be such a cosmic blowout that all of Earth is doomed.

Zane has no powers. He has no hope of commanding armies. Zane's lips thin as he glances behind me, shifting my attention. I turn to look over my shoulder and the scythe is yanked from my grip.

My gasp fills my world, and everything turns into slow motion as I pivot back to Zane, meeting his wide, terrified gaze.

Zane has the scythe in a two-fisted grip, owning it. He took it from me with the same intent I had taken it from my father on the day after Thanksgiving. He wants the job. Breathing be damned.

A ding sounds from my Book of Fates.

I can't look at it.

I can't breathe.

I can't take it back from him. If I inadvertently touch him, I'll siphon his soul. Making this all so much worse.

"Why did you do that?" I scream over the roar of the cyclone that overtakes us.

He sends a shaky smile and shrugs. "The world is better with you in it."

Oh, how I want to rip it from his grasp, but deep down I know, either way, Zane is dead. My book says so, and this time, I have no control over the outcome. I lower the electronic pad, which has his name blaring on the screen like a silent siren of doom, and wish the book into a charm before I drop it. The book shrinks and attaches to my charm bracelet like it always does at my command.

No sooner have I taken care of the Book of Fates than the essence of Death peels from every cell, dropping me to my knees in sheer agony.

Being drawn and quartered would have been less painful, but I remain lucid as every stabbing pain wracks my body. Death's essence intertwines around Zane—looping, testing, surrounding him—before it gathers between us, still pulling the last tentacles from within me. Then it shoots into Zane's chest in a mass of blinding light.

Zane bows backward with the force of it. His arms flail to his sides as his body lifts from the ground. He looks like Christ on the cross with his arms wide out and his head tilted back. A silent scream of anguish frames his face. I have no idea how he holds onto the scythe, especially with his eyes rolled back in his head so far, but he grips the rod with the whitest knuckles I have ever seen, almost as if he knows how important it is to keep a grip on that magical rod.

After the last of Death's essence rips from my cells, small orbs free from me. One circles around me as if it recognizes me, and then shoots out of the vortex encircling us. I have no idea what they are, but the release of that light makes me feel freer than I have felt since my parents showed up at Alex's house a little over a week ago, like I finally woke from a horrible nightmare.

Zane lowers to the ground with the scythe still in his grip and then his arm falls across his body, pinning the weapon to his chest, and the light surrounding us fades. The house comes into view and I scan the yard behind me.

I now know why Zane had taken the scythe from me. My eyes widen at the legion of angels just outside the marred crop-like circle that

Zane and I are in, frozen as if the events of the past couple of minutes had them unsure of their task of ridding the Earth of a duel-deity.

I pray Zane's death won't leave me in their crosshairs. If it does, this isn't about holding both roles in perpetual fortitude. This is just a power play. If that's the case, I am more than willing to yank every soul from them and destroy it with fiery wrath.

Their eyes fall to Zane. My Zane, whose chest doesn't move with the cadence of life. His stillness and ashen complexion announce his death as loud as my Book of Fates had.

I want to crawl to him, to touch him, to breathe air back in his lungs, but he remains still, with that damned scythe laying across his chest.

Zane sacrificed his life for me.

Tears blur my vision, and I close the distance, but resist reaching out. I cover my face, ignoring the whoosh of the sliding glass doors. It isn't until a hand touches my shoulder that I look up into my father's eyes. He crouches next to me and wipes a stray tear off my cheek.

"I need to go," he says softly and gives me a sad smile.

"Why?" I blink, not understanding why he'd abandon me when I need him the most.

"It's part of the deal. You should know that better than anyone." He glances at Zane to make his point.

But I don't know. He hadn't died when I took the role, so why now?

If he had known, I would bet my life that Zane never would have done this. He would have never sacrificed himself knowing someone else would die instead, especially my father—because without a soul, this was the end for him.

He will turn to ashes the moment his life is snuffed out.

My chest squeezes. "Don't go, Daddy," I sob. "Please," I whisper. I can't have both of them out of reach, one permanently, the other figuratively. "You don't have a soul. If you go with them, you'll cease to exist, just like that reaper."

He takes my hands between his and squeezes gently. "Have a little faith. Besides, I need to teach Zane a few things before he comes back." My father hooks his thumb toward my dead boyfriend. "Things you safeguarded us from. Otherwise, he will be more of a menace to the living than you can imagine. Your touch may strip souls, but his will kill."

My heart lurches in my chest. "But..." I glance at Zane.

"His touch kills the living, and that includes you, Melissa." He slowly stands. "So, let me go train him in Purgatory and try to release our old friend while I'm at it. Just don't move him, okay? You can throw a blanket over him if that makes you feel better, but do not let anyone touch him."

I nod. I don't want Zane gone into the reaper realm forever. I need him for so many reasons. He promised to help me sort out this abysmal touch curse, to make it disappear.

"I love you, Missy. Promise me you won't do anything stupid, no matter what happens," my father says.

I nod, thinking he's talking about Zane. "I promise." Tears spill, creating hot paths down my cheeks.

He smiles and then he turns and heads toward the angel horde in a gait that's more arrogant than humbled. When he spreads his arms wide, it's not in a manner of surrender; it is pure mockery.

"No!" A muffled voice comes from inside the house, yanking my attention that way. My mother struggles to break free of Alex's grasp. She looks like a wild woman trying to scratch her way out as she screams.

When I look back, I catch the sharp edge of a golden sword sticking out of my father's back. Now I know why my mother is going ape shit. I climb to my feet as well, bellowing the same "No!" as my mother.

I want to rush them, slaughter them for killing my father. The only thing that keeps me in place besides the angels' warning glares is my father's last words. If I attack, he'd perceive that as a stupid move, and I promised him I wouldn't do anything stupid.

Without the power of Death in my veins alongside Fate's energy, I cannot win a war waged with the angels. But that doesn't stop the devastation from filling me. How is my father supposed to train Zane when he's dead?

The blade disappears, pulled from his limp body, and I expect him to turn to ash like the reaper. But he doesn't. He just crumples to the ground. My mind snaps to the orbs circling us when Death's essence transitioned into Zane.

Could that have released the souls trapped inside me? And following on the heels of that thought: *Does this mean I'm no longer cursed?*

My mother collapses inside the house. She sobs his name over and over, and my heart breaks for her. The angels gather my father up, and in a whirlwind of smoke and light, they all disappear, but not before one of them points at me as if they aren't done with me yet.

A part of me wants to throw myself over Zane's body. If I die, so be it. At least I won't have to see the horrified sorrow on my mother's face every day of her life. But that's another stupid move, and neither my father nor Zane would be happy with me. Zane probably would be more pissed than he already was.

I need something to cling to now that the only human being I really care to hug is gone, and I have no idea if he'll make it back to me or not. So, I resolve to fix this damn curse, so when he comes back to me, I can kiss him into oblivion.

Besides, although Zane's actions seemed to defuse the angels' wrath, I don't know if any of us are truly safe from Heaven's retribution.

The End

Continue reading the next installment of THE DEATH CHRONICLES II on the next page with REAP THE DEAD.

Reap the Dead
Chapter 1

W*HAT THE HELL HAVE I done?*
I stare at the staff of the scythe securely clasped in my hand and then move my gaze to hers. Melissa Ramsay's wide violet eyes stare back at me with the same horror filling my soul. My heart hurts, and it's not an emotional reaction. The pain shooting down my right arm scares me just as much as the fear in Missy's eyes.

She warned me. She said I would die. Damn it all, I thought she'd be able to keep me alive like she did her parents and everyone she brought back from the dead.

At least the angels behind her have stopped their advance and seem more uncertain now. Missy didn't see them arrive, but I did. They came to annihilate Missy because she harbored both Fate and Death in her beautiful body, and Heaven just couldn't abide with one person holding all that power. That's what made me grab Death's scythe. There were simply too many of them armed with vicious-looking swords for one girl to take on, even if she *is* a true badass.

Unfortunately, if the angels have their way, there will be no future for anyone. Slaughtering Missy while she holds both roles of Death and Fate ends the world. Although I'd like everyone to believe I am sacrificing myself for the world, it's a lot more selfish than that.

I'm in love with Missy, and have been since I first saw her when we were seven or eight years old. I want her alive. I want a future with her. As odd as it seems, taking on Death is the only way I can guarantee that. That is, if Heaven isn't gunning for her just because she is unique.

Even with my motives driving me, dying sucks. My muscles clench against the pummeling discomfort. But no matter how bad this gets, I cannot let go of this damn stick. If I do, my forever with Missy is doomed.

A wind vortex circles around us, and it's like being in the center of a tornado. The mixture of salt air and the smell of rain fills the space, along with the distinct sickly smell of Death that clings to every cell of mine.

"Why did you do that?" she screams over the roar of the cyclone overtaking us.

"The world is better with you in it." I want to kick myself for how fucking corny that sounds, but it is all that comes to mind. Because declaring that I'm in love with her at this precise moment would be in poor form. My existence is better with her in it, but I don't know what the Hell my world is going to look like when this is over.

Tears fill her eyes and the book in Missy's other hand shrinks into a charm on her bracelet. Right now, I kind of wish I had the power to put this scythe on a necklace chain like she could do with a thought because it's damn heavy. I don't know how a petite girl could wield this mother effectively, but she didn't seem to have any issues with it at all. As far as the ability to shrink her Book of Fates, that's one of her new magical enhancements. She can conjure and change the physical properties of things. It's pretty boss if you ask me, but she'd give that power up just to be able to hug again. You see, when Missy took over for her parents, she inherited a nasty curse. She cannot touch anyone. If she does, she siphons their soul.

The wind whips around us, and she falls to her knees. Her face morphs from sad to a wince, like she is in exquisite pain. Her mouth opens and a scream barrels out, but I can hardly hear it above the wind and the rush of my pulse clinging to my body. Her agony ripples across her features as black smoke peels from her skin.

I want to wrap my arms around her and hold her tight, but I can't, not if I want my soul intact. And I have a feeling if I try to console her, the angels will see the soul transfer and kill us both on the spot. And I will never see her again.

My chest constricts. The force almost makes me let go of the scythe so I can try to keep my heart from flying through my rib cage in a bloody mess.

Dying doesn't compare to the anguish of seeing Missy suffering. I didn't think my taking the scythe would cause her any pain. I was as wrong about that as living through this ordeal.

The last of the black smoke exits her, and she sags on her hands and knees. Five orbs, three made of pure white light and two made of murky darkness, dislodge from her and float around us before beelining it out of the center of the wind tunnel we are in.

The smoke gathers, curling around me like a deadly caress. Each time it touches me, it feels like the stab of a knife, but it doesn't leave a mark. As it gathers in front of me, swirling at a frenetic pace, my labored heart pumps harder, as if it knows that blackness is the end of everything.

Then it slams into me, and I do scream the way Missy had. Every inch of my body feels like some invisible being is flaying me over and over and over until all that is left is a bloody pulp. My arms fly wide and I'm weightless and yet bound in agony. It reminds me of some creepy cross-like symbol.

But through it all, I still grip that damn scythe, even as my life bleeds out of my damaged heart.

And then darkness yanks me under, suffocating me, and I cannot draw a single breath.

Reap the Dead
Chapter 2

SOMETHING NUDGES MY SHOULDER, and the contact jars me awake. For a moment, I think I'm in the same panic room that Missy and I slept in last night. Her Papa had insisted she get sleep and the safest place in their house was that room. But it had no windows, so the blackness was just as complete as what is surrounding us now. I can't even see my hand in front of me. But then my fingers scrape on the cold, rough stone underneath me.

"Where the Hell am I?" I ask, not expecting an answer.

"The Other," a scratchy voice says from somewhere in this dark stone cavern.

I run both my palms over the rocks and the jolt in my chest has panic flushing me. The scythe is no longer in my hand. I need to find it. I roll onto my hands and knees, and start searching with my hands in frantic circles that widen with each pass. My breath wheezes as my throat closes. If I don't have it, that means I am not Death, and I died for nothing.

"It's not here," a raspy voice tears through the black, closer than it was before.

I think I recognize the voice and that shakes me even harder. "Mr. Ramsay?" *He was alive at the house. I punched him to get to Missy. What the Hell? Did they kill us all, anyway?* "How are you here?"

"It's part of the deal. When the torch is passed, the former Death dies," he says, but he sounds like he has marbles in his mouth. "But the angels interceded and here we both are."

Sadness envelops me. If I had known Missy's father would die, I would have thought twice about taking the staff from her. She must be doubly pissed at me for all this. "Where is here?"

"The Other. It's not Purgatory. It's not the reaper realm, certainly not Heaven, but I have entertained that it may very well be Hell, except the fuckers can't get in there, either."

"Why is it so dark?"

His sigh nearly fills the void we are in. "It's not dark. It's just... Other."

His explanation makes zero sense. "Did I just irreversibly screw things up?"

He doesn't answer right away, and then I catch a grunt and the sound of flesh pounding flesh. A sound I am intimately familiar with. And it layers a chill through me to the point my teeth chatter.

A chuckle emits from the blackness, and I'm no longer sure Missy's father is here with me. Or if he is, we aren't alone. My stomach drops.

I blink to adjust my vision, but it's useless.

Something solid connects with my chin and my head snaps to the side with the force of the impact. I roll onto my side, covering my head with my arms. This is my immediate instinct whenever the beatings begin: roll up in a ball and protect my head. I never fight back. Not with my mother's warnings echoing in my head. She always told me he would back off before doing too much damage, and while she was alive, that was the case.

But the moment she died, his temperament went south, and my broken bones became routine.

"Little bastard," another familiar voice growls. When a steel-toed boot connects with my stomach, knocking what little air I have left in my lungs out, I know why the voice sounded familiar. This must be Hell because I'm trapped with my father.

Another kick connects, this time on the back of my head, and my vision blooms into white lights. I'm living Thanksgiving morning all over again, and this time, there's no Dr. Ryan to magically heal me after.

"Leave him alone," Mr. Ramsay says in a weak, sluggish voice, as if he's just coming to.

"I'll stop when he's finally dead!"

Another kick lands and the crack of ribs echoes, followed by the same debilitating pain on my right side that almost killed me on Thanksgiving.

I need to escape.

I concentrate on the shuffle of feet and lower my arms, preparing myself for another blow. I'm not disappointed. The heavy boot smashes into my arm. I move faster than I think possible and grab my old man's leg, yanking him off-balance. When he teeters over, I climb on shaking legs and turn, moving away from his muttering curses as fast as my injuries allow.

Except I can't see. I don't know where I am, or what else is in this dark cavern with me. My flight reflex is screaming, along with every bone in my upper body.

Damn it, I need light.

Brightness flares all around me, and I freeze in my tracks, squinting at the sudden bloom of light that is just as blinding as the darkness.

Missy's father sits in chains, squinting against the light just like I am. The chains anchor both his wrists and ankles into the stone so he can't lift his arms to block the light. He also has very little room to defend himself either. His face is what I imagine mine looks like. Bloody and battered.

My head snaps back. My scalp screams in protest as a fistful of my hair is yanked. My growing rage bursts into a furious rush in my veins, sending a jolt of adrenaline through me, and I spin, throwing my first punch at my father. He looks just as deranged as he did when he attacked me at the house. His hair stuck up in random tufts, and his dark eyes carried the same hatred I've always seen. I roar as my fist lands in the center of his chest with a satisfying crunch.

My father stumbles back and looks down at his chest. The point where my fist connected blackens, as if my touch killed his skin cells, and he charges at me with fury blazing in his eyes.

I sidestep enough so he misses a direct hit, but the force of his shoulder into my side knocks me off-balance and I slam into the wall, wincing. The pain knocks my energy down a couple of notches. The light seems to fade as well.

My father comes at me again, and I have no room to maneuver. My chest takes the crushing blow as he slams into me, intending to break every bone in my torso.

He steps back and throws his favorite right hook. The one that makes me see stars. And this time is no different.

Time slows as I fall. I catch Missy's father's horrified gaze, and then my head bounces on the floor and everything drops into the black again.

Reap the Dead
Chapter 3

FLESH POUNDS AGAINST FLESH in violent succession, and grunts of pain fill the dark. I have no idea how long I've been out, but it sounds like it was long enough for my father to get sick of kicking my unconscious body.

"Stop," I whisper through cracked lips. The motion sends threads of agony from my jaw and cheek through to the crown of my head. White spots fill my vision and I think a few of my teeth are missing.

Ethereal light fills the cavern, and I squint against the brightness. A winged being crouches next to me. "Will you reap the dead?"

I blink at him like he's on drugs. "Isn't that my job?"

The angel pinches his nose and shakes his head. "Those stolen from our grip and those who are not supposed to still be alive."

I glance toward Missy's father to see another punch connect and blood spurt from between his already swollen lips. Yet he still shakes his head at me. I know he doesn't want me to abide by Heaven's command. Frankly, neither do I, but I am on the edge of passing out and I need a reprieve from my father's punches.

I look the angel directly in the eye. "Who?" Just the whisper of the word stings my swollen lips.

"You need to start with that little harlot Fate and then bring the rest of the ones she stole from our grip back home."

Wrong answer. It's so wrong that I laugh at him, even with my shattered chest. The Heavenly host must be daft if they think I'm going to harm that woman. "Reap Missy? Over my dead body."

He reaches out and touches my forehead.

SOMETHING NUDGES MY SHOULDER, and the contact jars me awake. I roll onto my hands and knees, confused as to where I am. A sense of déjà vu grips me, and I feel the stone under my palms. The blackness is so complete that I can't even see anything. It's as if I've been struck blind.

"Where the hell am I?" I ask, not expecting an answer.

"The Other," a voice full of pain answers from somewhere to my right.

I splay my hands on the stone and it dawns on me what I'm missing. Heat envelops me as panic flushes my skin. I'm not holding the scythe. *Shit. Does that mean it all went to hell?* I lean back on my knees and rub my face. I had it when the smoke hit me. I had it as my last mortal breath was ripped from my chest.

"What the Hell happened?"

"The fucking angels happened."

Those four words chill the heat right out of me, leaving me shaking in this black cave. He warned me that if I did anything stupid, the angels could gain the upper hand. He said Tom had been right. They were dicks. But I didn't think the upper hand would mean him locked God knows where with me. Besides, he was alive when I died. "Mr. Ramsay? How are you here?"

A heavy sigh sounds. "We've been through this a dozen times."

What the Hell is he talking about?

Before I can voice my question, I'm knocked onto my back by a mean punch. "I guess I deserved that." I rub my cheek.

"That wasn't—"

The sound of a fist hitting bone and then the distinct sound of a body falling echoed in the space. Along with the rattle of chains. The echoes in this space make it confusing as to where the sounds are coming from.

"Mr. Ramsay?"

"He's a little tied up right now."

Now that was a voice I'd never forget. My muscles seize as I climb to my feet. My limbs are shaking, and I turn slowly, trying to get a bead on where my father is in the dark. There is no sound, but I know in my heart where this ends. It ends with me no longer breathing.

My father wants to beat me to death. Just like he tried to do on Thanksgiving.

"Little bastard," he growls from behind me.

I spin around, right into his fist. I stumble, but I'll be damned if I go down. Because that is the end of me. His steel-toed boots are made to break bones.

Maybe this isn't the Other. Maybe it truly is Hell, because I can't think of anything more horrific than to be stuck in a room with my father for eternity.

I'm tackled full-on and knocked into a wall. My head bangs hard enough for my vision to bloom into white lights. Before I can shake it, my father punches me as if I'm a human punching bag and he's a prizefighter in training.

Each punch knocks the air from my lungs and one out of every three hits cracks something, whether it's my arm from trying to block, or my ribs. The mother fucker is stronger here than he's ever been at home.

He sends an upper cut into my chin. Between that and his mean right hook, I'm falling. The rocks jolt my broken torso as I land. This is it. Now his boot connects with my stomach and I groan. I'm not quick enough to cover my head and his steel tip smashes my cheek.

I'm living Thanksgiving morning all over again, and this time, there's no Dr. Ryan to magically heal me.

"Leave him alone," Mr. Ramsay says in a weak, sluggish voice, as if he's just coming to.

"I'll stop when he's finally dead!" Another kick lands and the crack of ribs echoes.

I need the bliss of unconsciousness. I'm beyond the point of Death—no mortal could withstand this type of beating—but the blackout doesn't come, just more pain with each sadistic kick.

"Leave him the fuck alone," Missy's father bellows, loud enough for my ears to ring.

Feet shuffle away in the darkness and my battered brain is glad until the sound of another beatdown echoes near enough for me to cringe.

Grunts of pain fill the dark, but at least it's not me who's getting beaten. And then the memory of who else is in the room with me flashes in my mind. Missy's father is in here, too, and I think he might be chained.

"Stop," I whisper through cracked lips, and the word sounds more like a lisp. I run my tongue over my teeth, alarmed by some of the gaps that hadn't existed before. The motion sends threads of agony from my jaw and cheek through to the crown of my head.

Ethereal light fills the cavern, and I squint against the brightness. A winged being crouches next to me. "Will you reap the dead?"

I blink at him like he's on drugs. "Isn't that my job?"

The angel pinches his nose and shakes his head. "You must reap those seized from our grasp and those who are not supposed to still exist."

Missy's father shakes his head and then my father slams his boot into the side of Mr. Ramsay's face. The kid falls over, unconscious. The same type of pure knockout that I've wished for over the last few hours. I'm a bit envious.

I look the angel directly in the eye. "Who?" Just the whisper of the word stings.

"You need to start with that little harlot Fate and then bring the rest of the ones she stole from our grip back home."

I tilt my lips into a smile. "Fuck you."

He reaches out and touches my forehead.

SOMETHING NUDGES MY SHOULDER, and the contact jars me awake. My skin flushes hot as I roll onto my hands and knees on the rocky and uneven ground. Echoes of pain reverberate in my head. I blink to let my eyes adjust.

I have a sinking feeling I have been here before and something awful is approaching in the dark. Panic transforms my mind into a sharp instrument just waiting for the gauntlet to fall.

"Damn it. Remember," a raspy whisper comes from near me.

Remember what?

My reflexes scream to ignore the voice, and I roll. A breeze licks my face as I climb to my feet, blind to what surrounds me. But I'm on guard now and listening for anything over my quick breaths.

Alarms sound in my head and I suddenly lean back, and that same wind blows against my face. But this time it's followed by a human growl.

My body reacts. I send a punch out with everything I have behind the force, and it connects with a body. Whoever I just slammed my fist into goes flying and the crash of flesh against something solid makes my lips twitch into a smile.

I wait in the dark for their intention to be announced by their next action.

"Little bastard," the growling voice says from the direction where my punch was aimed.

My blood runs cold.

This must be Hell, because I will never forget that voice. It tormented me day after day, right before fists knocked me out. That voice belongs to my father.

And I'm stuck in a pitch-black room with him, and he sounds as if he is on quite a bender from the fury in his tone. My stomach sinks. But I'm more on guard than before because I know his intentions. He wants me dead.

A second rasping voice comes from behind me.

"Zane," the voice says through labored breath.

Who the fuck is Zane?

I think I recognize that voice, but I'm not sure. Besides, right now, I'm more concerned about where my father is in the room. My heart pounds as I close my eyes and concentrate. The scrape of something over the rocks behind me sends a chill down my spine.

I turn toward the scrape. It is in the same direction as that second voice. It isn't dark on this side of the cavern and my eyes widen. My father has a knife to a kid's throat, and the kid looks like he's seen better days. It's as if my father has been beating him for years. I can relate. It's what he did to me for as long as I can remember.

But the only memories I have are of my father beating me. My mother is a hazy memory, but one I don't wish to lose. Still, a nagging feeling inside me tells me I should know this kid. I just can't retrieve the memory.

"Don't." I slowly shake my head.

My father smiles, but then the room gets squint-worthy bright and my father's evil chuckle ceases. It's as if he has been frozen, although a small bead of blood drips down the kid's throat. His breath still comes in thready bursts, as if he is afraid to move.

An angel appears and crosses to stand before me. "Will you reap the dead?" he asks.

I raise an eyebrow and glance at the kid. He shakes his head, even with my father's knife cutting into his throat. But I'm not sure why he's telling me to say no. Instead, I shrug and refocus on the angel. "Who do you want me to reap?"

"That little hussy Fate and everyone she ever brought back from the dead."

The walking dead. That doesn't sound like it would be too hard, except I don't know exactly what this angel is asking me to do. "How?"

The angel smiles, and the kid closes his eyes like he just lost his last hope.

"Strike them down with your scythe and you will never have to return here to the Other," the angel says.

My gaze moves to the sadistic smile frozen on my father's face, and I nod. I can do that.

"If you falter, he will burn in angel fire for the rest of eternity." The angel points at the boy.

An instinct to protect the beaten kid in chains flares inside me. I don't understand it, but I can't seem to ignore it. "I won't, just as long as he burns." I point to my father. I want that bastard to suffer. Something deep inside me breaks, as if the last frayed thread of hope just shattered.

The angel snaps his fingers, and my father is engulfed in white flame. At first, he doesn't make a sound. And then a scream of anguish echoes on the walls, and it satisfies a deep-seated hatred in my soul.

I trade a glance with the kid. Tears track down his cheeks and he just shakes his head. The disappointment written in his features tightens my throat and makes me want to take back my agreement.

Then the angel says, "Remember your task." And he taps my forehead.

Reap the Dead
Chapter 4

MY EYES OPEN TO the black, but this time something heavy lays across my chest and I am holding a round rod in my right hand. It is quiet, and I reach my left hand out and soft fabric caresses my palm. I am not on the rocks in that cave anymore.

What's more concerning is I have no idea where the Hell I am.

When I sit up, a creak sounds from beneath me and a covering slides off my body. I remember the feel of a bed well enough and I wonder yet again where I am, although a part of me does not care at all. I'm just thankful that I am no longer in that godforsaken cavern.

I climb to my feet and walk forward as if a shadow of a memory is guiding me, although the darkness hasn't been my friend and seems to hide deadly enemies. So I hold my breath with each step, waiting for a strike from any direction. When my hand brushes a light switch, I push it up and the room lights up.

Relief sweeps through me. No one else is in the room. But I know damn well that could change at the angel's will. I run my unsteady hand through my hair and take stock of the room. There are two entries, but neither of them operates with a handle. The number pad on the wall signifies the door requires a code to open.

That kind of blows. Instead of dwelling on the inability to exit my accommodations, I focus on the room itself. The bed I woke on seems to be laden with dust, as if no one but me has been in this room for ages. Except the pile of clean clothes on the couch and the surfaces of everything else look like someone was maintaining the space. It's all very disconcerting.

I glance at the staff I'm holding and look up. The blade glistens in the light, and I raise an eyebrow at the badass scythe in my hand. This mother would have been handy to have in the Other. With one swipe, I could decimate my father and be free of that horror.

It's something I can imagine Death carrying, if Death were truly a being.

A chill skitters down my back as if someone just crossed over my grave. I shake it off and look more closely at my clothing. It's stiff and uncomfortable, as if it had dried on my body. What I can see of my bare arms looks grimy, like I had been playing in a dirt mound before I fell asleep in the bed.

I stare at a small sigil on my wrist. I don't ever remember getting a tattoo, but a little circle with dots around it like the four points on a compass intrigues me. I try to wipe the dirt away to get a closer look, but all I seem to do is move the dirt in circles.

A door midway down the length of the room catches my attention, especially because it has a doorknob. I certainly hope it's a washroom and I can get this dirt off my arms. Crossing, I swing the door open and engage the lights. A smile spreads across my lips at the full bathroom until my gaze lands on a mirror across from the door. I blink at the reflection and turn, glancing over my shoulder to make sure someone else wasn't in the room with me.

A man stares back at me instead of the teenage face I remember. The forehead knits together as I study the reflection, stepping closer to inspect myself. The same green eyes I've always seen look back at me. When I run my palm across the scruff on my face, it's like rubbing sandpaper.

I'm grimy enough to consider the shower instead of just washing up in the sink. Pulling the curtain back, I am relieved at the spotless porcelain of the shower. I don't dare touch the plush towels for fear that the layers of grime on my skin will leave them just as grimy. I need a good scrubbing before I will dare touch the pristine white towels. A set of liquid soap, shampoo, and conditioner sits on the small corner shelf of the shower, just waiting for me, just like the razor and wrapped soap on the edge of the sink along with the cellophane-wrapped toothbrush and travel box of toothpaste.

All this tells me I am expected to be here.

Although, I don't have the foggiest idea where *here* is. I'm just thankful to be away from the continuous beatdowns from my father and that rock-infested cave.

I close the door and lean the intimidating scythe on the sink before I strip and turn on the hot water. I do not know how long it's been since I took a shower. Hell, it could have been yesterday or a year ago for all I know. The level of grime and crud on my skin clues me in that it has been much longer than normal.

By the time I turn the water off, my fingers have pruned, and my skin glistens it's so clean. The towels are as plush as hotel towels, and I dry my face off, towel dry my hair, then wrap the soft terry fabric around my waist. The steam is so thick in this small space that I open the door, so I don't suffocate.

Opening the door helps make the air breathable, but it does nothing to un-fog the mirror. Using the nearest neatly folded washcloths, I wipe a swath clear. Dark eyes stare at me from over my shoulder, startling me. I spin around to face the stranger and grab my scythe in a defensive reflex.

A woman stands a few feet away with her hands on her hips. I have never seen a woman with a robotic arm, especially one encased in gold or brass. It's cool enough for my mind to stall. My gaze finally snaps back to her face when I realize I'm being rude by staring.

"It's about fucking time your ass woke up," she snarls and crosses her arms.

I blink at her, not taking kindly to her tone at all. "Who are you?" I grip both my towel and my scythe as my muscles tighten with the stress of the unknown.

"Mandy," she says, eyeing me in a way that makes me shift. Like I *should* know her.

I can't read anything on her face except annoyance. "Is this your place?" I point my chin toward the room. I don't dare release either the towel or the scythe.

Mandy's mouth pops open, and then a crease appears between her eyes. "No. Why do you ask?"

Caution paints her words, making me more on guard than I was before. There's only one other conclusion, and maybe she knows the codes to let me the Hell out of here. "Is it mine?"

She laughs at me and then stops when I don't join her. "You really..." She shakes her head and bites her lower lip before asking, "Do you know who you are?"

I find I really don't know the answer to that question. My memories are filled with beatings and very little else. I remember my mother died. But who I am? That's as much of a mystery as this place is. Another memory sparks. The kid in the Other. *What had he called me?* "Z...Zane?"

She steps backward with wide eyes, and her cheeks lose their rosy color. "Holy..." She wipes her face and then runs a hand through her hair, looking completely frazzled. "What the Hell did they do to you?" Her voice shakes and she slides backward a step.

"What did who do to me?" Some internal alarms sound and my wrist of the hand holding my scythe itches. I glance quickly at it and the sigil is glowing.

Her eyes follow mine, and she takes another step away. "The angels. What did they do to you?" she hisses.

I weigh my answer as the sigil on my wrist burns. I'm not sure whether I should disclose my deal with the angel or not, but something inside me tells me I should, even though I don't think the angel would agree. But then again, the angel let my father beat the snot out of me before he intervened. "They offered me a deal."

"What kind of deal?" She pales even more and takes another step away.

I look up at the scythe and shrug. "I reap the dead."

"No shit. You are Death, with a capital D. That's your damn job. That's all our jobs." She rolls her eyes at me and seems more agitated now.

"I'm Death?"

"Yeah. You have the scythe, don't you?" She points to the rod I'm holding. When I nod, she asks, "What else did you promise them?"

The burn on my wrist nearly makes me drop the scythe. I don't know why the mark is reacting like it is, but it's pissing me off even more than this strange conversation. "They sent me to reap Fate, and all those she brought to life." I paraphrase the angel's directive, trying not to wince.

Mandy's lips draw into a deep frown and then the air pops, and she's gone.

For a moment, I expect the room to fade into the darkness of the cave. When it doesn't, I step out into the room and turn in a circle, looking for a logical explanation for her disappearance. I even look under the bed. But whatever manifestation she was, she is gone.

I rub my face and turn in a circle one more time until my gaze lands on the mirror. I could drive myself batshit with trying to figure out what just happened, but right now, I need to get this scruffy beard taken care of. Then I'll unravel this new mystery.

Reap the Dead
Chapter 5

THE MOMENT I FINISH pulling on pants and putting on the button-down shirt, my wrist burns again and the room tilts. I grab the scythe because for some reason I feel like if I'm not holding it, the world will go to shit in an instant.

I blink against the wavering walls and nearly drop to my knees at the sight of the rock cave again. My hands are empty, and my scythe is nowhere in this cave. This time the lights are on and that kid isn't anywhere to be seen, but my father certainly is there. And the bastard isn't burning like he had been when I made the deal.

He lunges at me and is stopped by a barrier that scalds his skin.

I can't help but smile. I really like the fact he's caged, especially because I am without a weapon, but that still doesn't erase the irritation scratching my skin.

The angel lands between us and stares me down. "Remember your task."

"Bullshit. You aren't delivering on your end," I snarl, pointing at my father. The fact he isn't engulfed in holy fire burns me to the core. He was supposed to be the one tortured for eternity, not kept in a cage to use as leverage over me anytime this dick of an angel expects me to do his bidding.

Darkness builds in the angel's eyes and he steps close, crowding me. "No. You need to meet your end of the deal before we will keep our word. Otherwise, I'll let him kill you over and over and over until there is literally nothing left of *you*." He jabs his finger into my chest. "Understand?"

I don't react immediately, not with the anger drilling a hole through my stomach. A part of me isn't as quick to agree as I was before. Maybe the slap of seeing my father not suffering has made me question my directive. Maybe it's as simple as waking in a place that wasn't this godforsaken cave that gave me a little perspective. Plus, wherever I had been laid out did not seem like a jail, even with the keypads.

But this place—this place is tailored to be just that. An eternal prison full of pain and anguish.

"The house you are in is full of those who require reaping. They are soulless creatures who don't deserve your mercy. Remember, they are monsters. Strike them down without fail."

I cock my head as he continues. An entire house of the walking dead. That didn't seem possible.

"Be warned, they will beg for their lives, but do not fall for their farce. Otherwise, you'll find yourself in a far worse situation than being here."

I glance around the room as doubt trickles down my back like a bead of sweat.

"Remember, Fate is a cold bitch who will try all sorts of tricks to get you to ignore your task, but she must be slayed or your eternity will be in this cave with him." He points to my father. "And that snotty kid who keeps warning you will burn instead."

I gulp and nod, vaguely remembering the person the angel is referring to. The one who referred to me as Zane. Deep within me, I feel a connection. A loyalty I don't understand. I don't want that kid to suffer.

"Anyone with blue eyes like ours must be put down. They are abominations and anyone in alliance with them must also be dealt with. They will destroy the order of the Heavens. They were revived from the dead and must be put down before the universe decides for us. Do you understand?"

I blink. "What if there are innocents in the house?"

The angel nearly growls. "There are no innocents living under that roof."

I'm still not convinced, and something tells me not to believe the angel, not without a valid reason. Doubt rubs me raw from the inside. "I thought you said to reap the dead. Those who Fate brought back. You said nothing about killing others." If I am to kill, I need a damn good reason. Being beaten for eternity wasn't enough for me to slaughter an entire houseful of people, especially if any of them are true innocents.

The angel pinches the bridge of his nose again and the buzz of the barrier evaporates. The angel disappears, leaving me with my father and his sadistic need to kill me. The lights go out, leaving me blind.

I change my stance and put my fists up like a boxer. I will not let him take me down without a fight. I'm just not prepared for him to rush me like a linebacker. He hits me dead-on and I fly onto my back. My head slams into the rock with a sickening thud. Stars fill my vision.

He lands on me, with his knees pinning my arms. One of his hands wraps around my throat and squeezes. "Little shit," he growls as he grabs a fistful of my hair and starts pounding my head against the floor. I try, but I can't buck him off.

Bright lights fill my vision as each slam of my head on the rocks jars my head until it hurts so bad I'm welcoming the darkness. But it doesn't come, just this slow suffocation accompanied by the bastard crushing my head with each terrible blow.

You'd think I'd be strong enough to throw this asshole, but I can't even wrap my legs around his body and get him off me. My eyes bulge with the building pressure on my brain from both the beating and the lack of oxygen.

And all the while, my father is laughing gleefully in the dark. How the Hell did I deal with this for so long without flipping out? An itch in the back of my battered mind tickles, but I can't reach it. Somehow, the answer is out there. I will have to dig that up right after I finish the angel's bidding.

Everything pauses and the lights come on like my random thoughts have been heard. The angel stands nearby, but the spots covering my vision don't get any better.

"Will you kill them all?" He crosses his arms, waiting for my answer.

I can't draw a breath to answer him and my head feels as though a giant stomped on it. I attempt a nod and my stomach sours from the motion.

My father is catapulted across the room, but his fingers leave welts on my throat. He lands in the area he was in when I first stepped into the cave. And I take a great inhalation, filling my starved lungs with air. I cough, and my head feels as if it's going to explode from the pressure. "At least show me what they look like," I wheeze out. Because, despite his directive, if the person isn't in his rolling deck of pictures, I'm not striking them down.

The angel snaps his fingers and a scroll of images flash. "I do not have a picture of Fate. But she is your prime objective."

My pummeled brain can't seem to keep up with the pictures, and I'm not sure I'll be able to recall them if any of the faces show up in front of me. Hopefully, my brain isn't as damaged as I think it is.

"Remember your task," he says as the pictures fade to black. "Or I will bring you back to the Other and let your feral father deal with you."

Reap the Dead
Chapter 6

MY EYES SNAP OPEN and I'm facedown on the floor. My head still throbs from the pounding in the Other. A reminder of what will happen if I fail.

I climb to my hands and knees in the same room I had been in before the angel pulled me back to beat me into submission again. I close my eyes and hang my head. What flows in front of my eyelids is the progression of pictures. Most of them have eyes that are unforgettable: bright, almost neon blue, like the angels.

For a moment, I consider rebelling. Killing isn't in my blood, but the consequences rub me like a mesh of barbed wire being dragged across my back. And it isn't my eternity that is making me hesitate. It's the strange boy burning in angel fire that gives me pause.

"They aren't human," I whisper, attempting to convince myself of my gruesome task. Squinting in the light with my throat as dry as sandpaper, I glance around the room.

Subtle differences make me straighten my back and sit back on my heels.

A new pile of clean clothes sits on the couch and the light in the bathroom is off. I could have sworn I hadn't turned it off when I stepped out into the room. And I certainly hadn't made the bed. Especially with clean linens.

But the oddest thing beyond that is the bottle of water on the table, like whoever neatened up the space figured I'd be thirsty when I woke. They aren't wrong, but it still is creepy as hell.

I slowly stand and glance around with my scythe still gripped in my hand. I stare at it like it's as foreign an object as anything else in the room. I wonder why it didn't come with me to the Other if it was in my grip here. No solid answer comes, so I cross to the bathroom and flip on the light because I dislike dark spaces.

It reminds me too much of the Other. The dirty pile of clothing is gone from where I had left it. I hadn't folded the towels, but they were neatly folded just the same. I lean over and take a whiff of them. They smell freshly laundered. A chill captures me at the thought of those faces caring for the room while I lay unconscious on the floor.

The air shimmers again and that figure who had surprised me outside the bathroom materializes. I stare at her, suspicious that perhaps she had been the one to neaten up the space. I don't get that from her at all. Frankly, she seems more battle-ready soldier than homemaker.

"Are you on the side of Heaven?" I ask, because I can't side with someone that has opposing allegiances.

She laughs at me. "Oh, Hell no."

The tattoo on my wrist burns and pain lashes through my head. Anyone not on Heaven's side is my enemy. I'm not sure whether or not that is my thought, but it is all I need to react. I swing the scythe. Mandy lifts her metal arm in defense and my scythe violently bounces off it, nearly throwing me on my ass.

I swing again, but before the blade reaches her, she blinks out.

"Come back here and fight!" I bellow at the ceiling, spinning around with my weapon at the ready.

The creak of the door catches my attention and I spin around, angry that I didn't take out that creature when I first saw her. But the blue eyes that peer through the door catch me off guard, and the face in one of the pictures appears in the crack.

His eyes widen at the sight of me.

I charge, raising the scythe, but the door slams closed before I can cross the distance. I swing anyway, burying the blade into the door. I yank it out and swing again. But no matter how many times I strike the wood, all it does is surface damage, as if the core is unyielding steel.

My blade doesn't break through, even though the sting from the sigil on my wrist demands I strike.

I dislodge my blade and pace across the space, cursing loudly as the blaze in my wrist poisons my mind. I need to get out of this room. I need to satisfy my end of the bargain. Otherwise, I am as doomed as I feel right now.

Reap the Dead
Chapter 7

I FINALLY CALM DOWN enough to position myself to the side of the opening, waiting for the next opportunity. Just when I think I missed my chance, the door creaks open. I hold my breath, waiting for it to widen enough for me to slip through. I catch his profile as he sticks his head inside the door, and then I burst through the opening before he can shut me back in.

Freedom gives me a rush of strength and my forceful exit knocks the man to the ground. He stares up at me with those wide, ethereal blue eyes and scrambles to his feet. My sigil brightens. This is one of the dead I have to collect. Even if I hadn't recognized his face from the slide show the angel showed me, I'd still need to cut him down.

Everyone in this house needs to be dealt with. Now. Sending them back to Heaven will sound alarms, and Fate will come running right into the edge of my blade.

I swing my scythe and it whistles through the air, hitting him at the crown of his head and slicing down as if he's made of butter, not bone. Nothing happens at first and then two halves fall to the ground. His eyes are still open and wide, as though he never felt his death.

I expect a ghost or a soul to come out of him, but nothing does. Just like the angel promised. These things weren't even human, and that fuels my need to destroy them.

"Run!" a scream follows.

I turn, swinging with righteousness, and my blade severs a petite blonde's head, and it rolls across the floor. Blood plumes all over the front of me from her headless body. A moment later, the body crumples to the ground as if it just realized it was dead.

The same absence of a soul grips me and catapults me forward.

Two kids bolt up the stairs at the far end of the room, screaming. Before I make it halfway across the room, a man appears at the bottom of the stairs. White wings fan out from behind him and light as pure as I've ever seen shines through him.

But his face is one of the souls I must reap.

I step forward and hit a solid wall that sends a healthy shock through my body. I leap backward and nearly slip on the slick puddle of blood seeping into the carpet. The sting of it sizzles on my skin and I glare at the angel-like creature.

A blonde appears from the stairwell. Another face I have been called to reap, except her eyes are not blue like the neon ones that flash from next to her. Her brown eyes are soft with fake concern.

"Don't hurt him. She will never forgive us." She sticks her hand out like a stop sign. "Calm down, Zane."

The angel from the Other told me this would happen. He said they would all beg for my mercy, but I was not about to listen. I cannot be swayed by whatever argument they try to launch, and the burn in my wrist is a stark reminder of my task.

I just hope their deaths will bring Fate to me. I want that bitch dead by my hands, preferably squeezing the life out of her. Again, the thought seems foreign inside my head, but I shake it away.

I step forward again into the electrified barrier and hiss as I jump back. The jolt hurts all the way to my teeth.

"Go," the blonde tells the angel. "Get them out of here." She nods toward the upstairs. "All of them."

I can't help but wonder how many more of the faces are in the house right now. My wrist twitches, scraping the scythe along the invisible fence caging me in. The shock isn't quite as bad through the metal, as if it is absorbing the energy instead of being scarred by it.

He glances at the blonde with a headshake. "Not until he's dealt with. I can't hold him in place indefinitely, especially at a distance."

"I'll be fine. I need to find out what happened with Nick. Now go, before Michael gets home and finds this." She waves at the dead soaking the carpet red.

Before the man leaves, he sends a glare in my direction and turns, bumping into a brunette barreling into the room like the place is on fire and her favorite puppy is lost in the corner.

When her lavender eyes land on me, a jolt as strong as the electrified wall zaps me, and it feels like my heart stops in my chest. For a moment, I can't draw a breath and I know deep down that this is who I've been waiting for. This is Fate, and she is as breathtaking as the angel warned.

My body reacts to her in a way that surprises me. I want to kiss her. Hell, I want to fuck her, but I know better. This is part of Fate's cruel trick.

"Go," she says, but her eyes are glued on me. When the man doesn't budge, she actually turns and pushes him. "Go!" she yells in his face, and points upstairs.

His jaw tightens, and then he marches out of the room.

"You, too, Mom," she says to the little blonde. And now I see some resemblance in the shape of their noses. But the black hair doesn't match, and neither does the age. They look maybe a year apart at best.

"I need to find out what happened to your father." The blonde turns to me. "Did you see Nick?"

I growl in response and test the barrier in front of me, yanking my hand away from the zap. But I welcome the shock. At least it puts me back into control and my entire body buzzes.

The barrier doesn't feel as strong as the first time I walked into it, and I wonder whether the number of times I've tested it has weakened it. Maybe playing this game of test and jolt with the force field is doing just that. I do it again just to be sure and this time the sting travels all the way up my arm but stops there.

"He has dark hair like Missy"—she points at the violet-eyed woman—"he has blue eyes, and probably still looks like he's eighteen?" she asks with a hopeful lilt to her voice.

I stare her down and test the barrier again, this time with the edge of my scythe to avoid the shock. The barrier crackles on contact. Although the blonde steps closer, the dark-haired vixen hangs back, studying me as if she doesn't believe what she is seeing.

"What? You've never seen Death before?" I snap at her and bang the scythe against the barrier again for show. I'm not even sure whether I should trust Mandy's explanation of who I am, but it's worth a shot. I want this woman to shake in fear at the sight of me.

She huffs. "I was Death before you stupidly ripped that scythe out of my hand ten years ago."

I cock my head. She can't be serious. Why would anyone *choose* to be Death? Least of all me. Besides, *she* is someone I would remember. I burst out laughing. "Bullshit."

She presses her lips together and her eyes actually gloss over with unshed tears, which surprises me because Heaven said she was a crafty and cold bitch. Her devastated look does not fit their description at all.

"We thought you might say that." She turns to the stairs and nods at someone I can't see.

An older redhead steps onto the landing with her fingertips sparking, and her picture flashes in my memory. She has the same ethereal blue eyes as the first idiot I cut down and the man with the white wings. Except the difference with this one—she has fiery wings.

Either way, she is also on Heaven's hit list. I blink and then narrow my eyes. This must be the devil's daughter that Heaven expects me to terminate. But the barrier is still a little too strong for me to break through without serious damage. I test it again, actually enjoying the shock that travels into my arms. It makes the sigil on my wrist glow as brightly as their eyes.

The redhead levels a wide-eyed stare, blinking rapidly as she scans the carnage around me as if she cannot believe I am capable of such destruction. She will learn the truth once I escape. She trades a quick glance with the one the blonde called Missy.

"We'll deal with the ramifications later. He needs to see," Missy whispers softly, as if the comment was not meant for my ears. But I'm tense enough to pick up every sound, even their flitting heartbeats pounding out their underlying fear.

The redhead inhales and then blows out of her mouth and nods. She closes her eyes and turns her palms toward me. The space between where she is standing and the barrier I am caught behind ripples and then morphs, capturing my full attention.

The sky is streaked with pinks and purples of a sunset. The ocean sits in the distance beyond an expanse of lawn broken by a pool and then a rock wall separating the grass from the deep, tumultuous ocean. A teenage girl stands on the grass with her back to us, with what looks like an ancient book in one hand and the scythe in the other.

The same scythe I'm gripping right now. Something about her stirs a need deep within me, and I nearly growl at myself.

The view switches from the girl outside to inside a house where many people are watching her. Every single one of them I recognize from the images the angels showed me. Every single mortal who must meet their maker today.

A ruckus pulls my attention to near the sliding glass doors, and a much younger version of me is struggling with a black-haired kid. He is attempting to stop me from going outside to the girl, and I deck him. My throat closes as I get a full view of the kid on the ground.

He is the same one my father threatened to kill in *the Other*. A sharp pain pierces my head, and I close my eyes for a moment. My wrist heats and I want to shake it, but the scythe is still in my grip.

Instead, I refocus on my younger self, who utters a half-hearted apology and closes the glass door behind him. He is unsure in his gait as he approaches the girl, as if he's afraid of her. Something makes her turn toward him. Her eyes carry a hint of fear, but it quickly turns into irritation as she glances toward the house and then back at the younger me before she juts her chin toward the house.

That's when I see them.

A swarm of angels. Thousands of them landing en masse on the grass and hovering over the water in the distance. And every single one of the winged bastards wears a scowl as they come toward us. I can only assume their intent is to wipe us all out. Me included. And that's the only logical reason I can think of as to why I grab the scythe from the girl.

No sooner do I have this weapon in my hand than a whirlwind swirls around the two of us in the yard, blocking my view. When it subsides, the girl is on her hands and knees, sobbing. My body is prone on the ground, with the scythe crossing my chest. Which is exactly how I woke up in the dark room I just escaped from. My chest is still, and my face beyond pale. I'm gray and I recognize the face of death.

The vision fades and I stare at the empty space, blinking. If what I am being shown is the truth, then Missy wasn't lying when she said I took the scythe. But the thing is, I have zero recollection of any of those events. I'm skeptical as I glare back at the three women. For all I know, that could have been a well-orchestrated hallucination peppered with just enough truth to make me buy it.

"You can go now," Missy says to the redhead.

"I love you, Missy. Be careful," the redhead says softly and gives her a hug. And then she flees up the stairs, out of sight.

I jolt at the sudden loss of one of my quarries, but there are still two in the room who I need to run my blade through. Missy is my primary target and the bitch Heaven warned me about. They said she'd try to trick me. They weren't fooling.

"The one you punched is Nick. Did you see him at all?" the blonde asks as she approaches.

I glance over her head at Missy and then back at her. Her eyes don't look like a monster's eyes, and for a moment, I doubt my mission. But then I remember: none of these monsters have souls. I lick my lips and give the slightest of nods, hoping she will close the gap for more information.

"Is he okay?" She steps closer. Just outside the barrier, looking up at me with imploring eyes.

Before she can move out of my reach, I turn my scythe and shove the pointed end right at her heart. "You can see for yourself," I snarl.

I don't know who is more surprised when it actually impales her, but I don't have time to pull it out when a wave of power knocks me clear across the room.

This time, an orb of white light surrounds the blonde. And I stare at it in awe, swallowing the doubt as the manifestation of her soul seems to form. The others didn't do that. They just ceased, like Heaven promised.

Movement captures my attention. Missy is charging at me and I'm on my feet, ready for her, tossing my doubt aside. Her hair whips as she moves and when she jumps into the air to execute a roundhouse kick, I shift my weight in time to avoid her foot slamming the side of my head. But she's now within reach and I grab her as she lands, knowing my touch is as deadly as my scythe.

I slam her against the wall and my hands wrap around her slim throat, squeezing. Her knee comes up between my legs with enough force for me to lose my grip for a moment, but the dull ache between my legs fuels my vengeance.

She's a fighter, and I lean my body against hers as she struggles and scratches my arms. But that's as far as she can get with the way I have her pinned. Her gasps and wheezes tell me she's still getting air and I press harder.

The horror in her eyes is mixed with something else, something I don't recognize until a tear escapes both eyes. It's the same look of heartache and betrayal I once saw on my mother's face when she caught that lying bastard cheating on her. The echoes of her sobs still give me nightmares, more than her deathbed goodbye.

A ding emits from Missy's wrist, and I stare at the charm bracelet as she pounds on my arms.

My gaze jumps to hers as my head feels as if something inside explodes. A flood of memories bursts forth through the prison that Heaven manufactured in my head. Like a picture show on steroids, the images flash through my brain. Not only images of this girl saving me in every way possible from the first moment I met her, but to the duplicity of Heaven's horrors.

I loosen my grip, but the damage is already done.

"Zane," she gasps.

"Oh, Melissa," I whisper, and my thumb passes over her lower lip. It blackens under my touch and I curse the gods. Tears fill my eyes as I finally recognize the woman I would die for.

Correction, the one I *had* died for.

And I am responsible for doing the thing I vowed never to let happen.

I am stealing her life with my touch.

I have to stop this.

She cannot die.

I don't care what the consequences are. I lean forward, capturing her mouth with mine. If she could wish life back into the dead, so could I, right?

She kisses me back with a sob, but then she goes slack, and I catch her, holding her to me as I fall to my knees.

My chest feels flayed open and my heart pummeled like it's been tap-danced on by a legion of reapers. I close my eyes and rest my forehead on hers, shaking from the realization that I just delivered her to those bastards on a silver platter.

"I'm so sorry, Missy."

I rock her as my tears fall onto her face. I press my lips to hers, wishing life even though I know deep in my soul I don't possess the kind of magic she does.

She wheezes out her last breath with my name on it and then stills in my arms. Her chest no longer moves and the feral beast Heaven created resurrects inside me, except it isn't aimed at their targets anymore.

Another ding comes from her wrist, and I bellow a wordless scream at the ceiling, vowing to kill every last goddamned angel in Heaven.

The End

Continue on the next page with KISSING FATE, the last installment of THE DEATH CHRONICLES II

Kissing Fate
Chapter 1

THE PHONE RINGS AND Papa Ryan's number flashes on the screen. He knows I'm working, so it has to be urgent. My heartbeat picks up, and I swipe the screen of my cell before putting it to my ear as I hold my breath.

"He's awake." That's all he says. That's all he needs to say.

My heart does a double tap in my chest. "I'm on my way." My hands shake as I end the call. My workstation is littered with chemicals and instead of just swiping them all into a bucket like I'm tempted to, I carefully stow each one in their proper storage compartment, taking deep breaths to stop my compulsion just to leave it all where it is. Abbott Laboratories would not take kindly to me leaving a mess and God knows we've had a few scares over the years of spilled chemicals combining into a toxic mix.

Once everything is stored properly, I cross to my boss. His greasy hair is combed back, and he adjusts his horn-rimmed spectacles as I wait for him to acknowledge me. He takes his sweet time and I'm nearly bouncing on my feet by the time he looks up at me. His sneer is all I need. It flares my festering wound. He has made it clear he doesn't like me, despite graduating at the top of my class in chemical engineering. He just thinks I got the job based on who my relatives are. He has no idea that I interned with one of the top executives, who then offered me a way to work my way up in the company.

I think he believes I am a threat to his job. I have no aspirations to manage people. This was just a way to pass the time. If he knew that, would he stop being defensive and maybe appreciate my creativity in the lab a little more?

"What do you want?" he snaps.

I take a deep breath, pushing my irritation down a notch. "I have a family emergency. I've cleaned up my workstation and need to leave."

I can see his argument launching and I mentally push the decision not to give me shit this one time onto him. I hate manipulating people, but it was better than starting a yelling match.

He blinks and then nods as my influence settles into him.

I'm out the door before he can come to his senses. I also avoid people on my way out because I do not want to get locked in some benign workplace conversation.

It's been ten years since Zane Bradley last took a mortal breath. Ten years of his body stowed in Papa's panic room. None of us thought we'd ever see him again, and I wondered whether he was ever coming back in my mortal lifetime.

Even the reapers didn't know where the angels were keeping him.

With Levi still locked and guarded by Heaven's griffin, I didn't have a prayer of finding him. I couldn't step into Heaven while I was still breathing, and none of us thought the angels would actually take Death to Hell.

We hadn't tried the jump to Purgatory, not with angels monitoring all the entries. While I'm still alive, if I choose to jump to Purgatory, I need to be touching either a reaper or Death, and neither of those were possible. One because touching Zane would kill me, and two because the reapers did not want to take the chance.

Even with my soul-sucking curse broken, they still did not want to bring me there to help search for Zane. Correction: Mandy didn't want to take the chance, and the reapers agreed with her.

Mandy warned me if the angels got a hold of me, while they had Zane stowed away somewhere, then their version of Armageddon wouldn't be far off on the horizon, and Zane's sacrifice would have been for nothing. So, I spent my days in college classes and my nights learning magic from Raven Ryan and studying sigils with Kylee Andreas.

I'm more highly trained in the dark arts than either of the Fates before me.

With Death and Leviathan in lockdown, Mandy had become my second-in-command. After all these years, she has been successful in recruiting reapers and strengthening the federation. She rules over the reaper federation with an ease that makes me proud. They are as loyal to her as they are to me. And Heaven has left the rest of my death collectors alone since Zane disappeared. Without Zane at the helm, I certainly need someone I can trust.

Zane's supposed to work for me, but I can't even call on him the way I can still call on the reapers. My mother says willing him to me is supposed to work, but it fails every time.

Even when we attempted to call him while we were in the panic room where Papa had placed his body—nothing. Not even a twitch. He remained dead but didn't decompose. There was zero loss of muscle tone; if anything, he seemed to bulk up. Zane Bradley remained suspended in time in a body that seemed to age, against all logic.

Ten years turned his boyish face into a man's, with stubble and all. And it was a face I dreamed of every night. I longed for those intense green eyes, and I could not wait to see him. My foot presses harder on the pedal, moving the car faster as the adrenaline kicks into my veins.

Zane is awake.

That thought brings both excitement and dread to the surface and I tap the steering wheel, weaving through traffic like a racecar driver. The angels aren't done with me. Not by a long shot. For ten years, I've been waiting for the other shoe to slam me in the head.

As I pull off the highway, Mandy appears in the passenger seat, and her hand trembles as she runs it through her hair. The sun hits her mechanical arm, sending golden prisms through the car.

"They've completely wiped his memories." She glances at me with haunted brown eyes.

I swerve at her comment and then take my foot off the gas to slow us down. "Explain," I say, but my heart is already pounding in my throat. I cannot imagine Zane not remembering me. I have never once considered an alternative. I had gotten so many invitations to date over the years, but I was waiting for him to come back to me, even with the underlying irritation of his choice chewing at my nerves.

"He's here to kill you and everyone you've brought back," she says and my heart stops beating in my chest. "He didn't even know he was Death."

That proverbial shoe nearly knocks me out. "Then we can't let him get out of that room." My mind rushes through the scenario and my stomach knots. *What the Hell did Heaven do to him?*

"Before all this, did Zane have a tattoo on the inside of his right wrist?" Mandy asks.

"No. Why?"

"He does now, and I think that's how they are controlling him." Mandy resumes chewing on her lip as she watches the scenery pass. "I think I've seen it in Kylee's book of sigils."

"Describe it."

"It's a little circle with dots around it, like the four points on a compass."

It sounds vaguely familiar. My mind shuffles through the sigils that Kylee drew for me, and I think I remember something that looks like what Mandy described. "I need to swing by Alex's house before I head to Papa's."

Mandy cocks her head.

"Kylee's book of sigils also has what they are used for and, more importantly, what we need to break the spell. And it will give me a chance to talk to Faith. If Zane truly doesn't remember, maybe Faith can jog his memory in some way." Faith Ryan, my adoptive mother, can project the past like an old movie projector. She calls it time jumps, but she hasn't used her gift because it has a devastating side effect. It rips the fabric between our world and the afterlife. Sometimes those rips are benign, like the ones that open portals to Purgatory, but sometimes her power rips holes into the underworld, releasing demons, or worse.

Considering the angels breached our reaper realm to get to Earth, what's a few escaped demons in the scheme of things? Especially if showing Zane the past makes him remember.

Besides, a little more supernatural activity would be good for the Ryans' family business. Tom Ryan, Faith's brother-in-law, runs a paranormal investigation agency and according to him, things have been slow.

As soon as I pull into the driveway of the house I grew up in, I glance at Mandy. "Make sure he doesn't get out."

"I'm on it," she says and disappears.

Kissing Fate
Chapter 2

I PULL THE KEYS out of the ignition and shove them in my pocket as I climb out of the car. The cool sea air hits my face, tingling as the fall winds tear over the water and wrap around the house. I glimpse the ocean as I jog to the front door. As much as I love York Beach, it had too many stark reminders of the horrors I dealt with ten years ago.

Holly and I moved to our own apartment in Portland after I graduated college and got the job at Abbott Laboratories. Our visits to York have become less and less frequent as our lives have become busier.

Besides, I needed some breathing room from the suffocating reminder that my future hung in limbo right along with Zane in the basement of Papa's house. Even now, visiting home splayed open the wounds that had partially healed with time. But seeing Zane in suspended animation hadn't allowed me to get on with my life. When we lived in York, it was a constant daily struggle.

Truthfully, I ran away from the pain. But no matter what I did, it always remained at the pit of my stomach, like some cancer eating away at whatever brief happiness I found.

My key slides into the lock and I pause, letting myself feel the full brunt of the situation before I enter the house and put it on my adoptive mother. My heart thunders at the thought of Zane awake. I wonder whether Papa has called them. That thought trips my adrenaline. I enter the house, praying they don't know. Praying they are safe.

The house is quiet and a lump forms in my throat. I shake the dread out of my mind. The house would be quiet, with only Alex and Faith living here. Still, my heart doesn't let up. It's almost as if a bomb is ticking and I have a finite amount of time before my world blows to bits.

I cross into the family room and my anxiety drops a notch at the sight of the redhead curled up on the couch with her nose buried in a book. She twirls a strand of her hair around her finger, announcing that either the book has her on edge or life in general does. Faith Ryan is a doppelgänger of my roommate Holly, which makes sense, considering Holly is her natural daughter. The fiery red hair and flawless cream complexion, along with their bright-blue eyes, and their propensity to twirl their hair on their finger when they are both unsettled, makes them seem more like twins than mother and daughter.

She looks up from her book as I head toward the stairs leading to my old bedroom. Her eyebrows arch and she glances at the clock. "What are you doing here?"

There's really only one thing that would bring me home during work hours. "He's awake." I head for the stairs. "And I need Kylee's book of sigils." I take the stairs two at a time and enter the room I used to share with Holly.

I rummage through the boxes in the closet until I find what I'm looking for. Moving the spell books aside, I pull out the sigil binder Kylee Andreas made for me. I haven't looked at it since Holly and I moved out a few years ago. But as I stand in the room, shuffling through the pages, I find exactly what Mandy described and my heart drops.

"Christ," I whisper as the sigil's description sinks in. It's a binding sigil that makes Zane Heaven's bitch. The only way to break the binding is to break the circle or sever the limb.

I carry the open book downstairs and fall into the chair across from Faith in defeat.

"That bad?" Faith asks.

"Mandy told me Zane remembers nothing." I rub my face and stare at the sigil in the book before meeting Faith's questioning gaze. "And he isn't the one in control."

Her face hardens and her lips press together. The last time the angels informed Faith Ryan of their intentions, she closed the only portal to Heaven that existed, blocking the angels from getting here so easily to carry out their plan. Being Lucifer's daughter put her high on Heaven's hit list, as well as those I brought back from the dead. Unfortunately, when she shut down Heaven's ability to get through to our realm, the heavenly host rammed through the reaper realm to get here and almost destroyed the entire reaper federation in their bid to destroy me.

The mama-bear part of her rears her head and her fingertips spark. She curls her hands into fists. "I won't let him harm you."

I let out a soft laugh. "I'm not worried about me. But I need your help." I take a deep breath and close my eyes, forging ahead. "I don't need your protection. I need your time jump thing to show him the night he became Death." I open my eyes and see her lips soften.

She shakes her head. "You know what happens when I do that."

"Lucifer doesn't exist anymore, and I promise, I'll help close whatever breach opens and help you gather the demons that escape."

"Missy—" she starts.

"If we can't jog his memory... I can't put him down. Killing him kills me, and leaves both posts open. You know what happens then."

The end of the world happens, which is the angels' end goal and the reason she closed the only portal to Heaven.

"I won't let you die." She flips her hair over her shoulder, looking more like her daughter Holly. It's an arrogant move, and I understand her reasoning, but it won't stop the end from being upon us all.

"If the angels win, you know the price." I don't want to impart my influence on her the way I had to on my boss earlier. She raised me and loved me like her own, so doing that will violate all the trust we have built over the years. "Please. If we can jog his memory, that may be enough to stop him without having to maim him, and without anyone dying."

She sighs. "If demons get out, people will die."

I close my eyes and lean back in the chair. "As shitty as it sounds, are their lives worth more than the world?" I look up at the ceiling, hating myself for the possibility of trading lives for the good of the world. It's not fair, and it's not right, but it's the only hand I have to play.

When I look at her, her lips are pinched in an unhappy frown. "Fine."

"Thank you."

"Don't thank me yet," she snips.

Before I can say anything to appease her frustration, Mandy pops in with her eyes wide and wild. "He's going berserk." She holds up her mechanical arm I created for her years ago. There's a clear dent in the metal and my heart drops.

I point to the book just to be sure, even though in my heart I already know. Heaven's betting on my unwillingness to harm him. "Is that the sigil?"

She turns the book toward her and nods.

Which means Heaven is in control of Zane unless I can break through to him. If not, I'm going to have to cut his wrist deep enough to sever the sigil, which will probably tear through all his ligaments, or chop his arm off completely. I shiver at the thought.

"Damn it all," I mutter and slam the book closed, tossing it onto the coffee table. I thought about astral projection like Papa taught me, but that would leave my body vulnerable to attack. "I'll be there as fast as I can."

Faith gives me a nod, gathering up her things. I don't even have to ask her to come. She heads to the garage as I jog out to my car. By the time I back out onto the street, the garage opens.

Thankfully, it's early November and the seasonal folks have bugged out of town. I bury the needle on my little sports coupe and mentally clear the road ahead of me as I drive. My left foot taps on the floor with impatience, even though I'm driving so fast I'm almost airborne. Holly would be proud of my driving skills today.

I turn onto Papa's street, and dings on my charm bracelet send my heart into overdrive. The Book of Fates delivers more names onto the list of the dead, and my heart jumps into my throat. I don't even glance at the charm. I'm still breathing, so it's not Zane, but that does nothing to calm my fluttering nerves.

The gate is already open to Papa's, and I slide into the driveway, almost nailing the post before I slam on my brakes, stopping inches shy of the side of the garage in the extra parking space allotted for guests. I don't wait for Faith. I don't need a lecture on reckless driving. Not when people have already died.

I tear the keys out of the ignition and bolt into the house, dodging Nana as she ushers Kylee's sobbing kids toward the garage. She doesn't say anything to me, but her calico eyes are full of fear and sorrow.

I run down the stairs and nearly plow over Papa. His dark hair hangs over his forehead, and his blue eyes blaze with fury. His hand is stretched before him and a vein pulses on his temple. His power fills the air.

My mother stands a few feet away with her eyes wide and her mouth slack with shock. Her blonde hair falls out of the loose bun on the crown of her head and her sunglasses are forgotten on her forehead, as if she had just returned from one of her morning walks when all this chaos descended.

I halt at the sight of Zane behind Papa's magical barrier. He's dripping with blood, growling like a rabid animal as he holds his gore-glazed scythe like a crazed warrior. His glare lands on me, and there isn't even a hint of recognition in his glowing green eyes. Only malice reflects in those irises, and I shiver under the intensity of it.

For the first time since I met Zane Bradley in grade school, I'm actually scared of the man.

It's only then that the stench hits me. Death in the form of iron and feces hangs in the air. The walls are painted with blood. There's even a splotch of red dripping from the ceiling. The raw amount of it sends a shock through me, as if I just walked into Papa's barrier. There's so much blood and only two visible bodies despite the carnage. I avoid looking at the bodies directly, but the head of Kylee Andreas pulls my attention. Her dead eyes stare sightlessly in my direction in a silent accusation. Her honey-colored hair, which normally flowed to the middle of her back in beautiful waves, was chopped clean at the point where her neck had been severed. A clear testament to the lethal sharpness of the scythe's edge.

I swallow the bile that creeps up my throat and refocus on the threat at hand.

"Go," I say to Papa without taking my eyes off Zane. Papa doesn't move and I turn, pushing him toward the stairs and the safety above. "Faith is coming. Now go!" I yell in his face. If Zane gets free of the barrier, Papa and his entire family are in mortal danger, despite their powerful gifts.

He still doesn't budge, so I send the mental order for him to obey.

His jaw tightens, and he shakes his head as if trying to rid himself of my hold. Then he marches out of the room. I know he isn't happy being manhandled by a whipstitch like me, but I just want my family safe, no matter what happens.

"You, too, Mom."

Before I impress my will on her to leave, she says, "I need to find out what happened with your father." Her imploring eyes leave me helpless, and I can't make her leave. I want to know what Heaven did with my father, too.

She turns back to Zane. "Did you see Nick?"

He growls in response, punching the barrier again. But it stands, sending sparks where he hit, and he yanks his hand away as if he's touched a flame too long. Yet he punches it a second time, like a feral wolf testing his electric fence.

"He has dark hair like Missy." Mom points to me as she creeps closer. "He has blue eyes and probably still looks like he's eighteen?" she asks with a hopeful lilt to her voice.

I can't help but hold my breath, too.

Zane scrapes the edge of the scythe along Papa's invisible shield. Sparks shower down on him. I stare, almost hypnotized at the sight of him. The shirt he has on hangs down open, revealing a chiseled chest. It's more pronounced now than it was ten years ago, and I cannot fathom that. Instead of just being skin and bones like someone bedridden for that long should be, he is cut like a god.

"What? You've never seen Death before?" he snaps at me and bangs the scythe against the barrier again.

I allow a huff of air to come out. This version of Zane is far too arrogant to stomach. It's time I brought him down a couple of pegs. "I was Death before you stupidly ripped that scythe out of my hand ten years ago."

He cocks his head and narrows his eyes. I have a moment of hope. Maybe that broke through whatever Heaven did to him. But my stomach falls when he laughs at me.

"Bullshit."

I press my lips together, and the tears almost come. I waited ten years to fall into his arms, and Heaven stole that from me just as surely as they stole my father. Mandy was right. He's been brainwashed. I glance up the stairs in time to see Faith climbing down. Sparks burst from her hands and the ends of her hair, and her eyes glow in the dim stairwell.

I give her a hopeless shrug and turn back to Zane. "We thought you might say that."

Faith enters what I will forever see as Death's killing room as opposed to Papa's basement. She nearly gags at the sight before her, but then her fire sparks turn the white of angel fire, bringing forth her fiery wings.

Like any power, Faith's ability to bring the past into the room with us has consequences. Yet, she loves me enough to create a breach or two in Hell in the hopes we can break through to Zane. Otherwise, we were all as good as dead.

I nod for her to go ahead. "We'll deal with the ramifications later. He needs to see."

She inhales and blows a long, slow exhale out of her mouth. Then she closes her eyes and turns her palms toward Zane. The space between where she stands and the barrier Zane is caught behind ripples and morphs.

Pinks and purples of a sunset fill the space, reflecting off an ocean view. The transformation of the cellar into Papa's backyard is humbling. The expanse of lawn is broken by a pool and then a rock wall separating the grass from the deep, tumultuous ocean.

I guess I never noticed just how beautiful the sunset was that day, but as I stare at Faith's vision, I sigh. The pending battle had wiped out my ability to see the beauty and grace all around me, but I think anyone in my shoes would be more worried about causing the end of the world than an ocean sunset.

My teenage self stands on the grass with an old-school Book of Fates in one hand and Death's scythe in the other, waiting for Judgment Day.

The view switches from the outside to the inside, where everyone is gathered at the door to witness either my victory or my death. But Zane isn't having it. He's struggling to get to the door. The door my father is blocking.

When he doesn't yield, Zane throws a right hook, knocking my father on the ground.

He mumbles an apology to my dad as he pulled the door open and stepped out. No one else attempts to stop him and he closes the door behind him, sending a final warning glare to those inside the house.

Zane's stride toward me isn't as self-assured as he seemed when he hit my dad and the closer he gets, the more tense his shoulders seem.

My younger self turns toward him, and I remember being so irritated I could have wrung his neck. If I could have touched him, I would have done just that, but I still had that awful touch curse.

With my back to the ocean, I missed Heaven's entrance.

No wonder Zane made the choice he did. If I had seen the thousands upon thousands of angels descending with scowls and swords intent on destroying, I would have done the same thing he did.

I blink, realizing if I had been facing them, I might have actually pissed my pants and quaked in fear despite the power I held. Zane saved me from their wrath that day, and as much as I have held onto my irritation with the way he went about it, a small part of me is thankful for his actions.

The rest of the scene I've lived through, so I close my eyes. Seeing Zane die isn't something I want to witness a second time. It nearly undid me then, and I can feel the tendrils of panic spreading through me again at the sound of his suffering.

My sobbing pulls my gaze back. If I had known then that his taking on the role of Death had nullified my touch curse, I would have crawled over and kissed him despite the ramifications.

The vision fades, and I swallow the lump in my throat before looking at Zane. He still stares at the empty space, blinking. I can't tell whether or not we made a difference. He seems lost in his own thoughts.

"You can go now," I say to Faith. If that doesn't break through to him, I'm not sure what will.

"I love you, Missy. Be careful." Faith pulls me into a tight hug. I know she wants to say more, but she releases me and scurries up the stairs. I wait until I hear the front door close and then turn back to Zane.

Mom has already crossed half the distance to where he stands. "The one you punched is Nick. Did you see him at all?" she asks.

Zane glances at me and his eyes remain guarded, as if he's still trying to piece together the puzzle.

"Is he okay?" my mom asks with a plea in her voice. Then she steps closer. Close enough to Papa's barrier for some of her hairs to stand on end from the electrical current. She looks up at Zane, and I can almost envision her puppy eyes.

Then I see it, the deep hatred etched in his face as he turns the scythe and jams the point toward my mother like a javelin shot.

"You can see for yourself," he snarls.

My eyes go wide as the point breaches Papa's barrier and pierces right through my mother's chest. Fury fills me, and I send a wave of power across the distance. It knocks Zane clear into the wall.

Losing my mother hits me, shaking me from my toes to my teeth. All I see is red, and wrath replaces the loss. I sprint into action, letting the white-hot anger rule over my actions.

This isn't Zane. It isn't the boy I loved. This is a monster that Heaven sent to wipe us out.

I charge, forgetting the one cardinal rule of self-defense: never let emotions rule your actions. I jump when I'm close enough to land a roundhouse kick to his head. I spin, expecting my foot to connect, but he bends back far enough for me to miss. I land off-balance and Zane grabs me.

His hands are on me. Death's hands are around my neck as he slams me into the wall. I try to get away by kneeing him, and all that seems to do is infuriate him more. I scratch at his arms as his angry green eyes glare down at me.

When his grip slips, I gasp for air, but then he squeezes harder. It's not just the lack of air that's killing me. It's his touch. He promised me he would never hurt me.

Tears slip from my eyes as his betrayal stabs deeper than any knife. If I had it in me, I would call on Heaven's blade and end him. But I still love the idea of *my* Zane, and if he's anywhere in there...

I need to break Heaven's hold on him. I need to destroy that sigil before it's too late. If I fail, he will go after the rest of my family, and I can't have that. I conjure my nail to be as sharp as an obsidian knife and then rake my finger across the sigil on his left wrist. Blood spurts out as I sever both sides of the circle with a deep cut that would be devastating to a mortal. But he doesn't seem to notice. His gaze still holds a hateful resolve, and death is creeping into my bones.

The Book of Fates dings and I don't know whether it's because my mother has finally passed or whether it's my name scribbled on the page. My brain is too fuzzy from the lack of oxygen to decipher the name.

Zane's gaze darts to my wrist. He blinks and his mouth pops open. His grip loosens as he looks back at me, his eyes widening as recognition flashes.

That's when I see it—his absolute horror of his own actions.

"Zane," I gasp, but even I know it's too late to fix what he started.

"Oh, Melissa," he whispers, and his thumb passes over my lower lip so lightly that I almost don't feel it. His eyes fill with tears and they track down his cheeks unchecked.

He does remember. My laboring heart soars.

He crushes my lips with a kiss as though he's trying to breathe life back into me. I kiss him back through a sob because it's a hopeless cause. He isn't a freak of nature like me. He can't raise the dead.

He lowers to his knees and rocks me, uttering, "I'm so sorry," over and over again through his own sobs. Everything hurts. My death isn't fast, and it is every bit as painful as when the essence of Death was ripped from my cells, but I can't scream through my crushed larynx.

"Zane," I wheeze out on my last breath, and the darkness comes. I just hope Heaven is ready for the likes of me.

Kissing Fate
Chapter 3

THE PAIN IS GONE, and I am falling through the darkness. In the distance, orbs of light approach, but before they can reach me, an arm circles around me, pulling me in a different direction.

I struggle against the grip until my fingers fall onto metal, and I glance down at a brass arm slung around me.

"Shhh," Mandy whispers in my ear. "I need you to cloak us if you can."

I glance over my shoulder at her. I have never cloaked myself before. I don't have the foggiest idea how to do that.

"Your father could make himself invisible if he wanted. I'm sure you can, too. So, do it, before the angels find us!" Her quiet voice carries the edge of panic as we land in a patch of thick bushes and she pushes me down.

Mastering the powers that Papa gave me had not been easy. But I had. And I can conjure things as easily as snapping my fingers, so cloaking us with invisibility should be a snap.

I close my eyes and think of a blanket in the same pattern as the bushes we are in between. Cloth stretches over our heads, covering us, and I glance up at it. I can't tell the difference between the bushes surrounding us and the blanket above us. But it leaves us blind. With Mandy's arms still holding onto me, her fast breaths tickle my neck.

Feet shuffle by outside the bushes; Mandy stiffens, and I hold my breath.

"I could have sworn they landed around here," a gruff voice grumbles.

"Gadrel tried to call Death in to remind him of his task in case killing Fate had triggered a memory, but he's having issues."

I trade a silent glance with Mandy.

"Go check the reaper realm. They have to be here somewhere."

The flap of wings nearly rips the blanket out of place. But I hold onto it with my mind. As soon as Mandy is sure they are gone, she glances at me.

"That's not exactly what I meant by cloaking us, but it worked."

I certainly hope it did, and carefully peel the liner back to peer out from our hiding place. "Where are we?"

"Purgatory. And Levi is over there." She points to a squat building in the distance and the griffin circling it. The deadly sentry doesn't stop; it just keeps circling and circling.

"I need to go get Zane and bring your body here before they figure out a way to get to it." Mandy doesn't wait for me to speak; she just blinks right out of the area under the blanket I have partially folded.

I'm not sure whether or not I should stay put, but I watch the griffin with interest, counting the seconds he takes to completely circle around the building. That thing hurt Mandy, and I find I want to go pluck its wings and de-claw the thing. Then I'd like to see it fight Levi.

I see a flash inside the bars, as if Levi senses me. But there isn't anything I can do right now to save him.

The air shifts and I turn. Mandy stands beside Zane with the scythe in her hand. Zane still has my limp body in his arms. At the sight of my slack form, my essence recognizes where it belongs, and I glide over the distance and slam into the flesh and bone that was once me, filling my skin again.

It's strange and awful and exhilarating.

My eyes blink open and I'm in Zane's arms. He stares down at me with tear-stained eyelashes. "Missy?" he says with a sniffle.

For a moment, I don't react. Then the last few minutes prior to my death comes barreling back and along with it comes the anger. I push out of his arms and he drops me. I roll and jump to my feet, turning on him.

"You killed my mother," I snarl. "You killed me," I add when he just blinks at me.

"I wasn't exactly myself," he says. "But whatever you did seemed to knock me out of it." He mops his face with his bloodied hand, leaving streaks of drying blood across his face like some primal war paint.

I am not sure he even knows what I did to break the spell, and I'm not inclined to enlighten him.

"How could you possibly forget?" I nearly screech. But I'm aware of how close to the griffin we are, and the fact that thing tore half of Mandy's arm off tempers my need to shout at Zane.

Zane presses his lips together and shakes his head. "You don't know what it's like to be beaten to death every hour of every day, only to relive it again and again and again." His knuckles whiten around the staff in his hand and he looks into the distance as his jaw muscles jump. Then he squints. "What's that?"

"The griffin guarding Levi," Mandy says.

The slow grin that comes over his lips makes me shiver.

"That's the angels' pet?" He glances at Mandy, twirling his scythe in his hand like a majorette. The blade glistens through the blood and gore still clinging to it. And then he steps toward the monster.

Kissing Fate
Chapter 4

"NOT SO FAST." I put my hand up, and he glances down at me with arched eyebrows.

"But..." He points the scythe toward the hut where they are keeping Leviathan.

"Levi can wait. If we go without a plan, we are likely to get maimed like Mandy did, or worse."

"I'm Death," he says with an arrogant puff of his chest that makes me want to take him down a few pegs.

Both Mandy and I burst out laughing, and irritation blooms in the tight set of his lips.

"You are not a fighter," I say when I finally wind down.

"I bested you, didn't I?"

"You got lucky. You can't do it again."

He hands Missy the scythe and steps forward until he towers over me. "If you didn't have that touch curse..." His head cocks and his eyes narrow.

I can almost see his brain working, assessing the last few minutes at the house. The hug I shared with Faith, and the fact he still has a soul.

Then he blinks and his mouth pops open. "It's gone?"

I do not want to give him the satisfaction of being the reason the curse was lifted. The fact he wasn't here for ten years still burns deep. But the way he is looking at me makes me shift and nod.

The edge of his lips curve into a cocky smile.

"Finish what you were going to say," I snap up at him.

"I'd kick your ass."

I grab the edges of his shirt and pull him toward me, kicking out my hip as I roll him over it into a flip that slams his back onto the ground. He blinks at the sky and then meets my gaze. "You had the benefit of your Death touch before, now you don't." I point at him. "And I'm still pissed at you for so many reasons, but this time I won't let my emotions drive me to be stupid like I did in Papa's basement."

I turn to walk away, and my feet are swept from underneath me. I land on the dirt and roll, but he's fast and on top of me, pinning my wrists to the ground next to my head. The muscles in his arms bulge in the shirt, nearly tearing the fabric, and his wrist still weeps blood where I cut through the angel's sigil. I can't help the arousal that flares in me, but I stuff it back into the dark corner of my soul where it belongs.

"I'm not as incompetent as you think I am," he actually growls down at me.

The flash of anger in his eyes gets my aggravation itching my skin like a flea attack. "Well, I wasn't useless either, but you made the damn choice to take the scythe from me and what did that get us? A hell of a lot more dead people than if you had just let me handle the angels without being such a chauvinistic asshole."

"I took the scythe to save you."

"Bullshit. You just wanted to be the hero of your own damn story."

He closes his eyes and takes a breath. "I wasn't trying to be a hero. I was making sure I didn't lose you. Stopping the angels from hurting you was part of it, but those bastards will never stop. They reduced me to nothing, all to make sure I delivered your dead body to them. Same with the Ryans." His eyes open and he searches my gaze. "You holding both the roles of Death and Fate had nothing to do with their vendetta."

"They killed my father, and you killed my mother." I will not mention Kylee or Gabriel being slaughtered in Papa's basement. Both of them were casualties of his angel-controlled wrath. At least he didn't kill Kylee's kids. If he had, there would be no forgiving him.

He nods. "I did." He doesn't make excuses, and that warms a part of my furious heart. "They have your father, though."

His weight settles on me and that rightness I remember when I was near him fills me. I shake it off as I try to wiggle out of his hold, but his hands are like vises. The same vises that strangled me to death.

"Where?" I say through clenched teeth and attempt to twist my wrist.

"The Other. At least that's what they called it." A dimple appears in his cheek as I continue to struggle against his grip. "Are you having issues?"

He has no idea what I am capable of, not with some of Papa's power running through me. And now that I have my body, I still have that angelic juice mixed in my veins. I imagine being as hot as a stove burner set on high.

His cocky smile slips, and he hisses and rolls away from me, shaking his hands as if they are on fire. "Damn it," he mutters and glances at me with wide eyes.

I climb to my feet and brush the dirt off my backside. "I'm not having issues at all."

Zane stares at his reddened hands and then glances at Mandy.

"She's more of a force now than she was when she held both positions, so if I were you, I wouldn't get on her bad side," Mandy says. "Although, with what you did back there, I'd say you were pretty well entrenched on her shit list."

I am not ready to disclose my new and exceptional arsenal of gifts. Not until I am positive he can't slip back under the control of the angels. Until then, I need to keep him at arm's length—even though my body definitely has other thoughts.

"Where is the Other?" I ask because I can't seem to pull any information out of any memories of Death or Fate that are embedded in my mind. The Other is a black hole with no references.

"I don't know. I thought it was Hell. Especially because they employed my father to beat me to death over and over and over, like a sick version of Groundhog Day." He lets out a sarcastic laugh. "Maybe that *was* the bastard's idea of Heaven." Zane shrugs and we both glance at Mandy.

The color in her cheeks fades. "The Other isn't something any of us have ever seen. I thought it was a myth."

"It isn't. Missy's dad seemed to understand what it was. But I was totally blind unless the angel allowed light in."

The more I hear of his time away from me in the Other, the more fury laces my blood and the more I want the angels to feel my wrath. I shake the thoughts out of my head and glance over my shoulder at where they have Leviathan caged.

"We need to get him out of there, but we only have a small window to get to him before the griffin circles back to the front. It's literally less than a minute between when he disappears behind the building and when he reappears on the other side." I glance at Mandy's arm. "You should hang back." I point at her.

"No, sir." She hands Zane the scythe and crosses her arms. "I'm not letting you get near that thing without me by your side to protect you."

"I'll go get him out," Zane says, like a macho idiot.

"We do this together." I glare at him. "Or you sit on the sideline."

"You can't make me sit this one out."

I bark a short laugh. "I can order you to stand down." I point at him. "Remember, I am your boss. So, do I need to issue an order?"

The frown that forms and the rounding of his shoulders announces his displeasure, but he shakes his head. "What's the plan?" he grumbles and kicks at the dirt.

I turn toward the target. "If we can't get him out in the time we have, we need to kill that thing."

Zane slowly smiles. It seems he's gotten the taste of killing and he likes it.

I shiver. The only life I enjoyed taking was Zane's father, but killing him after I stripped him of his soul made it possible for the angels to intervene on his final destination. That was on me. I glance at the griffin in the distance and that same righteous justification fills me.

"Or at least subdue it until we can free Levi. I think our friend will want the honors of ending that thing." In my heart, I know Levi wants his chance to set things right.

"It's Heaven's lapdog," Zane says.

"Yes. And Levi gets to destroy it. Not us." I point at him. "Do you understand?"

"Fine." He rolls his eyes. "Let's get on with this."

Zane takes the position on my right and Mandy steps to my left, and we start toward what could be another disastrous decision.

Kissing Fate
Chapter 5

THERE IS TOO MUCH space between us and the prison gate that holds Levi. Walking will put us in the griffin's cross hairs. I stop and take Zane's hand in mine. He glances at the connection and then meets my gaze.

When I take Mandy's, I stop and wait until the griffin has rounded the nearest back corner and then close my eyes, wishing us all in front of the gate holding Levi in. Wind blows through my hair and when it settles, I open my eyes. The three of us stand in front of the gate.

Levi turns his head in our direction and my heart squeezes at the condition he is in. Ten years of lockdown and angel wrath has left him nothing more than a husk of himself. The monster I remember has been replaced by a blackened creature, and I am stunned into inaction.

Zane stands next to me with the same sorrow-filled, open-mouthed gape as I have, and I snap my mouth closed.

Levi's gaze goes to the scythe in Zane's hand and then snaps back to mine.

"A lot has happened since you were locked away," I whisper.

And then the flap of wings fills our world.

We all spin with our backs to Levi's prison.

The griffin opens his beak, and a high-pitched squeak that reminds me of a mouse comes forth. It's such a disappointing sound from such a frightening beast. At least a lion's roar would have done it more justice. Even a blackbird's caw is more ominous.

Even so, his talons and back claws are deadly. It flaps its wings above us and the wind it produces plasters us against the bars.

I force my arm out straight, with my palm facing him, and yell a spell that Raven had taught me. "Vel prohivere non morieris!" It is supposed to stop a person from attacking me. Of course, the temporary spell only lasts a few minutes, enough time to get far enough away from the assaulter. Although it was meant for rapist or muggers, I thought it might be enough to at least stun the griffin.

Unfortunately, all it does is infuriate the beast, so I tap into my more potent powers. I yank my arms down and the griffin falls from the sky as if an invisible rope had hog-tied the thing.

"Use the scythe on the lock. I can't hold him forever," I snap, straining to hold the griffin in an imaginary noose. Each time the thing claws at my invisible binding, I have to grit my teeth. It's as if his claws are tearing my flesh.

Metal meets metal with a scream behind me. I can't take my eyes off the bird thing as I listen to Zane's attempts. When a creak breaks through the reverb of metal, I step to the side, still holding the griffin fast.

The growl that comes from the cage has even me shivering, but the griffin stiffens, and its eyes grow wide. Leviathan's beastly snarls are what a magical monster is supposed to sound like, not the delicately small squeak of the griffin.

A streak of reptilian skin darts past me, with jaws wide. I hold tight because I don't want the griffin to lay one filthy claw on my Levi. As Zane said, this was the angels' pet, and I wanted it in pieces. Feathers fly, followed by fur.

When I'm sure there is very little fight left in the bird, I loosen the tight reins, but I don't let go altogether because I want to feel its departure from this realm. I want Heaven to know their pet protector has been torn to pieces.

If I had my druthers, I would have just launched Heaven's blade at the bugger, but that tool was on lockdown and I would only grab it if there were no other way to win. With Levi gleefully devouring the griffin, I didn't need to make a grand show of terminating the monster.

My Book of Fates charm dings and I close my eyes, pulling forth the information in case there is something else that needs my attention. The bell tolls for the griffin. I smile and fully release my hold.

"Leave something for them to find," I say, and Levi looks back at me with a maw full of dripping feathers and fur as if I'm spoiling his fun. "Seriously, I want them to know."

He growls, but drops what's left of the mangled body and approaches us. He sniffs Zane and lets out a low warning growl, showing his ferocious teeth. In his natural form, he looks like some weird combination of Godzilla and a dragon. His jaws are powerful enough to snap the strongest steel. And yet when he turns his snout to me, that growl ceases.

"I need you in dog form." I place my hand on his snout.

His head tilts into my touch and shrinks into my trusty German shepherd, who immediately tackles me and laps my face. It's as though he truly is a dog and not an epic monster. I wrap my arms around him and squeeze, hugging him with everything I have.

"I missed you, too, but we have to get back to the lake house before something happens to the rest of my family."

Kissing Fate
Chapter 6

W ITH ONE HAND AROUND Levi's collar and the other clasped in Zane's hand, I look to Mandy on the other side of Levi. "Can you get us to the lake house?" The cottage by Mirror Lake in Brooksfield, New Hampshire, is our family's designated emergency spot. It's also the place where I met Mandy for the first time and gave the reapers human forms.

Although Papa owns it on paper, it has always been Steve and Jennifer Williams's home in the sticks. And since Papa sold their penthouse in New York City after Faith took out

Lucifer, it was the only place left for Steve and Jennifer to live since I brought them back to life ten years ago.

"Yes." Mandy nods, but she looks at Zane. "You cannot touch anyone but the three of us, understand?" She points at him with her metal finger. "You are toxic until you can figure out how to protect them. And I don't mean you'll make them sick—I'm talking with even a brush against someone, you kill."

"No shit." He chews his bottom lip. "It seems the only real power I have is killing."

I refrain from rolling my eyes. "There's likely to be some backlash for what happened at Papa's." I'm not sure if Michael Andreas will be of the right mind not to attack Zane. And Damian and Naomi may very well be in the same court of anguish.

His frown deepens, and he nods. But I don't have time to deal with his guilty conscience right now. Instead, I focus on Mandy and when she closes her eyes; I feel the pull.

This is the first time I've consciously transitioned from the afterlife to Earth and it makes my entire form tingle before I free-fall through the realms. It's like flying and I smile with the exhilaration until I land on my feet, jarring my body back into existence.

The sun just breaks over the mountains, lighting the frost-covered lawn and making the yard look silver-coated. I look up into the big picture window of the cottage. The soft glow of the light inside illuminates a full-length breakfast table and a few of the early risers sitting with their back to us.

I turn to Zane. "You might want to go into the woods and wait while I go inside. Mandy, you can go with him and make sure he doesn't get into trouble." I point toward where Paradise Cove used to be. The only known portal to Heaven existed on this property until Faith Ryan closed it when she learned the angels were gunning for me.

Now it's just an overgrown cove with crunchy moss. It'd be the last place any celestial would look for Death.

I glance down at Levi. "Make sure they are safe." I nod toward Mandy and Zane. He looks dejected, and I pat his head. "I'll be back. I promise." I crouch down, giving my favorite monster a hug.

"You might want to change before you go in. You smell hideous." Levi turns his snout away.

I glance down at myself and blink in disgust. My pants are soiled and my shirt is marred with blood. One glance at Zane, and I realize why. Back here in the land of the living, we still have the gore of the dead splashed all over us. I close my eyes and let my conjuring magic swell, cleaning both of us until we are left with pristine clothes. I even clean the scythe until it gleams.

But I leave Zane's white shirt unbuttoned. I quite like the view of his ripped chest. I realize I'm objectifying him, but right now, I need something that reminds me of what I am fighting for, and what better view than the body I've dreamed of against mine for the last ten years? I want him to remember what he is fighting for, too, just in case Heaven gets their grubby hands back on him. I take a deep breath, debating. And then the perfect memory surfaces: the way he looked at me when I came back from my showdown with the reapers.

I close my eyes, envisioning the way the leather fit on my body, the cut of the bodice, the flare of the duster skirt and the thigh-high slits. He sucks in air between his teeth, and I open my eyes to that hungry spark in his eyes that I remember. I can almost hear the expletive falling from his lips as he scans me.

His eyebrow raises, and I shrug in response, allowing a ghost of a smile to form.

"Any chance you could teach me how to stow this somewhere so I'm not carrying it like some horror movie reject?" He glances at his scythe. "I don't want a charm bracelet, though." Although the symbolism of the scythe is necessary, for Death to always have that staff in his hand is a ridiculous standard. He can't put it down. Not without putting his livelihood in jeopardy, not to mention his existence.

"All you need to do is will it to be so," I say. "But you have to be able to make it appear in your hand again. It's all mental will and imagining it happening."

He closes his eyes and creases of concentration appear on his forehead, but nothing happens.

I'm thinking he really has no powers besides being Death.

His eyes open to the staff still in his hand and he glances at me. "I suck at this."

I close my eyes and imagine a miniature scythe hanging from a golden chain around his neck. That cool rush of air flows through me, and I am pleased when I open my eyes. A golden-linked chain hangs around his neck with the silver scythe hanging on a loop. The way it sits on his chest stirs a deep need.

"Better?" I look away from him, dousing the heat centering in my belly at his intense gaze.

"Much!" Levi says and trots toward the entrance to the woods, as if I had asked him instead of Zane.

"Go on," I say to him as I shoo him toward Levi.

His smile falters as he plays with the charm on his necklace. "I, um. I'd rather not." He glances over his shoulder at the path that Levi stands on, waiting, and shifts from side to side. "I don't want to lose sight of you right now." He sucks in his lower lip and avoids my gaze.

I tense until he finally looks at me. His green eyes shimmer as he glances around.

"What if this isn't real?" He grips the necklace so tight I think he might snap it. His chin trembles. "What if I wake up back in that place?"

His words crush my insides. I cross to him and take his hand, steeling my emotions. "It is not safe for the people inside to have you near them."

His lips curl down into a frown, but he nods. At least he, of all people, understands my need to keep my family safe.

"Besides, you have Levi to protect you." I point toward the woods and then I turn his hand so he can see his wrist. "I broke their ability to pull you away. See?"

For the first time since the battle in the basement, he looks at his wrist and blinks at the deep cut interrupting the sigil on both sides of the circle.

"That's how they were controlling you." I tilt his chin, so he looks at me. "They can't find you anymore. I promise."

He reaches out, cups my face, and softly runs his thumb across my cheekbone. "I hurt you. I can't take that back, but I plan on trying to make it up to you for the next hundred thousand years."

"I know. Now go before someone sees you. I need to break the news that I died as well, so you need to be scarce while I smooth this all over. Understand?"

He chews on his lower lip and glances up at the house. "Too late." He juts his chin toward the window.

I turn and splay my fingers out, taking a protective step in front of Zane. Michael Andreas, Kylee's husband, marches across the lawn with his fists clenched and his hateful blue-eyed gaze locked on Zane. They say Michael looks like his namesake, the Archangel Michael. His great-uncle. You see, Damian, Michael's father, is the Archangel Gabriel's son. They all have dark hair and that olive skin so prevalent in the Greek isles, but they share the angel kin's blue eyes. It's a trait that is unmistakable, and I can only imagine what the archangels look like.

"Stop," I yell, pulling his gaze to mine, but he doesn't slow down.

"I should have ended both of you ten years ago," he growls through clenched teeth.

I conjure an invisible wall between us, and Michael smacks into it. He stumbles back and spins toward the house, rubbing his nose.

"Let me through, CJ!" His voice echoes over the still lake.

His insinuation that Papa put up the barrier to stop him almost makes me laugh. "Papa didn't do that," I say.

His gaze swivels back to me. "What?"

The sharpness of his clipped tone makes me wince.

My hands are still splayed, but instead of just a gesture of placation, they were actually holding the wall in place between us and Michael. I needed a little more concentration to create and hold something versus Papa, who could create a barrier and go about his day while it's held in place.

"I put that there." I take a breath. "He was under the angel's control. He did not know what he was doing."

"He killed Kylee!" Michael snarls.

"And Gabriel, and my mother." I swallow the knot in my chest as Zane's sins drop from my lips. "And me before I could stop him."

Michael blinks at me, but his hands remain fisted. "I don't care. I am going to kick his ass."

"I'm not holding you back because I'm worried about him." I meet his gaze. "I'm holding you back because his touch is Death."

"I don't care!"

"I do. You have kids. And Kylee would be pissed if I let you die because of your own stupidity!"

He presses his lips together and looks out at the lake. The sheen of tears glazes over his eyes.

"Michael, my father wasn't able to teach him to protect us from his touch. And they have my father in the same place they had Zane for all these years. They brainwashed him."

"And you believe him?" he snarls at me.

I turn and grab Zane's arm, twisting it so Michael can see the ruined sigil. "You know what that is, right?" I point to it and wait. He had been around enough while Kylee was schooling me in the different sigils. He saw the drawings and I'm sure when they went home at night, he'd ask her questions that perhaps I hadn't.

His glare morphs into wide-eyed recognition, and then he glances back at me. His hands uncurl slowly.

"Your anger is misplaced." I drop Zane's hand. "You and I want the same thing. I want payback, too," I say, but I still hold the mental wall in place between us. I don't trust Michael. I know all too well how much the loss of a loved one affects the mind. "Unfortunately, I had to break the curse while his hands were around my throat."

I thought the need for vengeance burning through me then was bad after the angels murdered my father, but now, every cell in my body craves revenge as much as I yearn for Zane's touch. Maybe someday I'd be able to indulge in those decadent wants, but today I have more important issues to deal with.

Like how to protect the people in this house. *I* can't protect them. I don't have the same authority to safeguard those I love from Death's touch like I had when I *was* Death.

Unfortunately, only Zane can grant that, and he does not know how.

"I'm sorry." Zane's voice cracks with emotion. "I didn't know what I was doing. I know that's no consolation, but had I had any control over my mind, none of that would have happened."

Michael's gaze drops to the ground and the muscles in his jaw jumps. When his eyes raise back up, there is a dark anger still there. "What are you going to do about this?" He looks directly at me.

I drop my hands. "I'm going to make sure you all survive whatever war the angels are waging. It's dirty and vile and hellish, and I won't allow those dicks to harm any of you."

"Your walls won't hold against Heaven," he says.

"They seem to be quite scared of Papa's shields." I cock an eyebrow, challenging him.

"The legion of angels I saw the day he died didn't seem to be scared." Michael waved at Zane. "If they really were plotting our demise, why wouldn't they have done it then?"

It's a valid question. "Maybe they were as shocked by Zane's actions as I was. I have no idea."

"They want everyone here to die. They have a real problem with Missy and the Ryans, and I don't have the foggiest idea why," Zane said. "But they thought they could use me as their weapon, and if Missy hadn't been smart enough to do this"—he raises his gouged wrist—"I would have continued coming until you were all dead by my hand." He bites his lower lip and shakes his head. "They stripped me of my memories and turned me into a monster that was far worse than my father ever was."

Levi and Mandy stroll back over to us.

"I guess we aren't hiding in the woods?" Levi says, looking between us and breaking the tension.

Michael actually smiles at the sight of Levi in drag. "I thought he was under the watch of a griffin." He waves at the dog by my side.

"He was, but when we set Levi free, he destroyed that god-awful thing. But we left just enough to let them know we are a force to be reckoned with." I smile, but it fades as the weight of what I need to do crashes down on me. "I just need to figure out a viable plan to defeat them."

Kissing Fate
Chapter 7

MICHAEL ANDREAS ISN'T THE only one at the cottage besides Steve and Jennifer Williams, as evidenced by the line of familiar cars in the driveway, so when we walk into the house, I envision a protective box around Zane, so no one inadvertently touches him while we are inside. I mentally measure a perimeter of a foot and a half on all sides of him just to be sure and create a clear, unassuming buffer to keep the rest of my family safe. Unless someone walks into the safety zone around him, no one will be the wiser.

Papa sits straighter in the chair with his lips set in a stiff frown at the sight of Zane. When his gaze falls to me, I give him a nod of acknowledgment. I've never been able to communicate telepathically with any of them, despite being given a dose of angel juice. I could only send out a mental SOS if I needed help, but even that had taken years to perfect.

"Where's your mother?" he asks when the door closes behind Mandy.

I take a breath and shake my head, shifting through the sudden tightening of my throat. "She didn't make it."

That's three casualties at the hands of the man behind me. The hostility in the room ratchets up a notch as silence falls over everyone.

It's early enough for the teenage kids to still be sleeping, but most of the adults are present. Besides Papa sitting in the recliner in the living room with a tablet in his hand, Nana is sitting at the table with Papa's parents, Ty and Jessica, along with Tom and his wife, Raven. It looks like they are playing cards, but I can't imagine trying to think this early in the morning. Although every single one of them has a steaming cup next to their hands.

Michael must have been at the table because there is an empty spot with cards face down, but now he stands with his back to us, as if just looking at us brings him pain. Which I can relate to. His parents are on the couch with their e-readers, too.

Neither one of the homeowners is present, but the sound of a shower running down the hall could be either Steve or Jennifer Williams. I'm just glad that the only cop in the bunch isn't here glaring at us with his own judgment.

It's bad enough that everyone is staring at us as if we are the enemy.

Well, all except Tom Ryan and his father Ty. Those two seem to stare with frank curiosity instead of open hostility. I guess they are the only true ones of the bunch who understand the stigma of being an outsider.

Either way, the attention is unnerving.

"But you made it out okay," Faith says from the kitchen entry. I spin in her direction, surprised to see her and Alex with dish rags in their hands. I had been so focused on Papa and the rest of the family that I didn't notice anyone in the kitchen.

I let out a shaky laugh. "No. Not quite." I trade a glance with her and press my lips together. "But I was able to break the hold the angels had on him before I bit it."

Fire sparks from her fingers as she narrows her gaze at Zane. "What do you have to say for yourself?"

Faith reacts exactly as I expected. She's always been uber protective of me. Sometimes even more protective than with her own daughter Holly. But I guess that has to do with having absentee parents for sixteen years of my life. They saw what that did to me and this was her way of making it up to me in my folks' absence.

Zane drops his gaze and shrugs. Guilt rolls off him in devastating waves. "I have no valid excuse," he says, owning a mistake that isn't his fault.

Faith's fingers don't stop sparking, nor does the glare soften.

I clear my throat. I can't let him take the blame for what the angels did to him. Ten years is a long time. I'd bet that anyone in this room would cave to that sort of brainwashing. Hell, I think Papa's father is the only one who could relate intimately.

I focus my attention on Faith and Papa. "You saw him," I say and zero in on one of Papa's memories. "Zane was as far gone as your dad was after Lucifer mind-fucked him."

Papa recoils in the seat as if I just slapped him. I guess that memory is as painful to him now as it was then.

I glance at Faith. Her fingers are still spitting sparks. "The angels are just as black-souled as your father with what they did to Zane. He was not himself. And if you have any doubt whether he snapped out of it or not, you have the ability to see for yourself." I wave at the space between us like a game show host showing a contestant a coveted prize. "You can also show us exactly how Heaven undid him." I cross my arms, cocking an eyebrow as I look from her flaming fingers back to her face. "If you are so hesitant to believe he is on our side, show us what happened so everyone can make their own judgment calls."

As soon as I utter the words, I want to pull them back. I really do not want to see Zane beaten to death. That will undo me just as much as it screwed him up. The thought of it happening multiple times a day, for ten years, leaves me cold and furious.

"Why are you so quick to trust him?" She fists her hands to douse her anger.

I suck my lower lip in between my teeth. I haven't told him about my infusion of Papa's power, never mind Raven's witchcraft lessons or Kylee's schooling on sigils. I don't trust that he is out of danger yet.

I don't trust him.

The realization drops my stomach.

"I don't," I finally say. "Not completely. But he didn't deliver me to the angels, and he did set Levi free, so I am trying to give him the benefit of the doubt." I glance over my shoulder at him, meeting his gaze. "He's going to have to earn my trust again." I look away, unable to stand the hurt in his eyes.

The area between us shimmers and morphs into the basement of Papa's house and thankfully the scene is of Zane strangling me against the wall and not the earlier carnage.

I'm actually turning blue and my skin under his hands has blackened. I'm staring up at him as tears streak my face and I'm trying to loosen his grip any way possible, but he doesn't yield. And then the tip of my finger morphs into a blade that I use to tear through the sigil on his wrist just as the Book of Fates dings on my charm bracelet.

Everything about him changes in that instant, and I see a glimpse of the old Zane as he stares down at me. The truth of what he is doing paints his face in a horrified grimace. His hands release their tight grip on my throat, but I'm too far gone.

Hell, he crushed my vocal cords and all I can do is hiss out his name.

He kisses me and then pulls away. Tears roll down his face as he apologizes over and over, falling to his knees with me in his arms. His sobs continue even as Mandy blinks back into the room and dislodges the scythe from my mother's dead body.

"You need to come with me now," she says and grabs his arm. All three of us disappear in a blink.

The air ripples again, and the cottage falls back into view. But before anyone can speak, the space transforms again. This time, the view isn't of Papa's house. It's a rock-formed cave.

I glance over my shoulder at Zane. All color bleeds from his face, and that says a lot, considering he's already dead. His trembling lips and wide eyes broadcast his absolute terror. His chest even rises and falls like someone close to hyperventilating.

The conversation outside flares bright in my mind. His fear of this cottage, of me, not being real is manifesting in the shakes accosting him. He can't tear his eyes away from the brutal truths being laid bare for all of us to witness.

I step closer and take his shaking hand as the image of his father strikes another debilitating blow.

Zane's attention snaps to our intertwined hands and then to me. His chin trembles and he blinks back the sheen in his eyes. He grasps my hand tight, and relief smooths out some lines on his face. His breathing calms and some of the color returns to his cheeks.

Being strong for him helps soothe that immediate need to pummel an angel in the same way his father is beating him, and I squeeze his hand as I refocus on Faith's time jump in front of us. I glance back in time to see his broken body fall to the ground, and yet his father still kicks him until the angel intervenes. When the angel offers Zane relief from the beating in exchange for my death, Zane tells the angel to fuck off, in so many words. Then that bastard touches Zane's forehead and the scene repeats. Over and over.

This was his existence for ten years. My stomach rolls, and I nearly gag on the acid. "Stop," I command after watching Zane get pounded to death five times in a row.

The scene disappears in a poof, as if I just unplugged a television. Silence fills the cabin, and I glance outside at the bright sunshine. How much time had passed while we watched Faith's time jump? Enough to move the clock to midday.

The next thought chills me to the core. *How many portals did Faith open by showing us this?* If the breaches she created are in Heaven or Purgatory, it may bite us in the ass. It's truly an odd feeling, praying for a breach in Hell, but that's what I find myself doing as I blink at the sun-drenched lawn outside the window.

Everyone is staring at Zane with the same abject horror coating my veins with a toxic need for vengeance.

Thankfully, I'm not an impulsive teenager anymore, or I would have blinked into Purgatory with Heaven's blade at my side and recklessly slaughtered as many of the bastards as I could. But that need is still there, fanning the flames.

Zane slowly pulls away from me, breaking our hold, and he turns toward the door. His movements are stilted, as if he doesn't know whether to walk or run, but he leaves the cottage in one hell of a hurry.

I glance at Faith and give her a nod. I know what she risked. I think some of the others know, too, because they talk in hushed tones. I can't deal with breaches today. That's a problem we will have to deal with some other time.

I turn and head to find Zane. He's already at the dock, sitting with his head in his hands. I can't imagine the confusion and pain he's stuck in right now, but he needs to get it all out before they come. There is no doubt in my mind that they will appear, but they have to find us first.

When I take a seat next to him and start softly rubbing his back, he says, "They are going to send him after me."

"Who?"

"My father."

My first reaction is to wince, but I suppress the urge. It makes sense. They know his weakness and will exploit it. My blood boils, creating a hot flush through my entire form.

"Good." I welcome a face-to-face with his father. This time I will not be as humane as I was the first time I killed him. I might be inclined to skin him alive with a spoon or something appropriately painful.

That bastard deserves a prolonged death. I'll have to noodle on that for a while to come up with a particularly horrendous way to kill him that will cause maximum suffering.

Zane stares at me. "What do you mean, good?"

"This time I won't be so nice." Hell, I even know some really horrific spells, too. The more I think about it, the more I smile.

"You scare me sometimes," he says.

I don't respond, but inside I'm feeling accomplished. Scaring Death isn't a small thing. But as much as visions of vengeance seem to quell the rising fury inside me, I can't let it lull me into not being vigilant.

I refocus on Zane. "We need to get you to tap into some ethereal magic." I meet his gaze.

"I'm not a part of your bloodline." He stares at me as though there is no magic inside him, but I know better. Every Death could at the very least hide and call the scythe from the ether.

"My mother wasn't of any special bloodline either, and she learned to conjure things when she took Fate's job."

His eyebrow cocks. "Really?"

"You have Death's memories in there." I tap his temple. "Take a look."

He closes his eyes. "I barely have my own memories and you want me to..." His head cocks like a curious puppy and then he grips the deck stair underneath us and his eyelids fly open. His great inhalation makes me smile.

I remember the sudden rush of memories. It felt as if I were plastered on the front of a speeding freight train heading toward a dead end. And from the look on his face and the rapid blinking of his lids, he is experiencing that rush right now.

He falls backward and stares up at the blue, cloudless sky above us before he wipes his face. "Goddamn," he whispers. "I'm glad I'm already dead. I would hate to pass this along to my son," he says through his hands. "Who made up that fucked-up rule?" He moves his hands and squints at me. "Seriously?"

I shrug. I never really took stock of the parameters of Death—the rules or the origins. But he is right, and I scan the lake in front of us. Heaven destroyed the original being that held both roles. A sour taste laces my mouth.

"Heaven," we both say at the same time and trade glances.

Zane sits up next to me and shakes his head. "Remember when you told me that everything you thought you knew about good and evil was all screwed up?"

I huff. "Yes."

"Well, I'm there right now."

"I've been there for ten years. Welcome to the club." I don't want to entertain this conversation at the moment. It always sends me into a dark place. "So, with all this new information in your head, do you understand the dynamics of conjuring?"

"With all this shit in my head, it's hard to figure out where *I* begin and end." He rubs his temples. "But yeah. I get some of it. Your dad was in the position the longest, by the way. Everyone else was only in the post for twenty-five years max. Some had powers, but some didn't. But they all could pull the scythe from wherever they hid it. Did you realize, before your grandfather, no one messed with time?" He licks his lips and glances at me. "You could have turned back the clock and not picked up the book or taken the scythe, you know."

I glance away from him and nod. I knew that. I even considered it. "There are always consequences to manipulating the timeline. The reapers would have kept coming, and others would have died."

He ponders my answer as he picks at a hangnail. "You could have still taken them," he says with a certainty I never had. "And then we would have been together without all this hanging over our heads." He glances at me. "I bet we'd be married by now." His lips twitch into a smile.

I narrow my eyes at him. "Do you not get what consequences mean? Take a long goddamn look at the consequences of my father and grandfather's actions." It was the reason I pushed that aside and didn't even consider it. "And we aren't married. Not even close," I spit out, letting him know in no uncertain terms that he is still in the doghouse with me right now.

I take a breath, getting hold of the aggravation. As much as his questions are irritating me, it's not him. It's that damn clock ticking in my head. The more we pussyfoot around this, the more dire things feel.

"Look, I am on edge. And rightfully so." I glance at him. "But right now, I need you to figure this out, because if I'm not with you and they come, your scythe is useless on the necklace I created." I flick the charm at the end of the chain.

He grabs my wrist with a malicious glare that is so out of character for Zane. And then his eyes clear, as though he forgot where he was for a second. His hold on me loosens. He shakes his head in a violent quick burst, like he's trying to rid himself of his demons.

"Sorry," he mutters and brings my hand to his lips, pressing the softest of kisses on my skin before he lets go.

I pull my hand into my lap, away from him, trying not to show the unease shuffling through my mind. *It's almost as if...* "Let me see that sigil," I say before that horrific thought fully forms.

He voluntarily holds out his hand so I can see the mark. He is healing, and the broken sigil is almost rebuilt.

I hate it when I'm right. "Damn it. It hasn't even been a full day."

He gulps. "Maybe we should keep this thing right where it is," he says with a frantic desperation layering in both his voice and his eyes.

Before I can speak, he leans in and captures a kiss. I'm too shocked to stop him. Not even when his hands cup my face, and he swipes his tongue across my closed lips. I open my mouth perhaps to argue, but I don't have the heart to stop him, not when his kiss is so magical. It lulls me into a putty he could easily sculpt, but the sirens inside me push him away.

Trusting him right now could get everyone in the house killed.

"We need to address that," I say breathlessly and point at the sigil.

"What do you suggest?" He stares at the thing that interrupted our kiss. Disgust pulls his lips back in a grimace as he stares at the thing that could control whatever powers he harbors.

I swipe my razor-sharp fingernail across it again, adding another deep cut to his flesh.

"Ouch." He pulls his hand away from me.

"I did that this morning at Papa's, and it's almost healed." I don't know how to address this problem short of chopping his arm off, and the thought of doing that makes my stomach churn to the point of being near physically ill.

He takes a deep breath and stares at his left wrist. He tilts his head back and forth as if he is silently arguing with himself, and then he finally nods and looks at me. "Cut it off." He holds his arm out to me.

I'm not crippling him. I recoil away from him, and I guess the horror filling me must be written on my face.

"Look, this thing is going to regenerate again and again. I would rather go without my hand than be locked away for another ten years."

"I...I can't." I cannot wrap my head around being the one to slice his hand off. The action is not within me. I can cut him all day long with my nail, but sever a limb? I just can't.

He climbs to his feet. "I'm sure someone in there would be happy to chop off my arm for me." He starts toward the house. "Maybe Levi will snap it off," he calls over his shoulder.

My mind swirls, and the dark truths unfold. I jump to my feet to intercept him. "Wait," I say as

I skid in front of him and put both my hands on his chest, making him stop. "There has to be another way."

The resolve is already written in the tight set of his lips. "Will you love me any less without a hand?"

My eyes roll. His physique isn't what I'm in love with. "For Christ's sake, why would you even ask that?"

"That's the only reason I can think of why you wouldn't agree to this."

I hate his matter-of-factness right now. His logic is flawless, and it burns, but I still can't wrap my head around it. "I'm just saying there has to be a way to burn that sigil out without you losing your hand. We have angel fire at our disposal." I wave toward the house.

His eyebrows arch. "So, you'd rather see my arm burned to the bone instead of chopped off?"

I close my eyes and that hideous vision blooms. "No. I'd rather you be unharmed, but I can't keep slicing your wrist with my fingernail when it's healing so fast."

"Just burning the skin won't remove it," he says. "They wouldn't put something on me that could be removed so easily, and you know that." He glances down at his wrist. "You cut deep, and that still isn't lasting. Besides, Mandy seems to do pretty good with a mechanical arm."

"Zane." I sigh, coming to grips with his decision as well as a child being told its bedtime right in the middle of their favorite show. "I don't have the stomach to do it. And we both know Levi won't be a clean cut. Besides, what happens to him if that thing still forms while it's in him?"

He opens his mouth and then closes it. "That would be very, very bad," he finally says.

Understatement of the year. That would mean they could control Leviathan. The griffin was scary enough, but a Heaven-controlled monster? The End of Times would be much better to swallow than that.

"Seriously, there has to be someone in there who would be willing to hack my limb off. I'd put bets on quite a few of them. It might even come to blows for who gets the chance to injure me," he says with a tilted smile.

His attempt at humor affects me, but I can't quite smile back. The subject is just too dark.

He puts his hands over mine, pulling them away from his skin before lacing his fingers through mine. His expression grows serious. "It's the only way to keep you and everyone in there safe."

I squeeze his hands and then pull them from his loose grip. He is right, whether or not I like it. "I know. But I still can't be the one to do it."

He nods and kisses my forehead and then heads around me toward the house.

I turn my back on the house, looking out over the lake. I'm sure there will be a line forming to hack his arm off.

Another dark truth bites me in the ass. It is not safe for anyone else to do it. Touching Zane in any way is a death sentence. Damn it. I really need to be the one to do it.

I head inside, where everyone is arguing about who gets to maim Zane. "I will do it!" I yell over the din, and shocked heads turn in my direction. "It's not safe for any of you. Even if you wear gloves."

Zane looks up at the ceiling and then closes his eyes. Just the reminder of Death being in the room with us chills everyone's enthusiasm.

"But, Faith, we might need your fire abilities to cauterize."

"What? Do you think he'll bleed to death? He's already dead," she says, but she steps next to me, anyway. She looks over at Michael standing near Hannah and his children. "Why don't you take them for a walk," she says to Michael as she nods toward the under-eighteen crowd.

Michael glances at Zane's arm and chews on his lower lip before he nods. "Sure," he mutters. "Why don't I take them to the store or something? I think we all need a bit of a break, anyway."

Unease fills me. Hannah is on Heaven's hit list, but I don't want the kids here to witness this. And perhaps a change of scenery would be good to calm some of the hostility still radiating from Michael.

Papa nods. "Maybe you can swing into the pizza place near campus and grab a few pies for dinner."

Michael nods and corrals the kids out the door.

We all focus back on the gruesome task in front of us. I straighten my back and glance in the kitchen at the rack of knives. None of them will be clean. I shivered at the thought of sawing through his flesh and bone.

Zane follows my gaze, and he sits in one of the chairs as if his legs suddenly didn't have the strength to hold him. He stretches his arm out, palm up, gritting his teeth like a part of him is fighting this solution. "Conjure my scythe. It'll slice clean through." He shifts so a good part of his forearm is hanging off the side of the table, enough to rid him of the sigil and then some.

"I don't know if I can touch your scythe." I glance at Mandy. Panic fills every fiber because the sigil is nearly whole again.

"I can do it," Mandy says, lifting the burden from my shoulders and I sag with relief.

Before the sigil completes and I lose Zane again, I conjure the scythe and he hands it to Mandy. My heart hammers against my ribs as if I've sprinted a half-mile stretch down the beach. It's an odd feeling, especially considering, in reality, I'm as dead as any corpse in the cemetery.

Zane looks at me. "Do you mind holding me still?" he asks and attempts a smile, but it fails miserably. "Just...just no one touch the hand because it'll probably still be toxic." He closes his eyes and pulls me close, burying his forehead against my chest.

I wrap my arms around him and hold him as tight as I can, but I'm shaking just as much as he is. I take a quick glance back. We have mere seconds before the circle completes.

Mandy doesn't give any warning; she can see just as well as I can. The whistle of the blade fills the room, followed by a thump on the floor.

Zane inhales sharply and his grip tightens. He whimpers against my chest.

Blood shoots out of the stump, surprising us all. I guess dead is a relative term when you are Fate and Death. Apparently, we can still bleed. My mind wanders back to the time jump. I should have known. He bled in the Other, too. I stroke his hair and whisper, "Shhh" as Faith steps in, pointing her hand at what's left of his forearm.

I close my eyes and the stench of burning flesh follows.

Zane's whimpers turn into a sob as his hold on me tightens. I cannot imagine the agony and my eyes burn with unshed tears. I take a long, slow breath and glance at Mandy, giving her a silent nod of thanks. She slashes the limb on the ground, severing the sigil in half again before she holds the scythe out, relinquishing it with a scowl that tells me she is just as unhappy about this as I am. I will the scythe back onto Zane's necklace and it dissolves in a swirl of light before settling in place on the chain around his neck.

"I'll put these somewhere that won't trace back to here." Mandy picks up the pieces of Zane's severed arm. The halves of the sigil glow for a moment. Then Mandy blinks out of the room, and I say a silent prayer to keep her safe.

I swallow the bile lining my throat and look at Zane's severed arm. The stump is blackened with lines of puss and blood leaking through the crusted end. It's not neat or clean, and I wish to God Nana could heal him the way she had healed Mandy years ago, but no one was safe from Zane.

"Can someone get me some burn salve and bandages, please?" I ask, even though I can hardly force air through my throat.

People move. Nana disappears from the room as Faith grabs a roll of paper towels.

"Don't," I say as she comes closer. "Just get me a couple crappy towels and I'll clean it up after I bandage him. Okay?"

She blinks at me as though I just sprouted three heads.

"It's Zane's blood."

"Oh." She steps back, putting distance between the table and where she stopped.

Alex heads down the hall and comes back with a couple old, ragged towels he dumps onto the blood, before he retreats into the kitchen with Faith.

No one threw up. I'm impressed. Especially with Zane, who still shakes in my arms. I continue my soft cooing as I slowly run my fingers through his thick hair. I don't know if we can suffer from shock the way someone who is alive can, but he has suffered a trauma, so I keep combing his hair and telling him it's going to be okay.

He folds his arm toward his body, and I reach out, catching him at the elbow. "I need to patch you up first."

He nods into my chest and then pulls away, turning toward the damage. I stop him, cupping his cheek and tilting his head so he is looking at me. Tears still flow down his face and he leans into my palm with his green eyes locked on mine.

I shake my head slowly. "Trust me. You don't want to do that yet."

"That hurt like a motherfucker," he says with a raspy voice. "But I don't feel the poison of that tattoo anymore. So, for now, at the very least, you are safe." He lets out a soft laugh as more tears slide unchecked down his cheeks.

I blink away the sting in my eyes and glance around at the remaining people in the room. No one is near the table besides Alex and Faith, and even they are as far into the kitchen as possible and they can't seem to look this way. I don't blame them. Zane's arm is gross.

Papa is still in the recliner, but he is looking at his brother in a way that tells me the two are doing that silent communication thing that twins usually share. Either that or they are having a telepathic conversation. He catches me staring at him and gives me a nod, like he approved of the sacrifice Zane just made for everyone.

Papa's father sits on the couch with a tablet in his hand. He's just staring at Zane's severed stump, but he isn't pale the way Alex and Faith are. He is more relaxed about the amputation than anyone in the room. But then again, with his past, this might just be another walk in the park for him.

The only one in the room who is just as green as I feel is Steve Williams, the former FBI agent. A nagging memory forms, but then Nana steps from the hallway, squashing whatever fragment of someone else's memory was about to surface.

Nana approaches with her medical bag, setting it on the table. She takes out items, lining them up as if she was going to be the one to patch Zane up. When she reaches for his arm, I clear my throat.

"Oh, I forgot." She puts the burn salve on the table next to the bandages.

I peel myself out of Zane's grip. "Look at Papa," I order and point toward the recliner in the other direction of where the patching action is to take place. "And keep your eyes that way, understand?"

Zane nods. "Yes, ma'am," he says with a weak voice, but he does exactly as I instruct.

I take the seat next to him and take a few deep breaths as I dip my fingers into the salve and scoop a healthy dollop out. This is Zane. He doesn't need me hurling all over his burned stump. My throat constricts, tightening against whatever thoughts my stomach might have. With another deep breath, I pick up his arm and cover the blackened skin with the salve, ignoring his hiss of pain.

When I finish bandaging his arm with Nana's supervision, I step to the end of the table and wipe up the puddle on the floor with the towels, wiping any trace of the horror we inflicted on Zane away. I breathe in through my nose, out through my mouth, counting breaths to keep the knowledge of what I'm doing away from my senses.

As soon as I throw the pile of blood-soaked rags in the garbage, everything hits, and I need air. I barely hear Zane calling after me as I bolt out the door. I'm at the end of the dock in a blink and my breath hitches in my chest. I drop

to my knees and dry heave as harsh sobs
constrict my chest.

I grip the edge of the wood and glimpse
myself in the water. My violet eyes nearly glow
with tears and each one that hits the surface
ripples my ugly cry even more.

Zane did that *for me.*

I wipe my face, attempting to get control, but
it's not happening. Not with the knowledge he's
given his life, his mind, and now his arm for me.
So why the hell do I still feel uneasy?

I close my eyes and the image of him
impaling my mother haunts me, followed by his
powerful hands crushing my throat with that
hateful glare as he squeezed the life out of me.

Heaven wedged doubt so far down in my soul
that I can feel its poison spreading through me.
Another tear drops into the water and a shadow
falls over me. I stiffen as Zane's reflection steps
closer.

I wipe my face, pulling the shattered pieces
back together before I climb to my feet and turn.
He still is something to behold, like a knight
right out of a dream. There he stands, with his
shirt still unbuttoned and clinging to his sweat-
kissed skin, his golden necklace gleaming in the
sun, making him look like a fucking god. It's
unfair that even as pale as he is, he can still
make the most attractive of men look homely.

Just the fact he came to check on me
hammers my insides and another round of tears
seeps out of the corner of my eyes.

He crosses and runs his good hand into my
hair, pulling me to his mouth. His tender kiss

melts me and hurts at the same time because I'm still questioning his loyalties.

I'm done wallowing in my confusion. I need to ignore that nagging voice that Heaven put into my head, because I want to trust Zane. I have a choice: let their poison cloud my perception, or let it go. That man choking me in Papa's basement was their puppet, not *this* immortal kissing me as if I'm his entire world.

Mental chains inside me shatter as the freedom of choice rings through my soul. I choose Zane, despite what those bastards tried to do.

I break the kiss and push him away with renewed energy. "We still have work to do before we can focus on whatever is between us." I wipe my face, focusing on winning this war. "Like you learning to conjure your scythe."

"I don't have the energy for that right now." His thumb caresses my cheek as he searches my eyes, pleading for a reprieve.

That's exactly what the angels are hoping for. For us not to be at our sharpest.

"Well, find it, because they already know they can't pull you back into the Other. Mandy bought us some time by hiding your hand somewhere, but once they figure out where *we* are, they'll be sending their worst to bring us into their control." I bite my lower lip and stare him down. "You're the one who said they won't stop. So, suck it up, and let's get to work."

Kissing Fate
Chapter 8

Z ANE'S FACE IS RED with concentration as he stares at the staff in his right hand. He successfully conjured it from his necklace before the sun set over the mountains a few hours ago.

The report of gunfire makes both of us jerk and turn. We had parked ourselves in the burned-out husk of Paradise Cove to practice and prepare for a battle we both know is coming. Apparently, those in the house with firearms decided dusk was a good time for practicing on the gun range in the woods on the far side of the property, too. It really puts a damper on Zane's ability to concentrate.

Zane's brow creases in irritation after like the twentieth shot. "Don't they know bullets won't do anything to an angel?"

"No. But those with certain sigils carved in them or spells cast on the bullets can, so I imagine they'd rather be sure of their aim because missing could prove disastrous."

His gaze swivels to mine. "How do you know that?"

"We should talk." I lower to sit on the ground and pat the space next to me.

He lays the scythe out in front of him and joins me.

"A lot happened while you were gone." I pick at a hangnail, trying to figure out how to word the things I've been keeping close to the vest.

He leans away from me, studying my profile. "There's someone else?"

I laugh and shake my head. "No, Zane. There has been no one else."

The creases of worry lining his forehead smooth out. But instead of relief, they are replaced by sadness. "You...waited for me?"

I meet his gaze and rolled my eyes. "I've been on one date since you died." I shrug. "Holly begged me to go out on a double date with her and one of her boyfriend's friends." I shiver just thinking about the greasy goon who tried to kiss me at the movies. I nearly knocked him out. "It was a disaster. But that is not what I need to talk to you about." I conjure his scythe back onto his necklace because I'm uncomfortable with it sitting within reach, as if the damn thing is calling for me somehow.

He cocks an eyebrow that I ignore. "What kind of disaster?"

I close my eyes and tilt my head back with a groan. "I broke his nose because he tried to kiss me, okay?"

Zane snorts laughter. "Really?"

"Yes. I heel-punched him right in the nose." My lips twitch into a smile. "And I didn't talk to Holly for a week after that."

His guffaw echoes off the lake. "I wish I had been there to see that."

"That's not what I want to talk about right now." I smack his chest lightly with the back of my knuckles. "I had a lot of training while you were gone."

He's still laughing. "I would have never guessed."

He's mocking me and I narrow my eyes. "I have a chemical engineering degree." I spit out the least of my educational endowments.

His laughter winds down. "Wait. You went to college?" He sits back and studies me. "Why?"

"Well, to get a job for one, considering I had no idea how long I was going to be here. I needed to hold my own. As a matter of fact, Holly and I have a nice, cozy apartment in Portland." I flip my hair over my shoulder.

"I was wondering why she wasn't here," he says, giving me all of his focus.

"She doesn't know about any of this unless Alex and Faith called her. But I would think they'd want her as far away from harm's reach as possible. I'm sure my phone has dozens of text messages from her by now, but my phone is in my car in Papa's driveway." I poke his chest. He's the reason I don't have it on me.

He nods, searching my eyes as if he's trying to get a glimpse of my soul. "But getting a degree and a job isn't what you want to tell me."

"I'm supercharged."

"No shit."

"No, I mean angel blood supercharged." I point toward the house. "So are Tom and Papa's dad. Papa thought we should be fully prepared in the event the angels attacked, so he shared a bit of his power with us. And let me tell you, that was a bear to control." I laugh lightly. "Someday I'll have to tell you the stories of that training, but for now, you knowing is enough. Plus, I learned how to cast spells and read those ancient spell books. Raven is a phenomenal teacher. Although the one she taught me to stun an attacker didn't really work on the griffin."

His slow smile of appreciation warms the chill right out of my bones. "I was wondering what the hell you were doing," he says. "But I just thought it was something Fate related."

I smile. "And Kylee schooled me in sigils." My smile fades at the mention of Kylee Andreas. "She made a book of every single sigil she ever ran across, along with what it does and how to counteract it. The book is probably still sitting on Faith's coffee table unless she grabbed it on her way out. The sigil on your wrist was in that book. So, essentially Kylee saved you from the angels."

His frown deepens, and he glances at his bandaged stump. "And here, all I learned in ten years is how to die horribly and kill without mercy." He looks out at the water, haunted by his own thoughts.

"You were able to call your scythe," I say, leaning into his field of vision.

He sends a sideways glance at me and then studies the moonlight dancing on the surface of the cove. Silence descends on us while he works whatever out in his head. "So, you were the one who threw me against the wall in Papa's basement?" He slides his gaze to mine.

"Yes. And burned your hands when you were holding me on the ground in Purgatory."

"So, you really could kick my ass from here to California and back." Half his lips curl into a lopsided grin.

I finally allow a genuine smile to form, and his eyes nearly glow in the darkness.

"Come here." He grabs my arm, pulling me into his lap.

This time I don't fight him, especially not when he delivers a kiss that sends tendrils of heat through my body. I wrap my legs around his waist, locking them behind him. I can feel his hardness beneath me as our sensual tongue dance turns more insistent. I thread my hands into his hair and circle my hips against him.

I'm not sixteen anymore. If for some reason the universe ends tomorrow, I want to know what it's like to be with Zane and not in that oh-so-innocent waking in his arms crap we spouted out ten years ago.

Zane groans under my lips as if he reads my intent. His hand slides from my hip, up my body until he cups my breast through the leather corset I am still wearing.

I have an advantage. His shirt is already unbuttoned, and with a handful of his hair, I pull his head back far enough for my lips to capture his throat. I run my tongue up the line of his neck until I reach his earlobe. Gently, I nibble, chuckling softly at the noise of contentment coming from his mouth.

"I dreamed of this," he whispers. "You in my arms. For years, it was the last conscious memory before I faded into the black. You. And those bastards somehow erased you from my mind."

He grips the back of my neck and turns, laying me out on the dried moss as he lays the bulk of his weight on me. He winces when his bound arm knocks against the ground, but he shifts and uses his elbow to prop himself up. The hunger sparkling in his eyes matches my own.

"I'd like to—"

A throat clears at the entrance to the cove.

Zane looks up with guilt written all over his face, as if we are still teenagers and have been caught in this compromising position. He rolls off too quickly and yelps as he puts weight on the stump of his arm.

"I'm sorry for interrupting," Mandy says. "But we have a problem."

I climb to my feet and offer Zane a hand in getting to his.

"What's the problem?" he asks, clearly annoyed at the interruption.

"The angels are coming."

I wave my hand in Zane's direction, and the scythe pops back into existence. Zane grabs it as I launch into a run toward the cottage and whatever hell the angels have decided to deliver.

Kissing Fate
Chapter 9

I CLEAR THE WOODS, with Zane and Mandy following closely behind. Holly is just getting out of her car when I see a shadow approaching her.

"Holly!" I yell, but it's too late. A silver glint swipes across her throat, and even in the darkness, the plume of blood that spurts out from both sides of her neck is clear enough for my vision to go as black as that jet of life juice.

Zane's father stands in the light with a deadly grin.

The Book of Fates on my wrist dings. "No!" I bellow and send every ounce of power toward him. Like a steamroller at warp speed, the power that Papa gave me rolls across the lawn, smashing trees and cars before it slams his father into the trunk of an ancient oak tree.

I hold him against it as I advance, crushing him with each stomp. My veins burn with rage.

Zane bolts ahead of me with the scythe raised in his hand. The growling yell that fills the space seems to calm my fury to a manageable level. When he approaches his father, he slows long enough to swing the scythe like a baseball bat. It slices the bastard's torso in half and his rotted intestines spill out.

I turn to Mandy. "Take him to Hell."

She grins and bows. "With pleasure."

Holly's glazed eyes stare sightlessly at the sky and the wail that comes from the door echoes my feelings. I fall to my knees and take her already cooling form into my arms, rocking her as tears spill on her upturned face.

Nana slides to a stop and before I can tell her it's too late, she presses her healing kiss on Holly's forehead and then looks at me. "Bring her back," she says.

I haven't brought anyone back to life since I was Death and Fate all rolled into one. I close my eyes. "Bring me her spirit," I whisper.

The air shimmers and one of the newer reapers stands near, but she doesn't have the light I expect.

"They got her before I could. It's like they were waiting. Like they expected bloodshed and death."

I am stunned and furious at the same time. My gaze jumps to the tree and then back. My stomach drops. "Did Mandy get through?"

She glances at the ground and shakes her head.

"Oh, for fuck's sake!" I cry and hop to my feet, spinning around in a circle as more people pile out of the house. "Papa, we need that barrier!" Zane had been on the money. Those bastards sent his father to do their dirty work.

Another gunshot rings in the distance and we all spin toward the shooting range. When four more shots ring out in quick succession and the lights in the shooting range flicker and die, I'm already running.

"Get everyone inside," I order, and then twirl my finger and point to Papa. "Set your force field to kill on contact," I add.

He nods and gathers Holly's limp body in his arms, and heads for the door, with Nana and Faith huddled together.

I focus on the woods, slowing down. My hope that Steve Williams is using the enhanced bullets is low. He's much more practical than that, and normal bullets won't do a damn thing to a ghost, as Zane so accurately pointed out.

I trade a glance with Zane as we match stride for stride together. A part of me wishes he would have stayed in the safety zone Papa is creating. "We can't go charging inside after this. Papa's barrier kills, mortal or otherworldly, so we have to be very careful."

I cross into the open clearing and there stands Zane's father with that smile I want to burn off his face. The angels must have intercepted Mandy. They were the only ones that could have repaired the damage Zane did before sending him back to do their dirty work.

Zane's father has Agent Williams on his knees, with a gun pressed to Steve's temple. The click of an empty magazine sounds, and Steve yanks away from his grip, sweeping Zane's father's legs from beneath him, before he rolls out of the bastard's reach.

I envision an electrified net made of metal anchored into the ground around Zane's father. It forms over him as quickly as a sandcastle being demolished by a giant wave, trapping him underneath.

He thrashes and hisses as the net delivers just the right amount of electricity to cause excruciating pain. As we walk by, Steve reaches out, catching Zane's leg. We both gasp, and so does Steve Williams.

That's when I see the spreading red on his shirt and the top of his jeans. We missed it earlier because he was bathed in the shadows. He opens his mouth, but blood bubbles up, gagging on whatever warning he's trying to give us. He had already been shot before we got here, and touching Zane relieves the pain of the bullets shredding his insides.

Zane and I trade a glance before he crouches down and leans the scythe on his shoulder in order to take Steve's hand. There is a softness and compassion in that motion that tightens my throat. He is ensuring the least amount of suffering given the current circumstances.

I conjure the only thing that will guarantee Zane's father will never come back from the dead to create more devastation. Two deaths in a matter of minutes are two too many.

Heaven's blade shimmers into existence in my hand. The blue glass of the knife reflects its own light, making the clearing brighter than just the moonlight. I grip the smooth handle, with the blade facing down. All it takes is one nick from this knife to snuff a life right out of existence. Faith used this blade on Lucifer himself. The devil's death somehow made me possible, and I am glad I possess such a powerful weapon.

His father laughs as he stares up at me. He has no knowledge of what's coming and all I can hope for is it isn't painless. I hope he feels the ultimate destruction in every cell. I hope being erased from existence comes with a dose of agony before he ceases.

I glance over my shoulder at Zane, and he nods. I know he wants to inflict more pain on his father. Hell, I do, too, but because I can't deliver him to Hell like I want, I opt for a more permanent erasure.

I crouch down and smile. "I wouldn't be so cocky right now." I hold the blade over his stomach and slam it down through one of the netting holes, careful not to touch the electrified metal. The tip of the blade breaks through the skin of his stomach just enough to draw blood and invoke Heaven's blade's wrath.

Before he can react, I pull the blade out and step away, sending the knife back to my ultimate hiding place. One that only I can tap into. It is just as secure as Kylee's arsenal of ancient weapons in her house in San Diego, mostly because she helped me create it and safeguard Heaven's blade with the most powerful sigils.

His father still laughs, but the joke is on him. I smile. "You are done."

His maniacal cackle turns into a curdling scream that echoes through the woods and across the lake. If I had my way, I'd make sure they heard his scream in Heaven itself.

I turn and put distance between myself and the effects of the blade. Neither Zane nor I need to be knocked out by the explosion. I'm not leaving us vulnerable for the angels to swoop in and take over our bodies. And I'm certainly not leaving Steve's body, either.

I crouch down and sling Steve's arm over my shoulder. As we stand, light flares over Zane's father and then the explosion I expect bows all the trees, and nearly knocks us over before it sucks back into itself like a black hole. The pop of air announces his father's true demise.

I glance at Zane as we head for the house. "The angels are going to be pretty upset. I just annihilated their second favorite pet right out of existence."

Kissing Fate
Chapter 10

MY NOSE HAIRS TINGLE as we approach the house. "Stop!" I yell, and Zane pulls up before he hits Papa's deadly force field. We are close enough to the barrier for me to feel the electricity buzzing. I take a shuffling step back.

The body of Steve Williams is getting heavy, and I try to shift the weight as best I can, but I nearly drop him. Dragging dead weight really isn't anything I trained for and Zane still holds the scythe in his hand, so he isn't helping as much as he would be if he had a second hand.

Damn it. Levi should at least be able to sense me by now. I blink and then look at Zane's weapon. "Nothing's going to come from the direction of the house, so cover my back."

He nods and unthreads his damaged arm from around the body. I sag under the weight and re-adjust my grip on the dead man while Zane steps behind me with his scythe at the ready.

"Hey!" I yell, pushing the thought out as well, just like Papa taught me. A beat passes, but it's enough to have my muscles screaming at the dead man's full weight.

The door opens in response. Papa steps out with the reddest eyes I've ever seen on him. He sniffles and wipes tears from his cheeks. The shock of seeing him cry freezes me in place.

His gaze lands on Steve, and he moves. For a moment, the barrier holds and then it snaps and reforms beyond us. It's not enough time for anything to get through without getting caught in the deadly force field, but the fact he had to take it down for even a second rubs me wrong.

He grabs Steve from my grip and that's when he realizes the man I'm carrying is dead. His gaze snaps beyond me at Zane, as if it's his fault.

"Zane's father shot him," I say, and he looks at me. "The angels sent him back here again. But that was the last time. I made sure of it."

Understanding smooths out the lines on his forehead. "Heaven's blade?"

I nod, transferring the weight of the body to him as we carry Steve back in the house and lay him on the floor in the back alcove, away from the rest of the crowd. Holly is laid out on the couch with her arms crossed over her chest like a fairy-tale Sleeping Beauty waiting for love's kiss. Now that the imminent danger is at bay, just seeing her lifeless body cuts deeper than Zane's scythe.

Zane's hand lands on my shoulder and he gives me a squeeze. I glance back at him, expecting the scythe to be leaning against his handless shoulder like it was in the clearing. Except the scythe isn't where I expect. It dangles from his necklace. Somehow, in the thick of all this chaos, Zane found his magic. He offers me a cockeyed smile that doesn't break through the sadness in his eyes.

The fact he found it deep within him instead of burdening me with the task just adds to the black hole I seem to be falling into. My chin quivers. He reaches for me, pulling me into his arms as tears blur my vision. The numbness of action fades away, letting the full force of Holly's death hit like the force of an F5 twister.

Hot paths flow down my cheeks and I can't stop them. I bury my face in my hands. My legs turn to spaghetti, unable to handle my weight, but Zane holds me in place and kisses the top of my head. It's his turn to whisper, "Shhh," in an attempt to calm the raging storm.

I don't know how long we stand this way, but I take a while to gain any semblance of control and find my footing. I mop my face and push away from Zane's chest, but I'm hesitant to leave the comfort of his arms. I'm not the only one crying in the house, either. Steve's wife is now sobbing over Steve's dead body, and Faith, Alex,

Nana, and Papa look as if they have allergies from Hell. Their noses are as red as their eyes and they are huddled near the couch where Holly is, clinging to one another in much the same way I had been clinging to Zane.

"Can you bring her back?" Faith sniffles and points to Holly.

I bite my lower lip and look at the floor. I had only tried once to revive the dead since the portal to Heaven was closed ten years ago. And that attempt failed. Zane hadn't come back to life, no matter how long I pushed or how hard I prayed.

With the hope sparking in Faith's eyes, I don't have the heart to tell her I didn't think it was possible to bring her back. Not with the portal closed. And even if it was open, if Holly isn't in Heaven, I am positive I won't be able to yank her from the angels' grip.

"I don't know." I peel myself out of Zane's strong grip and cross and kneel on the floor next to Holly. "Just so you understand, I don't know if this is truly possible." My chin quivers as I lay my hands on Holly. She's cold to the touch, reminding me she isn't just sleeping.

I close my eyes and concentrate. All my memories of Holly flow through my mind, from when we were little all the way to sharing dinner the night before Zane woke. It squeezes my chest. I wish the breath of life back into her.

Time slows as I push my will into her, but that magic wind shift never comes. When I open my eyes again, she remains gray and cold to the touch. Tears blur my vision and spill over, leaving hot paths down my cheeks. All I can do is shake my head.

The collective hope in the room falls, along with my head. I drop it until my forehead touches Holly's.

"I'm so sorry," I whisper and look up, meeting Faith's gaze. My skin burns with disappointment.

Faith sucks her lower lip between her teeth and nods as tears escape down her cheeks, too.

Jennifer Williams is close enough to Zane to reach out and grab his hand. He tries to yank it away, but she holds on as Death's poison infiltrates her living cells. He finally pulls his hand away.

"Why would you do that?" he gasps.

Jennifer smiles up at him even as her breath labors. "I don't wish to be here without him." She falls over onto Steve as the stench of urine fills the room. My Book of Fates dings another tolling for death.

Zane's horrified gaze meets mine and my heart drops. I did not put my protective barrier around Zane when we came into the house this time. And then Zane closes his eyes and bows his head. The creases on his forehead deepen.

"What are you doing?"

"Trying to protect everyone here from me. So *that* doesn't happen again." Sweat pops out on his forehead and his fist clenches. The muscles in his jaw tighten. When his eyelids fly open, I feel the power slide through the house. The walls even sparkle with it, as if his power to kill is now nullified within this home. "I think I did it." He meets my gaze with wide eyes of wonder that is misplaced in the current environment.

I know something happened, but I'm not a hundred percent certain it will work, especially with his difficulty shrinking his scythe and willing it back to its deadly form, which should be an inherent power of Death.

No one moves to test it out, which I'm thankful for.

"We have to do something about the angels," Papa says.

I am at a loss as to what to do. "I can call the reapers, but the angels still can smite them." I climb to my feet. "If the angels come, I'm not sure our collective power will be enough to protect them, and the casualties..." I can't finish that sentence. It's not something I want to entertain. "I don't think Zane and I can beat them without help."

"We'll stand by you," Papa says.

"It's very personal now," Alex says. Bitterness laces his voice, along with something dangerous—like a caged lion.

"We all stand with you," Damian, Gabriel's father, says. He glances at Tom. "If the archangels were here, they'd stand with us, too. They were pretty much done with the militant attitudes of the whole lot of them."

An idea forms and I cock my head, glancing at Zane.

He narrows his eyes at me, as if he's trying to read my mind.

"But the archangels don't have their grace. How would having them on our side work?" I look at Damian.

"They are still a force to be feared, but the lower angels ganged up on them and forced them out of their stations. They've been demeaned and ridiculed ever since, and they did not agree with the attack on Missy. I'm sure they'll be even more angry with the Death of their blood by the angels' order."

"If they were here, Faith and I would be more than willing to give them the grace we harbor. Especially if it means the angels suffer." Papa glances at Faith and receives a nod. "Maybe then you can bring her back," he adds and waves at Holly.

Unfortunately, I don't know if I can ever bring Holly back, and it saddens me to the core. However, I might be able to bring the archangels here. It would be riskier than releasing Levi had been, especially because neither Zane nor I know our way around Purgatory.

I glance at Levi laying on the floor. He meets my gaze. "That would indeed be risky, but the reward if you release them and can bring them here will be the complete destruction of the lower angels."

That sounded like a hell of a reward. I looked at Zane.

"What do you need?" he asks.

"I need to get near the entrance of Heaven, and then I need you and Levi to watch my back, because I don't think I can pull them out of Heaven if we are under attack."

"Stealth mission." He nods. "I think I can do that. But can I ask a favor?" He holds up his bandaged stump. "Can you conjure up a mechanical hand for me like you did for Mandy?"

I close my eyes and the only thing that comes to mind is a metal hand like what I saw in one of those old movies on late-night television. It's shaped like a hand, but all steel. That soft breeze filters through me, and I open my eyes to Zane with a Terminator's hand.

He's just staring at it. "Um. Maybe one that actually works?" He smiles sheepishly at me.

"What do you think I am, a mechanical engineer?" I raise an eyebrow at him. Maybe if he had taken the time to conjure up something, it would work.

He blinks at me. "I just assumed you made Mandy's arm," he says after a moment.

I had, but like Zane's, it was just for show.

Papa's father laughs from the table and raises his hand. "That would be me. I'm the one who wired her arm so she could use it."

"Think you could do the same for me?"

Ty Ryan's gaze falls to Jennifer Williams's dead body near the door. "I kind of enjoy breathing," he says.

"You'll just have to live with it like that until we can figure out how to make it work." I start toward him.

"I protected everyone here already."

"How sure are you that it worked?" I don't hold back, because if for some reason it didn't work, another person will die. We can't have that. Period.

"I felt his magic," Raven says from the hallway. "And I'm sure enough to test it out."

She starts toward him, and he splays his good hand in her direction.

He licks his lips and then shakes his head. "I don't want anyone to risk it."

The door behind him opens, and Smoke and Phoebe enter the house. Smoke pats Zane on the arm and steps around him. "Good to see you up and about," he says and then stops at the sight of Steve and Jennifer dead on the ground.

Zane stares at his arm where Smoke touched him and then his wide gaze looks up at Smoke, like he's waiting for the inevitable. A few beats pass and nothing happens.

Smoke glances around at the alarm on everyone's face. "Did I grow a second head or something?" He looks at Papa. "We came as fast as we could. What's going on?" And then his glance lands on Holly's prone form on the couch.

"Shit. It's starting again." He pulls Phoebe close in a protective reflex.

Zane backs up and leans on the wall next to the door, mopping his face with his good hand. Relief sags his shoulders, and he tilts his head back, closing his eyes for a moment. Then he looks directly at me. "That will only work within these walls." He glances around the room. "It won't work anywhere else, so if we're outside, please avoid touching me, unless you have a death wish."

"Fine, but what the hell happened to you?" Smoke points to Zane's robotic hand.

"I had them cut off my arm above a sigil the angels branded me with. It's how they controlled me. As for this"—he waves at his new robotics—"Missy conjured it for me."

"Jesus," Phoebe whispered. "Who else did you kill besides them?" She waves at the bodies in the house.

"He didn't kill them." I don't want them to think these deaths are his fault. "The angels did this."

"He killed Kylee and Gabe," Michael Andreas says from the corner, and his voice carries every ounce of bitterness radiating from him. His break out with the kids did not seem to cool his hostility at all. If anything, it ramped it up a notch or two.

"And I killed Missy's mother and Missy before she could break the hold that the sigil had on me." He holds up his dysfunctional mechanical hand. "So, this was necessary to keep everyone else safe."

"And we were just contemplating whether whatever spell he did in the house would nullify his Death touch. Thanks for being the guinea pig," Ty says to Smoke from his seat at the table and raises his coffee cup in a silent cheer. He looks at Zane. "Let's have a look at the hardware she created for you."

Zane takes the seat opposite him and lays his arm across the table, bracing himself for whatever discomfort the procedure is likely to cause.

Ty takes his arm and turns it this way and that. "I'll get you up and running in a jiffy so you can go get those cantankerous bastards."

Kissing Fate
Chapter 11

IT TOOK TY A little over an hour, along with an infusion of Valerie's healing powers, to connect the circuits to Zane's nerves so he could use the mechanical hand as efficiently as his normal hand. I have to admit, seeing each metal finger touch his thumb, and then his robotic hand clench and open, is gratifying. It makes his loss a little less severe.

He smiles at me and then glances at the bodies near the door. His smile sours. And he gets up, crossing the distance to Steve and Jennifer's lifeless bodies. He crouches down.

"I'm sorry we couldn't protect you. I promise we will find you and set you free from whatever horrors those bastards are delivering." He holds his good hand over their bodies and closes his eyes, dipping his head in concentration. The bodies disintegrate into ashes and then swirl across the room in the form of a dust devil before he sends them up the fireplace chimney. It was eerily similar to what I had done to his father after I stole his soul and snuffed out his life, while Zane and I were both alive and fleeing Heaven's wrath.

No one says a word. Not even me. I'm speechless because I thought he couldn't readily tap into his powers. Yet he had shrunk the scythe when we came into the house earlier. It seems, in the last few hours, he has somehow gotten proficient with his magic.

He crosses to Holly and extends his hand.

"No. Leave her." I can't watch her turn to dust. It isn't her time and I'll be damned if I let her death stand. We just need to find where the angels have her soul locked up. My bets are on the Other. But that won't stop me from trying to pull her back when I'm in Purgatory. If I can't, I pray the archangels will be willing to find and free her, along with my father.

If the angels followed through on their promise to escort all those in this house to Hell instead, the underworld better be prepared for the chaos I will rain in order to release my family and friends from eternal damnation.

Zane pulls his hand back with a nod. "We can't leave her here long," he says, and I understand. Decomposition is a nasty side effect of being dead. "You might want to keep her in a cool place, just in case this takes longer than a day or two."

Faith's lips press together, and she trades a glance with Alex. They nod, but neither of them make a move to follow through on the suggestion. Instead, Faith crosses to me.

"Are you sure about this?" she asks as she reaches out. Her hands land softly on each shoulder and she makes sure I am looking at her. "I can't bear the thought of losing you, too."

It's a little late for that, but I don't utter those words. My heart isn't beating. My life was already snuffed out. Now I'm the deity Fate, and can come and go with a blink of air. It's a weird dynamic, to say the least.

"You won't. I'm not giving up this book." I point to the Book of Fates charm on my bracelet. "Besides, it seems Zane is coming into his own already." I glance over at him. "So, I'll have two forces watching my back."

I'm still uneasy about going to Purgatory, but with Zane and Levi, I think we will be okay. It's a move no one expects, so there is a measure of surprise that will work in our favor.

But there is still one problem: Papa's deadly barrier.

I blink as a new thought comes to mind and I glance at Smoke.

"How did you get through Papa's barrier?" I knew his deadly force field still surrounded us. So logically, Phoebe and Smoke should have been toasted when they hit it. But here they stand, unharmed by it.

He pulls up his shirt sleeve and shows us a sigil tattoo on his arm. Phoebe does the same.

"We all have them," Phoebe says.

I turn to Papa and point at her. "Why wasn't I told about that?"

He blinks at me and opens his mouth to speak.

"Because we didn't trust that Heaven was done with us," Alex says before Papa can speak. "And if either of you were used against us, we needed a safeguard that wouldn't compromise anyone else's safety."

I turn to Michael because I don't recall seeing that sigil among the pages Kylee had drawn.

He shakes his head. "Just like you won't find the sigils we all have on our shoulder blades."

"I know about that one. I was there when she drew it on everyone," I snap. "How does it work?" My gaze snaps to Papa.

He shrugs. "For us, it just does. And if I'm touching you, you can come through without issue."

I hold out my arm. "Draw it on us so we can get through, to go to Purgatory and bring the archangels back."

No one moves to do as I ask. I glance around the room, feeling like an outsider for the first time within my family.

"We can't put any more lives in jeopardy," Papa says. "I love you like my own, but you have to understand, we can't take that risk either." He glances around and gets small nods. "Paradise Cove is the safest place outside of here to do what you need to. I can let you out of the barrier, but you'll have to do that telepathy thing when you get back for me to come get you and the archangels.”

Papa crosses to me. “It’s not you we don’t trust—” he starts, and I put up my hand.

“You obviously didn’t trust me enough to tell me. Does Holly have that same tattoo?” I don’t remember seeing her with any tattoo and the only way she has one is if it’s somewhere super private.

“Yes.” Faith won’t meet my gaze. “She has it on her butt cheek.”

I glance at my dead roommate. My best friend. The one who knows me better than myself most days. I wipe my face, accepting this dichotomy of information and try to ignore the burn of betrayal.

“Fine.” I turn toward the door. “Let’s go.” I pause as another truth dawns on me. I turn back to Papa. “You can’t touch Zane outside these walls.” Seven words slam silence on the room. “Hadn’t thought of that complication, did you?” I can’t help the snark. “If I’m touching him, I’m a conductor of his power. And I’m not leaving him at their mercy.” I turn back and punch out my arm, turning my wrist to the ceiling. “So, if I am going to go on this insane mission to save all our asses, you have to put your trust in me. Otherwise, our best chance at surviving is gone.”

Papa looks between the two of us and then down at the floor, shaking his head.

“She’s right,” his father says from the table.

Papa turns and glares at his father. Some silent communication starts.

"You know she's our best chance." Ty crosses his arms.

"Your father's right," Jessica Ryan says from beside Ty. She covers his hand with hers. "And you know he's got the same touch as Eric, so don't be so quick to dismiss him."

Papa jerks at the mention of his older brother. One who is still locked in Heaven and hopefully not being manipulated by the angels. Somehow, that thought gets swept away. Eric Connor was more along the lines of a seer than anyone else, even Ty.

But I hadn't had the forethought to call him from the dead ten years ago. Although, right now, I kind of wish I had. I'd like the benefit of seeing what's coming.

Papa sighs before he trudges across the cabin to one of the kitchen drawers. He comes back with a pen, keeping his gaze down as he approaches, as if he is aware he did something underhanded.

"I don't know how many you can bring with you," he says as he draws a new sigil on my skin. "So, you may need to make multiple trips. If I were you, I'd land in Paradise Cove just to limit your exposure. It's warded, and only those with pure intentions toward this family can enter and exit."

"You know we were there earlier today, right?"

His gaze lifts to mine. "We weren't sure where you went. But that still doesn't prevent them from getting into his head again."

I could stand here for the rest of eternity arguing with him, but I don't. There isn't any way to curtail his doubt. Not with the deaths of what they consider family members still so fresh.

"I get it," I say softly enough for him to hear. "But he had us chop his own hand off to keep us from harm."

"That isn't lost on us, and it makes this harder for everyone here." He meets my gaze. "But he still took your life. And right now, I'm having a hell of a hard time with the fact that my son's kids are both dead."

I open my mouth.

"I know he didn't kill Holly. But all this angel shit has left an enormous hole in my soul, so you just have to deal with our uber cautiousness." He finishes the drawing and steps back, capping the pen. "When all this is over, I'll spar with you and you can try to kick my ass then, okay?"

"I've never bested you in the dojo," I mutter.

"You've never been angry enough at me to use all your skills." He meets my gaze, and his lips form a ghost of a grin before he nods at the door. "But we have some angel ass kicking to dole out first. Go get our secret weapons."

Kissing Fate
Chapter 12

I STAND IN THE center of the moss in Paradise Cove, looking between Zane and Levi. My nerves are jumping, making my stomach feel decidedly sick. We are risking falling right into the angels' hands and I'm not prepared for a battle in a land that I only have two allies.

Levi rolls his eyes. "Just get on with it."

"Where is the safest place to show up in Purgatory that's near Heaven's gates?"

"You know there isn't a true gate, right?" Levi says.

I close my eyes. "Yes, I know. But I do not know where the safest place is that the angels won't be. They intercepted Holly. It's likely they've intercepted Steve and Jennifer. So, wherever souls appear, we cannot land."

Levi nods. "I know a place."

I raise an eyebrow. It sounds like more of a come-on than a plan.

"I had time to roam whenever I chose," he says, a little offended that I have the audacity to question him.

"Sorry, Levi. You'll be in charge of the landing when we do the jump, okay?"

"Yes. I will stay in this form unless I sense danger. My transformation will be your warning if things are amiss."

That's a pretty large warning signal and I'm okay with that. I glance at Zane.

"Works for me. I'll cover your back while you do your thing," Zane says.

I step to Levi's side, wrap my hand around his collar, and Zane threads his hand through mine. "Navigate away." I close my eyes, wishing us into Purgatory. The transition feels as though I'm falling through space. I imagine an astronaut who loses their grip on the space station while doing a famed spacewalk must feel like this. Weightless, yet moving at such a speed that everything is a blur. I nearly laugh. It's like stepping into a wormhole.

When my feet hit the ground, it's the crunch of snow underfoot that snaps my eyes open. The mountain range we are in the middle of reminds me of the pictures I've seen of the Canadian Rockies or the Swiss Alps. The scenery is stunning, with whiteness in every direction, coating the peaks and valleys around us. Unlike the brown wasteland Levi had been locked in when we rescued him.

"Where are we?" I whisper, taking a quick glance at the same awe on Zane's face before looking at Levi.

"Heaven's gate is a couple miles in that direction." He points his muzzle toward the right. He turns in the opposite direction. "And Hell is almost a continent away in that direction." He sniffs the air. "You better get to it. They know we are in Purgatory, but it is vast enough to give us a little time."

I release both of them and drop to my knees. I have no pictures to rely on for these four beings like I had for some of the others I pulled from Heaven ten years ago. I only have Papa's memories to pull from. I splay my fingers in the snow and close my eyes, shuffling through his remembrances. Shuffling through his time in Heaven to zero in on the faces of those I was about to call.

A crackle of thunder bangs in the distance, making me jump. The wind picks up and Levi's low growl is all the warning I need.

"Michael, Gabriel, Raphael, Uriel," I command.

The air shifts around us, and I open my eyes to four very confused mortal-looking men. But their faces and their auras tell me exactly who they are. As if that isn't enough to confirm their identities, their dark-haired, Mediterranean flair, along with those piercing blue eyes, confirm it. There is zero chance of mistaking their heritage.

Not when Gabriel looks like his son's doppelgänger and Uriel matches Ty Ryan as if they were poured from the same mold. Uriel reminds me of all the Ryans except Tom. Tom is more a mold of Raphael, softer and more nurturing despite his obvious tendency toward sarcasm. The resemblance is remarkable. It's as if the angels stamped themselves into mortal DNA and replicated their images.

Michael is the one I'm most unnerved by. He is almost Zane's equal in the looks department, but his chiseled jaw and high cheekbones were a little too perfect for my taste. As is his powerful form. Even without grace, I want to shy away from his presence.

Their eyes land on the scythe in Zane's hands before dropping to me. I stand up slowly and spread my fingers wide with my palms facing them, trying to placate the anger radiating from them.

"CJ Ryan needs your help."

Every one of them cross their arms.

I'm not prepared for their blasé attitude. I thought invoking the name of their distant grandson would at least garner support, but Michael's glare never falters. Neither does Uriel's or Gabriel's. But Raphael seems to be more focused and less pissed.

I close my eyes. "I need your help," I add, and try not to shake in their presence. "I need to bring you back to the cabin."

The sky lights up with a burst of lightning, followed by a thundering clap. And they glance up. Michael's jaw tightens and a fire flares in his eyes, as if he's just itching to kick someone's ass. When his gaze falls to mine, I swallow hard.

"Before the angels find out we are here," I add.

"Why should we help an abomination like you?" Michael says.

"Because agreeing to help me also helps your bloodlines." I'm not giving up. Not when I have them literally within reach.

"We are as helpless as they are against the angels," Uriel snaps.

That is an argument I can counter. "Not with your grace." I lift an eyebrow, hoping it's enough to pique their interest. Enough of an enticement to get them to follow me back home.

Their arms slowly uncurl and fall to their sides. Interest sparks in their eyes and they all exchange a glance.

Triumph fills me, but I keep the need to jump up and yell out a rebel "Yes!" under wraps. "If you know who I am, you also know who raised me. I'm not blowing sunshine up your ass. I'm giving you a chance to get your grace back and re-establish your place in Heaven."

"You might want to hurry this up," Levi says as he faces the direction away from where he said Heaven's gate is. The hair on the back of his neck rises.

Michael's eyes narrow. "What do you get out of this?"

I tap my foot out of sheer nerves. If Levi transforms, it will already be too late, but if I don't give the angels an answer, they won't come. "My parents get to have their happily ever after, and I get my best friend back. The angels have my father and CJ's granddaughter, and they've vowed to wipe out humanity. This is the End of Times unless you step in and help."

Their gazes swiveled to Zane as if my answer is not enough. "And what do you get?" Uriel asks.

"Retribution for the last ten years of torture," he says, glancing over his shoulder at them. He didn't even try to sugarcoat his intentions.

I shift my weight, nervous that he just screwed us out of the help we desperately need. My gaze goes to the growing storm overhead. Levi's growls become consistent, along with the thunder.

Time is running out.

"If they find us here, they will lock us up and strip us of our memories and send us back down there to reap the Ryans, and every drop of angel blood will be eradicated from Earth." My heart rockets in my chest. "You may think that's all hunky-dory, but they will take your kin and lock them up in Hell for an eternity of torture. That's their promise—that none of us will ever see each other again. So, if you don't want that, take my hand and I'll get you to your family."

I grab Levi's collar with one hand and Zane follows suit, grabbing his tail in case the connection of both of us touching his collar would somehow infect the angels with his Death touch. It didn't seem to affect the angel in the Other, but he wasn't taking any chances.

I stretch out my free hand, reaching toward the angels.

"Last chance." If they don't take me up on this offer, I have to get out of here before they show up and we are outnumbered.

"Damian and Naomi too?" Gabriel asks.

I nod.

Gabriel steps close and takes my hand. He turns to Raphael, offering his free hand and the chain forms. Uriel is the last one and not a moment too soon.

With the connection complete, I close my eyes and wish us all back to Paradise Cove. The pull this time is more sluggish because I'm dragging four beings with me. It feels as if I'm wearing gravity boots and not the wild free fall that I felt coming here. My grip on Gabriel's hand slips, but he somehow shifts his hand to swallow mine in his, as though he knows if we lose this connection, I won't be able to find him ever again.

The landing is rough. I can't keep my balance and tumble onto my ass, losing the grip I have on both Levi and Gabriel. I'm the only one who seems to have this issue. Zane follows, landing with one leg bent as he falls to his knee. He had the forethought while I sucked us through the ether to stow his scythe. It glimmers in the moonlight on the chain around his neck. He looks like Thor as he lifts his head to look at me through messed-up bangs. I have to stifle a giggle, but glancing toward the archangels helps.

They are on their feet, as if it were just a stroll along the river and not some ethereal mega slide that slung us to the earth. They stuck the landing and the amusement on their faces unnerves me. It's cocky, almost like we are beneath them. What they don't realize is Zane could reap them with a swing of his scythe. No one, not even the angels, can run from Death.

"Where's our grace?" Michael asks.

"CJ and Faith hold your grace." I climb to my feet. "They are this way." I head toward the path and wave for them to follow. I move aside to allow Levi and Zane to cross in front of us.

The archangels stop at the edge of the path as if they can't cross over from one side to the next. I glance over my shoulder at them. Uncertainty flashes over their faces.

"If you notice, Paradise Cove isn't what it used to be. There's no barrier between the moss and the woods like there was when it was..." I search for the word. "Operational."

If memory serves me, or at least the memories of others passed to me through Papa's transfer of some of his powers, Michael and Gabriel both breached the barrier from Heaven's gate to here when they battled Lucifer, so their hesitation certainly vexes me.

I reach out my hand again, because their stall seems to be more permanent than just a moment. Michael takes my hand and crosses over with me. Then drops it as soon as he is in the woods.

"You all don't need that," I say, meeting Uriel, Gabriel, and Raphael's gazes. They cross over without my help and give Michael a subtle smirk.

Michael responds by marching up the lawn, muttering under his breath until Zane steps in front of him and holds out his hands. The movement triggers the motion sensor and the backyard lights up with all the spots pointing right in Michael's face.

I'm sure if people inside didn't know we were here, they certainly do now.

"Stop!" Zane yells.

Michael just rolls his eyes, squinting in the light. But he does as Zane says.

"There's a barrier we can't touch," he says. "Papa—I mean, CJ—set it to kill, so..." He stands in the zone that Papa deemed safe before we left.

Lightning traversed the sky and thunder pounded in the distance.

"Shit, they're coming. Just stay put," I say to the archangels. Before anyone can argue, I drag Zane and Levi across the barrier and then cross it again to where the archangels stand.

If we go in a line with me leading, there's no way the last one wouldn't feel the effects of the barrier. So, I step into the middle of them and grab Uriel's hand in mine and Raphael's hand in the other.

"Grab their hands. Now!"

Uriel takes Michael and Raphael grabs Gabriel's hand, and then I step forward. The barrier sizzles, sending unpleasant tingles through me as I pull the four angels through with me. I'm not the only one who felt the effects, but at least everyone is functional.

"Go inside, now!" I point toward the house, issuing an order, one Zane can't refuse. The frown on his face deepens, but he turns and trudges toward the cottage. "Go!" I yell at the archangels. "Before they see you!"

Papa rounds the corner and avoids Zane, but he crosses to the archangels as he eyes the sky with concern. "Come on," he says and leads them away.

I don't follow, and both Levi and Zane stop before they round the corner.

"What the hell are you doing?" he snaps. The cords in his neck stand out as he mentally overcomes the order for a moment.

"I'm testing a theory. Now go before they see you and Levi."

He turns and marches toward the house with Levi by his side. I'm surprised Levi obeys, but I guess they both realize that I'm betting on multiple surprises, like the archangels and Levi all wrapped into one frightening force. I'm not sure they know he's left Purgatory. Zane's father didn't see Levi, so the angels only know that I have control over Zane.

I don't want the angels to know for sure. At least not yet.

I wait until they are in the house and the curtains to the outside world have been drawn before I turn toward the storm. I want to see the angels underestimate this force field. I want to see someone toasted in the barrier.

Anger rakes over my skin, and I embrace it. The thunder and lightning isn't nearly the level it was when the angel army approached Papa's the night Zane became Death. I think it's a test of their capabilities after being absent for so long.

I would love a hand-to-hand fight. The last angel I had a fight with wasn't really all that badass. But that was when I held both Fate and

Death in my beating heart. I stripped that bitch of her soul before I used Heaven's blade on her. That was a lesson I am glad I learned in single-handed combat. The blowback from the destruction nearly knocked me out. It's why I don't have that weapon on my charm bracelet.

I shake the memory away, step through Papa's barrier, and shift into a ready stance, glaring at the storm.

Two angels descend from the storm cloud, and I can't help my grin. They have no idea what kind of force I have become. And they have no clue what awaits them in the house behind me.

They smile as if I'm just a normal human and then they send what looks like angel fire at me to smite me. I put my arms up and envision a shield. The fire curves around me, spreading over the barrier behind me like a fan. When it subsides, I drop my arms.

It's my turn to give them a dose of their own medicine. I shoot my hands out with a bellow of anger, launching my power at them. Although I hadn't moved from their assault, the result of my magic knocks them clear into the middle of the lake. They splash under the water as if they were shot from the stratosphere.

It's enough for now and I turn, crossing Papa's barrier. A banshee-like scream makes me glance over my shoulder as one angel comes at me, dripping wet, with a sword at the ready.

The minute the heavenly being connects with the force field, she bursts into a fiery ball, wailing as the power of Papa's barrier cooks her right out of existence.

I look beyond her at the other being, who halts a few feet behind. His face is scrunched in a mask of fury, and I tip my head with a smile and point my finger at him as if it's a gun.

"You won't hold up to all of Heaven's angels," he growls.

"We'll just see about that, won't we?" I head back inside. I want all of Heaven's angels to come, because I cannot wait to see the celestial bloodbath.

Kissing Fate
Chapter 13

“WHAT THE HELL WERE you thinking?” Zane yells when I walk into the house. All the lights are on, giving the living area a warm glow.

“They can’t smite me.” I smile. It’s something I’ve wondered for years, and it gives me insight into why they fear me. It has nothing to do with me harboring Death and Fate at one time. And even though Zane told me that, I needed to find it out for myself.

"But what if you had been wrong? That was reckless." He steps closer, towering over me. His eyes are nearly flaming with anger.

"I wasn't, so don't get your panties in a wad." I try to step around him, but he grabs my arm with his robotic hand.

"I'm serious, Missy. And I'm not the only one who isn't pleased with you." He waves at the remaining household behind him, including the four statues standing in the middle of the living room with scowls as deep as the mid-winter snow.

The group seems lighter. I scan the faces. Ty is still here with his wife. Papa and Nana stand next to Alex and Faith. Smoke sits in the alcove with a book and Phoebe steps out of the bathroom. Tom, Raven, and Hannah are on the couch with a board game laid out on the coffee table, playing with Damian and Naomi. And then it hits. The missing link. The same one that came after me a lifetime ago. "Where's Michael and the kids?" I ask.

"We sent them to Connecticut to catch a flight to San Diego," Damian says.

Unease fills me, and I glanced at Papa.

"We thought with the focus on you and this place, it would be best to get the kids out of here. Plus, their place in San Diego is a fortress."

I had been out west to Kylee and Michael's place. It was indeed a fortress and Papa's right. If the angels are focused on me, they'll slip through without an issue.

"You promised us our grace," the Archangel Michael says with narrowing eyes.

I had been outside long enough for at least one transfer of grace to occur, but there was an underlying current in the room. I look at Papa and Faith. "What's the problem?"

"They aren't willing to help us bring Holly back," Faith says.

I take a breath. "It's really not up to them. I just need her and anyone else stuck in the Other to be brought to Heaven where they belong."

Michael recoils, taking a step back. "There was no mention of the Other." He looks between me and Faith.

Zane turns, facing him. "They had me trapped in the Other for ten years," he snaps. "They captured my father's soul and reanimated that bastard. He beat me to death multiple times a day for ten. Fucking. Years. They need to be stopped." His scythe appears in his grip. "So, if you aren't on our side, you will not live to see this end." His eyes glow with green malice.

Michael stands tall, along with Uriel. The battle angels square their footing. I bet if they had wings, they would be all aflutter at the thought of bloodshed.

There is entirely too much testosterone flexing in the room.

"Look. The deal is two-fold. Your grace for helping us. And helping us means defeating the angels who want to kill us and freeing the rest of our family who are stuck in the Other." I look between the four of them, and the irritation in Michael's eyes speaks volumes. He does not like ultimatums and I'm betting if he could give me a smackdown, it would make him very happy.

Gabriel steps forward and places a hand on Michael's chest, defusing the tension. "It's not that we aren't on your side. We just cannot fathom the Other's still in Creation. We dismantled it after Lucifer created Hell."

"Apparently not." Zane doesn't fold under the explanation. His eyes still carry a hardness that I've only seen when he was being controlled. It's unnerving, especially considering he's standing in the room with a room full of angel descendants.

Gabriel trades a look with his angelic brothers. "If they've reinstated that house of horrors, then we have a bigger problem than just the angels themselves."

"What do you mean?" Zane asks before I can.

"It means it's a literal land of nightmares. It's used to strip prisoners of who and what they are and mold them into anything the angels desire. Lovers, warriors, slaves..." Gabriel trails off with an unhappy scowl.

Zane's scythe shrinks back down and attaches to his necklace as if the answer satisfied some deep warning bells. He folds his arms, unimpressed. "What exactly are you willing to do about it?"

"We can't do anything without our grace," Uriel says from behind Gabriel.

I step between Zane and the angels. "Will you help us defeat the angels and get my family out of that hellhole?" Without an answer, I'm unwilling to allow Papa or Faith to relinquish their edge. The grace they harbor amplifies their power and has since before I was born.

"If we get our grace back, yes. They must be stopped and the Other must be destroyed." Michael blatant stare down makes me shift.

"Will you get our family out of the Other before you obliterate it?" I know I'm splitting hairs, but they didn't fully agree to my terms and Tom's old warning that all angels are dicks echoes in my mind.

They exchange glances and finally nod. I wait because a nod is not a verbal contract.

"Yes, we will get your family out before the Other is destroyed," Michael says with annoyance, inclining his eyebrows. "As long as you give us safe passage through Purgatory," he adds, looking straight at Zane.

"Fine by me," he says, as if he's the sole owner of the world between Heaven and Hell.

"Just as long as you never set foot in the reaper realm ever again," I add and jut my chin out. Angels have been screwing with the reaper realm for a decade now.

"Fine." Gabriel nods.

I stare at the four of them. Graceless archangels. "Before they give you your grace back, can any of you tell me why? Why now? Why, if they wanted to destroy us all, why wouldn't they have done it ten years ago or any time since?" Seriously, that is a question that's been nagging me. "Is it personal?"

Michael purses his lips, studying me as if he has an answer. He trades a glance with Gabriel. "My guess—they weren't powerful enough before. But if they've been leveraging the Other, not only have they been stripping their victims, they've

535

been feeding off the fear that thrives within those walls.”

“Like a vampire?” Damian asks.

Michael’s gaze softens as he glances at his nephew. He nods. “Yes. And it takes a while to amass enough energy to attempt to destroy God’s plan.”

Well. Shit. I don’t say the words out loud, but I do glance at Zane and then turn toward Papa and Faith with a nod. “Who’s first?”

Michael pushes forward ahead of his brothers. And without a word, crosses to where Papa stands.

“Take a seat.” Papa points to the chair next to the one he slides into. As soon as Michael settles in the seat, Papa dips his head and closes his eyes, covering his heart.

I’m enthralled with the ball of light as it forms between his hand and his chest. It bursts from underneath his fingers, letting out a light so pure I have to squint to see as he pulls it away from his body.

Papa pauses, staring at the light, and then looks up at Michael. There is a yearning in his eyes, as though he doesn’t want to let go of something so pure. He takes a deep breath and slams the ball of light into Michael’s chest, even as a grimace forms on his lips.

The archangel lights up as if he swallowed the moon and moonbeams bled from his skin. It seems to nearly burst from every cell, like the body before us can’t quite harness it. Everyone shields their eyes, but I can’t tear my gaze away as full and powerful wings of pure light form on his back. When the light dims, the wings remain and they are pristine white, like what Papa sprouts whenever he reaches fury on the emotion spectrum. The archangel surpasses my expectation when he flexes his wings. The light slowly recedes but doesn't fade completely. Michael takes a deep breath, as if he is content to be whole again, and then he sends a glaring smile in my direction, as if I should shake in my boots instead of the angels who stand against us. He points at me. "You and I need to have a word in private."

Oh fuck, no. I'm not interested in having a cage match with the Archangel Michael. Especially considering the only way to get that grace back is to rip his heart out and eat it. Stealing grace differs from giving it willingly, as Papa just did. And I can see the malice in the angel's eyes.

"Just as soon as we are done here." I want to make sure the rest of them are healed before I agree to a private conversation with a fully charged archangel.

"Uriel, you're up next," Papa says and repeats the transfer of grace.

Each one is just as glorious as the previous one, and Uriel and Gabriel are just as refreshed as Michael with their grace-infused wings.

Unfortunately, the transfer didn't do the same for Papa. He leans back in the chair, looking more exhausted than I've ever seen him. He glances at Alex. "Think you can handle the barrier for a bit?" he asks.

"Sure, Dad." Alex closes his eyes.

Power rolls out from him, and it tingles as it travels through my form, expanding outward until it crystalizes together with his father's. It's heady to think either of them could crush this Earth in a fit of rage. But they never have even given it a thought.

Papa gets up and pats Alex on the back before he heads down the hallway. Nana follows, with her brow furrowed in worry.

Faith waves to the chair, and Raphael takes a seat.

He reaches out and takes her hands. "You do not need to do this," he says.

"We need you powered up," Faith says with a smile that isn't natural. She's hiding something, and I cock my head as she does the same thing Papa just went through, except she hands the grace to Raphael instead of pushing it right into his chest. Her hand trembles as she does, and her cheeks go pale.

I've never seen fear so acute in her eyes. Raphael must see the same thing I am seeing because he takes his grace and peels a piece off, pressing it back into Faith's chest.

She bows back as it seeps back into her cells. Her hair glows, and just for a moment, those fiery wings appear before they fade away.

"To keep that balance with Lucifer's grace," he says with the softest smile, and I find I want to hug the healing angel. His heart is bigger than all of them put together. He presses the remaining grace to his chest. Light shines through him and his wings. His wings are tipped with golden highlights. It's as if the healing angel is the most beautiful of all.

When the light settles and all four of them are back to their former glory, Michael grabs me by the upper arm. "Now." He hauls me toward the hallway.

Levi scrambles to his feet with a low growl, and I put my hand out, silently telling him to stand down. His ears flatten, but his growl ceases.

Zane steps in front of us. "No one manhandles her," he snarls, but at least he hasn't conjured his scythe. Yet.

Michael's eyes narrow. "This coming from the one who took her life so callously." His cool voice deflates Zane, but he doesn't yield.

"Step aside, boy." Michael's wings snap as a warning.

I do not want a violent confrontation between Zane and Michael. That would not end well for anyone. I meet Zane's concerned gaze. "I'll be fine. He just wants to talk," I say, although I have a feeling that is not what the archangel means to do. I think I'm in for a serious fistfight at the very least, but I keep my voice as calm as possible. "Really, I am okay." I smile, but it's not a reflection of the fuming inside.

He gives me his "Are you sure?" look and I nod. Zane steps aside, but I can tell it's with reservation.

Michael drags me into the farthest room and slams the door behind him. He tosses me toward the master bed, and I bounce off the mattress, nearly falling to my knees.

I catch myself and straighten with a glare that matches his.

"No one gives me an ultimatum," he growls, sounding more menacing than Levi had.

But I laugh at him, anyway.

His face flushes red, and he points at me. "You are a menace," he says softly, now that we are away from the group, and his tone immediately sets me on guard. It's worse than the barreling growl a moment before. He stalks across the floor, staring at me with his intense eyes until he towers over me. "One that needs taming."

"Taming? What the fuck does that mean?" A thousand ants march across my skin, and I try to suppress the shiver of aggravation. He's in my personal space and I do not like it at all. I try to slip by him.

He corners me against the wall, framing me in with his arms and his outstretched wings. He leans in and I put my hand firmly on his chest, locking my elbow in place to keep him an arm's length away.

"What the hell are you doing?"

He blinks as if he's never been turned down before, but then his gaze narrows. "I'm teaching you a much-needed lesson in submission." He rips my hand from his chest and slams it against the wall.

I laugh at his audacity. "In your dreams." I step closer and then pivot, flipping his winged ass over my back onto the floor in a textbook jujitsu move.

"I'm not a little Earthly tart you can decide to play with. I'm Fate, so show a little respect."

I step away, creating distance and time to react to whatever his next move might be. In a blink, there's a crack of his wings and I'm slammed into the wall with his arm across my chest, blocking me in.

"I'm an archangel. You show a little damned respect." His wings flutter.

He's close enough to see the golden flecks in his blue eyes, along with his true intent. And it's anything but pure.

"You don't dictate to Heaven's avenger."

"I fucking saved you from being a second-class citizen in Heaven, and I made it possible for you to be restored to your former glory. I can take it away just as easily." I place my hand in the form of a claw over his chest, letting my nails dig into his flesh through the thin shirt he wears. "I know how this works. The way Papa gave you back your grace was the nice way. There is another way, and I'm perfectly capable of executing that ritual."

Tom Ryan had told me how he stole Lucifer's grace from Damian, and how he made Faith rip his own heart from his chest to get the grace that Lucifer was after. Eating the heart of an angel is gross, but right now, I'd happily do it to this asshole.

He reaches out and grabs my charm bracelet. "Two can play that game."

I freeze and stare at his hand. If he claims the Book of Fates, I pass on. Like Heaven or Hell—or, in this case, probably the Other...at the gleeful hands of the lower-ranked angels. I move my gaze back to his, conjuring up as much of a glare as he is wearing. Neither of us is bluffing, and I calculate my odds of getting to his heart before he can yank the delicate chain from my wrist.

Slowly, I flatten my palm on his chest, yielding to his bluff.

His cocky smile, like he just won the prize at the local fair, sets me off, but I don't react, because he still has his hand wrapped around the chain holding the Book of Fates to my skin.

"That a girl." He releases my bracelet and glances down at my chest, rising and falling in the tight leather corset. He meets my gaze and has the audacity to run his hand up my arm.

Now, I react. My knee slams between his legs with all the power I have. He actually lifts off the ground from the hit. His entire face reddens, and he falls to his knees, groaning. Although I want to slam my fist into his upturned face, I resist, and step around him and cross to the door. I pause with my hand on the doorknob.

"I trust this ends whatever you thought you had rights to." I don't even look back as I leave; I just shut the door behind me and walk back into the living room with a new and violent determination.

"For the record, before anyone else decides to be galactically stupid like the mighty Archangel Michael, I belong to Zane Bradley. I am his in every sense of the word, so just don't be an asshole, or I will have your balls on a platter." I level a glare that really sets the mood in the room. I meet Tom Ryan's gaze. "You, my friend, are totally on the money. *All* angels are dicks."

"Did he try..." Zane hooks his thumb over his shoulder toward the back bedroom as his face reddens.

"I took care of it." I meet his gaze. If Michael comes back out here like a wrecking ball, then he can conjure his scythe and eliminate the fool, but for now, hopefully feeling his balls in the back of his throat should be enough to tame that mother.

Zane's lips thin and he does not heed the warning in my silent communication for him to leave it the hell alone. Instead, he turns to march down the hall and give Michael a beating.

"I wouldn't get into a fight with him," Damian says. "He's kicked my ass a few times when I was a vampire, and vampires are notoriously strong."

Damian's warning didn't slow Zane down, either.

"Leave it alone," I say, and Zane turns to me with a hardness in his gaze. He does not like it when I issue an order. Especially one when I can tell he feels as though he shouldn't have let me go down there to begin with.

He chose the scythe. He's the one who has to obey Fate. I'm his boss for eternity and although I don't enjoy ordering him around, sometimes it's for his own damn good, like right now. This little glare of his is just nothing more than him mentally telling me we'd be having a talk about this later when all this angel crap was done.

I look forward to that conversation.

Michael limps back into the room, looking a little demeaned as everyone stares at him. He comes within striking distance of Zane, and although I stopped him from walking down the hall and confronting Michael, I am not fast enough to stop the punch he throws.

It catches Michael in the side of the jaw, sending him sidestepping into the living room wall. His wings flutter as he straightens and squares up for battle.

Levi moves in front of Zane. It's the first time he's willingly protected him without a direct order from me and for a moment all my piss and vinegar is gone, replaced by a sappiness I hate and one that earns me a side eye from Levi.

Michael eyes the dog warily.

"I would have expected that kind of behavior from my father," Faith says to Michael, and crosses her arms. "But not from an agent of Heaven."

Michael's nose twitches and a sneer passes over his features, before it is replaced with the proper embarrassment. His cheeks turn a rosy hue as Faith's words sink in. Losing is not something this being takes lightly, and he's had his fair share of it in the past half century.

He relaxes his muscles and gives her a nod, as if he's thanking her for reminding him what he truly represents. "I apologize. That was not...right," he says to me with a slight bow. But he doesn't quite meet my gaze and him not adding a litany of excuses to the end of the sentence makes his apology more acceptable.

"Fine. But if you do anything that stupid again, I'll let Leviathan eat you." I point to the dog sitting in front of Zane. My favorite monster would gladly take out all the angels if he could, and he'd be satiated for centuries.

"With pleasure," the dog says in that deep-toned voice that spreads fear in every single one of his enemies. It seems the archangel is not immune to fearing my cohort, because he pales a few tones.

"You have Leviathan here? On Earth?" Uriel asks with wide eyes.

"Where the hell have you been, mate?" Smoke asks from the corner. "He's been hanging with Death for the last fifty years."

"And he hasn't eaten humanity?" Gabriel asks.

"No. You really didn't know what he was when we were in Purgatory?" I stare at them, dumbfounded. "Besides, what the hell makes you think he would eat humanity?"

"Our father said he was unmanageable," Raphael said. "That's why he had him chained near the gates of Hell in Purgatory."

"I was unmanageable for your father because he was as much of a dick as the rest of you." Levi bares his teeth in a low snarl just to make his point.

"Seriously? God chained him up?" I ask.

"Your father sounds like a royal dick," Zane says at the same time as I gawk. "Levi's a pussycat," Zane adds and pats his head. Levi just looks over his shoulder at him, like *are you kidding me?* "Missy's father set him free, and he's been part of the family ever since."

"He's hunted demons with me," Faith adds. "And got me through the lower realms of Hell when I closed one of the portals we jumped through by accident."

"And those angel dicks locked him up and had their griffin guarding him," I add. "But we took care of that god-awful thing."

Raphael's brow arched. "You dispatched the griffin?"

"Yes, sir, we did." I smile. "The three of us are a force to be reckoned with." I stare at Archangel Michael as I speak.

"That is because you are Fate," Michael snaps back at me.

"Dude, she was a force long before she became either Fate or Death." Zane moves across the room to sling his arm around my shoulder in a way that shows his claim.

I shake his arm off my shoulder. Although I announced I was his in no uncertain terms, that he has to physically mark his territory in some way is irritating. I give him the side eye in case he tries that again.

I glance around the room. "Now that we are all playing nice with one another, and the archangels are all graced up, we need to focus on a plan." When no one offers an immediate idea, I sigh. "The angels are coming back, and they are coming in full force. So how do we play this?"

Ty leans forward from his spot at the dinner table and rubs his chin. "We have some key points of surprise and if we stage it correctly, it likely will overwhelm them." He turns the pile of papers he has in front of him around so we can all see.

I cross to the table and look down at the stack he's turned our way. His elaborate drawings are impressive, to say the least. I can only draw stick figures, so seeing the likenesses of all of us makes me glance at him.

"How long have you been drawing those?" I ask.

"I've been doodling for a while. Basically, since you left to get them." He points at the angels.

"That's what, only a couple of hours?"

He shrugs. "It was tough to figure out the right progression, and I think this approach is the best out of all my thoughts." He doesn't even acknowledge that his drawings are beyond perfect.

I stare at his thought-out approach, still awed by the detail. Zane isn't on the front line with me. Neither is Levi. And the archangels are missing. The only ones standing with me drawn in intricate detail on the first piece of paper are Papa, Ty, Tom, Alex, and Faith. The powerhouses.

"This is what they expect." He taps the paper. "They probably expect Zane, but they do not expect this." He flips the top page over and there is a likeness of Zane, along with Levi. Even the scale seems right, with the cross between Godzilla and a dragon representing Levi's native form. Next to them are other beasts. A tiger. A hawk. I blink at the third drawing. *That can't be right.*

"Is that a saber-toothed tiger?" I point at the prehistoric death machine that probably could give Levi a run for his money. "Where the hell are we going to get that?"

Ty points at Smoke and raises his eyebrows. "If I'm not mistaken," he says.

Smoke shrugs. "That's a pretty good likeness."

Both Phoebe and I spin to look at him.

"I assume you can still shift," Ty says. It isn't so much a question as a statement.

And damned if Smoke shrugs. "Beats me. I haven't tried since Fate released me from being a housecat."

Phoebe still stares at him with an open mouth. "You were that? Why didn't you ever turn into that while we were hunting demons?" She's still blinking fast, like the dots are not connecting right.

He chuckles. "Fate cursed me into a housecat," he says. "If I could have had my natural form, I would have gladly donned it to protect you from those damned demons." He wraps his arm around her waist and pulls her into a tender kiss. "But I'm no ordinary saber. I'm twice the size of any in recorded history." His grin is infectious, and I smile in response.

We have a mammoth saber-toothed tiger at our disposal. I can't help the feeling of hope that intertwines with the dread. The last paper shows the archangels descending between us and a sea of angels as far as the paper will allow. It's daunting, at the very least.

If raw numbers determined the winner, we are sorely outnumbered based on his drawing. Even if I call upon the reaper federation, the numbers are still too skimpy.

Ty reaches out and covers my hand. "Trust in yourself," he says softly, while Phoebe and Smoke still chatter about his secret shifter form.

"Show me. Shift now." Phoebe waves to the living area and captures my full attention.

I want to see this, too.

"You really want to see me in fur again?" he teases and steps away from people. "Please have a blanket ready for when I shift back because I'll be naked, and I don't need all the alpha males in this room jealous of my endowments." He winks at Phoebe. His grin fades as he dips his head in concentration.

Phoebe grabs the throw blanket off the back of the couch and holds it tight to her chest as she keeps her gaze locked on Smoke. Every set of eyes is on him, including all the angels. I think the raw curiosity has us all holding our breath.

The cords on his neck stand out with the effort to shift, and his hands clench. When his eyes open, they're decidedly the golden green of a feline with elongated pupils. His eye teeth grow to razors in his mouth and he tilts his head back, letting out a roar. Fur spurts from his skin and an instant later, he drops to all fours and lowers his head.

It looks just as painful as having the essence of Death stripped from your cells. I shiver. When he finally completes the shift with a bone-grinding crunch, the beast takes up most of the living room and his mouth is head height for most of us in the room. He flexes his front paws and his nails glisten like deadly knives.

He roars at us and then purrs at Phoebe, rubbing the side of his head against her until she giggles and pushes him away.

Despite his endearing feline actions with Phoebe, he still is terrifying. I wouldn't want to be on the opposition. Between Smoke's alternative form and Levi, I would be running for the hills while trying to control my bladder.

"Damn glad you are on our side," Zane says. "He's almost as terrifying as Levi." Zane says exactly what was running through my mind.

"And I assume you two can still shift," Ty says to Naomi and Damian.

They nod. "Yes. That's inherent in our blood."

"Well, let's see." He nods to the living room where the saber-toothed tiger takes up most of the space.

"I'm not sure we'll all fit in here," Damian says.

"Humor me," Faith says. "I'd really like to see what our backup team looks like outside of what's on paper." She looks over her shoulder at Ty. "Despite the exemplary detail of your drawings."

"Fine," Damian says with an eyeroll.

Their transition lacks the effort Smoke displayed. One second they were in human form, and the next they transform. Naomi is a fraction of the size of Smoke, but her white tiger is especially intimidating, especially with the bright-blue angel eyes.

Damian's hawk is nearly the size that the griffin was, but when he caws, it's exactly the sound I expected from the griffin. Fierce. There is no room for him to spread his wings to give us an idea of his wingspan, but based on his size, he could carry a full-grown man in his talons with no problem.

It's humbling. They are an impressive lot, and I can only imagine what they will look like when Levi joins them in his native form. We can't see that until the time comes, because the cottage would be demolished if Levi snapped into his natural state. I glance at him, and he gives me that tongue loll of a canine laugh.

Even the archangels seem to shrink away from the beasts in the center of the room. After all, they were made to destroy immortal scum like demons and now the lot of lower angels.

"That's awesome," Phoebe says. "Now change back so we can finish looking at Ty's strategy and see if we need to tweak it."

Damian and Naomi flip back, fully clothed, just as fast as they shifted. But Smoke's transition back to human seems just as painful as his original shift. Bone grinding on bone and tendons snapping back in place makes me shiver.

And he wasn't kidding. His sweat-soaked body is completely naked when it finally snaps back together. At least the view of him is limited to a quick flash before Phoebe throws the blanket around him. But what I do catch makes me envy Phoebe for a second. I glance away until he's properly wrapped.

Smoke remains kneeling on the ground, catching his breath as he clings to the blanket around him. When he finally looks up, his face is drawn with exhaustion. He climbs to his feet unsteadily.

"You okay?" Phoebe puts her arm around him.

"I just need a drink and a little nap." He turns away from us and disappears into the back hallway, with Phoebe helping him.

She comes back and grabs the nearly full carton of orange juice and gives us all a tight smile before she heads back to wherever he is laying down.

Two of our mighty warriors are down for the count, and I trade a glance with Ty.

"They'll be fine by the time this battle begins," he says, easing my worry. He is very good at reading people without the benefit of telepathy, although he possesses that gift, too. But his tap into the human condition is much more subtle, like his so-called glimpses into the future.

Although Jennifer Williams had been a natural clairvoyant, Ty gets his from his angel heritage. Papa once told me that even before he and Tom were born, their father had made arrangements for their guardian to be Steve Williams. That was some eight years before Steve came into their lives. I remember the goose bumps that spread over my arms at that story.

I glance up from the ornate pictures and over my shoulder at the rest of the folks gathered around Damian and Naomi. They are still fawning over the shifters, and I have to let out a quiet laugh. I turn back and stare right into Ty's frank gaze.

"Are we going to survive this?" I ask outright, because of all the people in the room, he's the one with foresight. Even my Book of Fates won't show me who lives and who dies. At least not those in this room because, believe me, I've scrolled through it several times over the years, trying to read the Fates of my family and found nothing.

He takes a deep breath and shuffles through the papers. He has many more drawings than what he showed us, and I pluck them from his hands. His wide-eyed gaze jerks up to mine.

I slowly shift from one page to the next. The pages show so many outcomes—from an explosion that cracks the earth in two, to the bloody battlefield and only Zane sitting by himself with his head in his hands, to me nearly breaking apart with light.

I stare at that one, because it isn't on the same battlefield. I'm alone in Paradise Cove, but not the burned-out husk it currently is. In the picture, Paradise Cove is reinstated.

Ty takes the drawings and pulls out the one with the archangels, placing it on the table as he rips the rest of them into little pieces without breaking my gaze.

"So, the archangels next," I say, trying to not let the tremor break my voice.

He nods. "If the Heavenly host doesn't back down, yes, the archangels come next," Ty says.

Our conversation seems to pull people back into the strategy talks. Neither Ty nor I mention his other drawings. I trust he has seen every possible outcome and has chosen the right one. If not, we are all doomed.

"There's one particular angel who I'm not letting leave alive regardless of whether or not he waves the white flag," Zane says, and everyone turns to him. "The rest of them, if they yield, then I'm okay with letting them go back to Heaven with the promise they will never step outside those gates again. But the one who tortured me—Gadrel…he's mine." He presses his lips together and his eyes flash a warning against any type of argument.

I'm okay with his need for justice, especially considering I want to skin the asshole alive just to relish his pain. And then use Heaven's blade to snuff him out of existence when I think he's sufficiently suffered.

I glance at the clock. The witching hour just passed, and I look around the room. "I think you all need to get some rest." I cross to the curtain and push it aside. "I'll keep watch in case they decide to attack while it's dark."

"I'll keep you company until my father gets up," Alex says as he picks up the drawings that Ty left on the table.

Ty and Jessica, along with Faith, Damian, and Naomi start down the hall.

"You sure you don't want some help?" Tom asks as he looks at Alex and twirls his finger. Raven waits with Hannah at the entrance to the hallway.

"I'm good, Uncle Tom." He gives Tom a hug and then shoos him off to be with Raven and Hannah.

Quiet descends on the living room, leaving me with Alex, Zane, Levi, and the four archangels in what looks to be shaping up to be a very long night.

Kissing Fate
Chapter 14

"I'LL SEE YOUR BET and raise you a..." Zane looks at the pile of junk next to him. An assortment of paper clips, staples, and pens lay in a pile. He pulls out a pen and drops it in the growing pile of desk supplies and counts out a dozen paper clips. "A dozen paper clips." He drops those on the pile and cocks an eyebrow.

Uriel frowns at the five cards in his hand and then folds them in front of him with disgust. "I'm out."

I look at my cards, biting my lower lip at the three aces, queen, and seven in my hand. I toss a pen and ten paper clips from my pile into the kitty in the center. "Call."

Michael fans his cards out, studying his hand. He toys with a pen and then sighs as he folds the cards and tosses them into the center. "Fold."

Raphael doesn't even look at his cards. He just adds to the kitty what is required to stay in the game and then tosses two pencils in. "I'll raise you two pencils." He grins and glances at Gabriel, who started this bid raise madness.

"Oh, for fuck's sake." Gabriel flips two pencils in. "I call."

Zane and I do the same and then all of us show our cards. My three of a kind doesn't hold water with two full houses and a straight flush. Zane smiles as he pulls the pile toward him.

This is how we've chosen to pass the night. Four angels, Death, and Fate around a poker table. It's almost a bad bar joke. Especially considering Zane has barely lost a hand.

I shuffle and then cock my head at the rumble of thunder in the distance. My heart leaps into my throat and I nearly topple the chair as I get up to pull the curtain back enough to see dawn's arrival and those ominous clouds gathered in the sky.

I spin toward the group. "Get everyone up. It's show time."

Levi jumps to his paws and barks. Alex sits up like a rocket on the couch. I'm running for the hallway, broadcasting a siren in my head that is sure to wake anyone who has an ounce of psychic ability. I stop in the middle of the hall and will every light in the house on, knowing that is more effective than knocking on doors as I make my way down the hall.

Tom is the first one in the hall. He looks like he slept in his clothing. Same with Papa and Faith.

"Papa, I don't think the barrier's up," I say, and he pauses.

His magic flows right through me as he forms the security perimeter around us again.

When we get to the living room, Ty turns to Zane. "You know what to do?"

"As soon as they land, I'll lead Levi, Damian, Naomi, and Smoke out."

He nods and looks at Michael.

"We will give it five minutes and then we will exit through the back door by the garage and ascend over the house to land in front of Missy. If they have taken that opportunity to attack, we will come down with all our glory and wrath."

He summarized the plan in a more arrogant way than Ty had directed, but at least he got it right.

Michael glances at the sigil Papa drew on his wrist. "And you are sure this will work?" he asks.

"Yes." I hold up my wrist. "That's how I got you all through the barrier without being toasted." I cross my arms again. He was there to see Papa draw it on all their wrists. Even Levi got a sigil, but unless he lays on his back for a belly rub, no one would be the wiser as to where his sigil is hidden.

Michael presses his lips together. "Did you not feel the barrier as we went through?" he snips at me.

"Yes. But believe me when I say if I wasn't leading you through, you all would have been torched. This time, you won't feel a thing passing through. But if they try to attack the house, they will be fried."

He seems to accept my explanation, especially because the rest of the people are nodding in confirmation.

"If they've attacked, you use the full force of your power to wipe them out," I continue, just to make sure everyone is on the same page.

Michael and Uriel nod. By the time this little refresher is wrapped up, the rest of the house is gathering around us. I glance around at the warriors and those who love them. "Nana, you need to stay inside with Phoebe, Raven, and Hannah just in case we need your services later," I say.

She nods, but I can tell she wants to be in the middle of the fight. After all, these bastards killed her granddaughter and the need for retribution flares in her eyes just as brightly as it does in Papa's.

I head to the door with my powerhouses with me. We march to just shy of Papa's force field as the sky lights up with a thousand lightning bolts. Alex takes his place on one side of me and Faith on the other. Tom stands by Faith, and Papa stands between his father and his son.

I reach out and take both Faith and Alex's hands, gently squeezing to show my appreciation to the people who raised me in the absence of my true parents. "I love you guys."

"Ditto." Alex squeezes back.

The rest of them clasp hands as well, and we stand as one united family.

The pre-dawn sky sends a chill traveling down my spine. "I hope no one takes a trip to the lake today," I mutter.

Faith snorts a laugh. "If they are, they're going to be quite surprised to see a war of angels in their backyard."

"Let's hope it doesn't come to that," Ty says. "The last time I battled here, I lost my head, and I'm quite fond of it. I'd rather not have a repeat."

We all look around Alex and Papa at Papa's father. He grins back with that brittle sense of humor that is so inappropriate that even I crack a smile.

"Dad," both Papa and Tom scold at the same time, as only twins can do.

"Come on. That was funny."

He really is unnerving when he grins the way he is, and I get why people used to call him the Angel of Death. Although I know he isn't, he certainly can embrace that persona at will.

"No. It wasn't." Papa sends a sideways glare at his father.

I glance at our merry band of six. Two on one side and three on the other, and I am again thankful they are on my side. Not only are we all supercharged, but we are all masters in jujitsu. Not one of us standing here is a novice in hand-to-hand combat.

The energy flowing between us tingles through my limbs. I am prepared for an army of angels, and when they land on the lawn a few feet from us and the line of angels spans the entire lake, I swallow hard. And then the angels part and my heart drops.

There in the center, with blades to their ethereal throats, kneel my mother, my father, and Holly. They all sport black-and-blue faces, split lips, and those bruises cover whatever skin is exposed. But my father's eyes are clear, and they meet my gaze. He sends me a wink, like he's reminding me of the last thing he said to me ten years ago.

Promise me you won't do anything stupid.

I tighten my grip on Alex and Faith's hands, knowing they are feeling the same need to rush to their rescue. That is exactly what the angels want. They want us to break formation, to rush in individually so they can slaughter us.

"Don't," I whisper loud enough for Alex and Faith and Papa to hear.

Power crackles all around us.

The angels holding the front line take a step back; their necks crane and their eyes widen. I smile as Levi steps into line by Tom, followed by Zane. On the other side, Damian, Naomi, and Smoke take their places by Ty.

Zane's scythe glistens in the morning light. He's the only one with a weapon on our side, even though the angels all carry swords.

An angel steps forward and Levi growls. I send a sideways glance at Zane and will him not to step out of line yet, but his face contorts with fury. Yet he stays in line, trading a glance with me. This is the one that tortured him day in and day out until he broke the boy I loved.

This angel is Gadrel. The bastard wanted a war? Well, he was going to get one.

Faith's hand clamps down hard on mine, as if she knows I'm about to launch at this bastard.

The angel points at me. "Surrender, and we will spare them." He waves in a grandiose manner at the spirits of my parents and Holly.

I narrow my eyes. They already slaughtered them. We have Holly's body on ice as a reminder.

"I didn't think Heaven's agents could lie." I glance to my right and my left, looking for confirmation, and receive a couple of nods before I bring my cold glare to the angel. "So, does that mean you are a demon in disguise?"

"I command the reaper federation to back me now," Zane says, straying from the script.

I try not to react, but I'm sure Gadrel catches the tic near my eye as irritation flushes my skin. But it's the way the angel grins at the order that sends ice through my veins.

I still have the power to annihilate reapers who want to do me or my family harm. That was inherent in my blood and not a thing passed to me when I took the role of Death. I close my eyes and call on that gift. The power to weed out the dark hearts and snuff them out. Dust to dust. Ashes to ashes. The power rolls out behind me, engulfing the reaper federation.

I open my eyes and a few ashes swirl in the wind. I allow a cocky smile to form at the horror etched in Gadrel's face. Oh, they didn't know I still harbored that power. Well, they were in for quite a ride!

Satisfaction fills me in a warm wave, and I keep hold of Alex and Faith's hands despite the itch to strike that angel dead on the spot.

"Patience," I whisper. More to myself than anyone, but it's waning in all of us.

Gadrel snaps his finger. The angels surrounding my parents swing their weapons. Blades whistle through the air and three heads roll onto the ground, rolling until they land near enough to set off a chain reaction in me.

They just beheaded my parents and Holly.

Unbridled rage fills me as their forms fade into the ground, back to whatever hell holds them. I tear my hands out of Faith's and Alex's grip, and launch forward beyond the barrier.

Angel fire launches at me from every angel, as though this were planned. Even Gadrel smiles triumphantly. Ty's pictures flip through my mind, and I gasp and throw my arms wide. Instead of blowing up, angel fire soaks into my body like an electrical current into a lethal battery, setting every nerve on fire.

Dark knowledge of their intentions scrapes my senses, and I bellow with fury. The angels just made *me* a celestial bomb. *I* am their agent for the End of Times. This was their plan all along. This is what they were biding their time for: to feed enough energy into me to kill the world.

And what truly sucks...I'm powerless. I cannot release any of what Papa gave me. I can't conjure a weapon. I can't use anything magical. If I do, what will result is the equivalent of the big bang itself, and I and everyone I love will be gone. Torn to shreds.

My body thrums with power. It's ripping through every cell, burning and gathering more power as it takes on a life of its own.

But I am close enough to Gadrel to land a bone-crunching punch into his nose. A fraction of satisfaction snakes through me as he falls on his ass and blood covers his immaculate clothing. But it isn't enough to wipe off that arrogant gaze from his face. It's as if he's laughing at me, like he knows a more heinous secret.

Zane's scythe swings, taking off the head of the closest angel. His face is set in a mask of rage and he swings again, slicing through another angel. He's like wrath embodied as he continues to slash. Levi joins him, tearing heads and wings as efficiently as I expected.

But Gadrel still holds that smug smile. He expects to survive whatever blast I create when I let this burning glory go. Which means if the Heavenly host can withstand the blast, Heaven can surely absorb the power without imploding.

Ty's pictures flip through my mind, but even with the outcomes scribbled on paper, I still want to eviscerate Gadrel. Unfortunately, I can't even call Heaven's blade to battle.

The rest of the group remains in place, which gives me hope that someone followed the plan. But when I glance over my shoulder, I realize it's not because they are following procedure; it's because someone is holding them in place. Alex looks furious about it and Faith is full-on flaming. But when my gaze falls on Ty Ryan, he meets my gaze. I see the warning in his eyes and can almost hear his voice whisper in my mind.

It's not time.

I have one chance to make this right, but in the meantime, these fuckers needed to pay.

Unfortunately, not at my hand. I know what needs to be done, and Faith is going to be even more pissed when I pull her from her chance at retribution.

That's when I see it. The angels' self-righteous smiles falter as their eyes lift to the sky behind me. The archangels descend and they take a double take at me. Michael's eyes widen and then he turns toward the Heavenly host with a mask of wrath more feral than Zane's.

I have a moment to relish the fear in the angels' eyes when that voice whispers *Now* in my ear. I spin and grab Faith's hand, yanking her away from the sudden rush of yelling angels.

I don't even have to give the order; everyone rushes forth to deliver justice, and it's absolute pandemonium.

"What are you doing?" she yells as I pull her toward the path to Paradise Cove.

"I need you to blast me a path, Faith." I glance back at her as I drag her with me. "They made me into a bomb."

She blinks at me, still wrapped in the shock of Holly's beheading, but she does exactly what I ask, torching any angel that comes at us from any direction. As soon as we are within the confines of Paradise Cove, I let go of her wrist.

"Open it back up," I say, out of breath. I strain to hold together my cells. I can feel the burn of power liquifying my insides. "I don't have much time," I add.

She opens her mouth to argue, but I point to the blackened moss. "Just like you did back then."

She still doesn't move.

"Jesus Christ, Faith. Do it! Heaven's the only place that can handle this power!" Trembles capture me in their grip and my voice wavers with it. "Otherwise, this is the end of all. This was their fucking plan!" I point toward the backyard. Her inability to grasp the need for her to act quickly is adding to my frustration, which, in turn, is adding to the speed at which their poison is growing.

"But..."

"Do it, before they bring the fight to us and I lose control." I point to the ground, hoping that breaks through whatever hesitations are holding Faith back.

Dawning widens her eyes, and she crouches, placing both palms on the ground. Under her hands, vibrant green moss replaces the black. The effect spreads, wiping out the scars she left when she closed the portal to Heaven.

Zane appears at the entrance with his scythe in his hand. It glistens with blood and gore. He's battered as well, but when he sees me, the worry lining his lips and forehead relaxes. The scythe shrinks and attaches to his necklace before he crosses to me, ignoring the regrowth making everything around the three of us flourish.

Neither of us belongs on this side of Heaven, but I need to be here. I need to release the power they poisoned me with before it explodes.

"Is it done yet?" I ask Faith.

"Almost."

"When you are done, run." I meet Zane's gaze. "Both of you."

He shakes his head and wraps his arms around me. "Not a chance."

A popping sound snaps the portal in place and Faith rises to her feet.

"Go," I whisper.

She glances at Zane and then back at me. Her eyes widen and she bolts. The moment she steps off the green moss, I look into Zane's eyes.

"Please go." A tear blurs my vision until it slips out, tracing a hot path to the corner of my mouth. I have no idea whether I will survive this, and I think he's aware of that because he threads his hand in my hair and kisses me.

I raise my arms to the Heavens and release the explosive fuel the angels fed into me. I cry out under his lips, and he takes that as an invitation to swipe his tongue across mine. The distraction helps the burn consuming me, and I kiss him back.

His grip around me tightens, pressing me against him as though he's trying to hold me together. I want to wrap my arms around him, too, but I'm afraid.

Not until this poison is bled from my veins. Otherwise, I will doom us all.

It hurts as much as when Death's essence peeled from my cells, transitioning into Zane ten years ago. But the way Zane is kissing me anchors me in place. His arms keep me from flying into a thousand pieces from the force of the angel fire. I rip away from his lips and tilt my head back, screaming with the power pulsing inside me.

He leans his head away from me, but he does not release me from his hold. In fact, I think he tightens his grip instead.

Heat fills my mouth. It burns my eyes. My hands feel as if I am holding onto a lightning bolt. The more I push to purge this, the louder and longer my scream goes. The exodus of power is immense, filling the glen with white light, blinding me.

And then emptiness weighs down on me, pulling me into the black.

Kissing Fate
Chapter 15

M Y EYES BLINK OPEN, and I lift my head from Zane's chest. One of his arms remains securely around my back, holding me to him. But he's laid out on the grass, with his other arm stretched out away from me. His mechanical hand is a mass of melted metal and his cheek facing me is reddened like he fell asleep in the sun.

Paradise Cove is in full bloom around us, and the light shining down from us above spreads over us like a fan. Fog rolls off the cove, diffusing in the rays.

"Zane?" I shake him, and he blinks, turning his head toward me. There is a very distinct sunburn line down his face, and I can't help but smirk.

He smiles up at me and winces. "My face kind of hurts," he says with a raspy voice.

"It looks like you spent the day at the beach and fell asleep in the sun."

He brings his prosthetic hand in view and stares at what is left of the metal before dropping it back on the ground. "I'm surprised we both didn't go up in flames." He looks back at me. He gently shifts me onto the ground and sits up, running his hand down the unburnt side of his face. He glances at me with a soft smile and then scans our surroundings.

"Where are we?" he asks. "Is this Heaven?"

"No, it's Paradise Cove."

His eyebrows arch.

"Faith reopened the portal for me. Didn't you notice the change when you came?"

He let out a laugh. "No. I was focused on you and the light that was bleeding through fractures in your skin. Gadrel said we were too late. That the world would end tonight. Those crazy motherfuckers made you their bomb. They fed you enough angel juice to wipe out the cosmos." He shakes his head. "That's when I ran to find you." He meets my gaze. "If you were going to blow to kingdom come, I wasn't going to let you die alone."

I palm his cheek. "I think you held me together."

He chuckles. "I don't know about that. But you certainly shot that shit out of you like a rocket." He holds his melted hand up and studies it. The smile fades and he glances around at the woods surrounding us. "Why aren't we ashes?"

"Because I shot my power into Heaven, the only place powerful enough to absorb it without exploding."

He glances up and I catch the glint of metal around his neck. At least his necklace and scythe didn't melt. My charm bracelet still exists, too.

I climb onto shaky legs and take stock of myself. I don't feel any different from before they shot me with their nasty poison. So, I glance at his mangled mechanics, envisioning them morphing back to the shape of a hand from the melted blob. When the metal creaks, I smile. I can still conjure.

He climbs to his feet, staring at the repairs I made. He taps his pinkie to his thumb, then his ring finger, middle finger, and pointer before smiling. "You conjured a working hand this time."

"I figured it would save us a few hours of time while Ty tinkers with it."

Next, I tap into the power from Papa, forming a wall between us and the path out of here. When he walks into it with a bang, I actually laugh out loud. "Sorry, just testing things out."

"And you used me as your test subject?" He rubs his nose. "You could have given me a little warning."

I close my eyes, evaporating the wall, and take my first step. My legs are unsteady, and I pause to get my balance.

"Are you okay?" He moves to my side.

"I didn't realize just how weak I am."

He slings his arm around me, giving me the support I need.

"By the way, I told them to hold that angel bastard until we returned," he says as he leads me out of Heaven's portal.

Zane certainly knows how to bribe the rubber right out of my legs. By the time we reach the end of the path, my gait steadies. However, the view of the backyard halts my progress.

Blood and limbs litter the lawn, and my heart leaps into my throat at the carnage. I cannot imagine what kind of losses we took and I'm afraid to ask.

"Who did we lose?" My unsteady question falls out of my trembling lips.

Zane pushes me forward a couple of steps and points to the area next to the bay window by the cottage.

My legs wobble as I scan all the faces that stood with me. Each one being tended to by Nana. There's nothing more than cuts and scrapes and broken bones. Everyone is still alive.

We did not lose a single soul in this celestial fight.

Tom nods my way, and all eyes turn toward me. I can't help the tears that spring forth.

Faith is on her feet and sprinting in my direction. I push off Zane, because I know she's coming to hug me. And he's still toxic to living beings.

Before she can get to me, a shrill cry comes from between the archangels.

"How? How can you be alive?" Gadrel bellows. The archangels have him bound and on his knees between them.

I hold my finger up to Faith, stopping her. Hugs can come later. But this asshole must be dealt with. Now.

I cross to the archangels and they lift him up to stand before me as if I'm his judge and jury, all rolled into one steaming mad entity.

"How?" I tilt my head. "I'm much smarter than you give me credit for. The only place that can absorb that much power is Heaven itself. And while your partners in crime were slaughtered on the lawn here, Lucifer's daughter opened the portal for me." I wave toward Faith.

"How could you!" he screams in my face.

"How could I what?" I tap my lip with my finger as I glare at him. "Reinstate Heaven's glory? The same glory you stole to make me into a bomb?" I glance at the archangels. "How could I give the archangels their grace back?" I shrug. "Break the spell you had on Zane?" I step forward, oozing menace, and he shrinks back. "How could I what?" I growl through clenched teeth.

I circle around behind him and pick up one of many discarded angel swords and slash with purpose. Two bloody wings fall to the ground as he wails, as though someone cut his balls off instead.

I come back to stand in front of him, close enough to relish the fear in his eyes. I shoot my hand out, formed in a claw, and puncture his chest. "Or how could I steal your fucking grace?"

My hand ensnares his heart, yanking it from his chest with a violent tug.

In one hand, I hold his beating heart and in the other, I will Heaven's blade from my trusty hiding place in the ether. The blade appears, glistening in the sunlight. "Or how could I snuff your ass right out of existence?"

I aim the knife at him and pause. I am not the one who deserves the privilege of killing this bastard.

I turn to Zane. "You get the honors," I say softly, offering him both the heart and the blade. "Unfortunately, to consume his grace, you need to eat his heart. As far as the knife, you know how to wield a blade."

He takes the heart in his mechanical hand and Heaven's blade in his flesh-and-blood hand. He stares at the heart and then at the angel. Instead of lifting the muscle to his mouth like I expect, he spears it onto the knife and then buries the rest of the blade into Gadrel's stomach.

"I don't want an ounce of his toxic being infused with my cells. It's better to wipe all of him out of existence," he growls, and yanks the blade back out. He hands the knife to me, and I send it back to my hiding place in the ether before any blowback can knock it out of my hand or an archangel can grab it.

Gadrel bellows to the Heavens, struggling in Uriel and Gabriel's grip. But there is no help there for him.

"Boys, you might want to step back," I say as we take more than a few paces away from the one who created this nightmare.

The archangels listen and drop Gadrel to his knees. They move out of the blowback range before the traitor lifts off the ground.

That same explosion of light followed by the sucking back into the universe occurs just before Gadrel pops right out of existence.

For some reason, it doesn't quite satisfy my need for vengeance, but it will have to do. The complete slaughter of the Heavenly host will have to do. Bodies float on the shoreline. The water laps red onto the beach and stains the dock with blood. Feathers float in clumps.

Levi is knee-deep in the middle of the lake, gulping up bodies like it's an all-you-can-eat buffet. I glance at Zane.

He glances down at me. "Remind me never to get on your bad side."

I smirk and look up at him. "Was that too far over the top?"

He snorts laughter. "Just a little. Almost as much as a prehistoric monster eating angel remnants." He waves at Levi.

He's right. We can't have him out there like this, especially because it's the middle of the day and he's likely to be seen. I whistle.

Levi glances at me, and I point to the spot before me. Annoyance passes over his reptilian face, but he obeys, trudging out of the water like a mad toddler instead of Leviathan, the most feared monster in all the realms.

He shrinks down to dog form and shakes the water from his faux fur before he trots over to the humans still breathing. I step toward my family.

"We are done here," Michael says, stopping me.

I turn as he starts toward Paradise Cove. This was only half of our deal. That wall I tested out in Paradise Cove erects, and Michael bumps into it with far more force than Zane. He bounces back and falls on his ass in surprise.

"Not quite." I cross my arms. "There's still a little thing called the Other that you need to take care of."

He climbs to his feet and picks up the closest sword. His wings flutter as he turns on me. Within a blink, Zane has the scythe in his hand, at the ready.

I tap my foot and raise an eyebrow.

"Listen, little one, I cannot get to the Other from here," he snarls at me and eyes Zane's gleaming weapon. His face twitches with frustration and he throws the sword on the ground. It's his way of yielding, but he isn't happy with either of us. "So, if you want your relatives out of there, I suggest you remove this barrier." He points in the direction he had been walking.

I blink at him, debating on whether or not to yank his chain. The fire in his gaze tells me I shouldn't. "Fine." I wave, dissolving the invisible wall. "But if you double-cross me in any way..." I point at him.

"What? You'll point me to Death?" he says, goading me.

"No, I'll come find you." Zane grins and points the scythe in his direction. "Even you can be reaped."

Michael looks at him as if he's about to launch into battle, but it's Raphael who speaks up.

"We will deliver your family from that prison, as we promised."

"How will we know you destroyed the Other?" I ask.

Raphael glides his gaze to Zane. "It is said those who have been imprisoned in the Other will feel its destruction."

Zane steps back next to me, satisfied with the answer. The scythe shrinks back onto the necklace and he puts his arm around my shoulder. When all four archangels disappear into the woods, he says, "At least we don't have to escort them through Purgatory."

"You realize, if they don't follow through, we're going to break protocol and storm Heaven to find them?"

He chuckles. "Yes. And it's pretty clear they do not want *you* in their domain."

We cross to the family. Papa stands unscathed, as he scans the decimation of the property. Even the lake flows red with the blood of the angels.

"I don't even know where to start." He sighs.

"Yeah, it's quite a mess." Zane turns and puts his hand out. Body parts turn to ash in the same way Steve and Jennifer did. Even the blood fades to dust. He twirls his finger and a funnel forms, filtering the remains into the stratosphere. It takes minutes to clean up, and he turns with a smile. "Better?"

"Can I hire you to clean my house?" Naomi says from a few feet away.

He chuckles under his breath. "I'm not that good at cleaning unless it's dead bodies."

"There is a basement that you *will* clean," Papa says, staring Zane down.

The reminder of Zane's killing spree puts a damper on the mood as we wait for the archangels to cash in on the remaining part of their deal.

Kissing Fate
Chapter 16

SINCE THE DANGER OF being slaughtered has passed, Damian and Naomi decide to book flights out west, and Smoke and Phoebe agree to drop them off at the airport on the way back to New York. Leaving us to deal with whatever fallout comes with the archangels and the destruction of the Other.

I'm uncertain they will follow through on their promise, but I don't share that unease with anyone else in the room. The infusion of knowledge I got from the angel fire blast was more than my brain can comprehend. It layers on the centuries upon centuries of Fate and Death's knowledge still locked in my head, not to mention all the crap that Papa transmitted to me when he gave me a bit of his supercharge. I guess when you share powers like he did with me, you also share memories. Papa's shared powers with Damian, Steve, Tom, Nana, and his father, Ty. And holy hell, Ty's memories were by far the blackest.

You'd think there would be some point where the information load would short-circuit, but it hasn't.

I glance out the window at the pristine yard and for a moment, it's covered in angel blood and body parts. A blink clears it away and replaces it with the colors of sunset.

Zane's hand reaches out and covers mine, as if he can sense I'm becoming overwhelmed with today's events. I twist my hand so I can thread my fingers between his, and I glance at him.

"The angels nearly ruined Heaven to end life on Earth." I sigh. "They siphoned the energy from the Tree of Life until it was nothing but a shriveled husk."

Papa's head snaps up and Ty's gaze moves from his delectable breakfast crepes on the stove to me. Even Tom stiffens in the chair. Jessica pauses with a handful of silverware grasped in her hands. All four pairs of eyes widen.

I didn't expect that reaction. "And when that wasn't enough, they charged themselves up on the Other." I finish what I was saying, studying the growing horror on their faces.

"They destroyed the Tree of Life?" Papa asks.

I nod. "But don't worry. That's where I focused all the energy they fed me. So, either it's back to full bloom, or I cooked it right out of existence. Either way, it was the only choice I had, short of ending the world."

"I certainly hope you didn't toast it. That tree houses the entire angelic bloodline. The angels that were killed today were not God's creations like the archangels. They were followers that ascended to the positions. I don't think you would have been able to ward off a smiting from the children of God," Raven says. "Especially since they are now all recharged with their grace."

I wasn't sure I bought her idea that the archangels could smite me, and I traded a glance with Tom. He gives me a shrug and I can't tell whether he agrees with his wife, or whether he thinks I'd kick their asses.

After all, I drove Michael to his knees once already.

"So, why target me?" I ask, instead of trying to shuffle through the celestial download.

"Power." Raven meets my gaze. "It's more of an educated guess, though."

Her guess feels right. "But didn't they already have power?"

She glances at Tom for a moment. "Yes, and no. If the world ends, they would ascend even higher on God's ladder. And to end the world, they needed an entity powerful enough to absorb their smiting enough to become a breathing bomb. That's where you came in." She smiles and tilts her head.

"So why issue the kill order for all of you?"

"That's easy. They have always thought we were abominations. Nephilim to them were the same as they were to Lucifer. Something to be used and then destroyed." Ty flips a crepe in the pan over the stove as he speaks. "It's amazing that we ever created trilogies." He glances at Papa. "But that also opened a lot of bitter doors up there. We were tolerated but if they ever actively went after the archangel's kin, there would have been an uprising."

"If they went after CJ directly, the archangels would never have let that stand, despite their station without grace. They would have taken Heaven back by force and the ground in Heaven would have run red with their blood. So, they targeted the next best thing. One without an angelic bloodline." Ty pours another dollop of batter into the fry pan.

"But they told me to kill everyone with eyes like theirs. So, in essence, they were targeting CJ and all the other archangel descendants," Zane says. He blinks and looks down at the table as a crease appears. "They showed me snapshots and said you were unclean and needed to be reaped."

"Sneaky bastards. You do the killing, and they have someone to focus the archangels' wrath on." Ty pours a cream filling into the pan and then rolls the cream-filled crepe onto a platter with the others. He garnishes it with strawberries and a dab of confectionary sugar.

I find I'm more focused on his breakfast skills than his words. All I know is I want that entire platter. I can almost taste the sweet tartness of the crepe. I catch his amused gaze.

"Thank you all for wiping the lot of them out," I say, humbled by their collective power. The anger swirls around me, heating my skin before I let it go. The release of the fury I've held so long lifts a horrendous weight from my shoulders and I have a moment of true freedom.

"They were the ones that were unclean." Zane glances out at the lake just as Ty Ryan sets the heaping plateful of strawberry cream cheese crepes on the table.

All my focus draws to the sweet-smelling confections, and even though this body no longer has the need for food to survive, I indulge. As the crepe melts in my mouth, I close my eyes, savoring the sensations. Sweetness laced with a hint of tart, smothered in creaminess that is divine.

Zane's purr of approval opens my eyes. He looks as euphoric as I am, and he sends me a closed-mouth grin. He swallows and licks his lips as his gaze drops to the plate with only a few crepes left. But before he can reach for one, his eyes widen, and his hands grab onto the sides of the table.

His entire frame shakes with some unseen force and his gaze slowly finds mine as if it is taking a Herculean effort to move his eyes.

I see the anguish in his irises, and I send my chair back and move like lightning to his side, wrapping my arms around him in much the same way he had held me in Paradise Cove.

Every muscle of his trembles as if wound so tight they are likely to snap. He whines under the pressure like a soft mew of a lonely cat.

"It's okay, baby. I'm right here." I stroke his hair, and my hand comes away wet as if his sweat glands had somehow come to life and gone into hyperdrive. I catch Papa's concerned stare, but he isn't looking at me. He's looking at Zane, or more than likely through Zane, at whatever it is Death is witnessing.

Papa's face pales and he shakes his head, meeting my gaze with more than just a little concern at this bizarre scene.

"They are destroying the Other," Zane says, his voice straining through clenched teeth. And then he slumps in the chair as if he has been unplugged. His head lolls and his eyes don't open when I nudge him.

"Zane?" I shake him, harder this time.

His eyes flutter open. "Holy Jesus," he whispers and wipes the sweat off his face with the hem of his shirt.

"What happened?" I ask, and everyone leans in, expecting an answer.

Zane just shakes his head. "Give me a minute to recoup." He leans back in the chair and presses both his flesh palm and his mechanical palm against his eyes.

We all wait for him to get his bearings.

"You said they destroyed the Other. Did they get Holly out?" Alex's voice holds an edge that I feel in my blood, too.

Zane drops his hands to the table and opens his eyes. "I honestly don't know. I'm still trying to wrap my scrambled brain around whatever the Hell that was. It felt like a nuclear bomb went off inside my body."

The archangels had warned us that those who spent time in the Other would feel its destruction. They weren't joking.

I have to trust that the archangels are true to their word in that they got those close to us out before decimating the place. I glanced outside, hoping I'd see Holly and my parents crossing the lawn, but nothing is out there.

I send my senses out, looking for them on this side of the realms. They are not here, so unless the archangels reneged on their end of the deal, our loved ones were behind the pearly gates.

If Zane had that type of reaction, my father probably was just as traumatized. "Where's Holly's body?" I ask.

"Out in the garage," Faith says, and her eyes shine with hope.

I nod. "Bring Holly's body to the lawn just before the path to Paradise Cove, please," I say before I head out the door with purpose. I certainly hope they didn't double-cross us. Because if they have, then I am ripping open my family's wounds once again.

I get to the edge of the woods and take a deep breath before I head down the path. I get to the lush entrance to Paradise Cove and, as I take a step to enter, I'm thrown back on my ass. The impact jars my teeth.

Wings flutter and I look up into the Archangel Michael's angry face. He stands on the green moss.

"You do not get to enter Heaven. You know the rules."

My eyes narrow. "And you don't get to enter my domain, yet the rules have never stopped you." I climb to my feet, squaring off.

He glances beyond me. "Where's your better half?" He brings his sharp gaze back to mine.

"In the house, recovering. I trust you have met all the terms of our agreement?"

He nods once. "Your father is recovering as well. He is with your mother and his parents are doting over him. It's nauseating." He rolls his eyes, and I cannot help but smirk. "I do have something for you, though," he says.

When Michael reaches behind him and then shoves a form through the barrier he won't allow me to cross, I am expecting Holly. But the stumbling body attached to the golden arm sends a fresh wave of excitement through me.

"Mandy!" I catch her, and she looks up at me, bewildered.

"You did it? You stopped them?"

I smile. "Yes, we stopped them, with the help of my friend here." I point to Michael.

Mandy shrinks back from the winged creature on Heaven's side of the barrier.

"I would hardly call us friends," Michael scoffs and waves us away.

"Uh. Aren't you forgetting something?" I am not about to let him dismiss me without delivering Holly, but what I want is the least of his concerns.

"No. I've met your terms. Your family is safe. So are the rest who died by Heaven's hands. Now go, before I step through this barrier and teach you a real lesson." He cocks his eyebrow at me and then turns and dissolves in the air.

But his wings still beat as he ascends, rippling the water of the cove and sending my hair back like I'm standing in a stiff ocean breeze.

Well, if the Archangel Michael won't deliver her, Fate sure the hell will.

I turn and march back to the yard with Mandy at my heels. Holly's dead body is in Alex's arms. He lowers her to the ground at my feet, meeting my gaze with a hope so thick it tightens my throat.

"She's safe." I glance down at her prone form, wondering for the first time whether this is the right choice. I glance at the living room window and Zane leans on the windowsill, still looking just as haggard as he did when I stepped out of the cottage. He gives me a nod.

The lump in my throat grows to the size of a watermelon and firmly wedges against my larynx. The expectations are clear on everyone's face. They expect me to raise the dead.

I kneel and put my hands on the ground next to Holly's stiff form. I close my eyes and envision Holly alive and vibrant and as carefree as she was the night before the world came crashing down on all of us. I can almost hear her laugh.

"Holly Ryan," I whisper, willing her back. Willing her out of Heaven's grip. I refrain from adding my parents to the list of the reborn. As much as I wanted them with me, I think they will fare much better living their eternity in peace.

The air around us sparks, creating flashes of light on my eyelids, and the air takes on a distinct ozone quality. Holly's sharp inhale snaps my eyes open. The body on the ground is still not breathing, and I glance up, staring into Holly's ghostly eyes.

Mandy steps back as if I've just opened the gates of Hell or something equally as horrendous.

I blink and sit back on my heels. I may have pulled her from Heaven, but I didn't get her back into her body. And I share some of Mandy's horror. I need her spirit to meld with her flesh. My mind races through the catalog of memories swarming in my head, looking for answers.

A vision startles me, and my gaze jumps to Tom Ryan. He stares at Holly's ghost. He sees the spirit world and always has. And he's forced a spirit back into flesh.

"Tom, put her back in," I snap at him.

He points to his chest and his mouth forms a small O, as if he doesn't understand my directive.

"Yes, you. You see her just as clearly as Mandy and I can. And you've done this before. Please. Put her back in her body, just like you did with your father's spirit."

Dawning widens his eyes, and he moves toward Holly without hesitation.

But it wasn't just Tom's actions alone. It was the combination of the healing magic that's been passed to Nana along with his that allowed Ty Ryan to live when he rightfully should have died.

"Nana, push some of that healing mojo into her body, please." I'm a little more diplomatic in my request with her because I've been taught to respect my elders. I've never ordered my grandmother around, not even when it's literally life and Death.

She does as I ask, and the moment she moves away and the healing light sparkles over Holly, Tom grabs the ghost by the arms and forcefully slams her spirit into the stiff form on the ground.

The air tingles and sparks. It's as if the magic inside Holly has awakened. Then Holly's body gasps and her back arches as a great inhalation of air nearly lifts her off the ground. Her dull red hair slowly turns vibrant with life as Nana's healing magic laces its way through her entire form. Her eyes fly open like two broken shades and her eyes glow angel blue instead of the dull shade of death. She blinks at the blue sky above us, repeating gasp after gasp until she falls into the cadence of breathing.

She is still too pale, but at least her chest rises and falls without having to attempt CPR. She slowly lifts her head and glances around at the circle around her.

"I heard Zane's awake," she finally says when her gaze falls on me.

I laugh and nod and glance at Mandy. My eyes blur and hot tears leak out, sliding down my cheeks. I capture a salty one in the corner of my mouth and sniffle as I look back at Holly.

When she sits up, I throw myself in for a hug before anyone else can.

"Hey, I just..." She trails off and just hugs me tight, as if the events leading up to her death suddenly surfaced. "I died, didn't I?" she whispers in my ear.

I nod. "So did I," I say softly and pull away, wiping my face. "But mine can't be reversed." I try to smile, but the corners of my mouth drag down from the tremble in my chin.

Holly cocks her head and sadness fills her eyes. "What happened?"

Something rumbles like thunder in the distance.

I jump back a little and glance at the sky, expecting storm clouds, but then Holly's stomach does it again. It's loud enough to make me break out with a shaky laugh.

"I think I'm hungry," she says.

"Grandpa made crepes, but I don't know if there are any left." Faith crouches next to her daughter. The two exchange a quick hug and then climb to their feet.

Alex steps in to embrace his daughter. He looks over her head at me and mouths the words *thank you.*

I didn't bring her back just for him. After all, she is my best friend, roommate, and, for all intents and purposes, my sister. I give him a nod just before he breaks the hug and turns toward the house.

"I'm sure your great-grandpa can whip up more of those crepes to silence that stomach of yours." He smiles.

Holly stops halfway up the hill. "I'll be just a second. Just make sure Grandpa makes me a plateful," she tells her parents and then turns to me. She waits until everyone else heads around the corner before she looks at me. "What happened?" she asks again, this time with a little more force.

I glance beyond her at Zane standing in the window and take a breath. "Zane wasn't quite right when he woke up." I bring my gaze back to Holly. "The angels had him all that time and they branded him with a sigil that gave them control."

Her eyes narrow and she crosses her arms, but I catch the sparks of aggravation dancing across her fingertips. She is just like her mother in that way. Both of them spark when they are aggravated. "Zane killed you?" she actually snarls and spins, catching him watching us.

Before I can stop her, Holly launches toward the house with her march of anger. If we were at her parents' house, the entire foundation would shake with each step.

I hurry after her. "He didn't know what he was doing." I grab her arm, but she yanks it from my grip.

"That is no excuse. The bloody asshole died because he didn't want you to get hurt and he has the audacity to kill you?" She huffs. "I'm going to kick his immortal ass."

She barrels toward the door.

"Do you want me to intervene?" Mandy says as she matches me step for step.

"No. Why don't you go round up what's left of the troops and let them know Purgatory and the reaper realm are finally safe from Heaven's wrath."

She looks unsure, as if there could be a sniper in waiting around any corner in our domain.

"If you want to bring Levi with you, that's fine, too," I say as Holly steps into the house. That seems to calm Mandy, and I nod for my trusty sidekick to follow my reaper general back to Purgatory. "Hold down the fort until we get there," I say and Mandy nods, blinking out with Levi by her side.

Holly corners Zane by the window and swings. He parries with his metal arm and when her punch is deflected; she pulls back. I can see her wide eyes in the window reflection as she stares at his mechanical hand.

Zane looks down at the focus of her attention. "I had them cut it off so the angels couldn't get in my head again." He splays both hands in the air, trying to placate her. "You know damn well if I was in my right mind, I never would have hurt her."

"Ten years ago, I would have agreed, but that's before you became Heaven's bitch." She shoves him back against the wall. "I'll never forgive you for taking her life."

"What they did—"

Zane is promptly cut off by her as she points a fiery finger at him. "I don't care."

Ty, her great-grandfather, leans over the table and places a plate of new crepes on the table. "Hey, hangry hellfire, why don't you eat something before you decide to set the cabin on fire?" He pushes the piled-high crepes across the table toward her.

She turns toward her great-grandfather and then looks at the offering. It's like a switch turns off, and all that occupies her mind are those delectable treats. Before another word is uttered, she is sitting and digging in as if she hasn't eaten in weeks.

That is the Holly I know and love.

Kissing Fate
Chapter 17

I PULL ZANE ASIDE while the family is eating their breakfast. "We need to do something important," I say quietly and pull him outside. Before he can ask any questions, I blink us away from the cottage.

When we get to our destination, the first thing that hits me is the smell. But then again, when you leave dead bodies in a basement for a few days, the smell *is* going to be vile.

"I don't want them coming home to this mess." I glance at Zane.

It's the first time he's really seen the damage he caused with a rational mind. He covers his nose with his wrist, grimacing as he scans the carnage.

While he's preoccupied with being disgusted by the bloated bodies, I conjure two beautiful urns inscribed with Kylee Andreas and Gabriel Andreas, respectively. I know it isn't nearly enough, but at least Michael and his family will have something solid to pay their respects to without having to clean up the mess.

"You need to do your clean-up thing, including wiping out the stains in the carpeting, but I need you to put their ashes into these urns." I cross and put them on the coffee table, closer to where the bodies rot, trying not to gag.

He stares at the damage he caused, turning a little green, but he nods and splays his good hand, closing his eyes.

"Try not to mingle the ashes," I say when the bodies reduce to ash.

A crease appears between Zane's eyes as he concentrates. Kylee's ashes rise into the air and swirl across the floor before siphoning into the urn with her name on it. Then Gabriel's ashes do the same into his urn. That left the bloodstains on the floor. Blood from Kylee, from my mother, from Gabriel and from Zane stains the carpet.

He opens his eyes and stares at the stains before he glances at me. "I don't know if I can get the smell out."

"I'm sure they can air it out in some way." I'm not sure they can, but with Papa's magic, maybe he can get rid of it. In the meantime, I conjure a dozen of those pine-scented car fresheners and pin them to the ceiling.

Zane closes his eyes again and this time ash particles lift from the carpet in spurts, as if Zane's power is waning. It takes some time, but he finally has all the blood and bodily liquids evaporated from the room. Although the stench still hangs in the air, mingling with the pine air fresheners, the cause of it is now scrubbed from the room.

I take his hand and force the transition back to the cabin. The cool breeze flows through our clothes like a giant eraser, giving us a clean forest smell instead of the gagging aroma of death.

The task weighs on both of us. The lighthearted banter inside the cabin just seems wrong in retrospect, but I understand the Ryans. They helped save the world. They have a right to be jovial. It just doesn't jive with the act of interring Kylee and Gabriel to their respective urns.

Holly glances at me from the couch. Her color is back, and so is that sleepy look of a healthy food coma.

"Where'd you go?" she asks.

"We needed to do a bit of a clean-up before you all head home." I meet Papa's gaze.

He slowly nods. "I appreciate that."

"Missy conjured some air fresheners, but you might need to do something a little more extreme." Zane stares at the floor, shifting from foot to foot. He seems like he can't quite meet anyone's gaze.

"Why?" Holly asks.

"We will fill you in on the way home," Alex says, saving Zane from more of Holly's fiery wrath. His voice carries a warning to not push for more information, but Holly isn't in tune with her father. She never has been, or she just ignores his cautionary tone.

"What happened at Papa's?" she asks me, because it's clear no one in the room wants to answer her, at least not while in our presence.

"People died, and it wasn't pretty." That's pretty much all I need to say. Holly meets my gaze and I try to convey to her not to pursue this line of questions.

"Oh." She blinks and gives me a subtle nod, and then a miracle occurs. She lets it go.

I guess it's inevitable that I'm more readable than her father. I could finish her sentences and she could finish mine. Living in the same space and sharing a bedroom for twenty-six years kind of does that to people. Even though we don't share the same bloodlines, we have always been on the same wavelength.

The water turns off in the kitchen, and Ty and Jessica step out, wiping their hands. "We're ready to head back home whenever you are." Ty glances at Papa.

I can't blame him for wanting to bug out now that the danger has passed. This isn't their home. They want to go get into comfortable clothing and kick back and watch a football game on television. Or have a family dinner together to celebrate they are still alive. I get it. If I were in their shoes, I would want to do the same, considering all we have been through.

Unfortunately, I don't get to go back to my old life, and I guess my expression must show that because Holly bites her lower lip and twirls a piece of her hair as she studies me.

"You're not coming back with us, are you?" Holly asks.

"No. I need to address some things in Purgatory and the reaper realm, along with locating any portals that were opened by leveraging your mom's time jump powers. But I'll be around soon. I promise."

"What about your job? The apartment?" she asks, reminding me of things I have to address in the mortal realm, too.

"You've got the apartment." I smile. "And I'm sure my boss will be happy if I never show up to work again."

She smirks at me. "So, what do I tell him if he calls the apartment?"

"Tell him I died." It isn't a lie. Besides, I could use some downtime now that the world isn't in danger of ending. I've never really discovered the possibilities with Zane, and ten years of fantasy scenes in my head are just itching to be explored.

She gives me a huge hug, squeezing me tight. "I get it. You want to be alone with him," she whispers in my ear so only I can hear. "I'd be shuffling everyone out of here if I were in your shoes."

I smile and hug her tighter for a minute. This is why she is my sister, even without the blood connection. She reads me so well. "I love you, sis."

"Love you, too," she says. When I pull away, she gives Zane a side eye and points her finger at him. "Take care of her," she orders.

"Always."

It's such a simple answer, and it warms my soul.

"Don't be a stranger," Alex says when he steps in for a hug.

"I won't. And you know how to call me if you or anyone needs our help, right?"

"Yes. And you've got our number, too." He kisses my cheek and taps my temple with a smile before relinquishing me to Faith for a final heartfelt hug.

Papa steps in after, and his hugs are always the best. I know I'm cherished by the family after one of his hugs.

Nana gives me a peck on the forehead, and I feel the tingle of her magic seeping into my skin. "That's a little to help you if you ever need it in our absence."

I hug her tight. I am going to miss them, but I know I can't hide out in the mortal realm forever, despite the sadness of leaving all I know behind.

"It's a brave new world. Embrace it." Tom gives me a quick hug, followed by Raven. Hannah is almost tall enough to look me in the eyes and this year she turns into a dreaded teenager. She hugs me, too.

Jessica and Ty are the last ones to leave the house, and Ty pats me on the head. "Don't do anything I wouldn't do." He winks and trades a knowing smile with Zane before he shuts the door behind him.

The rumble of cars down the driveway fades and then silence descends. I still have my back to Zane as I watch the last of the dust settle. My stomach flutters. There's no one else here and no pending doom hanging over our heads.

I take a deep breath and turn, but Zane wasn't looking at me; he's looking out the bay window at the bright sunshine bathing the lake. It's not the ocean, but it is still beautiful the way the sun creates slivers of diamonds on the surface.

He must sense me staring at him and he glances my way with a playful smile dancing on his lips. He looks around the cottage.

"We are alone."

Heat rises in my cheeks when he turns fully in my direction. The white shirt I fitted him with still hangs open and the miniature scythe catches the light, creating rainbows through the room as if it's a prism instead of steel.

I'm not sure I can move. I'm caught somewhere between the want heating me from the inside and nerves marching across my skin like a thousand spiders.

I have no experience beyond our kissing session in the cove. *What if I'm not what he wants?*

That fearful thought freezes me in place, but his eyes sparkle with everything I'm feeling, and he kicks into action, crossing the distance to pick me up and pin me to the wall. His lips crush down on mine, unleashing a kiss that sucks the air right out of my lungs.

His mechanical arm finds its way to the small of my back and his flesh-and-bone hand slides down my neck, settling on the curve of my chest. He actually purrs under my lips, like he's content just to kiss me and rub his thumb on the side of my breast.

His lips break from mine, only to follow the line of my jaw down my throat. Before I have a chance to catch my breath, the ripping sound of fabric makes me blink.

I look down at my ruined bodice as it falls to the floor around my ankles. He grins up at me like a man who knows he's in a little bit of trouble but too far gone to care.

"You can conjure another one." And then his mouth greedily covers one nipple and then the next.

I thread my hands through his hair, content to let him lead, to be pampered by his mouth. But then he picks me up and turns toward the hallway. He stalks into the master bedroom with me in his arms and lays me out on the bed as if I'm made of china.

He steps back and drifts his gaze from my head to my toes and back. "Do you know just how beautiful you are?" He peels his shirt off and climbs on top of me. He hasn't undone his own pants, yet I'm without a stitch of clothing underneath his weight.

I smile. I've been told several times over the years, but not one of them had the level of adoration in Zane's eyes.

He cups my cheeks, searching my eyes. His grin fades as shadows of doubt clouds his eyes. "What if I'm not enough?" he whispers, staring into the depths of my soul.

"I've waited ten years to be in your arms," I say.

He chuckles and dips his head. "Way to put the pressure on." He slides his gaze to mine, and that doubt is replaced by humor and something feral underneath.

"You once said you wanted to kiss me into oblivion."

He twirls his hips gently, rubbing his hardness into me in a way that heightens every last nerve. "Is that all you want?" he teases and nips at my throat, sending chills through me. "Me to *just* kiss you?"

I can't answer. I'm not sure what exactly I want from him, but this is certainly a good start and I do not want him to stop. Ten years of fantasies and not one of them left me speechless from his touch. But he does. Every brush of his hand, every kiss, every swipe of his tongue strips me of any hesitation.

"I want more than that." I finally breathe out the words, panting with the symphony of sensations.

He pauses, and that playful smile turns serious. "You've never..."

I shake my head, and he sighs, but I can't bring myself to ask the same.

He caresses my lips with his thumb. "Despite my reputation, this is new to me as well." He looks between our molded bodies. "I've never had such a beautiful woman at my mercy," he purrs and then grins. "And I am going to savor the moment, if you don't mind."

He doesn't wait for me to answer—he swipes my lips with his tongue. But when I open my mouth to capture a kiss, he moves to my jaw, licking down my pulse line, creating a delicious heat mingled with chills that turn my skin into a relief map of goose bumps.

He moves down my neck, covering my skin with butterfly kisses that have me whining for more every time he shifts and they disappear, only to reappear lower on my body. He is magical in his ministrations, coaxing his name from my lips with every new sensation.

Tingles, heat, chills, and everything in between accosts me as he toys with my breasts. And just when I think I can't take it anymore, he moves lower, sending my senses into overdrive.

He slides down farther, pushing one of my legs up and over his shoulder, opening me up to his hungry gaze. He lines my inner thigh with kisses, nipping his way to my core. His tenderness and playfulness twist together until he finally settles between my legs. The moment his tongue swipes my sensitive bud, I nearly buck from the sudden rush of heat that fills every pore.

My eyes fall to half-mast as he manipulates my body in a way I thought impossible. He continues, encouraged by my moans until my world explodes in physical pleasure. Then his fingers explore me, teasing, testing, all while his tongue circles in the spot that has me grabbing a fistful of his hair.

I pant and whine as his mouth moves away from my pleasure center. His eyes are so green they glow with crazy need as he crawls up my body, kissing his way along my skin until he captures my mouth in a hot kiss.

Without warning, he fills me with a single thrust that shatters a cry under his insistent mouth. I arch into him as he initiates me into womanhood. There is no pain like Holly told me there would be. The only sensation I have is fullness and a desperate ache deep within me, like being stretched nearly to the breaking point.

It's odd, and he pulls away from the kiss to gaze down at me. He moves languidly and his eyes close as if he's savoring each motion. He certainly is creating a new form of ecstasy within me with each slow stroke.

"So, *this* is what my friends bragged about in high school." He grins and circles his hips as though he does not want these overwhelming sensations to end.

I let out a laugh. Holly never told me sex was *this* mind-blowing. She didn't seem all that impressed with her first time—or the last time she screwed around. She obviously didn't have anyone like Zane playing her body like a concert pianist. I hope to the Heavens above that she finds someone who takes her to another realm the way Zane does to me.

My eyes roll back with the force of the next wave and I dig my nails into his biceps, letting out a moan that jump-starts him into motion. His hips move faster, creating delicious heat, sparking wave after wave of orgasms until I think I'm going to scream loud enough to rip the roof off.

He groans my name, and every muscle stiffens until he drops on top of me, trembling.

"Fuck," he whispers, drawing out the word like it's almost revered. He props himself up on one elbow and traces my lips with his finger.

I twitch from the sensory overload, smiling in my post-euphoric state. "I believe we just did," I whisper as sleep tugs at the edges of my vision.

He smiles, but looks just as exhausted as I feel.

He rolls off me, creating an emptiness I am not prepared for. I whine in response and he pulls me onto his chest, looking up at me. The cool metal of his mechanical hand sits on my right hip, a stark contrast to the warmth radiating from my left hip, where his human hand squeezes ever so softly.

"I'm thinking of a small nap before we try this again?"

The way his eyebrow raises makes me chuckle. Although every muscle is begging for sleep, my libido has other ideas. I circle my hips, grinding into him, and the Angel of Death comes alive underneath me.

His eyes sparkle with renewed vigor. "I guess a nap will have to wait."

He pulls me into a kiss that ignites a fire deep within me. I can't help the giggle that surfaces. He doesn't know it yet, but he has awoken the vixen in me, and I want to ride my incredibly hot, immortal boyfriend into oblivion.

The End

ABOUT J.E. TAYLOR

J.E. Taylor is a USA Today bestselling author, a publisher, an editor, a manuscript formatter, a mother, a wife, a business analyst, and a Supernatural fangirl. Not necessarily in that order. She first sat down to seriously write in February of 2007 after her daughter asked:

"Mom, if you could do anything, what would you do?"
From that moment on, she hasn't looked back.

Besides being co-owner of Novel Concept Publishing, Ms. Taylor also moonlights as a Senior Editor of Allegory E-zine, an online venue for Science Fiction, Fantasy and Horror, and co-host of the popular YouTube talk show Spilling Ink.

She lives in New Hampshire with her husband and during the summer months enjoys her weekends on the shore in southern Maine.

Visit her at www.jetaylor75.com to check out her other titles and sign up for her newsletter for early previews of her upcoming books, release announcements, and special opportunities for free swag!

9 781963 769159